THE BALLAD OF URIAH

MIKE MACKESSY

PRODUCTIONS

Dedication

I dedicate this book to my wife, in thanks for her help in reading and re-reading what I write. Thanks for your help in editing and getting through the process of preparing another book. Thanks Gwen, for allowing me to devote time to this book. Thanks for allowing me the time to get my things done.

Nick Wale
A great publicist, thanks for the covers and all you do to help. It's very much appreciated.

1

SAN ANTONIO 1883

I TURN 70 TODAY. I'VE LIVED MOST OF THEM YEARS IN the heights of the Great Stoney Mountains and spent time in the wilds of a young Texas. I've got little but memories saved. Unless you count my collection of wounds and scars. I carry three pistol balls, two rifle balls, and a Blackfoot stone arrowhead deep within this old body of mine. They are all too deep to mine out, or lay dangerously close to veins and muscles. But that's okay. I only feel them when the weather changes. The ones still inside me don't concern me as much as the lead balls and the stone or the steel arrowheads that have scared the outsides to this old body.

Forty years ago today, I did one of the hardest things I would have ever imagined. I shot down an old and dear friend. In addition to my birthday, today is the fortieth anniversary of the darkest day in my long life. I was responsible for turning the man into the outlaw he would become. If I had only left things as they were when I entered the Cheyenne village, maybe this would not have been necessary. Maybe? I must tell you that fight began over 45 years ago. He was at one time my best friend. Then he went bad. I did not then, nor will I ever, keep a willfully lawbreaking man in the company of my closest friends. That's exactly what he was, both an outlaw and a close friend. Let me explain.

My journey began as a 16-year-old boy from back east. I was in school where someone left a newspaper in a café next to the school and I picked it up. I read of the mountain man rendezvous and was hooked. Even the name, Rendezvous, brought to my mind vivid scenes of a mountain life, trapping, trading, and of course Indians. In the late 1820s I got caught up in the saga of life west of the Mississippi River. The newspaper chronicled the mystery, putting a name on the rumors, causing me a restless excitement by hinting at and outlining my possible success or ruin. I am not a gambler, but I was willing to take a seat at this game. Even without knowing or understanding the rules and pitfalls. That newspaper yarn set into motion the beginnings of my foolish plan which led ultimately to me gunning down my desperado friend. Bear with and excuse an old man his windy tale as I recount for you this difficult turn of events.

———

1829

I consider myself a man of deed and daring. As such I sprang into immediate action implementing my long-term plan. Thanks to a relatively wealthy family I was away at school. I lacked for nothing. I gave myself a year to gather my "Possibles", visiting several nearby general stores, outfitting myself with everything I reckoned needful for the looming journey. Rough working clothes, a flannel shirt, long-johns, boots, a thick leather belt, a large hunting knife, a camp knife, and a hat. I purchased two .45 caliber, single shot, flintlock pistols, a .45 caliber American long rifle, powder horn, balls, and extra flints. I made holsters to wear both pistols on my belt and a large possibles parfleche. I left home and school, outfitted for a life in the Great Stoney Mountains, as true Mountain Men call the Rockies, at seventeen years of age.

The weapons and their accruements are in addition to the gear I already own that I brought with me from home. Like my Ol' Faithful .45 caliber Kentucky long rifle and a pair of .45 caliber pistols, my familiar wood axe, a knife I made for myself, and my possibles. I believed I was a proficient hunter, evidenced by those few years spent providing for me and my family, when Pa wouldn't or couldn't hunt with me. Boy was I miss-took.

I added two packhorses, pack frames, six heavy duty canvas panniers, rope, a saddle suitable for the west, saddlebags, and filled four of the panniers with supplies. I bought coffee beans and a grinder, a frying pan, Dutch Oven, a plate, two cups, three different sized spoons, and a pot big enough to wash dishes in or make a stew. I added candles, matches, and a deck of cards. That's when I remember a bedroll. I choose two wool blankets and a canvas sheet to cover them in. I have everything I need except a destination.

After paying for all my gear, I pile it in my room in a house I shared with four other students. Under threats of the most grievous kind I warn the students to leave my new gear alone. I was on my way to the livery stable for my riding horse. I was intent on buying two packhorses.

"Just a minute now son," says the owner of the general store as I explain my intentions. "My brother is the owner of a livery. Why don't I go with you? I'm sure I can get you a good price on those two packhorses," says the helpful store owner and clerk.

"Thank you, sir. I'd welcome your help."

"That's quite alright. Come on I'll introduce you."

I follow him out of the store and down the street. Introductions are made. Questions as to my riding experience are asked. I dis-remember my answers, but I know they are not quite accurate. The three of us engage in a highly spirited discussion about horses and packhorses. At the end of it all, I am the proud owner of two excellent packhorses. I know today that the intentions of the shopkeeper and his livery owner brother were not pointing in my favor. How I bought such fine animals I'll never know. They were the best pair of horses I ever owned. I bought two pack saddles, saddle blankets, saddlebags, head gear, reins, and lead ropes.

It's true I know how to ride, but just. I get the pack frames secure on my horses, to the surprise of everyone watching. I successfully lead them back to the general store. I take my time packing my gear. I understand balance is important. After a couple of hours my horses are loaded and secured. I'm dressed in new duds. I buy a second set of jeans and a shirt for just in case. I set up both possible bags for pistol and rifle. I thread both knives and both holsters on the belt. I throw it around my waist and close the buckle. I carry my new rifle to my saddle horse. Ol' Faithful is tied to the first packhorse. In a pommel holster ride my second pair of pistols. Under the close supervision of the crowd of friends and well-wishers I climb onto the saddle, shoulder my rifle, and taking up the neck lines to my packhorses, promptly leave town and school.

I must mention the name of this town, Kansas City. The stores and liveries are familiar with outfitting trappers heading for the Rocky Mountains, attempting to make their fortunes trapping beaver and hunting buffalo. They assume I am one of them. That assumption serves me well. They do not dare risk the ire of the fur companies. There is too much money involved. The fur companies take things like overcharging very seriously.

Many years down the trail, as I look back, I realize this is one of my first big breaks. The store owner tells me the railroad is looking for track layers and hunters. He felt sure I could find a job there. Truth to tell I could use the job. I have goods but no money. I ride east looking for the railroad tracks. Well I find them sure enough, but getting a job is not easy. They think I am just another runaway kid. I reckon in a way I am, but not like many of those other runaways, I am prepared. After haggling, swearing, and dire threats I am offered a job. It's not the job I want but I take it. I start working five and a half days a week as a track layer. At first the work is back breaking hard. After six months I grow strong enough that I get used to the hard work. I start hunting on that half day Saturday and on Sunday. I make more in that day and a half than as a track layer. I save all the money I can; I have a goal. I am going to trap beaver in the mountains.

At times it is hard to keep that goal towards the front of my mind, but I do. The saloons with whiskey and willing women do not tempt me, after my first encounter. I had to try both. Finding a deep disappointed in both, I vow to save my money.

Several things happen to me during those three years I work for the railroad. First, I grow to five foot and nine inches and stop. I gain muscles and strength, tipping a scale at 200 pounds. The results of such hard work, not an extra pound on my frame. I learn to fight using fists and knives. Fist fighting is easy, the knife fighting comes harder, but I learn from the many cuts I receive. I become a crack shot with rifle and pistol. I learn to clean and skin game. I learn anatomy and apply it to fighting and hunting. Three years is plenty, I've had enough. It's time, at twenty years old, to head for the mountains. It is 1833.

I visit a general store in Kansas City to re-outfit myself, buying three additional packhorses and all the supplies I'll need for a year. I learn from talking to mountain men in town what the trip and a life in the Great Stonies will need. I make a list. That's what I give to the clerk. After packing it on my horses I am ready to earn my living as a trapper.

I ride to the quay. I want to book passage on a sternwheel steam ship sailing north to the Missouri River, towards the Yellowstone River. After much searching, I find a boat ready to leave, buy passage for me and my seven horses, and walk aboard.

"Horses and trappers keep to the bow. No exceptions. You'll find stalls. Help yourself to what you'll need. You will sleep there also. You will take meals with the crew. Questions?" says the second in command, who is also a steward of this small sternwheeler.

"I heard I could earn wages by helping to load and stack firewood. Is that true?" I ask him.

"It is, if you can do the work. I pay fifty-cents at each stop."

"That's not what I heard. I will work for the $1.50 offered at each stop. Take it or leave

it," I tell him with hands on my hips.

"Fine, I'll be leaving it," mad at being found out by a mere lad.

I reckon him to be the one that shot my bedroll. The man by the horses returns to my camp carrying a pistol in each hand.

"Don't shoot mister. I give up," says the third man at my coffee pot. He drops his pistol to the ground and stands up. The man with the two pistols aims them in the direction of my shot. I shoot him with the second rifle. He falls dead.

The third man is motionless and moaning. I step out of the grass holding two pistols in front of me.

"Why you're just a kid," he says, pulling a knife and rushing me. I shoot him with both pistols, stopping him right in his tracks. I drop the empty pistols on my bedroll. I reload both rifles. Carefully walking to the road, I smell and hear the horses before seeing them. I creep ahead. There are three horses tied to a bush. I untie them and bring them into my camp. I saddle my riding horse, pack my camp, and load my four packhorses. When ready, I check the bodies of the three outlaws. I collect three more rifles and six more pistols. In their pockets is very little else. I take their knives, not wanting them to get into the wrong hands. I pack their rifles, pistols, and possibles on my second packhorse. When ready, I put out my fire with the last of the coffee, then ride out. I ride after the sun rises. Beginning to fall asleep in the saddle I know I need to stop. Up ahead is a thick grove of pine and fir trees. I decide to stop and make camp in the middle of the trees.

This site has been used many times as a camp. I find a rock-lined firepit next to a grassy field that will hold all my horses. I string a picket line after leading them to the creek to drink. I tie them all to the picket rope and hobble them. I unsaddle my riding horse and unpack the others. I bring the pack carrying coffee and supper fixings to the firepit. I make a quick meal of buffalo hump steak and coffee. Now I'm really tired. I fall asleep as soon as laying down.

———

Indian Attack

I'm saddling my riding horse after securing panniers to the pack frames on my packhorses when I hear...a lot of someone's riding towards me. Too far away to tell who they are, so I back away from my horses hiding in the grass with my weapons. It's four Indians. All of them act excited, their eyes are big like they're enjoying something. There is blood on their hands. Each one of them has been painted in blood. The sight in front of me is horrifying. In addition to the blood, they are wearing feathers and bristle with weapons. I'm frozen until tearing my eyes away from the grizzly scene.

I lay my four pistols in the grass in front of me. I shoot the biggest warrior with my rifle, lay it aside, and pick up two pistols. My right-hand shot stops a second Indian. I wound the third warrior with my left-handed pistol. He staggers to a stop, but he's not out of the fight. The fourth one is on me before I can pull my knife. I get three good punches in before the wounded one begins hitting me from behind. I turn to hit

In the dark I am kicked awake. The sun is about an hour from rising. The camp is preparing to move out. I am untied, led next to a horse, and the same warrior takes up the end of the rope. He rides, I run at his side. We cross a creek. I fall into the water to drink. The horse stops. I keep drinking. Two warriors help me rise. He rides off. I follow. From there I lose track of time.

Later that night we enter a big camp. I'm tied to a tree like a yard dog. They feed me and allow me water. In the morning they come for me. Apparently, these Indians are trying to trade me to another bunch. They have no use for a half dead captive. The second bunch refuse all offers. In retaliation I'm beaten by the angry warrior that hates me. He takes my boots, tears off my vest and shirt. Striped of my jeans, they slice the long johns off my limbs. Dozens of little cuts and nicks bleed as I'm spread out on the sand. Others hammer stakes into position for both legs and both arms. Spread eagled and tied to the stakes, they leave me behind as they ride away with their mules and my horses. All I can do is watch helplessly as the Indians ride away laughing at me. The angry warrior is the last to ride off. He cuts me using my own knife from belly button to chin. It's not deep enough to kill me, too fast, but leaves me covered in blood. All the insects I never knew living in the plains and foothills attack me.

I about freeze through the night. The next day I bake under the sun. The parts of myself that I can see have turned a bright red, burned by the relentless sun. Most of the cuts have closed with dark, angry, scabs. Through the day vultures are attracted to the dead mule next to me. That is what's left from yesterday's supper. By midday of the second day a small flock of them evil birds fly overhead. I can see them. Powerless and abandoned, all I can do is watch. Every time one lands, I scream to chase it away. Soon my feeble threats do not move them. Gradually the stronger ones begin setting down, picking at the dead mule. The others follow their example. The carrion birds are feasting. I've screamed myself hoarse. As the sun prepares to slide past the horizon ending my third day staked out life a hide drying in the sun, I hear a horse walking towards me.

I hear it stop. I'm wondering if they've sent a man back to take care of me. At this point I do not care. Every joint in my body is screaming out in withering pain. The sun feels like it's burned through my skin down deep into my bones drying every bit of moisture from my beaten body. I try hollering. The pathetic sounds escaping from my dry throat will not alarm anyone, but I keep it up. A swollen tongue keeps getting in the way as I try to make a sound. I see a shadow slowly approaching.

"Well now, what do we have here?" asks a voice. I cannot see the man who is talking. I hear the metallic sounds of horseshoes on hard rocks. I hear leather creaking as he climbs to the ground. I hear sand crunching under...moccasins.

"*Are they back to finish the job?*" I scream inside my head. The desire for an end to the pain and suffering is quickly replaced by a new fervent wish to live. That spark starts a fire in the center of my being.

"*I will get my revenge,*" I tell myself.

I start wiggling again, trying to pull up the stakes holding me. All I have succeeded in accomplishing is rubbing raw spots around each wrist and ankle. I can feel new blood flowing down my weak limbs.

"Hey boy take it easy. Stop your wiggling. I'm here to help. Hold still while I cut you lose," adds the voice. Exhausted, I stop, expecting a bullet, not help. I watch a knife pass across my eyes to cut away the bonds on my wrists. All I can see is a pair of worn brown moccasins walking by me. Free, I try to move my arms from their spread-out position. Both arms and legs refuse to work, to follow my simple directions.

"Easy now, I have water but take only a sip at a time. If you take too much your stomach will spasm and you'll lose what you've drank so far," says the voice of the moccasins. After that first cool sip the canteen disappears. I'm too weak to fight or object. I wait. I used to know that boots and shoes and especially moccasins cannot talk. Wherever I am now, they do.

"Who did this?" asks the moccasins.

"*Indians,*" I rasp out, mouthing nothing aloud.

"Don't talk. I'll ask a question, nod or shake your head to answer. I'm afraid you might have damaged your voice." I nod my understanding.

"They heading west?" I nod.

"You were with a group?" Another nod.

"Do you have kin close by?" My first shake.

"I passed two dozen mules pushed by ten Cheyenne. There were also a dozen real nice

horses with them. Is that your bunch?" I look into his eyes as I nod, yes.

"I'll bring you with me, don't worry I won't leave you. I can tend you until you're ready to continue on. Did they attack here?" I shake my head.

"South?" A nod.

"How far south?" Nothing, I don't move.

"What is south of us? Platt River?" earns him a nod.

"Did you notice the rubbish they left behind?" Another shake.

"Anything I find is yours. Take a drink. That's it. Now you wait until I return before taking your next sip. I'll be right back." I watch as he walks around the old campsite. He chases off the carrion. I'm sitting up against a big rock. It's warming me from the night's cold. I must have fallen asleep. The next thing I know a rough hand is shaking me awake.

"Wake up, time for another sip. I didn't find much. I got you a knife, a pistol, and a rifle with a broken stock. Don't worry I can teach you how to fix it. Take a sip. We need to ride. We'll make camp away from here. Can you stand?" I nod. He helps me stand. I've got an extra pair of buckskins. They'll be big on you, but they'll cover you. Stand still while I get them on you." I nod. The pain as the buckskins climb up my sun-damaged legs is brutal. After bearing all I can I fall, folding into a whimpering ball of burning flesh.

"I'm sorry son. I thought that would help. You need something to protect you from more burning under this sun," he tells me. The next time I open my eyes he's tearing through his packs looking for...something. I have no idea what. I close my eyes, once again.

"I knew I had this. Just had to find them," I hear. I pry open my eyes, slowly turn my head to look at...I don't know who is helping me. He shambles over to me.

"Hey boy, this will help. I got a mess of this silk...I reckon they might be blankets.

Anyways we can cover you in this silk. It may not hurt as much as regular clothing or buckskins. Here, let me help you up and we'll see." He helps me stand. He wraps the silk around my shoulders. For the first touch it burns, but the pain fades quick. He leads me to a saddled horse and helps me into the saddle. He covers my legs with a second sheet of silk. Taking a third sheet he drapes it over my head.

"What's your name?" I croak.

"Sorry son, I reckon I should have introduced myself earlier. I'm Micah. I'm what they've taking to calling, a Mountain Man. If you can, what's your name, son?"

"Uriah."

"That's a fine handle. I knew another Uriah, back a couple of years. He went under fighting them Blackfoot. Yes sir, Uriah was quite a man. I reckon you'll shape up to be quite a man too. Something like this always makes a man stronger than he was before." I look at him as if he's lost his mind.

"I know it don't feel like it now, but mark my words, Uriah, it will work out just like I say. And when it does, look back fondly on this Ol' Mountain Man." All I can do is shake my head at the crazy old coot. He's the one that's been out under the sun too long, not me.

After a longer drink from the canteen we head out. Walking at my side he leads the horse and two packhorses out of the deadly camp. I know we're heading south. Five days later we reach the Platt River. My voice is no better. I'm weak but the long, knife-cut up my belly is healing. During our stops to make camp he works sewing the silk sheets into pants, a shirt, moccasins, and a head cover. I wear the silk garments during the day. It is almost unbearable rubbing sunburned skin against anything else. Every day I feel a bit stronger. We stop at the river.

"Are we making camp?" I rasp out.

"No, I want to take a look for anything they may have left behind." All my supplies from the packs thrown out by the Indians are gone. The camp looks like no one has been through in years. I sit, waiting, discouraged. Micah returns with my old hat, and my saddlebags.

"Are these yours?" he asks me.

"Yeah they are," I tell him. He hands what he's carrying to

me. I open the saddlebags, they're empty. I put my hat on over the silk covering my head.

"Thanks," I tell him, a little bit is better than nothing. "You didn't happen too find my boots, did you?"

"No, sorry that's all they left behind. Don't worry I'll show you how to make moccasins and once you've worn them, you'll never want to wear boots again. You ready to tell me what happened?" asks Micah.

"I reckon I can. I'll tell you the highlights and fill it in later."

"Tell me however you'd like. We can talk as we travel. I don't like the feeling here." I start relating the tale. Beginning from leaving home to the Indian attack to the trying to trade me, I tell Micah everything. He puts a name to the Indians, Blackfoot and Cheyenne. He tells me about the connections between the Blackfoot and the Cheyenne. How they trade between each other, especially captives. I'm feeling drained at the end of the telling.

"We can't stay near here. This is one of the main War Roads for the Blackfoot Nation between Canada and the States. It's well used. I hate to do it, but we need to keep moving and right quick." His warning hits home. I wearily climb onto the extra packhorse and hold on as we ride north by west.

I notice the day is turning to dark. Micah shows no sign of stopping. As the sun sinks below the horizon we ride off the path into the trees. I spread my silk blankets and fall asleep. The next thing I know strong hands are shaking me awake.

"Uriah, wake up," he tells me.

All that comes to mind is the Indian attack. I sit up, grab the broken rifle, and prepare to bash open Micah's head. He easily blocks my weak swing of the rifle.

"Whoa up there Uriah. I've got coffee and grilled venison for you."

"Sorry Micah, I was thinking they were back."

"No, they ain't here. Just us. Eat up, there's more if you want it," he tells me. I have a second helping. I feel stronger every time I eat. This is the most I've been able to keep down since the...incident.

The next weeks, I reckon it's only weeks, I really don't know, but they pass quick. We ride every day, making a new camp every night. I have no idea where we're heading, or where we're going. When I'm healed enough to take an interest in the things around me, I reckon it's been six weeks. We're heading for the foothills, the beginnings of the Rocky Mountains. We turn north and west towards the mountains. In addition to the stories about the Rocky Mountains, I've read everything I came across about trappers and mountain men. In the early, very early mornings he leaves the camp. A couple of hours later he returns bearing game, usually a deer. Sometimes it's a turkey, or a handful of grouse, once an elk, and twice a bear. In addition to the meat he works the hides.

I'm wearing moccasins I've made myself. Micah showed

me how to fashion pants and a shirt from elk hide. The sunburn has stopped its burning glow. I'm dressed and feeling stronger. For the first time in two months I see other people. We've reached what looks like an Indian village. I look at the buffalo hide teepees and the women and kids standing by them. The men, their warriors have gathered together to welcome us. Micah is well known. As we ride into the village all activity stops, everyone heads for the recognized and distinguished ol' mountain man. We make our way through the press of bodies to the central lodge. Standing outside, two chiefs greet Micah as a long-lost friend. I stand behind him by myself. I'm terrified of the Indians. I'm ready to bolt for the wide open. I'm sweating and my limbs are actually buzzing. I'd run but I'm froze in place. I close my eyes and cover my ears blocking the sights and sounds of the din around me. I feel rough hands pull my hands away from my ears.

"What do we have here? It looks like this urchin is afeared of us. How's come you be afraid of us boy?" asks a dirty, foul smelling hulk in front of me. I'm cowering inside of myself. "What's the matter with you boy? Answer me when I'm talking to you," yells the heap of leather and fur.

"John, leave off the lad," warns Micah.

"Why Micah? What's special about this cowering lump?" asks the bully walking away from the group.

"I rescued him. The Blackfoot left him spread out and naked under the sun for what looks like three, maybe four days. The Blackfoot cut him up first. Took everything from him. You all know how it is. This was six weeks ago," Micah tells the silent crowd. I am not the first to experience Black-foot tortures. I am, however, a member of the select few that have survived and have lived to tell the story.

"I'm sorry Micah," says another trapper digging through his possibles. He opens a finely beaded leather bag, with-drawing a handful of gold coins. Placing them in Micah's hand he says, "I want this to go on account to the lad. It will help him resupply. If you need more coins, let me know and I'll cover all his costs at rendezvous." He turns and walks away, stopping at my side. He bends down to whisper in my ear.

"Sorry for the roughing lad. My name is Cyrus. If you ever need anything, tell them to put it on my account. If I can ever be of a help all you need is to let me know," he tells me, after spreading out a buffalo robe. "Sit and rest," he tells me with a hand on my shoulder.

"Thank you," I mutter. Cyrus walks away. The crowd is quiet for another minute. Then, at the sounds of a running horse, all at once merry making erupts. The loud sounds are foreign to me. A pitcher of water arrives at the buffalo robe I'm sitting on. I lift up the pitcher of drinking water enjoying the cold travelling down my still dry and parched throat. I dare not waste a drop. I am so involved in savoring the water I do not hear the crowd quiet for a second time. I place the empty pitcher on the robe, smack my lips, and sigh. I have never enjoyed water as much. Well that first sip after three days under the sun was perhaps better. Much better. That's when I realize everyone is quiet and everyone is staring at me.

"What?" I ask a bit more forceful than is needed. No one moves. No one speaks. Another trapper reaches into his poke, withdraws a handful of coins, drops it. Adding to the pile untouched on the robe, he walks to his horse. A hand to my shoulder and a smile as he passes, he jumps onto his saddle and rides out. A stack of leather and fur is started on the robe next to me. It grows in height through the day. Members of this village bring me gifts, buckskins, and furs. The gathering is quiet. I'm stunned.

"Why?" I ask.

"Many men have been found under similar circumstances as yourself. However, not many of them survive their ordeal. You are a member of an elite company. These rough and tumble men are paying you their best compliment. Accept it as such."

I am truly speechless. Random thoughts are running through my head. I'm confused and embarrassed.

"All I did is live," I try to explain.

"That is the reason for their expression of...well, marks of respect and honor to a unique and noteworthy man."

"But I did nothing."

"You survived. To that end you've earned their reverence, respect, and admiration. To all of us this is the beginning of an outstanding reputation, that will follow you the rest of your life. To these hard men, what you did is unique in our world." I am shocked and speechless. I sit on the buffalo robe and finish another pitcher of water. I wipe my mustache and beard, smiling glad to be alive.

"Where are we?" I ask Micah.

"We're at Rendezvous, son. This is what us trappers and mountain men live for. We turn in this year's fur for next year's possibles," he explains.

"I thought this was an Indian camp."

"It ain't, but there are Indians here. No Blackfoot though. Most of the white trappers are camped further down the trail. We'll head down that way when you're strong enough."

"I don't want to keep you from what you need to be doing. Let's go," I tell him. I stand to leave with Micah at my side.

"Let's get you outfitted," he tells me. The bright summer sun blinds me as I stand. I am led down the trail to a second camp. The throng of unkept men in dirty leather and fur carry my gifts of leather and fur. Micah has my collection of coins. I forgot all about it. I reckon I'm not as healed as I thought I was. Thinking all of this to myself, the group of us stops. Standing in front of us are two trappers. Both mountain men hand me the leads to a horse. The first is a riding horse complete with saddle, rope, bulging saddlebags, bedroll, and pommel holster filled with a pair of pistols. The packhorse wears a pack frame filled with three packs. One to each side and one sitting on top. Cyrus stands in front of the crowd.

"We've all pitched in to outfit you. I've had this extra rifle for years and never had to use it. I'd be proud if you'd accept it." He hands it to me as another man steps out.

"I've had these extra possibles. I'd be right proud if you'd take them." Another trapper hands me a powder horn. Still another a thick leather belt. They form a line handing me equipment, tack, and camp gear. I receive a knife, war axe, two more pistols, bars of lead, tools to make .54 caliber balls for both rifle and pistol, blankets, a winter's hat made from a plush red fox. Still others hand me a coat made from the best grade of Hudson Bay Blankets. Last in line are the local Indians. Most are friends and partners to the trappers. From them I receive a set of finely made buffalo hide pants, moccasins, a war shirt, cape, and gloves.

I must admit a fly lands in my eye, both of them, releasing a tear or two. I notice others in the crowd wiping at leaking eyes also. When I can hold no more, a pile begins growing in front of Micah and me. As they drop off their gifts they disappear. I hear the sounds of celebrating from the camp. I'm stunned and speechless. Micah hands me a heavy leather pouch with fancy bead work all around it. I carefully open the drawstrings. Inside I see the glare of gold and silver coins. Quickly I draw it closed.

"This is too much. I should give them back the coins," I tell Micah.

"Not if you want to keep your good name and reputation. Each one will take it as an insult if you give back a part of their gifts. No, you best keep it and be thankful. Sometime down the trail it'll be your turn to help someone who's undergone similar circumstances. You share what you can with them when you can. That'll be thanks enough."

"If that happens, they won't know I'm doing it in the names of these men."

"They all gave freely, not wanting any praise or recognition," says Micah.

"Alright, how about I go and thank them?"

"It's already done. Doing any more will only cause embarrassment. The best you can do is ride out, now, with me." I do. We ride for a couple of miles heading north by a bit west. We come on a creek with a sandy bottom and a good crossing. I reckon this to be the proper time to wash and change clothes. On top of my new packs is a bundle, a towel and bit of soap. I take the small bundle and the larger one holding my new buffalo hide clothes, to the creek. I wash both body and hair, thoroughly. The sting of the sunburn is gone. The long cut up the center of my body is healed along with all the little cuts. It feels good to soak in the cool water. I'm surprised when I see Micah walk into the water. My body can use the soaking and the cleaning. Feeling refreshed I walk out of the water. As I'm getting dressed, Micah gets out to sit in the sun while he dries.

The soft-cured buffalo hide pants and moccasins feel good. Much better than the silk coverings. I put on one of the cotton shirts gifted to me. It's too warm for the war shirt. A hat tops off my outfit. The fox fur hat joins the war shirt waiting for cooler weather. At the packhorse I add two pistols, the knife, and the war axe to my belt. I load the rifle and the four pistols under the watchful eye of Micah. He looks through my possibles bag, taking out or adding as he sees fit. When he is satisfied, he hands it to me with the powder horn. Both ride over the left shoulder, just like Micah shows me. Dressed and outfitted, carrying loaded weapons, and with two packhorses carrying my extras, I follow Micah to the mountains. We are on our own.

That's when I stop and ask Micah a burning question. "When did you have time to turn in your fur and resupply?" I'd hate to think he missed out because of me.

"I did that when you was sleeping. I got what I need. Don't worry yourself," he tells me.

As we enter what he calls the for-real mountains I perk up. The air is refreshing. The views spectacular. I am eating meat every day; this is a new occurrence. I'm quickly regaining my strength. I repay Micah by helping with camp chores and duties. I cook, clean up, fetch water and firewood. As I grow stronger, he begins my education. It starts with Micah instructing me on shooting, the proper way. I am quickly proficient with my .54 caliber, percussion cap American Long Rifle. I had some skill, but with Micah's coaching I become a deadly shot, with both rifle and pistol. He moves on to skinning and cleaning the game animals I shoot for supper. I learn how to brain-tan the hides, the Indian way. He teaches me about plants that are good to eat and the ones that have medicinal value. I learn how to cook over an open fire. I begin drinking coffee without sugar and cream. But most of all I'm regaining my self-respect and confidence, by doing everyday chores. I quickly realize my pride is returning. I don't know how he does it, but he helps me in many different ways.

I begin to notice changes in the air, it's growing colder. The hardwood trees begin shedding their colorful leaves. The days are growing shorter, the nights appear longer. Without telling me about his plans, we arrive at an Indian village. I quickly learn it's a Crow village. After a talk with who I take to be the chief, we walk with an escort to a lone buffalo hide lodge, at the far edge of the village.

"This will be our home through the winter. We're here to trade for hides and furs. Most important I want you to learn how to live in the wild. It will help you in whatever way your life turns after leaving here."

"Who are they and why will they help me?" I ask him.

"They are a small village of the greater Mountain Crow people. I've traded with them and lived amongst them for over ten years. I've found them to be helpful, kind, and excellent teachers. You can learn many things from them, if you open up and let them teach you."

"I'm here and I have a lot to learn. I'll learn. Thanks Micah. Thanks for what you've done for me."

"Help me unload the packs and we'll prepare for the cold time. In two days, we go buffalo hunting." I unload the packs and bring them inside the lodge. I learn it's a 25 buffalo hide lodge, one of the big ones. Micah needs it to house all his trade goods. Four of his six packhorses carry trade goods. I help set out all our typical camp gear, coffee pot, Dutch oven, stew pot, cups, plates, and spoons. All this came from my packs, gifts from Rendezvous. After arraigning things, we drink coffee and eat the last of our venison. Micah's packs carry supplies necessary to make it through the winter. The packs hold exactly what I would expect, flour, sugar, salt, and coffee, with dry beans, and cans of fruit.

"I have enough supplies for us both. What we don't have is meat. That is what we're after come morning."

"Buffalo? I've never actually hunted buffalo. The ones I've shot have been targets of opportunity. How we going to do it?" I ask him.

"We will take up different positions around the herd. I reckon twenty-five animals will see us through the cold months. We'll make jerky, but most of it we'll cut into smaller portions and place them all in the trees around us. Tomorrow we'll make platforms high up so critters can't get to it. After we get back, I'll show you how to fix your old broken rifle using buffalo sinew and hoof glue," he tells me.

"How we going to get twenty-five buffalo back to this village?"

"I've got horses in the great horse herd. We'll used travois like the Crow use. I have a pile of poles in back of the lodge."

The Hunt

We are up early, eat, and finish a pot of coffee. Our saddle horses are staked behind the lodge, close at hand. The pack-horses have been released into the general herd. The herd boys have marked my packhorse with Micah's mark. The herd boys have them ready for us before the sun rises. Carrying rifles and possibles we walk outside. Micah's first packhorse is fit to an extra-long travois carrying the poles for the other travois. We are ready to leave the village, taking our place in the long line of horses. Our first stop is to the horse herd and picking up the rest of our packhorses. We're bringing thirty horses tied together with neck rope. Four hours from the village we stop. Micah ties his horse to a tree.

"Is the herd here?" I ask impatient for the hunt. I do not see any animals.

"They should be on the grassy plain the other side of these trees. Come on." I jump down, tie my horse to a tree and follow Micah. In front of me is a sight I'll never forget. As far as I can see there is a dark brown, undulating mass of buffalo. They are drinking from the creek and feeding on the hearty grass in the valley. There is no way I could ever count them. I am speechless.

"See that wallow to our left? About thirty yards from the herd?"

"No, what's a wallow?" I ask.

"That's where they roll in the sand. Over time it's formed

into a depression, a bowl in the grasslands. That's where I want you. Try for twenty animals and remember what I've told you. Most important is making clean and quick kill shots."

"I remember."

"Good, then go. I'll be to the right," he orders. Taking a canteen, with my possibles over a shoulder, and carrying Micah's extra rifle I walk towards the buffalo. I don't look back. I expect the herd to run when they see me, but they don't. Only one or two animals pay attention to me. These are the sentinels, my first targets. Carefully I pound in the two shooting stakes. I place my possibles to my right side, pour out twenty rifle balls, and a pile of patches.

I sight in behind the shoulder of the first cow that noticed me. There is a clump of mud over the target, but I need her to take a step forward. She does. I set the first trigger. Taking a breath, I settle the sights on the clump of mud. Releasing half, I begin pulling back the hair trigger. I do not hear the explosion launching the lead ball. Nor do I notice the push of the rifle into my shoulder. I smell the rotten eggs of burnt black powder. As the wind catches the foul cloud, I watch my first buffalo shot from a hide, fall sideways to the prairie grass.

I quickly reload using a patch of silk around the lead ball. Micah says the ball will fly faster and further with a silk patch. I aim at the dinner-plate sized target behind her front leg as the second sentinel wanders over to sniff the downed buffalo.

I repeat the firing steps. My second animal falls. I pick new targets until I have ten animals down. I run a wet patch down the barrel to both clean and cool the rifle. The patch comes out dirty. I run a second wet patch, then a dry patch.

Now it's time to get back to work. I repeat the firing sequence until I have twenty buffalo down. I run wet patches down the barrel until they come out clean. I run a last patch with a small dab of bear grease down the barrel. I reload the rifle and put away my possibles. I pull up both shooting stakes, stand, and walk to the horses. A couple of pats reassure my horse I'm back. I dig out the sharpening stone, my skinning knives, and my big butcher knife. As I inspect the sharp edge Micah walks up.

"How many down?" he asks me.

"I counted twenty."

"How many balls?"

"I used twenty-three balls for all twenty animals,"

"That's good for your first time. Now the real work begins. Let's get to it."

"Wait a minute. How many did you shoot and how many balls did it take to get them?" I ask.

"I got twenty-five down with twenty-five balls. Now can we get to work?"

Working together we take the horses to the left, my side. We gut each animal as we make our way over the field. Pretty soon I get the feel for what we're doing, and the work is faster and easier. When all the buffalo lay gutted, we bring in the horses.

I imitate Micah as he ties two travois legs to a packhorse. He lashes smaller branches crossways on the travois. Using the horses, we push and pull one buffalo on each travois. The sun is well past its center point when we finish.

"Clean up and it's time to ride," says Micah. I wash my knives and both hands before climbing into the saddle. Micah leads off pulling the leads to the packhorses. I follow, last in line. Our four-hour ride out turns to a five-hour return. We stop in a small grass field behind our lodge. As soon as we arrive, a swarm of village women swoop on the buffalo. Using horses, Micah and I get the buffalo off the travois. Two of the herd boys untie the travois and stack the poles in a pile. They collect and move the horses off the small grassy field. When all the travois are empty, the herd boys lead our horses to the main herd. Our saddle horses are tied in front of our lodge.

Working together, the women of the village attack the buffalo. They get them skinned, cut off the head and begin the butchering process. Before the legs are cut off the sinew is collected. Younger girls break open the skulls collecting the brains for tanning hides. Micah collects the chunks of buffalo. Young boys climb to the platforms. Other boys toss them the chunks of meat. They make piles on all the platforms then cover the piles tightly with canvas. The hides are laid out hair side down to dry. Bones are gathered, broken, and the marrow is collected. The broken bones are taken far from the camp where they are claimed by the village dogs. No one wants a Grizz in camp attracted by the gut piles, bones, and drying meat. Horns are collected from the broken open skulls. All the hooves are collected and boiled to make a glue. Stomach bladders are used for carrying water. Long slices of meat from legs and necks are placed over small fires to dry and smoke into jerky. The globs of yellow fat are collected, placed in Dutch ovens, and simmer over low fires. Nothing from the buffalo is wasted.

Each worker takes what they were promised, payment for their work. The work is finished in the dark, all that is left in the grassy field are the hides. In three days, the women will return to begin working the hides into soft cured robes.

From our forty-five buffalo we end up with thirty-five hides to be worked into soft-cured robes. We have the meat from thirty-five buffalo sitting, aging, and protected on the platforms high in the trees. We also keep half of the sinew collected, a pot full of glue, and a small paunch of rendered lard. The rest is part of the price paid to the women, kids, widows, and orphans who reduced our buffalo into useful parts. I reckon it a price well paid.

Later that night every family roasts fresh buffalo for supper. Micah and I enjoy a pot of fresh coffee with our meat. He shows me how to mix bread dough thick enough to wrap around a long stick, set it close to the fire, and how to bake the dough on that stick into bread. It's a feast.

"That was one of the best meals I've ever had," I tell Micah as I sit back with a refilled cup of fresh coffee.

"That's true. Tomorrow I'll teach you how to work with sinew and the glue that was made from the hooves. I'll show you how to repair that rifle of yours that we found left behind by the Blackfoot."

"Thanks, that will be a good skill to learn," I tell him.

"That's true. No telling when you might have to make similar repairs to weapons or equipment. I also made arrangement for you to learn fighting skills."

"What kind of skills?" I ask concerned.

"Wrestling, knife fighting, how to use a bow, and how to fight using a war axe. Those are all skills that will keep you alive down the road."

"Thanks Micah," I tell him. Thinking about what happened to me at the hands of the Blackfoot envelops my mind in a dark black cloud. I need to learn how to dispel this blackness.

———

Repairing the Rifle

First thing in the morning, right after the new day's sun clears the horizon, school in the primitive arts begin.

"Bring out that busted-up rifle," commands Micah. I carry it out along with my possibles.

"Sit down and watch carefully," he tells me. Taking the rifle, Micah binds the broken stock closest to the hammer with a rawhide lace. He tightens it as much as possible checking the fit between the cracks. Letting off the pressure of the binding, he coats both sides of the crack with warmed glue, then retightens the binding. He spreads the glue forced out of the break over the entire stock along the break. Using small strands of the sinew prepared last night he begins wrapping it tightly around the break.

"See how I did that?" he asks me.

"Yes, I do."

"Good, now you finish it. I'll watch and advise, as necessary." I take the rifle and begin wrapping the break in sinew. When I've reached the rawhide tie I stop.

"Now what?" I ask.

"Take the glue and spread it over the sinew evenly." I pour glue over the sinew from a spoon. I spread it with a leftover rawhide square. It is sticky and cooling. I work faster. When it's covered to the leather tie Micah stops me.

"That's good. Now we'll tie it from one of the lodge poles until it dries. After a couple of weeks, it should be dry enough to repeat the process. I reckon three times will make it strong enough to shoot. Now pick up your materials and put them away until next time." He helps me tie the long rifle to a support pole inside the lodge.

"That's good. Put your war shirt on, it's time to learn how to fight Indian style." For the rest of the day I am shoved, hit, punched, kicked, prodded, and bruised. I suffer in silence earning the respect of my teachers and the young men not yet old enough to begin real warrior training. I stumble to the fire pit. I am tired well beyond anything I've experienced so far in my short lifetime. Micah sees the expected outcome, a thoroughly defeated, me.

"Sit right here Uriah. I've got coffee, buffalo hump, and bread ready for you," he tells me, bringing me a plate of food. I devour it. He refills it, once, then twice. I finish the coffee. I stand to enter the lodge.

"It ain't time to sleep. You got one more thing to do," he tells me.

"I don't have the energy nor the strength to do anything else tonight."

"No, it ain't like that. We're going to the hot springs. A soak will do you good." I follow Micah out of the camp, to the river. Before the river gets to the camp, a feeder creek meets the river. Walking up this feeder creek less than a mile is a natural hot spring. I shed my dirty buckskins and moccasins to walk into the hot water. At first it burns. I stand still. In the space of a couple of minutes I continue into the water. It reaches my shoulders burning away the day's aches and pains. I close my eyes surrendering to the comfort and heat.

I wake all of a sudden spitting water. Micah is laughing. I'm surprised and don't understand what has happened.

"You fell asleep and toppled into the water. You're fine. We best head back so you can sleep this off," he tells me. I walk from the water; with the only real friend I have through that first long and cold winter.

Every day is the same, only my helpers change. I take heart in that. I learn that they are as tired and worn out as I am. Every night I visit the hot springs. After the first month I get a selection of new instructors. They are older boys undergoing warrior training themselves. The third month and another team of older teachers. This batch are warriors, but young warriors. The fourth month I learn from older, established warriors.

At first the going is tough. I learn quick, gaining strength, and winning more contests than I lose. I am assisted in making a lance and a buffalo hide war shield.

———

Learning Crow Ways

I can fight like a Crow, using bare hands, knife, war axe, lance, and bow. I can follow a trail. I have learned how to imitate many animal sounds. I can start fires under stressful and trying conditions. I can use a bow and arrow to consistently bring home game. I can talk in Crow holding a conversation without thinking of the English word and its Crow equivalent. I will never be the equal to a full-fledged Crow warrior, but I no longer feel defenseless.

Early one cold winter morning I wake to hear screaming women and shouting men. I jump from my buffalo robes.

"What is it?" I ask Micah, fully knowing he doesn't know any more than I do. I'm dressed and tying my moccasins.

"Could be a raid. We best hurry." Micah grabs his rifle, pistol belt, and possibles. I throw my belt around my hips. It carries my knife and war axe. I take up my bow and a quiver of two dozen arrows. As I pass out the doorway, I take up my lance and shield. I'm out before Micah. I see an unknown Indian on a horse trying to grab a Crow woman. Without thinking, in a habit formed over the last five months, I launch my lance. It flies true, taking the unknown warrior through the chest. I tell the Crow woman to run behind me. Before I can pull my lance from the dead Indian, I see more horsemen riding through our camp. I bring out four arrows, place one on the bow string and hold the others in my bow hand. I release without thinking about aiming. The arrow strikes true, four enemy down. I walk ahead looking for targets. Twice more I release arrows, all are killing shots. The girl is behind me, she's carrying my lance and gathering the loose horses. I've lost track of Micah.

I continue ahead. Seeing two more horseback riders attacking friends in the village I loose two more arrows. The girl rushes out to collect both horses. I run past her. The noise is fading. I hear the girl behind me groan. I turn in time to see yet another warrior trying to knife her and take the horses. I don't have time to loose an arrow. I charge ahead. We collide crashing to the ground. In the smashup, I drop my bow and the quiver falls from my shoulder. We are separated by six feet. I draw my knife and war axe, roll to meet the dazed warrior, and try to brain him with my war axe.

Groggy, he moves his head, my axe bites him in the right shoulder. He cries out, pushing me away with a powerful left arm. I gain my feet, waiting. He gets up. He only has a knife in his left hand. We circle around each other. He feints, I don't move. He tries another feint. I see him smile. He must think I'm a trapper or a mountain man wintering with the Crow. With a sneer he lunges at me. I duck down, driving my shoulder into his right side. He cries out as I bury my knife in his back. He pulls away before I can pull it out. The sneer has not left his mouth. But his eyes don't shine as brightly as they did.

I stagger back, hoping he'll take the fake. He does. With a war cry, the sneer, and his knife, he rushes me. I trade hands, now I'm carrying the war axe in my left hand, leaving my stronger right hand and arm free. He tries a wide, fast cut from his left side. My left arm stops it. With my right I grab his right arm and twisting, throw him over a shoulder. He lands heavy. The fall has knocked the breath from his chest. I fall with both knees onto his stomach. I'm seeing red. Everything is tinged in a red haze. I've never experienced this before. I wonder if this is the Berserker rage that I learned about in school.

Looking into the fading light in his eyes, I plant my war

axe in the top of his head. I hear a satisfying thud. The air leaves his body. All sounds of the fighting around me are still. I look up expecting to see another Blackfoot warrior from the invading war party. I don't. I see most of the village in a circle around me. They are all watching the fight. I pull my axe from his head. The warrior I could never best during training walks up to me.

"You won. The scalp is yours." I look at him not understanding what that means. Not seeing comprehension in my eyes, he says, "watch." Bending down he grabs the warrior's long hair in one hand. With the other, he scalps him. He stands, handing me the grisly trophy.

"You have more scalps," he tells me. Micah walks to me.

"You've got it to do. If you don't, they may kill both of us and I ain't ready to go out that way. Get to it," he tells me in English. I look down and see two scalps in his hand. I retrace my steps to each of the kills. Without thinking I reach down, grasp a handful of thick greasy hair, and cut around the scalp. I lift up and the scalp separates with a squishy sound. Carrying the nine scalps to our lodge the village breaks out in shouting. I listen. It is shouts of victory. The girl I saved brings me nine horses and my lance. The warrior, Raven, places his hand on my shoulder and screams a wild war cry. Something deep within me is released. I join him shouting with all the power my abused throat and lungs can release. This gets the other warriors going. It is complete havoc. A fire starts in the front of the head peace chief's lodge. Everyone disperses. Except Raven and me.

"You must collect a weapon from each warrior you killed. If they were on horses, you must collect their horses. You counted coup on the last warrior before killing him. You have performed the warrior rites concerning your kills. These are your trophies."

We walk together back to each kill. I take their weapons, all of them. We turn back to walk to my lodge. The girl holding the horses is standing in front of us. She also has my lance and shield that I have lost track of.

"What do you want?" he asks her in a rough manner.

"I am holding his horses. He gave them to me after killing the warrior trying to take me away," she tells him looking at the ground.

"Is that true?" he asks me.

"Yes, I saw him trying to take her. I threw my lance and got him. I took a hold of the horse."

"Did you give it to her?"

"I handed her the reins to hold and told her to stand behind me so I could fight without her being in the way," I explain to the warrior.

"Stay here with the horses until they can be marked and taken to the herd," he tells her, taking my weapons from her and handing them back to me. With a last look he walks off.

"What was all of that about?" I ask Micah.

"I ain't sure yet," he tells me in a low voice.

The wounded are being treated. The few dead prepared by their families. All others are cleaning up for the celebration. Before noon all traces of the fight are erased from the village.

"What about the enemy dead?" I ask Micah, confused.

"The society responsible for guard duty has to clean up the camp. They failed to stop the attack. They are held responsible. They have to take care of the enemy dead too."

"And us?"

"You may be one of the guests of honor. I've not heard of another warrior getting nine kills this morning. To the warriors that is a big deal. It makes you a warrior."

"What about the horses?" I ask, still ignorant of many Crow ways.

"He's trying to reckon who owns them," Micah tells me. I have a feeling there is more to it than what he's explained. I don't know enough to ask the right questions.

"You best wash up and get ready for the celebration," he tells me. Just then two herd boys walk up. They confer with the girl, then come to me.

"These are your horses?" the oldest asks me.

"Yes, I killed their owners. Who were they? Who attacked the camp?" I ask.

"They were Blackfoot," he says spitting at the ground.

"How many were there?"

"We counted twenty killed and recovered eighteen horses. I will mark these as yours." He was one of the ones that laughed at me as I learned to fight. Right now, he is not haughty, but reserved, maybe even afraid. I watch the girl slowly walk away. I go to the hot springs to wash.

When ready, I wipe down my cleanest buckskins, dress, and walk to the lodge. Standing in front is my lance and shield. The scalps have been tied to the lance. While I'm looking at it, Micah comes out.

"There you are. That was brought back for you. It shows all of your kills and awards. It's big Medicine."

"Okay. I'm hungry, let's eat." Together we walk to the main lodge, the fire, and the celebration.

Sitting behind the fire are the tribal elders. Seated in front of them are the village's main warriors. Behind them stand most of the village. As I walk up, I see the main peace chief stand. Someone calls out names. Those called walk to the fire. Raven and another chief pass out eagle feathers. Each feather represents a kill. I am called last. Micah tells me as I'm called. I stand and walk forward.

I am handed nine feathers. Raven is holding my lance displaying the scalps. He attaches the eagle feathers to my lance.

"During the day when you are in the village this lance and your war shield will stand outside your lodge. At night and when not in the village it will retire into your lodge," he tells me slapping my shoulder. I return to where I was standing. I don't pay attention to what all else is said. I'm hungry and want to eat. Thankfully, the meeting breaks up.

47

I am escorted to the fire where buffalo humps are cooking over coals. Raven cuts off a slab and hands it to me. I thank him and begin eating as I walk away. Twice more I return for another portion. Afterwards I return to my lodge. I have no idea where Micah is, and I really don't care. Now that I've eaten, I'm tired. I wash my hands before climbing under the buffalo robes. I hear someone entering. I think it's Micah until I feel another body under my robes. I pull it off me to see what's going on. It's the girl.

"What are you doing here?" I ask surprised.

"I am here for you," she answers with a smile.

"You don't have to do this."

"I want to." I can talk no longer, nature takes over.

In the morning I wake to the smells of coffee and grilling buffalo. Nothing is on the fire; it must be outside. It's cold but has not snowed, yet. It is expected any time. I walk out and it's the girl, she smiles at me, says good morning, and hands me a plate with meat and a cup of coffee. I sit to eat. Halfway through I begin wondering where Micah is. His horse is gone. I hand her my plate and cup and return to the lodge. All his gear is gone.

"Where did Micah go?" I ask her.

"To his new lodge," she says pointing to a new lodge next to our old one. I had not notice it. I walk over and yell for him.

"Micah, you in there?"

"Yeah what do you want?"

"Why'd you move out?"

"Too crowded."

"What, come out here and talk to me."

"Can't."

"Why not?"

"Busy," he says. Then I understand. He's got a woman. I've got a woman. What? I return to the fire confused.

"Why are you here now?" I ask still confused.

"I belong with you now," is her simple reply. I don't know what to do. I accept a second plate and cup of coffee.

2

SPRING 1834

I AM THE NEWEST ADDITION TO THIS TROOP OF TRAPPERS. Right now, I'm kneeling hidden behind a pile of blowdowns, in the middle of the most fervent prayer in my relatively short life.

"Oh God, if you'd see fit to let me live through the next couple of hours, I promise I'll go back and make things right," I pray, not knowing if I am going to last through these present circumstances.

I lay still concealed from the sight of the Blackfoot war party intent on finding me, a trespassing trapper. I was repeatedly warned about crossing the creek. The south bank is safe but do not, under any circumstance, ever cross the river to the north bank. The Blackfoot constantly guard their territory. However, I have a bad habit of not taking good advice. There are five Blackfoot looking for me. I feel reasonably sure

I can survive the coming fight. After all, I'm driven by hate and protected by this Hawken rifle and four pistols. Each weapon is a .54 caliber, single shot, flintlock. I'll have to make each shot count. I don't want to fight a Blackfoot warrior with a knife and a Crow war axe. I can and have fought with both weapons, it's just that I don't want my life to depend on them.

From under the lowest log in the stack I watch as the war party closes in on my position. I have a plan, of sorts. Slowly easing from behind the windfalls I sight my rifle on the closest Blackfoot. As my finger tightens on the rear set trigger, all the forest sounds stop. The ever-present wind also stops. In the back of my mind I consider this as strange. Carefully moving my finger from the set trigger, quickly forward to the hair trigger, I align the sight blade, centering it on the closest warrior's chest. Taking a breath, I let out half, while beginning pulling back on the hair trigger, and holding the sights steady on the man's chest. The hammer releases, striking the flint, igniting the powder in the pan. The lead ball is hurtling down the barrel towards the target. The rifle makes its familiar kick straight back into my shoulder. Opening my eyes after the shot I see the target falling to the ground. Surrounded by a cloud of foul smelling burned black powder, *"now is the time to get busy,"* I think to myself.

Setting the rifle against the logs I pull a pistol with each hand. Bringing up the first heavy pistol I sight on the closest Indian. Time slows down. I watch myself making the necessary movements extremely slow. Even my hearing is slowing.

The warrior's cries don't sound right. I center the sight blade on the warrior's chest, and again time stops. The first pistol shoots, hitting the brave in the chest. I drop it. Changing hands, with the second pistol I sight on the third Blackfoot. The sound of the third shot brings time back to its regular speed. I am dropping the second pistol while drawing the next two. The draw seems slow. These two pistols rest further back on my belt.

Finally facing the last two screaming warriors, with loaded and aimed pistols, I fire both at the same time. The two Blackfoot are so close they bowl me over. The shots ignite a small fire on both warriors' leather war shirts. The last thing I remember seeing is the cloud of spent black powder flowing by on the breeze. The lights go out as I fall back. My head connects with another downed tree, a log in the pile.

Coming to I see white clouds floating in a bright blue sky. I hear the wind passing through the trees, kind of whispering as it flows past me. I'm still clutching the second pair of fired pistols. Opening my hands, I let them go. I try moving my head, left, right, forward, and back. Not too much pain is good.

"*I reckon it's time to get up,*" I reason with myself.

I work my hands slowly to my side. Ready to push up, I try sitting. At about a forty-five-degree angle, the real pain hits, like running into a rock wall. The world turns dark. Once again, my head falls to the forest floor.

Coming to sometime later, I'm unable to discern the passage of time. I try a second time to sit up. Success. *"Next move,"* I think to myself, *"is getting to my knees."* Kneeling is successful. Now to stand. When the forest and the sky above stop changing places, I find I can support myself.

Standing, I take a survey of my surroundings. The forest is making the normal noises. The wind still blows. The five dead Blackfoot are in front of this impromptu fort. I pick up my pistols. The rifle is still where I left it.

"Grateful, that's it. That's this new feeling," I say out loud. It's a new one for me, one I'm not real familiar with. While I reload, I'm tossing arguments back and forth in my head. I can't ignore it. With weapons reloaded it's time to inspect the bodies of each Blackfoot. I take a weapon from each. Leaving them as they lay, I pick up my dropped traps and head back to camp.

A heaviness is relieved from my shoulder as I'm crossing the river. Safe on the south side I turn around. Unfamiliar words form on my lips, *"I'm truly sorry. I wish things might have been different. It's my fault. I crossed the river. I knew better. They told me."* They are unfamiliar to me, as far as Blackfoot are concerned. Ever since they left me for dead, I've carried a hate for them. I don't feel it now.

A different heaviness returns after turning my back on the north and trudging to the trapper's camp. On the way I have time to think. For maybe the first time in my short twenty-three years I face myself directly, square on, without glossing over any blemishes. I don't like the result. Somewhere deep down inside of me a new feeling is rising. Can I put words to it?

A branch breaks, the crack of snapping wood reaches my ears. I stop behind a tree. All of the previous conversation flees, pushed away by fear and caution. Slowly I set down the heavy traps. The chains softly clink and chime as they pile on the ground. I ready the front two pistols, then my rifle. I'm as set as I can get.

There's a movement. Leather and furs amidst the trees. "*Friend or foe,*" I wonder?

Another flash. How many? Then a voice, "You don't reckon he crossed the crick now do you?"

"I hope not," replies a deep voice. The voices of the trappers I'm working with, friends.

"Hold up. I'm here. I'm fine. I was on my way back to camp," I say out loud.

The two trappers stop. "Is that you Uriah?"

"Yeah, it is boys. There's no one else here, just me."

"You been out all morning. We got to worrying."

"Thanks, but it wasn't necessary," I say to assure them, walking slowly to meet my partners.

"We best get back to camp. I thought I heard shots about an hour ago," says Asa the trappers' leader.

"You did, that was me. I run into five Blackfoot. I killed them all. They won't be returning."

"Oh, now Uriah that's a good one. I've seen you shoot.

There's no way you could outshoot five Blackfoot," argues Silas.

"I did, and I took a weapon from each. I'll show you at camp."

"That tears it, Uriah. I warned you about crossing the creek. Now all bets are off. We're going to have to move the camp. They'll be after us for sure," replies Asa.

"I'm sorry Asa. I don't know why but something in me makes me do what I'm told I can't or shouldn't do concerning the Blackfoot. I reckon deep down they still owe me. I done it and I'm right sorry about it," I confess now that I've been caught.

"Good for you being sorry, but now the rest of us have to suffer because of your cussedness, Uriah. If we weren't so far from other trappers, I throw you out of our camp," says Asa, working himself up.

"I'll understand if that's how you want it Asa. I won't fuss about your decision."

"We'll talk about it at camp, later. And I want to see those weapons Uriah. But for now, we need to make tracks for camp." The trio of trappers increase their pace. They do not offer to relieve me of part of my burden, chains, or traps. In their frame of mind, I must carry my own load.

As dark settles around the woods and the trapper's camp, the nine men gather around the central fire. Each man carves slices from the chunk of elk slowly roasting over a bed of hot coals.

"Uriah show us what you done," asks Silas.

From the haversack carrying the spoils of today's fight I bring out five knives, three war clubs, two war axes, and a necklace of grizzly claws and one made from eagle talons.

"Boys, I'm sorry about causing you trouble but I couldn't help it. I got all five of them. These are their weapons. I want the necklaces, but you are all welcome to pick out something. If you don't have one yet, them are some nice war axes there."

The trappers are looking at me like they are seeing a new man. I have only reluctantly shared souvenirs claimed from a fight. This is something new.

"What happened to you out there Uriah?" asks Erastus.

"If you can't choose, do you want me to hand them out?" I offer, ignoring the question. That breaks the spell. Each of the eight men make a choice. Two war clubs lay unclaimed. "Perry, I want you to have this war club. I know you didn't want me to join your party after rendezvous and that's okay. Take this as a gift from me." I hand over an ornately carved club. A branch with a large knob at the end, the knob has been whittled into a walking bear. The entire length of the club is rubbed smooth and sealed with pine sap lacquer. Although the bear's form is complete, hard use is proved by slight dents in the wood.

"Thanks, Uriah, but if we vote you out, these fine gifts won't change things. I didn't know you, and the things I did hear about you, well let's just say most of it wasn't good. I took a chance on you. Knowing what I do now, I would not have taken you on. Now, it ain't personal but I have these other boys to think about. You've put us in a dangerous position. Them Blackfoot will be seeking after us for revenge. Just because you're still mad at them. I understand the why, but you've put all of us in danger. A fight with them Blackfoot is never good. They hate us white trappers. I truly don't know how you killed five of them. I'm not sure that's a good thing or not. We got some talking to do. Why don't you wander over there away from the fire? Not too far and take your rifle and possibles. In fact, take a walk around the camp for me. Then check on the horses. I'll invite you back with an owl call," orders Asa.

I sling possibles over a shoulder, pick up my war axe, fix it in my belt, then take up my rifle.

"If something ain't right I'll call in with a quail." With that I am gone, silently slipping between the trees. I wrestle with himself. I have to face the consequences of my action. I let my hate overrule common sense and knowing I made the wrong choice doesn't sit well with me. If I would have stopped and thought about it, I wouldn't have done it. But I didn't and now have to pay the price. In this period of self-evaluating I find myself coming up short.

"*Why do I still hate the Blackfoot?*" I ask myself.

The owl sound brings me out of this thinking. I'm with the horses. After looking them over really good I head back to the fire.

"Uriah we'll tell you straight out. We voted you out of the

camp, but since we need to move, you can stay with us until we find another camp. Then it's you and your eight horses on your own. Winter's coming soon. You can find the Crow and winter over with them again. Next year at rendezvous turn in your plews and do it again. We won't tell anything against you if asked."

"Okay Asa. That's better than I deserve. I'll pull my weight until we part. Thanks."

"We'll be breaking camp in the morning. You'll still need to pull your watch, understand?" says Perry

"Yeah, I do. Thanks."

We finish eating and drink the coffee pot empty. It's my turn to make the coffee for the night guards. Everyone likes my coffee. I don't just dump in the grounds. I use an old sock to hold the grounds. When I make the coffee, the others don't need to use their teeth to strain or sift the grounds.

The night passes quiet. We moved camp so often everyone knows their tasks. Each of us packs his camp gear, hides, and plews on packhorses. Each trapper has enough packhorses for his camp gear and traps. And another one or two for his plews, depending on how good of a trapper he really is. Asa leads us south by a little east. I can tell we are heading closer to Crow country. We have all spent winters with the different tribes and look at them as friends and are looked at as friends. Once we feel clear of the Blackfoot we can slow down to trap as we pass creeks and rivers. I am expecting to be asked to leave any day now. I'm not anxious about being on my own. Since leaving Micah I'm looking forward to it.

We've set up camp using our time to trap and hunt heading away from Blackfoot country. The trapping is good. We are well away from Blackfoot lands. The plews are piling up. Two more horses are used to carry pelts, leaving only four packhorses not carrying loads. We all will have a good showing come rendezvous. They have not mentioned my leaving, yet.

As always happens when you let your guard down, misfortune occurs. To us nine trappers, it occurs in mid-afternoon, as some are bringing back beaver pelts to be cared for in camp. Five of the trappers are in camp attaching fresh plews to round willow forms. Two other groups of partners are heading for camp after collecting their plews. The two groups of two trappers are attacked the same time as the camp. A large force of Blackfoot has divided their forces, attacking three locations. I'm with the horses.

The first pair of trappers drop their plews to fight back. Armed with a rifle and a single pistol each, the first group of trappers take down three braves. That leaves two Indians. Each Blackfoot attacks a trapper. It's a knife or a club fight. Perry using the club gifted to him to quickly dispatch the warrior he's fighting. He runs to assist his friend. Again, using the club he kills the warrior fighting his friend, but he's received two deep cuts. One to the right arm and one across the ribs. They grab up their plews and run to camp. Timing a lull in the shooting, the first pair make the camp.

The second attack is on a pair of mountain men still setting their traps. They kill two of the attacking Blackfoot before the three remaining warriors attack the pair. One trapper is killed before the last warrior runs off, wounded. Silas, grabbing his friend's rifle, pistol, and possibles is quickly reloading all his weapons. Silas begins his run back to camp, leaving behind plews and his dead partner.

The third attack is at the camp. Four trappers are fired on by three rifles and many arrows. The rifles shot by the attacking warriors are all clear misses. The Blackfoot are better with arrows. Three trappers fight wounded. However, they each account for a warrior. The three wounded can shoot but cannot load.

The first pair of trappers run into camp. Settling in, they begin reloading their weapons and reloading for their wounded friends. The trapper on his own decides to wait before entering our camp. He sits with two rifles and two pistols, loaded and ready.

As the Blackfoot attack the camp, he notes the rising clouds of burnt black powder. Sneaking as close as possible, he begins whittling down the number of attacking Blackfoot warriors.

Prior to the attack I am on my own, checking on the horses. I'm carrying a rifle and four pistols. I've acquired the pistols on days just like this, picked up from dead comrades.

Today I have accepted my fate. I was preparing to separate from the others. But now I reckon I'll lend a hand against these Blackfoot invading our camp. Taking a spot behind a large tree I wait. I know the Indians will come for the horses. I'll be here when they make their move. I reckon I'll stop them. I set my rifle aside, this close it will be all pistol work.

I notice the birds have stopped whistling and the squirrels have stopped running from tree to tree. The warriors are coming.

"There's a movement," I think to myself. *"Wait until he's out from the tree. Almost... there he is take the shot."* Aiming the pistol, keeping the front sight on his chest. *"He still doesn't see me."* When the shot goes off, I'm half surprised. I see the forest through the cloud of burnt powder. Safe behind a tree I reload the pistol. While adding it to the back of my belt I see movement from the corner of my eye. I take out a second Blackfoot creeping along the forest floor towards the boys in camp. Behind the tree I reload the pistols, replacing them in my belt. I'm ready and waiting with a pistol in each hand and two extra in my belt. I don't know how many are in front of me. I spot more movement. Two warriors are coming to see what happened to their comrade.

"Can I take the shot and change hands to shoot a second time before he's on me? No?" the internal discussion continues. Another thought, *"I've got to try."* I step out with both pistols extended. Both front sight blades find their chests. Both pistols fire. *"Quickly, now what? Take a better look."*

One warrior is down. *"It worked, reload, wait and listen for the one I missed,"* the internal conversation warns me. A dry limb snaps behind him. Taking a knee, I turn. I lay both empty weapons down and draw my second pair. Looking from the side of the tree I'm hiding behind; movement gives away his position. *"He's right there, coming to me. Sight on the chest and pull the trigger."* Spinning from the tree I thrust the pistol against the chest of this enemy and fire. The first look on the warrior's face is astonishment, quickly changing to realization, then accepting his fate. I push him away from me. His buckskin shirt is on fire. The Blackfoot falls into the detritus covering the forest floor smothering the flames.

I reload my pistols, double checking the others on my belt, and try catching my breath. I remember my rifle. I go back to the tree, find it, and check the powder and the flint. I can't sit still; I've got to move. I hear more firing at our camp. I stop to check the bodies, taking all their weapons. I don't want them falling into other Blackfoot hands. I make a pile of the weapons and plunder behind a tree. I'll come back for it. I need to move, now, to help. Before leaving the tree, I move the pistols to the front of my belt and add a club from the pile of loot. Carefully walking by the side of the horses I'm heading for camp. I wait after hearing firing from the camp. I'm torn. I know they need help, but the horses are important too. The waiting gets my head swirling and my stomach burning. It's not from fear or from the fighting but from anxiety over my friends and partners. *"What to do?"* More internal conversation.

I hear the faint cracking of a dry branch. A warrior is walking towards him. I cock both pistols in my hand. Kneeling, I'm looking around the tree for him. *"Where is he?"* There about forty yards away, a single man approaches, he's carrying a knife and a war axe. Do I shoot him from the safety of thirty yards? Or do I meet him with similar weapons? He stops, he's looking. Is it for me or for my friends? I stand. He yells and begins running. Aim and pull the trigger, it fires, a good hit, straight to the chest. The warrior begins stumbling, slowing from his short run. He's coming for me. I can see the pain and the hate in his eyes. He's going to fight me if it is the very last thing he does. I reckon it will be.

I'm aiming the second pistol, pulling the trigger, feeling the recoil, seeing the cloud of burnt powder, smelling the sulfur, the wind clears the area. The Blackfoot is dropping to his knees. A sharp look at me and the warrior collapses to the ground, dead. I reload and wait, hiding in the trees. *"Four warriors lay dead from my hand. Can't think about that now,"* waiting. *"They keep sending warriors to the horses. The horses must be important. I'm going to remain here,"* I decide stopping the internal worry and debate. I find a bush to hide in that I can see in both directions. I ready weapons and wait.

At our main camp, the fight continues. The Blackfoot attack in pairs or triples. The trappers can handle those attacks. They won't be able to handle a single attack of the whole group. Why haven't they made that attack? All I can hear is rifle and pistol shots. As long as I hear shooting, I know they're still alive and fighting.

Unknown to me, two of the trappers are pin cushioned by arrows. They lay dead. The trapper's camp is down to four men. As the warriors with bows step out to shoot, the trappers shoot them down. A heavy silence settles over the woods. I can almost feel it. It has been a while since I've heard a shot. The Blackfoot must have left but are any of my friends left alive? My mood is as black at the night.

I hear voices but can't make out the words.

"Asa, how many do you think we've killed?"

"I know six for sure. Could be more, and maybe more wounded."

"Sounds like they were attacking by the horses too."

"Yeah and it ain't going so good for them. Uriah is over there."

"Good."

"How long do think they'll keep this up?" asks Perry

"They've lost a lot of men. I don't see them continuing much longer. Now that it's dark they may pull out. But stay sharp, we ain't done yet," warns Asa

The birds come out; the squirrels are running from tree to tree. They've missed the last of the afternoon's sun to feed. They are making up for lost time now. The peaceful sounds chase out some of the dark from my head and soul. Above the camp an eagle sounds off. The darkness settles in. I need to move.

"Hello, the camp," I yell, breaking the silence. "I'm coming in. They have pulled out. We got most of them. How'd you boys do?"

"Hi Uriah, it's good to see you. We lost four. Peter and Lewis with Jed and Jacque. Was that you by the horses?" asks Asa.

"Yeah it was. They are safe. I checked their ropes and hobbles."

The five of us surviving trappers get to the business of burying our friends. We dig the grave deep, lay them to rest together, and fill the last two feet in with rocks covered by soil. There are no markers. The Blackfoot will dig them up and desecrate the bodies if we make markers or leave the grave recognizable. We drive the horses over the graves on our way out come the morning. There is no evidence of a grave to see or find.

The five of us surviving trappers equally divide our dead friend's gear and plews between us. We load horses with packs of camp goods and plews. I'm given a horse carrying three packs of beaver and a horse carrying three packs of mixed furs. That's alright with me; they are still a bit mad at me. I'm better off now so I'll not say a thing. When ready, just after the sun rises, Asa leads us south, away from the battle site, to the mountains.

A week later, in the morning before heading out I have news for my friends.

"I won't be going to rendezvous or wintering with you. I'm heading to Kansas City and this time next year I'll find the Crow."

"Why?"

"I'm going to sell the furs I have and reoutfit myself. These Blackfoot have left me very little. It's time to take care of myself. I will be back."

"In spite of everything, you'll be welcome in my company," says Asa.

"Thanks. Who knows, you may find me wanting to winter up. It all depends on what happens in town."

"Good luck."

————

Kansas City Summer 1834

I'm leading nine horses, five are carrying plews, one carries a mixed bag of furs and two carry camp gear. I head east to Fort Union and the riverboat landing. Instead of riding and generally following the river to Kansas City, I hope to take a faster, yet not necessarily any safer steamboat. The double-deck, side-wheeler I'm hoping to catch is about 100 feet long by 30 feet wide. The last one arrived with new trappers, horses, and needed supplies for the fort and for the American mountain men in the area. I hope to catch it for the six-week ride south covering about 2,300 miles.

I arrive at the firewood stop on the river. The pile of wood is still high. I reckon they haven't passed by yet. I set up camp to wait on the boat's arrival. I don't wait long. Mid-afternoon the next day I hear the steam whistle of the boat letting the stop know they're on the way. Except all that's here is me and my horses.

It doesn't take the captain long to figure out whoever stacked the wood is gone. While the crew loads the wood, I talk to the captain. He agrees to take me and my horses on, as long as I will provide my rifle against Indians or pirates. That is an easy decision.

I secure the horses and packs of pelts towards the bow of the ship. Before setting off, the captain cautions me about keeping out of the way of the working parts of the boat, especially the two spars called grasshopper legs. The spars are used to move the boat when it runs aground. The two spars act like crutches lifting the boat over and across whatever ground has stopped the boat. They are used a lot by the crew on this river.

This trip takes an additional week due to unscheduled stops for wood cutting details. A handful of usual firewood stops are not ready for the boat. The ship's crew has to cut wood, load it, and stack it. The captain reckons it's an Indian scare that has stopped the usual wood cutters. I volunteer to help, earning favor from the captain and the crew. I also receive a discount on my passage fare. The horses are unloaded and allowed to graze at each stop. The trip down river provides me ample opportunity to think and to plan. However, on arriving at the conflux with the Mississippi River, above Kansas City, I land without a strategy. It appears I possess the will but not the way.

Walking off the boat to find a buyer for my plews I notice frenzied activity along the waterfront. Curious, I begin looking for someone to ask about it. Up head are a handful of buckskinned plainsmen. I ride up to try and talk to them.

"Hello there," I say to a man sitting his own horse.

"Hello yourself," answers a Plainsman.

"What's all the activity about?"

"Indians have attacked the river boat. These men are trying to figure a way to go after them and are building up their courage to do it."

"That ain't hard. Just saddle up and get gone," I add.

"For this bunch that's easier to say than to do," he laughs.

"Good luck to you. Where can I find a fur buyer?" I ask him.

"Why do you want one of them critters?" he asks me with a shake to his head.

"I need to sell my plews."

"All right, follow me." The horse-back watcher walks us down the inside edge of the gathering bunch. Some move out of our way on their own, others we push aside, and some the horses move. At the river's edge the ferry area is in a frenzy.

"There you go. Right down the second street off the main street, and parallel to the river. You'll smell it before you see it. Good luck to you," says the Plainsman.

"And to you," I add to the horse-backed watcher, turning to lead my horses and their burdens to the tannery.

"Wait a minute," shouts out someone at the edge of the crowd. "We need them horses.

Mister. I'm asking nice on account we don't know you. But right this minute my men are fighting Indians. I need your horses to help them."

"First off, you ain't getting my horses," I say pulling two pistols. "I just came from there and I didn't see any sign of Indians. If there is a fight, it's a ways upriver and you'll need to take a boat to get there, not ride horses. Them Indians won't be there by the time you ride there. If you do make it, by that time it will be days after the end of the fight. I advise you to let me pass."

The crowd of men grows quiet and sullen.

"He's right. You'd best leave him alone," says one of the biggest men I ever have seen.

Everyone backs away from me. That's when they notice I'm holding two pistols. The crowd moves back even further. I'm hearing words like heathen, back woodsman, trapper, and the best one is Mountain Man all spoken as slurs. I take the names as an honor, but they are slurring the words as if they'd be a curse word. I replace the pistols in my belt and move my horses down the street parallel to the river when the whistle on the boat I just left sounds. I wave to the big man who spoke up for me.

That's when I notice an ornery old cuss approach the barge's rope tied to the landing. He's carrying a big double bit ax and looks like he knows how to swing it. I grab my Hawken from the saddle scabbard. That gets the attention of a few troublemakers. They point me out to the axe man. He shakes his head and walks to the rope.

"How hard is it to get a new rope?" I shout to the ferry's captain.

"Real hard, I reckon. Why do you ask?"

"They're about to try and cut your rope" I tell him.

"We'll see about that."

The ferry man removes a Kentucky Rifle from a scabbard fixed to an inside wall of what passes for an office on the Texas deck of the side wheel boat I rode down river.

He rests the full wood stock on a post. He's sighting when the men around the axe man see the ferry man with his rifle. They scatter. The axe man raises that big double bit axe. The captain fires. The ball lands at the feet of the axe man causing no harm. He grins then begins laughing at the captain.

"*I can't let this happen. The captain treated me just fine,*" again with the internal conversations. "*That's enough,*" I yell at myself. I pull my rifle. I aim at his legs; I don't want to kill him. Correct the sight picture by raising it up, I fire. The axe man drops the axe like it's on fire. All the group is looking and pointing fingers at me. My shot hits the axe-head at the handle, separating the axe from the handle and sending a terrific shock through the handle.

"I don't think they'll be messing with the rope anymore," I tell the captain. He's looking at me with a big smile and a gleam in his eye.

"I reckon that's a two-dollar shot," he says, climbing down the stairs to the edge of the dock and handing me back my coins. Two dollars is all that the captain charged me for my ride south.

"Well thank you," is all I can think of to say.

"You'd best make for the tannery right quick in case them rascals try to get the law on you. You'll be long gone."

"Why would the law be after me?" I naively ask, genuinely wondering.

"That bunch thinks highly of themselves and you just one-upped them," answers the captain. It's time to head out.

Before I can ask further, the captain walks away. I climb into the saddle, turn, and wave my thanks. As I ride off, we're absorbed into the crowd. My destination is a couple streets from the waterfront. I'm looking to sell my plews. I ride to the building. No one is there. A sign says they will not be buying any more beaver pelts. Underneath that sign is another. It reads, bring them to the Richardson Building, and gives vague directions. I follow them two streets back to the water-front and three streets south. There it is. The Richardson Building. I can smell chemicals, plews, and something unidentifiable.

I stop my horses in front of the building. As I'm climbing from my saddle a man runs scurrying out the door.

"You got beaver plews under there?" he's asking me, almost running to me.

"Yes, I do. These horses are carrying plews, furs, and buffalo robes."

"Good, don't climb down. Quickly now, move your horses to the back. Come on man, hasten it up." He is in a frenzy.

I do. In the back I see a press, scales, vats, and people working at tables.

"Move your horses to the tables, please." My packhorses are quickly lined next to the tables.

"Shut and lock the gates," he shouts. "Alright now, let's unload these horses and see what we got," says the short man.

"Wait a minute." I shout back.

"What's the matter, you change your mind? You don't want to sell your furs?" he asks me in a flurry of words.

"No, I do, but I don't know how much they're going for. What are you paying for good furs?" I ask him. He's standing by my horse looking up to me.

"I'm paying $4.50 for grade MB beaver fur. The price goes down from there."

"Alright, go ahead and unload," I tell them. He comes around to talk to me.

"I'm Adam Richardson. And you are?"

"I'm Uriah. I trapped, skinned, fleshed, and stretched each one of these beaver. These furs are some of the best you'll ever see. I've got fifty in a bundle and three bundles on a horse and five horses. That's 750 plews in all."

"I'll take your word for it, until we count them all. I don't want to cheat you if you've got an extra one or two."

"Shouldn't, I bundled them myself. Well, I should say we bundled them all together. Maybe it is a good idea to get an accurate count. Some of my old partners couldn't count past twenty. And that horse carries three packs of mixed fur."

"Can I get you something to drink while we wait?"

"If you have a cold beer, I would be thankful. I haven't had a beer in two years. I really would like one now that you've mentioned it."

The man, Mr. Richardson, waves his hand and a boy comes running. "Yes sir," he says.

"Go to the hotel's bar. Tell them it's for me. I want a pitcher of cold beer," he says to the runner, giving him a half dollar coin. The kid is off running in the streets.

"It's a warm day, what you say we go sit in the shade at one of those tables?" asks the shorter man.

"You lead, and I'll follow." He does. He finds a table out of the July sun. I didn't notice how hot it was until we get under the shade.

"What about my horses? Do you have water?"

"No, I don't. I'm still new to the business. I've only been open for about six months.

I'm still learning the business. I know of a good livery

down two buildings. I'll send a runner and have ten stalls, water, and grain ready for them when they are unloaded."

"That'd be right nice of you Mr. Richardson. Thank you."

"Think nothing of it. You're my first sale direct from the mountains. I hope to get more," he says with a sigh.

"I think I can help with that."

"What are you going to do after you leave here? If I may so bold as to ask."

"I'm heading for the general store to buy me some new clothes. Then to a barber for a hot bath, a shave, and a haircut. Why?"

"Well you see, I was just wondering if you knew your way around town and the best place to get what you've outlined?"

"Now that you've mentioned it, I don't. All I know about Kansas City I've learned by passing through on my way to the mountains." I know more, but I wasn't going to begin that discussion with him.

"How long are going to be in town?"

"Long enough to resupply and head back out. Maybe a day or two. I reckon I'll leave the morning of the day after tomorrow. Why?"

"Where are you planning on staying?

"Again, I haven't thought that far ahead."

"If you can trust me, I will get you a room for two nights that has a bath, and a barber downstairs. I can have one of my girls go to the general store for you. All I need is some sizes and a list of colors."

"I appreciate that, but what's it going to cost me?"

"Nothing. I'm going to offer these services as extras to get furs. Why? Don't you think

"Oh yes, it'll work just fine," I assure him.

The cold beer arrives and talking ends. Mr. Richardson walks away from the table to get the promised matters moving. He sends his sharpest secretary to the store for clothes. She has an eye for sizes and colors. He sends another one to the hotel with instructions to secure a room for two nights, a room with a bath. She arranges the services of a barber, laundry services, and a stable.

The unloading is complete. Another group of men take the horses, except for my riding horse, to the hotel's livery.

The tally is handed to Mr. Richardson. He walks back to the table to show me.

"Your tally was a bit off but they're all excellent furs. The count is 755, at $4.50 each. That's, $3,397.50. And those mixed furs are 70 buffalo robes of the highest quality. I will pay five dollars each. That comes to a total of $3,747.50 How would you like the money?"

"What do you mean?"

"You can have it in paper money or gold coins. We can put some in the bank and I'll give you however much you'll need while in town and to resupply. It's up to you. I can pay you with $20 gold double eagles. You'll be carrying 188 coins."

"I didn't realize that. How about we put some in the bank and I'll take some coins?"

"Good, come inside and we'll get it done."

I follow him into his office. He takes his seat behind a big desk. I am surprised, it is cleared of papers.

"How much do you want?"

"Let's say $1,000 in coins."

"Alright, here's a check for the rest, $2,747.50. We'll go to the bank right now and deposit it," says Mr. Richardson, handing me $1,000 in gold double eagles.

"First I need to strip my gear from my horse so he can join the others in a well-deserved rest." I walk back out to him. He looks back at me like it's about time you got to this. I unload my saddle, saddlebags, rifle, and all the other gear. One of Adam's boys will take him to the hotel's livery. I load my gear into the buggy we are taking to the bank. The banker comes out of his office to greet us. We exchange handshakes. All three of us walk back to the banker's office to complete the paperwork. There is one part that throws me.

"In case something happened to you who is the account to go to?" he asks me.

I tell them for now make it to Mr. Richardson. I don't know anybody else. I leave the bank with 10 twenty-dollar gold coins. Our next stop is the Kansas City Grand hotel.

Once again, the manager comes out to greet Mr. Richardson. I am escorted to a room with a bath. My gear is brought up in a cart. I agree to meet Mr. Richardson in the lobby for supper. I follow the best dressed man I've ever met. He hands me the key at the door of my room, spins around and heads back to his counter. He did tell me to let him know if I needed anything else. I couldn't think of a thing, well maybe new clothes. I was getting a lot of sideway glances with my buckskins in the company of the well-dressed Mr. Richardson, the banker, and the hotel man.

I open the door and can't believe my eyes. The room has three rooms. A front room, the bedroom, and a room with a bathtub. I am impressed. I fill the tub with hot water, as hot as I can stand. I drop the buckskins in a corner. They are still wearable, just needing a good airing. I scrub, then soak until the water turns cold. I get out and the biggest towel I have ever seen waits for me. I am half afraid to use it, but I do. And there laying on the bed are fresh store-bought clothes. I did not see who brought them in or when. I reminded myself to keep aware.

Even in the city I must keep my guard up.

There are jeans, shirts, socks, a leather belt, and new boots. I get dressed. I didn't want anything fancy, just good work clothes and that's what I got. When I am dressed, it is time to meet Mr. Richardson for supper. It is good to eat something I don't cook for myself. We both order the American Steak Dinner. I wash down the best steak I've ever eaten with a cold beer. To finish the meal, we have a piece of hot berry pie with cold iced cream on it and coffee. All of it is great. I'm feeling spoiled.

The next morning, well after eating another great meal, I go to the general store recommended by Mr. Richardson. I need to pick up supplies and trade goods. First, I need a hat. I walk around looking at everything displayed in plain sight. It's a wonder I made it two years without all this...when I'm interrupted.

"May I help you find something?" asks the most beautiful girl I've ever seen. My brain won't let my mouth and tongue work properly. "Is there something in particular you're looking for?"

"Yes, a hat. I need a hat for when I return to the mountains."

"I see. You're one of those trappers," she sneers. She makes the word trapper sound like something my boots picked up in the corral.

"Yes, I'm a mountain man; I've trapped some and hunted some." What an idiot I am. I can't even talk in sentences.

"Our hats are over here. I would recommend a wide rim, to keep all that sun off your face." I realize she's as nervous around me as I am around her. Somehow that settles me. I follow her advice. I pick out a second set of clothes, a third shirt, and a long sheepskin coat. I lay everything on the counter and she's adding up the total. I add two bandanas to the pile. She tells me the total. I pay it. I leave the list of supplies and let her know I'll pick them up later this afternoon. She helps me to the door. I'm carrying one box and she's put two on the boardwalk, then shuts the door. I'm on my own. I make it to the hotel carrying the three boxes. The man at the desk hurries over with his cart. Once again, he takes my gear in the three boxes up to my room.

I can't sit in the room any longer. I'm not used to the walls and ceiling. They feel like they're closing me in a small box. Once away from the hotel, I pass a gun store. I venture inside. There on the wall, behind the counter, is something I've never seen before. The store owner smells a sale.

"Can I help you?"

"Yes, you can. Those pistols and rifles look different than the ones I carry. What is the difference?" I ask him. He begins explaining the differences and the good points of percussion cap versus flintlock. When he's finished explaining, he tells me it is possible to change over flintlocks to accept the percussion caps.

"I've got six pistols and two rifles all flintlock. How much to turn them into percussion cap weapons?"

"I can do it all for five dollars."

"You can begin with these and I'll bring you the others directly." We shake. I turn around to head back to the hotel. I return with both rifles and four more pistols. I watch him work for a handful of minutes, grow bored, and leave the shop. I return to the general store. The bells over the door announce my entrance.

"You're back. We have your order filled and waiting for you out back. Would you like to settle up now?" asks the store's owner and clerk.

"Yes, I would." He hands me the bill. I double check my list against theirs. It's all there. I dig the banker's check out of my wallet in my possibles. With great care and precision, I fill out my name and the total amount payable to the store. With a flourish I hand it to him."

"I will be taking this directly to the bank," he announces getting out of his work apron.

"I'll be out back loading my horses. I intend on trapping for another season and returning this time next year. I'd like to do business with you again but…"

"That will wait until I see if this voucher is good," he snaps at me. I will be using a different store for supplies next trip. I don't tell him, yet. He storms out of the store. I can't understand what he's mad at. I head for the back of the store. The clerk follows me out. I look at him.

"Just following orders, ain't personal," he tells me.

"What does he expect me to do?"

"Ain't my place to say." I look through the stacks of supplies. It looks all here.

"I'm going for my horses. I expect to see all of this here when I return."

"It will be," he assures me. I get back leading my horses as quick as possible. The store owner is waiting for me. I line up the horses and bring the panniers to the boxes of supplies.

"I must admit, I was skeptical that your check was good. I'm happy to say it is," he tells me, like this is a great revelation.

"I knew that. Wasn't a surprise to me."

"I look forward to helping you next year."

"I ain't convinced you'll be my first choice in general stores," I tell him.

"Why is that?" he asks me, surprised and shocked.

"Trust goes both ways Mister. I trusted you and that trust was not returned. I don't believe I can work with someone who I don't trust and who don't trust me."

"Well look at it from my point of view. I don't know you. I don't..."

"But you know Mr. Richardson, the banker, and the hotel man, right? If they do, then I reckon you should have also."

"I apologize Mr. ah..."

"Uriah. That's all I got to say to you." I do not stop working while we're talking and can see that it annoys the store man. Inwardly I smile. I concentrate on my work. As I place the panniers on the pack frames, I balance the load, then secure it. I climb onto my saddle and lead my horses away from the general store. The store owner and a clerk watch me the entire time. I reckon he expects me to steal something. He's not so good at judging men.

It's late enough that my weapons should be finished. I lead my string of horses down the streets to the gunsmith's shop. I tie my saddle horse to the hitchrail and walk in.

"It will be better if you take that string behind the store. I can have someone keep an eye on them for you. Out front I don't trust anyone passing by."

"Thanks, I'll do that." The bells above the door announce my leaving. In only a few minutes I tie the string of horses out back. True to his word a worker carrying a shotgun is there to watch my horses. He shows me where the back door is. I walk in and make my way to the front desk. As I walk through his shop, I can't help myself from looking at everything on the tables and the walls. I'm impressed.

"How much do I owe you?" I ask him.

"A dollar each comes to eight dollars. Anything else?" he asks watching me look over his shop.

"Yes, I need .54 caliber balls, powder, and the percussion caps." The gunsmith puts what

I need on the counter. I look up and he tells me what I owe him. I lay the amount on the countertop.

"You may need to get accustomed to the caps after shooting flintlocks for so long. Outside of town to the east is an old quarry. That's where we all go to shoot new weapons."

"Thanks, I'll do that." Finding the old quarry is easy. I lead my horses to a small grove of trees next to a creek. I tie them to a picket rope where they can reach both the grass and the water. I set up the five bottles the gunsmith gave me for targets.

Not knowing what to expect, I am pleasantly surprised when the rifle fires and the bottle shatters. Two more shots at rocks farther way and I switch to my second rifle. Again, it shoots the same, just a bit quicker than the flintlock. Now for the pistols. One at a time I shoot the first ball at a bottle. Two more balls and I get the feeling for how they shoot. I think I've got it. Now it's time to clean them all. I move to under the trees. I begin with cleaning the rifles.

About halfway through the chore I run into trouble. Or rather trouble runs into me. Trouble in the form of two drunken ruffians. They've been out celebrating, heard the shots, seen me firing, and approach my camp.

"Hello, the camp," yells out the more drunken partner. I can tell trouble is heading my way.

"It would be better if you continue on. I'm not in the mood to be trifled with," I answer. On reaching the quarry I have changed into buckskins, my gun belt is slung around my waist, and I'm cleaning my pistols. Both rifles are loaded and close at hand. The horses stand loaded but relaxed.

"Don't be unsociable. Sure, we been drinking, but I can smell your coffee. That would sure be nice right now."

"Like I said, move on. Don't come in. You've been warned."

"Oh no, Jess we've been warned," laughs the bigger drunk.

"Come on Dave, let's move on. It ain't worth it."

"Don't tell me you're scared of a lone city boy playing mountain man. Come on, let's meet this city boy who thinks he's all it."

The two drunks stumble into my camp on the trail through the rocks. Seeing my ten horses, Dave pipes up. "Hey

Jess, maybe he'll let us ride one of his extra horses' home, so we don't have to walk the whole way."

"I don't know Dave. Let's not mess with the man's horses."

"Come on boy, sides there's two of us and only one of him. You know I ain't never been beat. Come on don't be an old lady." Entering the camp, they see the fire, the coffee pot, and the bedroll, but no person.

"See Jess we scared him off. Now, what was his, is now ours. Come on," laughs the drunk, stumbling into my camp.

"Just a minute you two, don't touch anything. Turn your drunken carcasses around and stagger out of here and to somewhere's else."

"We ain't leaving mister and your big talk don't scare me," boasts the drunk bully.

"You'd better grab your friend before he gets you both killed."

"Come on Dave, now, let's go. This ain't a man to trifle with."

"Both of you shut up. I'm going to sit and have me a cup of coffee, you both can..." he never finishes his thought. Instead I pick him up by the shoulders of his filthy shirt and walk him around the fire to the road and toss him bodily onto the road.

"He picked you up like a bushel of leaves Dave. That tells me it's sure enough time to

go," pleads his quickly sobering friend.

"No man is going to do that to me," he says turning to get his first look at me. Standing in front of the drunken bully I'm only five feet nine inches tall, but I'm backed by two hundred pounds of work-hardened muscle. All he sees is a shorter, now riled, mountain man, dressed in leather and fur. He doesn't see I'm carrying a belt shoved plumb full of handheld weapons. Nor does he recognize I have a rifle pointing at his bully head.

The bully takes a step back. Slowly he reaches down into a boot and brings out an Arkansas Toothpick. "What do you say? Put down that rifle and face me with a knife," he taunts me.

"Is there another way?" I ask the bully's partner.

"None he'll listen to now. Don't kill him. He's my only friend," pleads his partner.

"I'm setting this down right here. If you go for it, I'll kill you. Do you understand me?"

"Yes, I do. I'm going to stay right here."

"Oh, come on," shouts the bully.

I pull the pistols and unfasten the gun belt. After taking out my fighting knife and the war axe, I turn to face the bully. I bend my knees and twist my head, loosening muscles.

The bully rushes in like I reckoned he would. The knife arm is easily blocked. The flat back side of the war axe connects with the side of his head. He stops still in his tracks, but he's not out.

"It will take more than that little tap," threatens the bully.

The drunk thinks he's smart by faking a rush, stopping, and trying for my gut. I drop the war axe, capture the bully's knife hand in my hand, and begin squeezing. The knife falls, bones grate against bones, breaking in his hand. As the bully gets ready to yell, I throw a punch to his nose, breaking it, and the drunk is down. The broken nose is gushing blood. The drunk tries to swing a punch with his one good hand, but it's lacking strength. I catch it. Looking the drunken bully in the eyes I force the arm up and behind the man. I stop forcing the arm when I hear the bone snap. I hit him in the jaw, breaking it.

"Stop Mister, you're going to kill him. Please stop."

Fighting the red haze, I kick the bully in his most tender of spots, let him go, and watch him flopping in the road like a fish out of water.

"When he tells the authorities I beat him for nothing, you'd best remember how many chances I gave him to quit. I'll be back through these parts and if anything ever comes of this, I'll kill both of you, and if necessary, your families. You should leave people alone when they warn you. Now get."

Knowing the authorities will be on their way, I break camp. Lying in the road is the bully's knife, it's a good knife. I pick it up, tossing it on top of a pack. I'll be long gone when the sheriff and a pose arrive with the two drunken, well maybe now sober bullies.

"This is where he was camped sheriff," says Dave.

"I don't want to pursue this sheriff. He gave Dave plenty

of opportunities to stop and for us to leave. He deserved what he got. He was asking for it."

"What kind of a friend are you?" yells the belligerent Dave, showing the beginnings of a hangover.

"Not your friend anymore. Not the way you forced that mountain man into fighting and almost killing you. He warned you."

"Now you're telling me this guy is a mountain man. Dave you're on your own. Maybe you did deserve what you got. It's been a long-time coming," says a disgusted sheriff.

"You can't talk to me that way, even if you are the sheriff," shouts Dave reaching into his boot for his knife.'

"What's the matter? Did he take your knife too?" That gets the posse laughing at the humiliated Dave. He storms off, east, in the direction of the mountain man. "You'll never learn will you Dave?" taunts the sheriff.

But Dave is out of hearing range of the posse. He has no intention of following the mountain man. He wants the posse to think he is. That is a true representation of his life, all show, no follow through.

Five miles ahead I'm still shaking off the red haze. When it comes over me, I am dangerous. That's how I collected half of those six pistols. Each is a token taken from fighting another mountain man and trapper. Ten more miles and the red haze is gone. The night is giving way to a new morning. I have fresh horses carrying light loads. I decide to continue on. That's when I remember the hotel room. "*I have no reason to return to the hotel. All that's there are the new clothes I bought for town. Returning for them will be a waste of three days. May as well keep going now,"* I tell myself.

Ten days later, following the Missouri River, I arrive at one of the firewood cache and camp spots used by the steamboats. I unpack the horses more than ready for fresh coffee. I wake with the sun already up and shinning in my eyes surprised I sleep so late. What's prodding me? A poke with a stick. Two boys.

"Hey mister, what you doing in our camp spot? Are you hurt or dead?"

"He ain't dead stupid, he moved."

"Don't call me stupid," says the smaller boy, punching his larger friend in the arm.

"Okay, sorry. What about him?"

"Leave me alone," I warn the boys.

"At least he talks. Come on let's go. He'll be gone by tonight."

"Does everyone want to fight me?" I ask myself. The boys realizing they may have bitten off more than they could chew, leave the camp on the run.

I get up, make a pot of coffee and clean up. Now I'm feeling better. "I need a plan." I can't organize my thoughts.

I am returning to the mountains. *"I will not go to another rendezvous,"* I vow to myself. Last spring Micah and I went to Rendezvous to turn in our pelts. We did well, until Micah got ahold of a jug of mountain liquor. I ain't against a man getting drunk if that is his wish. And I certainly would not stop Micah on his way to his first bout of drinking in almost a year. But I will not tolerate a drunken bully. Micah is a mean drunk. We fought and it was either leave rendezvous, take a beating, or kill Micah to get him to stop. I left. I felt bad about it but...well anyways. I reckoned I couldn't return to the Crow and that made me even more angry at Micah. That's when I fell in with Asa and his boys. I already recounted how that turned out. It was my fault, and I feel shame for getting good men killed. I do not want to face Asa and his new crew. Where does that leave me now?

I feel a melancholy approaching. The best way to duck it is to go hunting. I secure my camp to spend a morning hunting camp meat. The effort has dispelled the darkness. I can think and make a plan.

3

RETURN TO THE MOUNTAINS FALL 1834

"A PLAN," I TELL MYSELF OUT LOUD TO MY ONLY
audience, my horses. "Who am I fooling? I don't need a plan
to understand the only thing I'm any good at is laying railroad
tracks and trading. I'm not much of a trapper. I ain't returning
to the railroad. No sir. I reckon we'll head back to the Stonies
for another season," I tell my horses.

I feel better after making that decision. Truthfully, it is
the only one I can make. I'm halfway to the mountains by this
time. I reckon I just had to get it right in my head. Talking to
my horses does that. I'm generally traveling back on the trail I
rode out on this past spring. I'm not in a hurry, as long as I
beat the snow. I keep my eyes open for the Cheyenne. I know
they are out, and I do not want to meet with them or the
Blackfoot, ever again. Well I take that back. I still owe them
for what they took and what they done. Given the right

opportunities I will try to even the score. But I ain't going out of my way to do it. I have set my mind to winter over south of the Yellowstone River and Valley. I'll find my own little valley to set my camp. I'll spend the cold months by myself trapping and hunting.

I do not remember much of the unremarkably dull traveling up to this point. I meet no Indians, no highway men, no Grizzly bears, and no particularly bad weather. I have my lodge up and my winter camp established before the first snow. The horses watch as I work. I spend a dull and repetitive fall and winter by myself trapping, hunting, and gathering fur. I choose not to be around people. Deep inside I've had enough of others. A lot of my circumstances I created for myself. I chose to leave Micah and the Crow village to link up with Asa's trapping crew. I chose to disregard Asa's one unwritten rule of not crossing the river and trapping in Blackfoot country. My selfish actions led to the death of too many trappers. I accept the responsibility.

Before, I roamed the mountains, trapping and hunting enjoying the life I led. Today, I do not. I am ashamed of myself and don't know how to change things. I cannot return to the Crow; I've burned that bridge. I can join a different company, but my past will catch up with me. Every night I think of my mistakes and how I could have acted different. I try to place myself in the future and how I can avoid similar problems. I've matured enough to understand my mistakes, but I don't feel I can continue in the mountains trapping and hunting on my own. For this season, I will. Deep inside I understand the dangers of being on my own. I don't care. I almost think I deserve what may happen. I'd leave the mountains, but they continue attracting me. They have a hold on me.

I do well trapping and hunting. Working keeps the doubts and troubling worries away. I teach myself to sleep with one eye and an ear open listening for my enemies, that I know one day will find me. Until then I'll continue trading with the Shoshone when I run into them. I winter alone, in a 25 buffalo hide lodge. My riding horse is hobbled in front of my lodge. The others spend their nights on a picket line and hobbled.

The cold, white, winter is wholly unremarkable. When the monotony and tediousness of the snow months spent deep in the Yellowstone's threaten to burst me asunder, I load my horses to hunt and trap a new and different area always returning to my lodge and winter camp. With no one stopping me, I pass a productive, yet lonely winter. As spring rolls around I decide to sell to Mr. Richardson rather than go to Rendezvous. He's the only one in St. Louis that helped me; well the banker did too. But I count Mr. Richardson a friend. I have to leave my lodge and the lodge poles. I do not have enough horses to carry it and my fur. I reckon it's oaky. My lodge was right where I left it this fall. I did it once, I can do it again. I know the perfect section of trees to leave it. So, I do.

Like the previous spring, this trip is remarkably dull traveling as I begin the return to St. Louis. I don't question the lifeless drudgery or the darkness and gloom inside me. I accept it as my penance. In my self-imposed separation I do not realize something, or someone has a protective hand over me. All I know is that I'm still mad at myself. I accept responsibility not in a whiney temper tantrum, but what I think is responsible like. I own my actions and mistakes and vow to do better. How? I have no idea.

I've taken down my lodge and cached the buffalo hides, covers, poles, and some extra camp gear. I fully intend on returning this fall. Life on the trail passes in shades of gray. As I reach the North Platt River color returns. I don't understand the how, but I ride alert. Seven weeks after leaving my winter camp to sell my furs to Mr. Richardson in St. Louis, disaster strikes.

––––––

Plews in River

I've got seventeen packhorses and an extra riding horse lined up behind me, all linked together by neck ropes. I stop in the trees before riding out from the trees, to the river. Everything looks undisturbed. There are no fresh tracks going in or coming out of the swollen creek. All the small forest creatures are making the right noises. The birds are chirping. The squirrels are talking amongst themselves; they have not issued any warnings to their companions. A warning concerning trespassers, especially trespassers mounted on horses and carrying weapons. The grass to both sides of the trail lays untrampled. No soil's been turned up. There's no evidence of horses passing through. Across the river as close as I can tell, the scene appears the same.

I tie the lead rope to the packhorses securely to a low branch. Leaving the packhorses in the trees, I walk my saddle horse out of the tree line to the water's edge. As I sweep my eyes back and forth, I look close at my horse's ears. They are constantly moving, turning, picking up all the local sounds. He is unaffected and peaceful. We walk to the water's edge. I need a firm crossing point. I'm looking for the gravel beach on both sides and where the river runs shallow. I find it. I am glad to see my sense of direction is working well. I don't see any big rocks in the middle of the river requiring a zig zagging crossing.

I've come to the place I remember. The gravel crossing is unobstructed. The river's level appears less than hip high. I urge my horse into the water. I'm looking at the bottom. Is the whole crossing covered in gravel? I can't remember. Is there any sand? I can't see any. The crossing looks good. I do not see any rocks displaced by horses crossing the creek. It looks like we're the only ones here. Perfect. I let my horse drink before making the opposite bank.

Over here the signs are the same. No tracks, no sand, only gravel, and the animal noises I would expect. I look to the sun.

It's just past midday. I'm thinking about making the crossing and setting up an early camp. I ride for the trail in the tree line. No tracks, no one has been through here. This is good. I turn around, re-cross the river, and ride to the line of pack-horses. They all are taking advantage of the stop and the green grass. With the horses chewing a last mouthful, I take up the rope and head for the river.

All of these horses have made countless creek and river crossings. Not a one of them is a spooky kind of horse liable to panic and cause me problems. I lead my packhorses into the river. My saddle horse makes his second crossing unfazed. I'm aiming for the tree line. I have nine packhorses on my side of the river, seven are in the water, and the last two are waiting for their turn to cross. I have the lead rope securely in hand when I notice the ears on my saddle horse are frantically swiveling, searching for the source of a new noise. I look across the river. That's when the Blackfoot attack.

Exploding out from the tree line on the opposite bank, the one I'm crossing over from, is a tight pack of five Indians. They are riding for the packhorses not yet across. To keep me from hauling on the rope and finishing the crossing, they shoot four of the horses in the water. Four out of seven fall from mortal arrow wounds. I shoot the lead warrior with my rifle. He falls to the grass, the first Blackfoot down. I secure my rifle over a shoulder and pull two pistols. I'm racing for the river's edge. There are four Indians trying to take the last four horses in the pack line. The live horses in the creek have stopped where they stand. I ride out of the river onto solid dry grassland facing my opponents.

My first two pistol shots take two warriors by surprise. Two more are down laying in the grass out of the fighting. There is only two left. I exchange the fired pair of pistols for the loaded brace in the pommel holster on my saddle. Drawing the second pair, I fire the right-hand pistol first. That warrior falls to the grass. There is one left. I aim with my left hand as my saddle horse is racing towards him. I fire and miss. I collide with the last Blackfoot warrior as I'm pulling my knife. Our horses clash. I'm falling. I kick away from my collapsing horse. Laying on the grass I see my horse struggling to stand. Now I'm mad.

I drop the pistol in my left hand to draw the war axe. I stand holding a fighting knife and a Crow war axe. I'd be ready if the grasslands and the blue sky would stop changing places. I hear and sense more than see the last Blackfoot running at me. Turning to face him, I stumble. That clumsy move saves my life. The war axe held by the warrior misses me. I twist. Now I'm facing him.

I remember practicing this move with the younger warriors in training, when I first arrived at the Crow camp. The actions happen without me thinking or trying to make them happen. His downward slash with the war axe misses, but not by much. I duck the blow. As he moves away, I use my legs to spring out and grab him. I'm dragging the struggling warrior to the ground. He falls hard, tail bone first. I hear a crack. The warrior cries out. I know he's hurt. He's trying to stand. He can't make it to his feet. The fall must have done some great damage. I tackle him from the side. Even a hurt and wounded Blackfoot warrior is a formidable enemy. I am not giving him a chance. My knife finds his neck. The fight is over quick.

I roll off him, to my back, laying on the grass. I'm watching the clouds pass until the sky and the horizon both stand still, in their rightful place. The collision and fall have disorientated me. I stand. When things settle to where they should be, I take a step. Then another. I walk to double check each Blackfoot warrior. As I stumble towards them, I'm hearing Micah in my head.

"Remember, more mountain men and trappers are killed by dead enemies than live ones," he warns me. That's his way of telling me to make sure the warrior is dead before getting too close. They are a danger no longer. I see my rifle. I check my possibles. The parfleche is still in place. Quickly I reload my rifle. Feeling better I reload the two pistols on my belt. That's when I remember my horse.

"Where is he?" I think to myself. Slowly I turn a circle looking for him. I move slow so I won't dizzy myself. There he is, standing at the head of the packhorses. I look him over, checking his legs, making sure he's okay. He is. I exchange the pistols on my saddle for the loaded pair. I look around at the destruction in front of me as I reload the second brace of pistols. Five Indian horses are milling at the river together

with five of my packhorses. Four packhorses are lying in the river, all dead, porcupined by Blackfoot arrows. Seven pack-horses are milling close to the water's edge on the other side of the river.

Leading my saddle horse, I walk to the dead Blackfoot warriors. I double check each one making sure they cannot attack me before taking their weapons. I cut the lead rope between the first dead horse and the last one on my side of the river. I secure the living horses to the rope. Climbing into the saddle I re-cross the river bringing my packhorses over with me. The five Blackfoot horses follow. I secure both groups of packhorses with the Blackfoot horses to trees near the first group of seven. Now I need to drag the slain horses out of the water.

At the water's edge I see all the packs on the four horses have broken open. I untie the pack frames. I think it'll help as I drag their bodies out of the water. I'll see if it does. With two ropes and two horses, I pull the dead horses out of the cold river water. We, my horses, and I, move the bodies of the slain warriors to the other side of the river away from my camp, on the other side of the river. To feel more secure, I move camp inside the tree line. I'll leave the dead Blackfoot for the next hunting or war party to find. I take their weapons and their horses.

The sun sits halfway from mid-sky and the western edge of the world. I have about three hours of light left to finish my work. The twelve packs of furs have all floated downstream about twenty yards, sinking into to a deep pool. I'll need to swim and dive for them. I quickly dig a firepit, line it with dry rocks, lay in a fire, and start it. I'm building up a bed of coals. While I'm adding wood, I prepare a pot of coffee. I set a flat rock close to the edge for the coffee pot to sit on. It's close to boiling as I strip down at the edge of the deep pool. I pile my weapons away from the water but close enough to grab quick, if needed.

I make the first dive to see if I can recover any of the twelve packs of fur. The water is clear but awful cold. I come out carrying one pack of furs. I pour a cup of coffee to warm up before making the next dive. I've counted ten packs, two have broken completely open. I reckon I'll bring up the ten full packs first. Each pack weighs about ninety pounds. This is going to take some work.

With the sun a full hands' width from the horizon I've brought up nine packs. On the next dive I bring up the last pack. I gather as many loose furs as I can, swim up, and drag them to the water's edge. I make three more dives. On the last dive I bring up all the furs I can save. After the last cup of coffee in the pot, I begin moving the furs from the creek's edge to the camp in the trees. I spread them out to dry, hair side down. I struggle getting that last bundle to the tree line. I'm beat. I've done all I can. I'll not reenter the water today

The cold drives me to the fire, to dry off, and dress. I build up the fire and make a second pot of coffee. When I'm warm enough to move and use my blue hands, I put meat on a stake and set it next to the fire to grill. I'm too cold and weary to mess with bread dough. Warmed inside I tend to the packhorses, unloading them and adding hobbles in the dark. I put them on a picket rope and hope they do not wander away in the dark.

That's when I remember the five Indian horses. They are standing next to my horses. I'll need four of them to carry packs. Wearily I get up and walk to the five horses, talking low and slow to each one as I add them to the picket line. I don't think they'll give me any further problems, tonight.

I wrap myself in blankets. Adding a soft tanned buffalo robe over the blankets I lay down close to the fire on a buffalo robe. Drinking coffee, I'm warming up, finally. I set down the empty cup but do not remember falling asleep. Waking with the rising sun surprises me. I'm warm lying under the buffalo robe. I don't want to move. I hear a horse walking behind me. Before I can turn over and look, I see a familiar nose and feel a friendly bump. It's my saddle horse making sure I'm awake and getting up. I reckon it's time. Before untangling myself, I add wood to the last of the fire's coals. When I stand after unravelling myself from blankets and buffalo robe, the fire is merrily crackling away.

I add new grounds to the sock and make a new pot of much needed coffee. Another slice of hump meat is grilling on a spit next to the coals. By the time I'm wearing dry moccasins and checking on the horses I smell coffee. I eat and finish off the pot while loading the horses with pack frames and packs of furs. I have a tough time getting the Indian horses to accept the heavy packs of furs, but I get it done. I clean my camp, climb into the saddle, and I'm ready to ride. The dead horses are far enough away from the river not to spoil the water. That's the best I can do. It's time to ride.

Saint Louis

I cross the river into St. Louis proper on a ferry. Eighteen packhorses are fully loaded, carrying my successful winter's worth of fur. Two carry camp gear. I'm riding my favorite saddle horse and leading a second. All together my procession of twenty horses is a sight to see. After crossing the river, I run into a bit of trouble. My timing is terrible. I'm crossing as many of the day laborers working at the docks are finishing their day. I'm leading nineteen horses. I'm dressed in buckskins and carrying my rifle. I have a second Long Rifle on my first packhorse. There are two pistols, a knife, and a war axe in my belt. The extra riding horses carry a third long rifle, extra possibles, and two packs of weapons, pistols, and a mixed bag of souvenired Indian weapons.

My possibles parfleche, tall moccasins, and war shirt are decorated with beads and porcupine quills in colorful Indian decorations and symbols. I have a couple eagle feathers stuck in the band of my wide-brimmed felt hat. There is a line of eagle feathers fixed to my Hawken also. Everything I own points towards spending a lot of time with Indians. I do not think about taking off or hiding the feathers and beaded goods once I reach civilization. I reckon I should have. My hands, face, and neck exposed to wind, sun, and all kinds of inclement weather have taken on a dark brown coloring. The only trait marking me as a white man is my long and flowing sun-bleached red hair reaching past my shoulders. I have taken to keeping clean shaved except for a long mustache that hangs down to the bottom of my chin.

Most people will recognize me as a white trapper or Indian trader. Those looking for trouble will look no further than my outward appearance. Unfortunately for me, many of the day laborers, the dock workers, and others, cannot look past my buckskins.

"Hey Chief, this is a White Man's town. What are you doing riding through?" screams out one of the men. His friends must have thought he was funny because most of them are laughing. Me, I choose to ignore him and keep riding, with an eye on my line of horses.

"Look at there, the chief is ignoring me. What do you boys think of that?" asks the bully. He receives no answer. When I hear one of my horses cry out in surprise or pain I stop. I've trained these horses to stay together when lined out on the trail, they will not stray. I flip the lead rope over the pack frame and ride back to see what happened. The bully has a thin rod in his hand and has hit one of my packhorses on the rump. I push him out of the way with my horse. Then get down.

"Lucky it's only a welt," I tell the bully, standing full height across from him. He stands an inch or so taller than me and is about as wide. He must feel safe.

"What would you do about it Indian man?" he laughs.

"I'm a trapper and a trader. I'll thank you to leave my horses alone. They've done nothing against you," I tell him, catching my reins to climb onto the saddle. As I boost up, I feel the whip of the thin rod against my neck. Without showing a sign of anything, I take my seat and prepare to ride. Until I hear the horse cry out again. Faster than they can follow, I have the bully laying on the ground with my knife at his throat. My war axe waits, ready to split his head open.

"If a one of you so much as twitches I'll split this man's head in two and come for you. Do we understand each other?" Pale, all of them slowly nod their heads. "I can't hear you. Speak up."

The crowd issues a feeble yes. I add my bladed weapons to my belt. The bully takes in a deep breath. He turns to me thinking it's his turn for threats. His forehead meets the barrel of my pistol. The hammer is thumbed back, and my finger is on the trigger. He wisely blows out the breath he was going to cuss me with. His eyes focus on my trigger finger.

"All of you walk away, now!" I yell, and they do faster than many of them have moved in years. "Not so fast. You are coming with me. I can promise you I'll pull the trigger if any of your friends try coming to your aid. Do you believe me?" There is silence. "Stay, while I climb onto my saddle." It is a feat to get my seat with that pistol tight against his forehead, but I get it done. "Now walk." He escorts me along my string of packhorses to the front of the line.

"Hand me that lead. If you run, I will shoot you." Taking a deep breath, he hands me the lead rope. We set off for Mr. Richardson's yard. Part of the crowd follows, well behind us. As I turn down the street to the tannery, a big-bellied town policeman pushes through the crowd up to me and the bully.

"You there, stop," he orders. I keep going, I have less than 50 yards to cover before reaching Mr. Richardson's gate. "I said stop, by the order of the law, stop now," he says, pulling his pistol. I've beaten him to it. I move my single-shot pistol from the bully to the policeman. That may not have been a good move, but by now I am mad clear through and not thinking clearly. A crowd is gathering around us once again. I'm forced to stop in front of Mr. Richardson's gate.

"What?" I ask him.

"What are you doing? You can't draw guns on citizens and certainly not on policemen. Get down, you're coming with me."

"I'm not. This man attacked my horses, twice. The only way to stop him is by threats against his person. I stopped his attacks and to ensure there are no more he is walking with me. He's the culprit not me." The policeman looks at me with a dumbfounded look. Apparently, he has never been questioned.

"Is what this mountain man saying true Martin?" he asks the bully.

"No, it ain't I..." The bully stops his lie when he sees my face clouding in more anger.

"You best tell the truth while you can, Martin," I tell him.

"I only hit his horse with a stick."

"How many times?" I ask him.

"Three," is his reply.

"Nevertheless, we can't have you lot rough up citizens like that. You're still coming with me," blusters the city cop.

"What about my horses?"

"That doesn't outweigh what you're done. Now get down."

"Just a minute, I have something to say," says Mr. Richardson pushing through the crowd.

"I don't care what you've got to say. It won't change things. I'm putting this rouge under arrest. Let's go."

"I'm afraid you're not putting anyone under any kind of arrest," says Mr. Richardson to the fat-bellied, now embarrassed copper.

"Step aside before I arrest you too," he threatens.

"That will be quite enough of that. I happen to be Mr. Richardson, and this is my business, and this man works for me. I demand..."

"Your demands go hang. I don't care who you are. Move, disperse."

"I am also his lawyer, and brother-in-law to the City Sheriff." This announcement stops everyone. "I've sent to City Hall for the Chief of Police, the City Sheriff and the US Marshal. In addition, I was witness to exactly what this bully did to the horse. I demand you arrest him and let my client go. Do it now, before I hold you accountable to the above-mentioned law enforcement officials. Or we can wait for them, right here. While we wait, give me your name."

"Why do you want my name?"

"You are going to be mentioned in the suit," answers Mr. Richardson.

"What suit?"

"The one I'm bringing against you personally, the City itself, and the City officials that hired you in the first place. And also, the bully who whipped this poor horse. Now both your names," says Mr. Richardson, ready with a pencil and his notebook. "You were involved in something this past winter, were you not, officer?"

"This has gone on long enough. Get gone both of you. Break it up," he tells the crowd, walking away with the bully in arm. I lead my pack string into the yard, directly in front of us. All the workers in Mr. Richardson's yard begin laughing and carrying on. The gate is closed as my last horse passes through.

"While I do not think they will be back, I suggest you

spread your blankets in the loft for the duration of your visit," he tells me.

"Thank you, Mr. Richardson, for getting me out of that. I truly hate this city," I tell him.

"Come with me while my men unload your horses and bring in your furs." I look back over my shoulder watching his men with my horses.

"I trust you. Let's go." We walk to his office while his men get to work looking through the furs and buffalo robes I brought back with me this year. I'm sipping my second cup of coffee as the foreman hands his boss a paper. He softly closes the door behind him.

"Let's see what they counted," he says, then gets quiet reading the list. "You've done well this year Uriah." Mr. Richardson gets out a pencil and adds prices to the amounts. He moves the paper to me. I look at it in shock. At the bottom is the biggest dollar amount I have ever imagined.

"Will you go with me to the bank so I can deposit this?" I ask him.

"How about I take the check to the bank for you. That will allow time for the unpleasantness to settle down. I'll bring you back a receipt, a check for your resupply, gold coins for your immediate needs, and your bank book. Will you trust me?"

"Of course, I will."

"Good, I'll be back. I'll have someone show you to the loft. I built a couple of rooms above the barn. You're not the only trapper and mountain man I buy fur from that has run into trouble in this town. I've had the first room cleaned, knowing you'd be here. I've got water boiling. Take a bath, change your clothes and I'll be back."

"Thanks for your help," I sincerely tell him, extending my hand to him.

"I should be thanking you for the high-quality furs and hides you've brought me. My business depends on yours. I'll have someone fetch you a meal from the café. You can eat after cleaning up," he says, shaking my hand. I watch him head out the front door for his carriage. I walk back into the yard. His foreman shows me to my room. He helps me carry my bedroll and saddlebags upstairs. I have my hands full with a ruck sack and three rifles. The tub has been filled and I can see steam rising. I undress and jump in, staying until the water cools. I dress in clean jeans and a store-bought shirt, with my moccasins. I'm told my meal is waiting in the office. I head over to eat. I've just finished when Mr. Richardson enters his office. He makes his way behind the desk.

"Here's your receipt, a check for resupply, a bag of coins, and your bank book," he tells me laying it all down on the table.

I look it over but really don't know what I'm looking at. I hand the bank book and the receipt back. "It's better protected in this office than in my possibles. I'm tired." I stand, take up the bag of coins and say good night.

"I will see you in the morning, Uriah," he tells me, as I open the office door.

I make my way to the room Mr. Richardson made for us mountain men. I remember thinking I should thank him when I see him come morning. I lay down on my blankets. I'm thinking how much I don't like the city. The next thing I know I'm waking with the morning sun in my eyes.

It will be a few hours before Mr. Richardson shows up at his office and I need coffee, now. I walk to the hotel I stayed at last time. At the desk they do not remember me. They do not want to let me into their dining room. The more I explain, the more the clerk refuses. Right then a young woman comes to my rescue.

"I don't mean to be impertinent or intrude but do you have the money for a meal?" she asks me.

"I do," I tell her. I bring out my bag of coins and spill it on the counter.

"I believe that will be more than enough to eat breakfast. Am I correct?" she asks the manager behind the desk.

"Yes, Miss Debra it is. Is this something you should be bothering yourself with? What will your father say?" asks the manager.

"He is not here, I am. I am making this my business, now let him in to eat. Or I promise you my family will never visit this facility again." The eyes of the manager grow big. He looks at me like he wants to skin me and nail my hide on the barn's wall.

"And make sure it is…" she stops. "You know, I am hungry too. Would you allow me to join you for breakfast Mr. ah…I don't know your name?" I'm lost in confusion. Why is she taking up my defense? Why is she interested?

"Sorry, it's been awhile since I've talked to a pretty girl. I'm Uriah," I stumble telling her.

"Pleased to meet you Uriah. I am Debra. Surely you jest about the long time since you've seen a pretty girl," she laughs.

"No ma'am, ah I mean Debra. I've not talked to a white woman in almost two years." I see her catch her breath, but she doesn't show it, much.

"Where have you been for the last two years?" she asks me quietly. I'm not sure what she thinks but to her there can be less than a handful of reasons for where I've been. I hope she doesn't think the worse about me. She also doesn't understand that asking that kind of question can get a man in trouble. I have nothing to hide so I tell her.

"I'm a trapper. I've been to St. Louis last year and of course this year. Other than that, I live in the Great Stonies." I tell her. I can see she doesn't understand, I try again. "What I mean is I winter in the mountains. I don't go to rendezvous for supplies. I sell my furs here in town to Mr. Richardson every summer. So, you see I'm not here much." She points out a table for us. A man in a suit pulls out her chair. I pull out my own.

"To start, Miss?" he asks her.

"Coffee and menus," she tells him. I watch as if this is done in a foreign language. I don't understand any of it. I do not trust myself with the heavy white mug and the pot of steaming coffee. Seeing my hesitation, she pours for both of us.

"Never mind the menus, bring us eggs, bacon, and grid-dle-cakes. Anything else you'd like Uriah?" she asks me.

"Maybe some fried potatoes," I tell her.

"Well you heard him. That's our order," she tells the man in the suit.

"Yes of course," he says ringing a small bell. I set my rifle in the corner behind me and my possibles with my hat on the floor.

"I do hope breakfast is up to our expectations," she sweetly says to the manager.

"You will be seated with this ruffian? Do you think that wise Miss Debra?" asks the manager.

"It is much wiser than trusting you lot to bring what he orders without my sitting here," she tells the shocked steward. They leave and we wait for our meal to be served. I know she wants to talk but I feel tongue-tied. I don't know what to say or how to begin. I feel relief when a cart in the company of four well-dressed waiters arrives at our table.

"I believe this will do, thank you," she tells the steward and the three waiters. We quietly watch them leave and close the kitchen door behind them. We are the only ones sitting in the dining room.

"Thank you, Miss...ah...."

"I am Miss Debra; you may call me Debra. How long are you going to be in town?" she asks avoiding telling me her family name.

"At this rate I will leave as soon as I sell my furs and resupply."

"May I take you to dinner? I'm staying in the hotel until next Tuesday. Father needs me out of the way while he entertains out of town business partners and acquaintances. Will you be ready let's say by 6:00?"

"Yes ma'am, I'll be ready."

"Good, I'll meet you downstairs." After that it's like the beaver dam broke. We are talking and laughing like old friends. We sit enjoying each other's company even after clearing our plates. Well, I reckon I should say after I finish our plates. Debra doesn't eat much, and I was eyeing her plate like a buffalo steak on the fire after a long day of hunting or trapping. Without a word she passed me her plate. I do not hesitate in setting in on everything that is on her plate. I polished off her leavings. I sit back and catch myself in time. I kind of swallow down the belch I was fixing to deliver. She seems to think that is hilarious. I swear these city gals do not have much to laugh at.

After exhausting all my stories, we get up to leave, ignoring the stares of the prim and proper city folk at their tables.

"Be seeing you," I say to her. She gets a sly smile on her

face and stepping up to her toes while pulling down my shoulders, plants a kiss on my cheek. I will admit that is a first. I do not remember settling the bill, the walk back to the yard, or really much of anything until seeing Mr. Richardson entering his office. I spend the day mending leather goods and brushing horses. It's a good time to catch up on all the gear needing tending. I lose myself in the work only realizing the time when Mr. Richardson says good night to me in the yard.

It's a darn good thing Mr. Richardson was holding a pack of clothes for me. They are the ones I left in the hotel room last year. Quickly I clean up and dress with one eye on the time. I'm waiting for Miss Debra sitting in the bar while keeping watch on the restaurant's entry. When I see her, I finish the beer in one last great gulp. I get up and make my way to her.

"You are here. I half expected you not to meet me," she says, planting another kiss on my cheek. Speechless once again, I let her navigate us to a table and order supper. I left my rifle and possibles behind, but we are still led to a back corner table. Debra never notices. In fact, she's talking so much I tune most of it out. That is until after we're seated, when she tells me her father wants to meet me. I come up short on hearing this. Her father? Why would he want to meet me? Why would she ever think of telling him about me? We've only meet one time, this morning. I'd better tread carefully.

"Excuse me Debra, why would your father enjoy meeting

me?" I ask her. She gets a lost and wild look in her eyes, then stops talking. I wait for an answer.

"I told him about our meeting this morning and how I intervened on your behalf. He has never met a mountain man, trapper, Indian trader, or anyone such as yourself. He told me he would like to. Why? You do not want to?"

"No, that ain't it. We hardly know each other. I didn't think you'd be interested enough to mention our meeting to anyone," I try explaining. I can't seem to say the words that need saying when I need to say them. I ain't too sure what's come over me.

"Well then, Father said Sunday at lunch would be a good time. Will you come?" she pleads. "Please do." I don't want to but how can I not?

"Draw me a map to your home and I'll be there," I promise her. She begins talking, only letting up to order us supper. I have no idea what we're having. The only words I recognized are coffee and apple pie after. This ought to be an adventure. I'm only half listening to her prattling on when the fancy-dressed waiter pushes a cart to our table. She actually claps and jumps in her seat as each dish is placed on the table. All I recognize is the coffee cup and pot. One of them fancy dressed lads grabs the pot before I get a hand on it.

"Would you like cream or sugar?" he asks, pouring my cup full.

"No, just like this is fine," I tell him.

"Very well," he says, standing back from the table. I wait

for him to walk away but he don't. I reckon he's going to hover the entire time.

Debra picks up where she left off. Giving me a long and very detailed account of a dance she attended last Saturday night. I'm still only half listening. I try a small bite of what she adds to my plate. After that first bite, I feel kind of silly. I remember back on some of the disgusting things I've eaten in the mountains when truly hungry. I reckon if they cook it in the hotel's big kitchen then it must be good, right?

To me it looks like a giant crawdad. I recognize the steak, but not all the sauces she tells me goes with them. I see several people eating the same large crawdads I've got on my plate. I watch her attack and crack the shell getting down to the meat, as she talks. I reckon I can set in on eating now that I've seen how it's done. It's different and very good. I refuse all the different sauces poured on my steak. I like it just fine right from the fire. I watch surprised as she washes her fingers in a crystal bowl of water. There are slices of what she calls a lemon in the water. Miss Debra tells me the lemon takes the fish smell from your hands and fingers. I never minded fish in the mountains, but like she keeps saying, I ain't in the mountains. So, I follow her example.

I finish my plate, then Miss Debra's plate that she has not really touched. It's holding more of the same things I just finished. She has not eaten more than a bite; she's only pushing her food around making it look like she's eating. While I'm watching her, she hands me her plate and I set in on it also. The crawdad is passable but a bit salty. The steaks are good. The best is the apple pie. With her pie plate in front of me I'm glad she don't eat hers. I clear the small plate.

I recognize most of the French she's talking with the head waiter. Many trappers are part French and over time I've picked up their words. I listen until they start talking about what we had for supper. I look up and quickly tell them in the French that I know what we just ate and please do not say anything more about it. That gets them to stop, but the looks on their faces, well I wore that same expression when battling Blackfoot Indians. I'm not sure me talking in the French I learned in the mountains was a good idea. I see several patrons hiding their laughter behind linen napkins. Directly after that the head waiter hands me the check. I can't make heads or tails from it. I show it to Debra.

"How much do I owe them for supper? I ask her.

"Fifteen dollars will cover it," she says smiling. I lay a ten and five-dollar coin on the table and stand. The well-dressed waiter helps Debra from her chair. He bows to her and we walk out. I'm tempted to ask what I said in French, but I've reached my fill of her and town life this night.

"If you walk me home, you'll know where to come on Sunday," she tells me. I had forgotten about lunch and reluctantly agree to escort her home. I am not paying attention to where we're going. She's still talking without stopping. I ain't listening to a bit of it. When she stops, I bump into her.

"Sorry, I didn't know we were stopping."

"This is where I live. Thank you for a memorable evening," she tells me.

"Glad you enjoyed it." That's when I remember she told me her Pa was entertaining business folk and she is staying at the hotel. But she's at home. I get a headache trying to reckon this all out.

"Until Sunday lunch, then," she says with her hand out. I'm thinking she wants me to shake with her. I grab her hand in mine and instead of shaking she pulls me towards her. I bump into her and before I can move away her other hand is on the back of my neck pulling me down to her. Our lips touch. I swear I feel lightning strike my body, travel through me, and into her. When she looks up, she is out of breath and smiling. After a second kiss she lets me go. Now I'm out of breath. She turns, opens the gate, and floats to the double front door that opens on its own. She tuns and gives me a shy wave, now that the butler is watching.

I turn in a daze. That was a surprising maneuver. She had me in a hold where I was powerless. She is going to be trouble, I reckon. I'm needing both eyes open wide come Sunday. I walk towards Mr. Richardson's yard thinking about everything but the kisses. I cannot dwell on them. I'm not paying attention to where I'm going. I see a door open, hear sounds of drinking men and shrieking women. I bump into one of three drunks pushing through the door.

"Watch where you're walking," shouts the one I bumped into. I keep going. Until I feel a hand on my shoulder. At the touch everything slows, my senses are heightened, and I can hear their heavy breathing. Turning around I notice the trio. I know what they're going to do. I grab the hand on my shoulder bending the wrist in a direction it ain't designed to go. While lifting the arm higher than the shoulder will allow, both cracks are a pleasure to hear. Suddenly I'm laughing. This is the perfect ending to a frustrating evening. Or rather to a year and a half of rough setbacks. I drop the screaming man.

The biggest one is facing me. He's taller and wider than I am. Good. I see him wind up to throw a haymaker. He's hoping to end this fight with one great punch. It ain't going to happen. I step back out of the path of his fist. As he goes by, he's out of balance. I grab an arm to use its momentum and bend it backwards I let him drop as we hear additional loud cracks.

The last man has drawn a belaying pin from his shirt. It's been awhile since I've seen one of these used as a weapon. He tries a sideways blow. I block most of it, but my left arm goes numb from the hit. He's smiling now. His friends are rolling in pain down in the filthy street. He's going to set things right. With my left arm numb I throw a right-hand punch into the side of his face. It lands but not with the authority I need to end this fight quick.

We face each other. He's lightly smacking his left hand with the wide part of the belaying pin. He's smiling. When the slapping stops, I know he's coming. I ram my left shoulder into his gut. Picking him up, I slam his body to the street. I see his head bounce off the cobble stones. His eyes cross. I bend down, using the callused end of my palm where it meets my thumb to flatten his nose. I do not see the pin come at me, connecting with my numb left shoulder. I scream, which he enjoys. He's laughing as he stands, blood pouring from his damaged nose. We circle each other looking for an opening. I'll give him one.

I fake a stumble. He moves in with the pin ready to brain me. Except I ain't where he expects. He looks at me as my right fist explodes his nose. Holding him up with my left arm I send a second fist his way, mashing his lips and loosening a tooth. He drops the belaying pin. I pick it up, but he does not notice. I give him a sideways tap to the ear. He will be hearing bells for a long time. I let him fall to the cobblestone road. I'm mad and seeing red. Both the men on the ground earn an additional smashed nose and a couple loose teeth. I kick the last one in the stomach before walking away. I keep his belaying pin.

I do not know where I am. I follow noise to another bar, enter through the door, and walk to the bar.

"Beer," I shout. The bartender looks at me twice. I reckon he knows better than to argue and quickly draws the beer. It's not cold but cool. I finish it in one breath. I place a nickel on the bar and walk out. I think I know where I am now. A half hour later I enter Mr. Richardson's yard through the Judas gate. At the horse trough I wash my skinned hands and face.

It feels so good I take my shirt off and dump a bucket of water over my head. Feeling a bit refreshed I'm left wanting more. I take off my moccasins and jeans. Using the bucket, I pour more water over my head and abused body. I make my way upstairs to my room drying off with my shirt and carrying the rest of my town clothes. I sit up laughing over what a fool I've been. The fight must have knocked something loose. I know simple and clear what to do, how to do it, and vow to carry through.

I fall asleep thinking about heading out the day after tomorrow. Then I remember I've not resupplied my trade goods yet, and something about Sunday. I can't bring myself to recall the thread of that thought before I fall into a deep sleep, the deepest I've allowed myself in over a year.

I'm awake as the sun begins rising, fresh as the new day, and quickly walk to the café on the corner. With the sun well past the eastern horizon I'm on my way to the general store recommended by Mr. Richardson. A different store from the one I used last year. They welcome me as I hand over my list. It's considerably longer than last years.

"It will take me all day to fill this order. Bring your pack string this time tomorrow

morning and I'll have it ready for you to load into panniers," says the owner.

"I will be here," I tell him. "And thanks."

My next stop is the same gun shop I used last year. A new man owns the store. He's not as personable as the old owner but agrees to have my order ready by this time tomorrow. That's all that matters to me. With nowhere else to be I walk around the shops in the blocks surrounding Mr. Richardson's yard. I revisit the café for an early supper. To be honest with you I prefer this food to everything on that fancy menu at the hotel. I should know by now that simple is better.

I spend the next morning packing my supplies into panniers and balancing the loads. I've got pack frames and loads ready for my string of horses. Thankfully placing the packs on the frames passes quick. I lead my horses and their burdens to Mr. Richardson's yard. I unload the horses leaving the pack frames in line for an early loading come the morning. That's when I remember.

If I hadn't promised to meet Debra's parents, I'd leave for the mountains right now. I did promise so I will meet them. I still don't know why she wants that to happen. I've only known her for a couple of days. I ain't anything to her.

I spend the rest of the day preparing the packs, the loads, and the horses for an early start. I check each horses' feet. With the help of Mr. Richardson's workers, we brush, feed, and water them. I wish I could ride out, but a promise is a promise. Even if it is to a spoiled, wealthy, city girl who I will never see again. I take supper at the café. The short walk back prepares me to lay down and call an end to the day.

Summer on the Plains

While out on a hunting trip, the Crow and their friend Micah hear rifle fire in the late afternoon. They elect to stop. The leader of the hunting party sends out scouts to see who's fighting. If they are friends fighting Pawnee, Cheyenne, or Sioux, the Crow may lend a hand. Otherwise they'll leave the fight alone. No Crow warrior will pass up an opportunity to fight and kill, take their weapons, and steal their horses.

Micah rides with this group of hunters. Deep inside he misses his newest friend the hot-headed Uriah. Micah accepts his part of the argument that made the friends separate. All he can do is hope to run across the younger man sometime in the future. Micah wishes Uriah well and truly misses him. Micah's been with the Crow since his friend's leaving. As the days pass, Micah can feel the white part of him melt away. He does not stop the process of becoming as close as is possible, a Crow warrior. Micah has adopted Crow weapons as well as their way of life. For the first time in a very long time Micah has found peace within himself.

Not many Indian's carry the white man's weapons, rifles, and pistols, yet. The Crow leader reckons it is a group of white men fighting Pawnee, Sioux, or maybe Blackfoot. If so, that may be a fight they will stay away from. They will decide when the scouts return.

"What did you see?" asks the hunting party's leader on the scout's return.

"As you thought it is a group of white hunters."

"Who are they fighting?"

"No one, they are hunting our buffalo," replies the scout in anger.

"I'm sure they will see the wisdom of paying you for the buffalo they have killed," Micah tells the leader. "Trading with the hunters rather than killing the group, hunting buffalo for the railroad is the better option. Done right this meeting will benefit both of us."

"We will see. Micah keep in the center of our group. I don't want them knowing you are with us," orders the hunting party leader.

"It's all right with me." In an extended line with the scouts in the front, the Crow warriors ride to meet the white hunters. The hunters have located a small herd of buffalo on a wide grass field between two ridges with a clear creek running through its center. The shooting stops as the Crow ride closer and the hunter recognizes them. There are two shooters with six skinners working on the downed animals. In their camp is a fire and two more men. A wagon is hitched to a team of four large mules. The skinners have just begun working. The two shooters watch as the remainder of the buffalo walk away, out of the killing field, onto the open plains. The Crow warriors ride to the men working on the twenty downed animals.

"Do any of you understand our Crow words?" asks the

leader. The hunters and skinners look at each other not understanding what was said.

"Do you want me to talk to them?" Micah asks from his position in the center of the Crow warriors.

"No, I will try talking with our hands." The leader begins making signs to the two hunters holding rifles. One of them, the older of the pair nods his head in understanding.

"Do you understand?" asks the hunting group leader.

"I do," he signs back.

"Why do you take our buffalo?" asks the Crow leader.

"We are making meat for the army forts and nearby towns. We did not know these are your animals," he signs.

"What did he say?" asks one of the riflemen.

"He wants to know why we're killing and taking his buffalo," repeats the old hunter.

"Didn't know they lay claim to all the buffalo. What do they want?" asks another skinner.

"Don't know yet but I reckon they'll want a part of the kills."

"If that don't beat all. Tell them no. We shot them and we're taking them," orders the hunter's leader, the second shooter.

"I wouldn't advise that John. They'll get a might skittish if we try to run rough over them. We'd be better off paying the fine in buffalo and not our blood."

"We got rifles, they don't," blurts another skinner.

"Except they can shoot six to eight arrows to our one shot.

Those are not good odds. Like I said, pay them," warns the older shooter.

"All right. Ask them how much they want." Using his hands, the older and wiser white hunter asks the Crow leader the cost of hunting his buffalo.

"How many did you kill?" asks the Crow hunter's leader.

"We have ten in the wagon and ten on the ground."

"Are you taking the skins and all the meat? Or just the tongues and humps?"

"No, we're taking it all and the hides. We ain't wasting any of it. We'll be taking it to the fort and the town."

"How far away is this army fort and town?" asks the Crow warrior, now concerned. The other white men can tell something has changed making the Crow a bit unfriendly.

"What's the matter with them?" asks the leader of the white hunters.

"They want to know how far away the fort and the town is. That's got them spooked a bit. I reckon they didn't know about it."

"Tell them a seven days' ride," suggests their leader.

"We need to be careful here John. They'll send a warrior to make sure we told them plumb center."

"Okay then, how far is it?"

"A five day's ride," he answers.

"Is that good enough?"

"It had better be," he tells his boss. Returning to the Crow he uses hand signs to convince the Crow they are a five-day ride east.

"Is what they say with signs true?" the Crow leader asks Micah.

"Yes, Raven, it is. The talker is not trying to deceive us. The other rifleman is their leader. He does not know our ways," he tells the leader in Crow. He turns back towards the older hunter to continue their conversation.

"I want the hides and a third of the meat," signs the Crow leader. The demand causes a stir among the Crow warriors. They all know the toll is high and the white hunters will argue.

"This could get out of hand right quick," thinks Micah.

"What'd he say?" asks the hunter's boss man.

"They want all the hides and one third of the meat. That's a bit high."

"Can you get him to accept less of the meat? Tell him we'll have to kill more buffalo to fill our wagons. Well go on and tell him." Slowly the older and wiser hunter turns to the Crow.

Using signs, he begins, "that is too much. We will give you all the hides and one quarter of the meat. We'll need to kill more buffalo to fill our wagons before returning to the fort and the town."

"What do they say?" the hunter leader asks Micah.

"What the old one told us is true. They will need to kill

more buffalo before leaving if we take half. He thinks that will make a difference to us," Micah tell him.

"We will accept the one quarter of your kills and the hides. Next time it will be better if you ask before you begin hunting. We will know when you come back. Next time we will want all the hides and one quarter of the meat. If that is acceptable you can hunt our buffalo," signs the Crow leader.

"We agree. I will look forward to meeting and talking again next time," signs the old hunter. He tells his boss the arrangement. Not happy about it, he accepts the decision. He is thinking on how to avoid Indians on their next trip out.

The Crow leader tells his men to cut poles for travois to carry the hides and meat to the village. The work will not be finished before the sun sets. The Crow move into the trees close to the creek for their overnight camp. The white hunters work until dark. They drop all the hides away from their camp but close enough the Crow warriors can finish loading the travois tomorrow. Both parties retreat to their camps in the dark. Not friends, but also not enemies, they watch each other cautiously through the night. The division will be finished come morning's light.

The Crow wake before first light as is their custom, in case enemies are waiting outside their camp. Micah smells coffee on the wind. He can't help himself. Pulling his blue enamel cup from his possibles, carrying a bow with a quiver of arrows over a shoulder, Micah walks to the buffalo hunter's camp. His long hair is covered by a cougar-hide shawl over his shoulders.

"Look what we have here," says the cook to the buffalo hunters just starting their day.

"Looks like he wants to fill his cup with coffee. Give him some Cookie," says the boss buffalo hunter. Micah holds it out the cook. He lifts the battered coffee pot, filling the cup.

"Leave room for some of this canned milk and two spoons of sugar," says the boss man. Micah watches as the cook adds a healthy amount of canned milk and the sugar. It's been a long time since he has doctored coffee like this. Micah takes that first sip, and it all comes back to him. He can't help himself. Micah quickly downs the whole cup, smacking his lips as the cup lowers. *"Now, that was good,"* Micah tells himself.

"Looks like he enjoyed it. Give him a refill Cookie," says the boss man. Micah takes his time finishing this one. Finished, he heads out of their camp with a wave of thanks.

"Now ain't that like an Indian. Leaving without a thank you," gripes one of the skinners. Micah stops in his tracks, looks him in the eye, and tell him, "thanks." That leaves them all speechless. Micah walks into the Crow camp.

The Crow have travois on all our extra horses made for the flint hides and the bounty of buffalo meat. Cookie and one of the skinners watch as they take a quarter of the tongues and humps off a wagon. By late morning the butchered portions of buffalo quarters are secure, and they are ready to ride to the village. The Crow warriors leave by mid-morning.

The Crow have been on the trail for only a few minutes when they hear war cries, rifle shots, and screams. Without orders, one scout turns back to the buffalo hunters. On returning he gives the leader a report. The Pawnee are attacking the buffalo hunters. The leader reads the expressions of his warriors. All are grinning and preparing for battle.

"Leave the travois here to wait until the fight is over. We will ride down to offer our help to the white hunters. If the Pawnee win with a short fight we will make war on the Pawnee. Prepare for battle, quietly," orders their leader.

Riding to the cover of the tree line, the travois are quickly lowered to the ground. Weapons are readied, bows with arrows, lances with shield, knives, and war axes. The quick application of paint assures the Crow of good medicine and victory. Leaving the horses out of sight on the back of the ridge with a young horse handler, the warriors are ready. They creep to the top of the ledge. The sight before them is expected. The Pawnee are killing the last of the white hunters. Several Pawnee are lying motionless on the grass.

When the victorious Pawnee begin desecrating the hunters, the Crow mount their horses. Lined together under the edge of the ridge they wait for the leader's signal. With all eyes on him the leader raises an arm. Quietly he extends it towards the waiting and unexpecting foes, the Pawnee. Riding to the top of the ridge they continue down toward the scene of the fight. Once spotted by the busy Pawnee, they knee their horses into a run and release their pent-up war cries.

Charging down on their shocked enemies frozen in place, the first falls before they react. Grabbing weapons, the Pawnee sing their death songs as they give battle to the Crow. Although fierce fighters, the Pawnee fall quickly. The speed of attack makes it possible to overrun their enemy before they can mount an adequate defense. Within minutes the fight is over. All the Pawnee have joined the hunters laying on the grassy plains. A couple of Crow warriors proudly show off their wounds. Now their work starts.

The horse holder brings the Crow horses into the bloody camp. He then begins collecting the Pawnee and the hunter's horses. Young warriors begin cutting poles for additional travois. Older warriors collect all the weapons. Micah collects the hunter's rifles and possibles. He makes a pack and adds it to a travois pulled by his second horse. Still others pour through the supplies of the hunters keeping what they can use, adding the spoils to travois. In the wagon Micah finds mountain riches, coffee, sugar, and cans of milk. He finds extra powder and balls for the hunting rifles. He keeps it all. It will trade for necessaries at rendezvous. In three hours, the Crow turn their backs on the battle site.

The return ride is spent with each warrior recounting his exploits during the short fight. They stop within sight of the village to wash and prepare themselves to enter the village in true Indian glory. They ride into the village clothed in battle honors and bearing an abundance of fresh meat, and other prizes of war. Each warrior receives a hero's welcome.

Around the fire the elders discuss what was learned from the buffalo hunters. The more they discuss what they know, the more they what realize they don't know. What the elders need to know can only be found by visiting the army fort or the town. No one in the village, except for Micah is fit for the task. Micah excludes himself. He's too much a part of the Crow village. The warriors agree. It is decided that Micah will make the journey to Rendezvous and bring back Uriah to answer all the elder's questions. The wisdom of this is quickly seen by the warriors and agreed upon.

Micah will get his chance to hash things over with Uriah.

4

ST. LOUIS SUMMER 1834

THE QUIET OF THE WARM, EARLY AFTERNOON AT THE tree shaded mansion, perfectly situated on top of the rise, is shattered by raucous arguing and vulgar quarrelling. Two family members are thoroughly immersed in shouting back and forth their view of the argument. A third family member, the mother and wife, cringes at the breaking of expensive glassware, bone china serving dishes, and porcelain tableware.

"You're being heartless. I thought my father loved me and wanted the best for me," says the crying nearly hysterical young girl, Miss Debra.

"I do," assures her father.

"Then why are you denying me the one man that will make me happy? The one man that I trust to protect me. The one man that I truly love. Why?" She wails.

"It is because I do love you that I forbid this marriage."

"How can you say you love me and then deny me this shot at happiness?"

"Because I know that in life you need more than just happiness. You need a man that can support you. A man that will keep you in and deliver to you the life you've been raised in and will expect. Now and well into the future. You need a man of means."

"You mean a man like you, don't you father?" she huffs.

"In many ways yes. I suppose I do. Look Debra, you need a man from your class, your station, and our social circle."

"I know, you've told me what I need. I'm telling you what I want," she says, stomping her foot in full tantrum mode.

"Enough. I have a compromise for you. Give me and him a year."

"A year for what?" she asks intrigued yet skeptical.

"A year to prove to me that he is the kind of man that deserves you. That he is the man that can and will make you truly happy. That he is the man equipped and ready to provide a future for you in the manner in which you have been raised and become accustomed."

"But how?" she wails.

"I will stake him to any enterprise the pair of you agree on. I will provide him every opportunity to make a success of that enterprise. If he can, in that one year, then I will grant to both of you my blessing and support. Do you accept?" he says challenging his only daughter.

"I suppose I must. But a year, that is such a dreadfully long time. I agree," she declares in the spirit of resignation and acquiescence.

"What sort of business does your young man envision himself undertaking?" asks her father for the first time during the argument actually intrigued.

"I don't know," confesses his headstrong daughter and only child.

"You've certainly talked about it, haven't you? You do know what he has planned for your future together, don't you?"

"To be brutally honest, we have talked without reaching any firm or binding commitments. However, I feel I can change his mind. I can maneuver him towards a sounder trajectory. Together we can machinate him by introducing the proper course. I know working together we can finesse him towards my more appropriate expectations."

"Is this something he is susceptible to? Is he amenable towards direction? Can he be swayed? Or is this your course? Have you brought forward or discussed this intention?" asks her father, sensing his daughter is telling him what he wants to hear and not the reality of their, shall we say, their relationship.

"While it is true I have not broached the subject openly, I had hoped we could do it together. I need him to change his present course. I cannot bear to think through or towards any conclusion he has chosen, or a path only he is aware of. And what he has in mind for me, for us, I have no inkling," she wails. "I am so confused."

"What exactly is this idea? And why are you opposed to it?" wonders her father, grasping at this key to ending their dalliance. The thought of their relationship causes him to shudder.

"Ever since he saw that darn ad in the newspaper, he's set his mind on trapping beaver. After a couple of successful years, he now sees himself accepted into the company of trappers and mountain men. He is set on returning to the wilds of the Rocky Mountains," she cries.

Inside her father celebrates victory. He knows she will never last a year. Without him constantly around, constantly wooing her, she will tire of his absence, and on the futility of this ill-fated union. He is rejoicing. Fur Trapper, indeed, beaver and the Rocky Mountains, never. Under no circumstances will a fur trapper ever enter into this family. At thinking the words, fur trapper, he shudders again. A year for a spoiled seventeen-year-old girl seems forever. This liaison is over, thinks her father. Internally he is wringing his hands and grinning in victory. In an instant he knows the part he must play.

"I do not think there has ever been a fur trapper in the family," he continues. He says fur trapper in the same tone of voice he would after stepping through a pile of horse plop laying in the street. The very thought of a trapper, a mountain man, an unwashed ruffian from the hinder lands, never!

"Maybe this new direction may benefit the whole family, you know new blood and all.

Bring him to lunch next week. We can discuss this with him in a more civilized manner," he concedes, seeing his plan coming to fruition, leaving his daughter malleable to his ends.

"Lunch next week is not necessary, father. He's waiting for me and an answer." She perks up at the thought of their meeting.

"And where exactly is he?" quips her father, the dead weight in his stomach turning to ice.

"Why, he's standing on the front porch."

"*Oh my*" he says to himself, "*that will never do. What if the neighbors see him? I can always say he is making a delivery. Yes. Well, why not settle this disconcerting matter right now? Yes, that's what I will do.*"

"You may bring him in. I'll arrange lunch with the cooks. After introducing your young man, go upstairs and bring your mother down for lunch," he orders.

"Yes father," she agrees knowing she and her man will triumph over every obstacle her parents cling to. He will earn their respect and agreement over a civilized luncheon. Slowly and carefully she walks to the double doors, the imposing entry into the ostentatious house. The doorman beats her there.

"Allow me miss," he says. He's enjoying the show.

Silently he wishes the young man well, but he knows he will not win this fight. The doorman is dressed in a fine suit. He reckons it cost him more than her suitor earns in a year. He opens the door. "You may enter," he looks up to the tall, man. His face registers the surprise he feels. This is no ordinary young man. In fact, this is not a young man at all. *"The afternoon will prove very interesting,"* he thinks to himself. The suitor to the young miss enters the home.

I stand my long rifle in the corner by the door, dropping my leather possibles strapped over a shoulder next to the rifle. I keep the pair of pistols in my belt with my fighting knife and Crow war axe. Seeing Debra, my eyes cloud over. I feel the tension in the air. Like the air before a summer storm. The kind of air that makes the hair on my arms stand straight. The kind of air you can actually taste as you breathe. I sense it intuitively. It's something I can't explain, it has to be experienced.

"Has he agreed to meet me?" I ask expectantly on the outside yet dreading the afternoon on the inside.

"Yes, and more. We're to sit for lunch. Father has questions and a proposal for you. Please, for my sake, listen through his discourse to the end. Do not take offense and leave. That is what he wants. Promise me," she pleads with me. From her pleading I know this will not go well.

"I promise," I say meaning it at the time. I wonder at what I have walked in on.

"Thank you my darling. Please leave the rest of your...

paraphernalia by your rifle." I carefully lay both pistols and my belt on the small table by the door. I almost feel naked and exposed. Taking my hand, she smiles, leading me into the formal dining room. The long table, able to seat twenty guests, is set for four. As we enter from the front, her parents' hand in hand enter from the side.

———

The Meeting

"It is good to finally meet you, young man. I have heard so much about you that I..." her father stumbles to an awkward silence after getting his first clear glimpse of me. Never failing to gain and keep the advantage, I charge ahead.

"I am glad to see the both of you. Likewise, Debra has told me much about you.

I must admit I am impressed," I tell them. *"To win the battle I'll charge ahead but is this a fight*

I really want to win?" I ask myself.

The head waiter seeking to end the awkward moment walks to the table to seat both of the parents. They both whisper a discreet thank you as they sit.

"My daughter tells me you both wish to be married. Is that correct sir," asks her father.

For the first time since this discussion began this morning

I'm feeling at a loss. Married? I never mentioned marriage. I am not interested in marrying anyone, especially her, this spoiled rich girl. I need to get out as soon as possible.

He's studying me as I sit in front of him. Yes, I am a man. Not one of his daughter's untried youth, which he expected. My hair is long, flowing to my shoulders. I am cleaned shaved but for what's being called a mustache. The ends of which are long trailing the sides of my mouth down to my chin. My hair is a washed out red, lightened from the many hours spent under the sun. From afar it would look almost blond. I stand five feet nine inches tall and tip a scale at 200 hard-earned pounds. That is if I ever manage to find a scale. Her father is slowly raking his gaze completely over me. Up one side then down the other. My wide shoulders and deep chest fill the leather shirt to just shy of the bursting point. A lean stomach leads to strong legs, the muscles can be seen working as I walk. The buckskin pants fit tight. My feet are covered by knee-high moccasins. Both my face and hands are baked to a dark brown, evidence of working under the harsh sun. My hands are not large, but my grip is strong. I know my strength and resist the urge to break her father's hand as we shake, during the welcome.

Her father notices the fine muscles in my hands and fingers as I grip a fork or a cup. Even to me the coffee cup looks small as I hold it by the handle trying to drink from it. I give up and set it down as carefully as possible. Her father expects to smell smoke, animals, sweat, and a host of unclean odors associated with the working class and outdoors men in particular. I made sure to clean my buckskins and take a hot bath this morning. The faint whiff of soap and cedar, I hope shatters his expectations. I've planned all of this to cause her father to reassess his position while sitting at his table, to his right side. Now I'm rethinking that strategy, if the prize is marriage to his spoilt daughter.

"You are not at all what I expected. Have you been to the mountains, already?" asks her father, genuinely interested.

"Yes sir, I have. This will be my fourth year."

"You must have started young," he says, the words tumbling from his mouth wanting to know the man sitting at his table.

"I was twenty the first year I spent in the mountains."

"That makes you twenty-four now?" adds her mother.

"Yes ma'am."

"What did you do prior to that?" she asks. Her father is glad for the interruption. He can marshal his thoughts.

"Before I left for the mountains, I work in a railroad camp as a track layer for three years. I left home at the age of seventeen."

"Your family must have been successful to enable you to outfit yourself and head to the mountains at such a young age."

"Yes ma'am, reasonably successful. I spent a year away at school before leaving home. I did not study that year, I worked, saved my money and outfitted myself with everything I would need to trap in the Stonies. Pa was only a decent farmer. We could not raise sufficient crops on that rock pile. He used his inheritance taking care of the family. At the age of ten I became the family bread winner. I supplied the family food, by hunting. I left home at the age of seventeen. I went to work in a railroad camp. I began as a road grader. I swung a pick and shovel. After six months I began hunting on my time off. I earned more supplying meat for the gangs than I did working on a gang. I saved my money. The work granted me the strength necessary to be successful on my own. After three years I left for the mountains as a trapper."

"I see. Were you a company trapper?" she asks.

"No ma'am. I was a free trapper heading out on my own. The Blackfoot attacked my camp. There were many Blackfoot. After what they did to me as a prisoner, well, I declared war on them Blackfoot. The rest is not fit for the table, but I will say I killed plenty of them. It was the kindness and gifts of the trappers and mountain men at rendezvous that helped me return to the mountains. I winter by myself trapping by myself. I bring my fur to Mr. Richardson every summer."

"What could that have added to?" asks her father, scoffing at my history.

"I own twenty-two horses. Plus my traps and camp gear and supplies. I have three rifles with possibles and six pistols. I have seventeen horses bearing three packs of trade goods, each. When I return next summer, I'll have twenty horses bearing three packs of fur each. My first year in the mountains I met an old mountain man. He no longer traps. He lives with the Crow. He invited me to winter with the Crow. I did for one winter. He taught me how to trade with the Crow and Shoshone. I sell all my fur to Mr. Richardson. I bank what I don't use for my resupply. One more year and I reckon I'll have enough to buy and stock my own horse ranch. You see that's my goal. I want to raise horses in a secluded valley somewhere in the Yellowstone area. But not just any kind of horses, no sir. I'm going to raise strong working horses. Crossing Mustangs with, well a Morgan or blooded work horse. I ain't too sure of the details, yet. I reckon I'll trade with the Crow for a stud or two. The Crow certainly know their horses."

"Young man, do you expect us to believe all of this?" asks father.

"Because you don't know me, I'll ignore the slight. But yes sir, everything I recounted to you is God's honest truth. Shall I continue?"

"Please go ahead," he mocks me with his attitude. I should stop but I can't. I don't have anything to prove to this man. So why do it? I don't know, maybe to wipe that condescending, disdainful, arrogant, and supercilious smile off his overfed, indulged, face. I feel myself rising to his baiting. I'm getting mad.

"At Mr. Richardson's yard I sell all my packs of beaver fur

and buffalo robes. They all rank 1MB. That means Number One Made Beaver. That's the highest rating possible. I trade for Indian-cured buffalo robes. I trap other critters for fur. Everything I earn pays for the next years' supplies and swag for the Indians. I restock for next year and return to the mountains. I've seen how little my furs sell for at rendezvous, so I've decided to make the long ride to Kansas City and sell my furs on my own. I can make money for myself instead of making the Company rich. It takes about five months to make the trip in and to return. I plan to get the most I can out of the trade goods I have. And I do. Except this time, it ain't all beaver. I have bear, fox, and buffalo. Well, long story short, I sell my furs for top dollar to Mr. Richardson. I made more money that I ever thought possible."

"Where is it now?" asks Debra's father in his patronizing manner.

"In the Kansas City National Bank, minus what I keep out to buy swag to trade with the Crow. I can sell any extra horses for top dollar. I buy better weapons, and a years' worth of supplies. After settling at the bank, I carry a couple hundred dollars in gold coins on me and leave the rest sitting in the bank. Next season year I hope to make half again as much as this year. If the Blackfoot or a grizz don't get me."

"How likely is that?" he laughs.

"What?" I ask.

"That the Blackfoot or a grizzly bear will stop you from returning?" asks her father.

"The Blackfoot are after me sure enough. So are the Cheyenne. They've made me an enemy. I kill a couple grizz every year. I reckon on a couple this year. Indian-cured grizz robe will bring in a lot of gold."

"That's quite a story young man," says father.

"You're welcome to talk to Mr. Richardson my fur buyer and the bank manager if you want to find out for yourself. That was only the highlights. A lot of what I lived through is not fit table talk." I reach into my buckskin shirt, take hold of my leather bag of gold coins. "This is half my coins. It weighs a bit less than a pound and a half," I tell the table while spilling out part of its contents. The gold coins pour out over the table. The look on her father's face, well it's priceless. I pick up the coins and replace the bag in my shirt.

"I did not show you that to brag, but to prove I am who I claim to be. I understand you do not find me worthy of your daughter. That's okay," I tell them standing. "I'll be heading to the mountains come morning. I'll be passing by the corner with my horses just after sunrise. If you still don't believe me, look for me come morning. I'm staying at Mr. Richardson's yard tonight and leaving early come daybreak. It was, well a pleasure meeting you. Good day." I turn on my heel and walk out of the dining room to the front door. It is held open by the smiling doorman. "Wipe that darn smile from your face before I smash it up," I warn him. He pulls a knife. I pull a pistol. In a hurry he walks away. I leave the door open.

I walk to Mr. Richardson's yard. I'm telling myself I'm

getting ready for the morning, but I know better. I'm riled clear through at the way they treated me at lunch. You know I didn't eat a single bite after taking that first sip of coffee. I was afraid of breaking that fragile cup. Now I wished I'd have...no, that ain't the right way for me to behave. I'm hungry, I walk to the café. A meal there always cheers me. Maybe it's the waitress, even if I don't know her name.

"If that's the way it's going to be, well I'd best stay in the mountains," I say out loud, not realizing it is out loud as I walk across Mr. Richardson's yard after supper.

"Things didn't go as you figured?" asks Mr. Richardson, overhearing my internal conversation.

"Sorry, didn't mean to say that out loud. You don't need to know my problems. I'm sure you have enough of your own."

"Nonsense, my young friend. I had a feeling they wouldn't accept you. No matter how much you earn from the fur trade they will never welcome you into their circle."

"How can you be so sure?" I ask him.

"Because I come from that same circle. I was the third son. I would never inherit. That goes to the first born. I was not fit for the army or the clergy. Those are the awards to the second and third son. Father agreed to set me up in a business of my choice. I had to make it work on my own. And thanks to you and many free trappers like you, I am succeeding."

"Do you miss that life?"

"No, not for a second. I'd much rather be here making my

own way. You have the start of a nice future. A future that's wide open to you, my friend."

"Thanks Mr. Richardson. I reckon I'll take my chances in the mountains against the Blackfoot and the Grizz. At least I understand them. I'll be pulling out come day light. I'm staying the night, but I'll be leaving shortly after dawn, once my horses are loaded."

"I won't be here, but the guard will be expecting you. If my men don't have anything to do, get them helping you. I'll see you next year. Good luck my friend, Uriah."

"I will see you next year." We shake hands. I wander to the corral where my horses wait for me. I have so many they've taken over one corral. I count them to make sure, all twenty-some are there. I pet each one before walking to my room upstairs. I feel almost naked having left my rifle, both pistols, both knives, and my possibles with my supplies in my room. I decide I want a beer before calling it a night.

I am stopped at the door of a nearby tavern by a large gatekeeper. I'd call him a bouncer.

"I'm wanting to go inside for a beer and you're blocking my way," I try telling him to head off what I think is coming.

"Sure, you do. Head on out and there won't be any trouble," he tells me while adding a set of brass knuckles to each hand.

"If you use those on me, well let's just say it'll be no holds barred," I warn him.

"Exactly how I like it." He tries throwing a punch, I dodge it, pulling a pistol from behind me, I level it in his face.

"Now what do you have to say?" He laughs at me.

"You ain't got the guts." I pull the hammer back, with my finger taking up the slack, I hear a woman behind me scream.

"What is the meaning of this John?" asks the head doorman.

"I was stopping this vagrant from entering the saloon when he pulls this gun on me," he tells the crowd.

"Listen, I just wanted a beer and..." I start. From the corner of my eye I see the bouncer ready a punch to lay me out. I knock the man against the head with my pistol. He's lying out cold, bleeding on the cobble stones outside. "Like I said," reaching down I hold up his hands wearing his brass knuckles. "He was fixing to use these against me."

"That may be, but you still need to move along before I call a policeman."

"What about that beer?"

"You can forget that right now young man," he tells me. The commotion draws the ire of the head doorman.

"Good day Uriah, what's the trouble here?" asks the owner of the gun shop as he's walking inside the pub.

"I was trying to throw this bum out when..."

"I was talking to Uriah, not you Harry. I suggest you shut up now." He does and tries to leave.

"Not so quick," I stop his exit. "Get back here," I tell him.

Looking at the disgusted doorman I continue. "Can I get a beer or not?"

"Of course, you can, Uriah," answers the gun store owner looking at the doorman almost daring them to say something different.

"These two stopped me, now I ain't one to hold a grudge but this day is one of my worst. So, I suggest you fire them before I kill them both," I scream. They are held in place by fear. "I'm not going in where I ain't wanted," I say changing my mind.

"Let's not be so hasty Uriah," says the gun store owner. One look at me he stops. "No, you're right. Come with me," he says. I'm walking away when there is another commotion at the door.

"I have a report of a robbery. What's going on here Harry?" asks a policeman to the doorman.

"It's only a misunderstanding. I have it under control," he explains. It should have settled everything but since he's here the policeman wants to do something.

"Do you want me to bring in the man causing the commotion? I'd be happy to do it," says the policeman to Harry the doorman.

"It's all under control, thank you officer." I'm watching from the edge of the crowd when the policeman catches my eye. I turn away to go, walking back to Mr. Richardson's yard.

"Hey, you, stop," he yells out. I have no idea he is talking to me. I feel a hand on my shoulder. I keep going. The hand contracts, gripping my shoulder through my shirt. I turn around. Seeing an angry man holding on to me I punch him, flattening his nose. He comes up with a Billy Club. I take it away from him, give him another punch, knocking him to the ground. The crowd moves away from us.

"This is quite the mob you have here Harry," I tell him. I leave the owner of the gun store to sort things out. I'm disgusted with humanity.

Without a pause I continue on my way. I pack the few clothes I left out, gather my second rifle and possibles, and slinging my gun belt around my hips I exit my room. I take the stairs to the bottom floor. There is a small crowd in the yard. I push my way through.

"There he is, that's the man that assaulted me," says a voice. I'm grabbed by two men. I easily fight them off. Seeing more coming for me I draw both pistols. Everyone stops in place and the yard is absolutely still.

"Harry you better straighten this up before someone is hurt. And believe me it'll take more than the likes of you all to get to me," I tell the yard. Harry walks in between me and the crowd, to stand by me. The crowd relaxes, all except the first policeman.

"That doesn't explain why you attacked me," he accuses.

"Why'd you put hands on me and pull that club. You never said you were police or asked me to stop. You along with all these other upstanding citizens simply assume I'm the trouble. According to Harry I'm not. It's all of you. If we

ain't done, let's finish this. If we are, stand aside." To empha-
size my point, I drop my saddlebags, still holding both pistols.

"That's not necessary. You can put up your guns," says a
voice in the back.

"Am I free to go?" I ask the yard. No one dare answer.

"This has been one big misunderstanding," says the voice
walking to me. I train both pistols in his direction. I've had
enough of this town. That's when things become clearer
through the red haze, it's the gun store owner.

"I'm the owner of the gun shop Uriah uses. I also have the
ear of the City Council. Officially, this is all a mistake and is
now over. Please, put up your guns Uriah ," he says.

"Why? So, the rest of them fine upstanding citizens can
rush me?" I ask.

"No, it ain't like that," says Harry.

"According to him and the policeman it is," I say pointing
a pistol at the bouncer, John, and the copper.

"They will be taken care of, trust me Uriah," says the gun
store owner. I never did get his name.

"I do, but not them. Am I free to go now?" I ask both men.
I am looking around for objections. There are none. Coming
through the door is the first friendly face I've seen all day, Mr.
Richardson.

"Let me through. I can help," he tells the crowd. He
makes his way to my side. "I know this man. He is a trapper
and mountain man, not a thief or an outlaw. In fact, he works
for me. I've heard enough to regret recommending your busi-

nesses to him. I also see a couple of restaurant owners who I recommended to him. Before someone gets hurt, I say clear my yard and leave. How about it? Or do I have to send a runner to the Chief of Police. Another customer and good friend of mine. I think that's a good idea. Harry, send a runner to bring the Chief and the US Marshal here directly."

"That ain't necessary," says the policeman who started the ruckus. "It's like he said."

"Harry?" asks Mr. Richardson.

"Go on and..."

"Be careful what you say next Harry. I'm having lunch with your employer tomorrow." The crowd is clearing. No one is left to stop me.

At the yard behind Mr. Richardson's tannery his crew is preparing my pack frames with three packs per frame laid in a long line. The horses are waiting for me to line them out.

"It might not be a bad idea for you to load up tonight and leave while you can. I do not think anything more will come from that disturbance, but just in case I suggest you prepare to ride out."

"That's good advice. I'll follow it this time, thanks. I need to do one thing first. Can we go to your office?"

"Sure. You boys get busy, we'll be right back," Mr. Richardson tells them. Sitting at his desk he asks me, "how can I help?"

"I need a pen and paper." He lays both on his desk. I

change the temporary benefactor to a permanent benefactor of my bank account, Mr. Richardson. I sign it and show him.

"Are you sure?"

"I am." We leave his office for the yard. "I reckon you're the only real friend I have.

Thanks for your help."

"Don't mention it. Boys bring out the packhorses," commands Mr. Richardson. I check the knots on each pack frame and on each of the three panniers. With all the help I'm ready to ride within an hour. I saddle my horse, add saddlebags, and bedroll. Each packhorse is tied to the one in front of it. I hold the lead rope controlling them all. With a wave, I'm off. Three of his best men ride with me, until I start on the Santa Fe Trail. I ride through the afternoon stopping as the sun begins setting. I'd keep riding but I don't want to wear out my horses. I stop at a small feeder creek, follow it off the trail onto the plains before setting up camp and resting the horses for the night.

I line up the horses and begin taking off packs and pack frames. I lead all the horses to a hastily set picket rope after drinking in the creek. I leave the packs lined up, covering them with canvas to protect them from dust and dew. In the morning I'll bring out the horses and reverse the process. I make a camp under the trees. I clean out the firepit, add rocks around the edge and start a fire. I reckon I have three more days' worth of beef steaks until I need to begin hunting. It's mid-summer, hot, but the traveling should be good. I have four months to reach the Yellowstone Valley and my winter camp or ride through the first of the cold winter months until reaching the Yellowstone's. The way I'm feeling right now traveling fast and alone sounds good. Then I remember Indians are not like town folk. They have already accepted me. I'll be welcomed to trade.

I sleep soundly through the night assured I've worked over all my gear until I'm satisfied all is ready for this long return ride. The brightness of the stars begins fading as the sun rises. It's time to load up. I bring out the horses one by one, load a pack frame then add three packs. After double checking the knots I return for the next horse. My saddle horse is last. I finish the coffee and a last bite of the baked bread, climb into the saddle, and lead my column west by a bit north. I have two sticks of bread and a cooked steak for a midday meal. This is my unchanging routine. The only thing that may change is if the horses need an extra day to rest. Or if I am unsuccessful hunting as we ride, and I need to dedicate more time to bring in camp meat.

Trouble eludes me until we reach the North Platte River. I stop for an extra day to rest the horses and to hunt. I want a buffalo. I take three packhorses with me to find one. I find a small herd and down a cow. The cleaning and butchering passes quickly and I'm returning to camp with two travois carrying buffalo meat. I smell a fire in the direction of my camp. I did not leave a fire going. Which means I have company. This can go one of two ways, depending on how many are in my camp and if they are drunk or belligerent.

I spot four horses, two are wearing saddles and two are wearing almost empty packs. I pull both pistols and hide them behind me, before riding in.

"Just helping yourself to my camp, are you?" I ask. I'm not giving them time to think or act on a plan.

"What makes you think this is your camp, boy?" says the bigger, dirtier man, the bully.

"Since the horses I'm riding are wearing the same brand as those horses on that picket line, well that makes it pretty simple. I'd appreciate it if you left now."

"We'll leave when I'm good and ready boy."

"And he ain't ready yet, boy," says the other man. They may be brothers. The second is obviously slow in his thinking.

"Don't take unkindly to my little brother. He don't mean it."

"I do. I want both of you out now."

"Or what?" That's when I pull both pistols. I admit I may have acted hasty but I'm plumb tired of bullies picking on me, making a joke out of my plans, and held to be of no account in the eyes of every man I've meet. I don't give them time to pull their weapons. I aim at both brothers and shoot. The right-hand pistol shoots center. The slow brother is dead on his feet. As he topples, the bully I missed center on, cries out.

"What'd you do that for. You done kilt us both," he cries, clawing for a pistol.

"I'd stop. You can live through this if you just go."

"We both know that ain't true." I pull the trigger on my rifle. Feeling nothing, I climb from the saddle, tie my horse to the picket line, and walk over to inspect the bodies. As expected, both brothers are dead. Standing over them I'm feeling, nothing. I reload. I go through the pockets of the bully first. He has a rifle, two pistols, a good knife, and ten twenty-dollar gold pieces in a pouch in his coat. I'm richer by $200. Truth to tell, I'd rather they had moved on.

The younger brother has a rifle, a good knife, no money, and no other weapons. Their saddle horses appear worn out but come from good stock. I unsaddle the first horse, piling the frayed blanket and the old saddle in the dust. The second saddle is in worse condition. It joins the pile. Both packhorses are also from good stock; they're just tired, worn out. Their pack frames and paniers are new and worth keeping. Looking inside the packs, I see they are empty. I tie a rope to a foot of each man to drag them out and away from my camp.

With their horses settled, it's time to care for the buffalo. I'll need to lay up a day to dry most of the meat for jerky. It'll come in handy down the trail. I wrap the parts I want to keep for camp meat in canvas. Searching by the creek, I find enough small limbs to make drying racks. The buffalo camp meat should last me until reaching the Yellowstone River. I tend to the four new horses brushing them, inspecting their feet, and making sure they eat and drink, then rest.

As the day ends, I do not waste time thinking about the

brothers. They sealed their fate by not leaving when they should have. I prepare bread dough and slice two steaks from the buffalo backstraps. I mix the bread dough thick, so it'll hold its shape and not run when I string it along a skewer made from birch wood. When ready I hammer five stakes into the ground. I string the bread dough over three stakes. I thread backstraps over two stakes. The five stakes are close enough to the coals to cook slow. Now it's time to dig out the coffee pot. I fill it with water from the swiftly flowing feeder creek. I've added a flat rock inside the fire ring ensuring it's stable enough to hold the coffee pot. I've learned the hard way how to successfully brew coffee. I've drowned several fires before settling on the flat rock idea. The last time was during a snowstorm. I was cold and tired when I reached for the bubbling pot, but instead of grabbing the pot, I knock it over. Not only am I out of coffee but the fire dies out, thoroughly drowned. I'll never forget that night nor the lesson learned. I sit at the fire until my meal is ready to eat. I enjoy supper, but I still have work to do before turning in for the night.

I keep my weapons close, in case of more uninvited visitors. As added insurance I move my saddle horse closer to the fire and my bedroll. He's the best night hawk I've ever camped with. He will warn me about anyone coming on the camp, man, or beast. This night I sleep straight through. I spend the day finishing the jerky chore. Supper is a repeat of last night's meal. After another complete night's sleep, I wake before dawn. The first morning's chore is adding kindling to the fire. After it catches, I'll add bigger sticks until I can set the waiting coffee pot on the rock. I leave my warm blankets to face the new day.

Two sticks hold bread dough, a third holds a chunk of buffalo. As my meal cooks, I begin loading my packhorses. I stop to eat. Then finish loading. I think about setting the four new horses loose but decide against it. I can trade them or sell them to the Crow.

Things go my way until crossing the Bighorn River. I'm close to the Crow village. All I have to do is follow the river north four days, then turn west. From there it's a matter of finding exactly where the Crow have pitched their winter camp. I must have let my guard down. I'm tired, the summer is giving way to fall, the days are shorter, and growing colder. I have a freshly shot deer on the last packhorse. I don't have to lead the first packhorse along the trail. Once I start him, he'll keep traveling in that direction, until I change it. I can ride up and down the line of packhorses keeping an eye on their condition and on the packs and not worry the lead horse will deviate from the trail.

I reckon I'm within a week of finding the Crow village. I ride from the front of the line of horses to the back, checking on how they're holding up. I'm midway when I hear a growl, then the horses stop. There are panicking cries from the horses in back. Quickly I ride to the back of the line. A grizz stands over the last horse in line, the one carrying the deer, one of the four from the brothers. A single swipe of his giant paw has killed the horse. The live packhorses run ahead. I shoot the bear with my rifle. He falls. I watch the head, know I hit it, but only see a trickle of blood from the hit in the chest. As I pull the right-hand pistol, the bear growls and stands. I shoot. The ball lands directly in his chest. I follow it with a second pistol ball. The bear's back on the ground. Two more pistol balls to the chest ensure he will not rise. I ride after the horses, leaving the bear where he fell. The horses have stopped after running ahead less than half a mile. The lead ropes are hopelessly tangling. I reckon it's time to make camp.

As I untie and untangle each horse, I drop their packs and tie them to a picket line. The last step is hobbling each horse. I don't do this unless they are upset and threatening to rebel by riding off, without me. Meeting a Grizz is threat enough. Two hours after shooting the grizz, all the horses and packs are where they should be, lined out for a quick leaving come daylight. I've made a camp alongside a feeder creek, started coffee, and that's when I remember the bear. I ride back to the grizz and my dead horse. Someone has beaten me to it. They're Indians, but I do not recognize the tribe. I ride into their camp. I'd better use the universal signs, there are five of them.

"Hello," I sign. They return it.

They sign asking if I shot the bear. I admit I did. They excitedly talk among themselves. I do not recognize the language; I know they are not Crow. I tell them they are welcome to the bear when it hits me, they are Cheyenne. They watch as I ride closer. The hide is valuable, but I'm so mad and frustrated I'm glad to give it away. I sign they are welcome to the hide. A leader walks to me sitting on my horse. He signs thank you, then asks, "What are you doing in the land of the Cheyenne?"

I tell him I trade for hides and furs. He tells the others what I said which gets them all talking. He invites me to come into their camp and share a meal. I tell him thanks and invite them to my camp if they want to trade. I'm taking a risk, but I reckon the value of a good outcome is worth the risk. I've not traded with the Cheyenne, only fought with them. I'm willing to try something new.

Their leader tells me they will visit my camp. I tell them to ride over when they are ready. I tie my horse to a tree by my fire. I can smell the coffee is ready. I'm on my third cup when the Cheyenne ride in. They tie their horses away from mine. That's fine with me. They walk to the fire. Taking seats, the lead warrior asks about the story of the grizz attack and the killing of one of my horses. Using signs, I explain as well as I can. He asks me if I've had to kill any grizz besides this one. I sign yes. They get to talking among themselves. I'm digging through my saddlebags for the necklaces of the claws from the five grizz I've crossed paths with. After retaking my place around the fire, I show them the five sets of claws. That gets them talking louder and more excited amongst themselves. I have no idea what they are saying.

A warrior hands me a parfleche holding the claws from the grizz. Another warrior adds strips of bear meat threaded over spits strung at the side of the fire. I sip coffee as we continue to sign back and forth, waiting as the bear steaks sizzle. The lead warrior cuts strips from the chunk of crackling and hissing bruin passing a piece to each man. I take the cooked meat and begin eating. We eat until we cannot force another bite down. With smiles all around we wipe greasy hands on our buckskin pants. They do not accept my offer of coffee. That's alright.

Now that I've eaten my eyes are growing heavy. The leader asks if we can trade. I tell him yes; I'll trade my goods for hides and furs. Without another word they turn aside spreading out their blankets and furs, settling in for the night. We'll trade tomorrow. I stand, take the coffee pot and cup to the creek, refill it, wash out the sock, and add more grounds for morning. My horse is hobbled next to where I spread my blankets. He has night hawk duties tonight.

I think my ears are playing tricks on me when I hear voices and horses approaching. The sun is only threatening to rise. Looking over I can only see one Cheyenne warrior as he sits up. The others slipped away during the night. The one who remained behind tells me he stayed in case others show up. He will vouch for me. I get up from my blankets, add wood to the fire and put the coffee pot on to boil. It's four different Cheyenne hunters. They sit their horses outside my camp. Using signs, I invite them in. Slowly they slip from their horses. One man takes them away as the other three come to the fire. In signs they ask permission to cook their meal. I agree quickly, offering them chunks of Grizz.

One man puts up end posts and a spit while another slices steaks from the chunk of bear. Another man threads them through the spit and sets them over the fire to cook. They refuse my coffee. The man taking care of the horses returns carrying a big pot. He asks permission to put it on the fire. I agree, curious about what he's doing. They tell me it's the fat from the Grizz. They are rendering it to make cooking grease. Bear grease is highly prized. I reckon they are hungry. They are not getting an early start on the day. They resist pulling off the bear, until cooked through. I'm amazed at how much they eat. The six of us are sitting around the fire quietly eating. When finished, they thank me and ask to see what I have to trade. I show them the packs of cast iron pots, Dutch ovens, frying pans, large and small pots, and spoons. These bring no response. They get excited after seeing the packs carrying new Hudson Bay wool blankets. I have sewing needles and threads, bolts of cloth, mirrors, tacks, and axes.

After a quick look, they invite me to their village to trade. They ask me what kind of fur I am interested in. I tell them beaver, bear, wolf, and buffalo, any well-tanned fur. I have many questions to ask them. But before talking further, they insist I load my packhorses and ride for their village. After watching me, they jump right in on helping fit the pack frames to each horse and adding the panniers. I double check the packs and tie the knots. I saddle my riding horse and am ready to ride. One of the Cheyenne rides off ahead of us.

Instead of heading west for the Crow camp, we head east by south for the Cheyenne camp. Three days later I ride into the Cheyenne camp. They greet the four warriors; glad they have returned and not been killed raiding or stealing horses. We stop in front of the biggest lodge in the camp. This is the teepee of the main peace chief. The people line up behind the four warriors and my packhorses. He emerges, looking around, sees the gathered warriors. A short exchange brings their focus back to me. The chief calls a name. The name is repeated through the camp. A young boy, a captive, slowly comes forward. The chief talks to him in Cheyenne. The nervous boy nods his head and turns to me.

"The chief says that I am to be your interrupter. I am to help you as you trade. I will show you to a lodge where you can unload your horses. They will be marked with your sign. When you want to leave, they will be returned to you. You may keep your best horse next to your lodge. Do you understand?"

"Yes, I do. What's your name?" I ask the boy.

"I am Nate."

"Are you a captive?"

"Yes."

"How long have you been here?"

"I was traded from the Sioux. I've been here four years."

"How old are you?"

"I don't know and before you ask, I don't remember my white name and I do not want to go back."

"Why not?"

"I am treated better here than my Pa treated me and my sister. She's dead. I like it here and I won't go back."

"All right. Lead me to this lodge."

"Follow me." He walks through the village without looking behind him to see if I'm still there. He greets several other boys near his age. He looks to be about 13 or 14. He's tall and strong looking. He's wearing buckskins and moccasins. He looks happy.

We've walked through the village to the east edge. Standing off by itself is a buffalo hide teepee. It looks like all the others. The boy holds the doorway open. I look inside. There is only a central firepit, outlined with rocks. I stand up looking at the boy.

"I will bring you fresh cedar limbs for your bed. I think you will get enough robes and hides through your trading to cover the ground and stay warm through winter. I will be working for you doing whatever you need. Like cutting firewood, fetching water, brushing your horses, and most important teaching you our language."

"Does that mean I'm to spend the winter here?"

"We don't know yet. It depends on how fair you treat our trades. We will have many furs to trade come spring. If we owe you furs and hides, then you can stay with us, if you want to. I think you will get more if you stay through the winter.

We have been waiting for a trader. No one has come to us. You are the first."

"Thank you. I think I will enjoy staying through the winter. Can I go hunting? How much will your services cost me?" I ask half in jest.

"My services cost nothing. The chief ordered me to work for you. I will be pleased to do it. If I don't, I'll have to go to work for a family, that I do not care for. If you can use a bow or a lance you may be invited to hunt. But not using your rifle," he tells me.

"Alright, I understand. Where will you be staying?"

"Here with you," he says, as if it's the most obvious answer.

"Okay. Let's unload the horses. I'll need a place to stack the pack frames inside out of the weather. When will the trading start?"

"When you are ready to begin. I will build a shelter for the pack frames after trading."

"Let them know tomorrow morning," I tell Nate.

"I will. Show me where you want this shelter."

"Right here," I show him. Together we unload the horses. I show the boy how to untie the panniers, how to stack them, and how to untie the pack frames. I show him where I want the canvas spread out. As we finish getting the packs off, the four warriors which brought me to their camp pay my lodge a visit. They lead horses bearing buffalo robes and many different kinds of hides. When the kid comes back with a load of firewood the trading begins. The trading starts with the exchange of buffalo robes. When I have all their hides stacked inside my lodge, they leave with many things that will make their lives easier. If the trades keep like this, it will be good for both sides.

Later, sitting around the fire in my lodge, it hits me. I understand this new feeling. For the first time in years I feel like I'm home. Nate is a good cook. I show him how I make bread. He's unsure at first but after trying a bite, he pays closer attention as I teach him. After supper he builds up the fire. My horse is outside the door, on night hawk duty. Everything is as good as I can possibly expect things to be. That worries me.

Internally I'm worried if learning I was a prisoner of the Blackfoot will adversely affect our trading. I do not know enough about their culture to learn how my status may change. I will need to keep my wits about me and learn as much as I can as fast as I can. But for now, I have work to do.

Trading with the Cheyenne

The next morning Nate gets me up early.

"The people will come as soon as the sun rises. You will be ready?" he asks me.

"With your help I will," I tell him. I notice the coffee pot on the fire with bread threaded on six skewers and mystery meat on four skewers. While the food cooks I show the kid how to spread out the canvas and how to lay out the trade goods in front of the lodge. We stop to eat. As we're finishing, people from the village arrive. At first, they look over everything I have laying out. They all leave without making a single trade. I look to the boy and raise my shoulders in the universal sign for, what just happened?

"They will be back. They wanted to see if what you have is worth their time," he tells me.

"Well is it?" I ask. He points towards the village. I see them returning but this time they are leading horses with travois bearing furs. I reckon they like what they see. Business is brisk. They are shrewd traders. The women make faces and show distain for the trade values of goods to furs. I sign okay and look to help the next villager. It never fails, the first one breaks in and agrees to trade. We pile the furs behind us. I keep the kid busy bringing out more goods replacing the ones rapidly disappearing.

When the warriors show up the women call it a day. Each one of them looks impassively at what is displayed. There is little haggling. They know I am giving them more than fair value for their furs. This is intentional. Not only do I want to leave with my hair, my horses, and my trade goods but I want to return next fall. Half of the axes are gone at the end of the day. I've exchanged a quarter barrel of tacks for a large stack of beaver plews. I'm surprised to see the warriors asking for mirrors. The mystery is solved when I see a handful of them practicing signaling to each other with them. Next year I will bring more. I make a note of that in my journal. I remember Raven saying I could only hunt with a bow and arrow. I ask every one of the warriors if they have a hunting bow and arrows to trade. So far no one does. I forget about it until the end of day.

Each warrior makes way for an old man. He is escorted to my lodge supported by a young warrior on each side of him. They are not holding him up as much as acting like escorts. He speaks with Nate for a long time. No one is trading during their conversation. When the old man folds his arms across his chest and nods his head, the trading is over. I'm watching this man. At one time, in his prime, he must have been extremely strong and a first-rate warrior. Even now in his advanced years I would not like to tangle with him.

"Sees Far has a bow, a quiver, and twelve arrows he will trade to you," says Nate.

"Good. What does he want for them?"

"The price will be high. Are you sure you wish to do this?"

"Yes. What is the price?" I ask now wary.

"If you make the trade, Sees Far will teach you to use his weapons."

"Is that it? Sure, I'll learn from him. Tell him yes."

"It will take the entire winter and be very hard. Are you sure? This is not an easy thing Sees Far offers you. He has not taught a warrior in several years. Many who start do not finish. He wants you to know before you begin that it will be hard, but he expects you to finish."

"Tell him I understand."

"Tell him yourself, Uriah."

"He understands English?" I ask surprised.

"Yes. Part of your training will be learning our language."

"I accept, Sees Far," I tell the aged warrior.

"We begin when the sun rises in the morning. Come to my lodge," he tells me in a strong voice.

"I will be there," I tell him. He gives me a look; one I can find no meaning behind.

———

Cheyenne Warrior Training

Before the sun breaks the western horizon, I present myself to Sees Far. Standing in front of his lodge I hear a voice.

"Is that you Uriah?" This does not sound like the old man I met yesterday.

"Yes, it is." A tanned arm throws open the flap. He pours out from the lodge. Before me stands a for real, Plains Indian warrior. He dressed in newer looking buckskins, from moccasins to war shirt. His war shirt is plain, undecorated, utilitarian. He is dressed to work. And work we do. He hands me a thick leather belt and a large parfleche. On the belt is a flint knife. The parfleche is empty. We walk to the edge of the camp. As we pass by something, he tells me its name in Cheyenne. I repeat it. By the time we get to the edge of the camp my head is too full of new words to remember the first ones. He is carrying a bow, a quiver filled with arrows, a lance, and a war axe. In his belt is a large metal knife. During our day he teaches me the basic moves of knife fighting, the Cheyenne way.

We start running. When we come to something Sees Far wants me to learn, we stop. He tells me in English then in Cheyenne. At this point I am only repeating the words trying to pronounce them correctly. We run all day. I've not run like that since I was a boy. By the time we make it back to the village I am tired. Sees Far is not. He leaves me at my lodge. Inside the kid has a meal on the fire. Ravenously I devour what is prepared. After eating he takes me to the hot springs. I soak in the hot water until my head drops to my chest. Waiting for me is a clean set of buckskins and moccasins.

The next day is a repeat. And so, it goes for two weeks. When I start remembering the words and names enough to repeat them to Sees Far, he rewards me with the materials to fashion a lance. I collect the parts during our run. At our midday stop he shows me how to build the lance. I return to the village carrying my first weapon made by my own hands. The next two weeks he teaches me how to use the lance as a tool and a weapon. The next weapon is the war axe. Followed by two weeks of instruction. Then a buffalo-hide war shield.

And last but not the least is the bow. Two weeks in only enough time to learn the basics.

By this time the snow is sticking and accumulating. We stop running and we begin riding, the Cheyenne way. I notice words are progressively finding themselves a part of my new vocabulary. Every day ends in the hot springs.

When the snow begins, I am allowed to trade in the afternoons. My training is managed in the mornings. When the accumulated snow begins melting, I realize the time is close for me to return to Kansas City and sell my winter's hoard of fur. I do not want to stop training nor leave the village. Returning to the city holds no promise for me. I do not want to go. Sees Far knows and understands.

On our last morning together, he sits me down and we talk. I've learned a lot from the old warrior. He makes me understand that I need to sell my fur, purchase more of the things this village needs, and to return to them. He hands me a list of their greatest needs. Nate and I begin loading furs into packs of compressed plews that afternoon. Two days later and I'm ready to ride. The village holds a feast my last night in the village. Before shuffling to my lodge, Sees Far tells me where to find them come my fall return.

Early the next morning Nate helps me load my horses. Many of the villagers bring us a packet of jerky or pemmican for my journey. I leave without looking behind me, sick at heart at leaving my new friends. This surprises me. I don't know if they understand what I've suffered at the hands of the Blackfoot. They have all seen the ragged knife scar from belly button to breastbone. I tell them it came from when I was a captive of the Blackfoot. I do not encourage questions. I don't believe they do not know about my history. Maybe they are as hesitant about telling me, as I am of them. This will take further reflection. Right now, I have miles to travel.

5

TO KANSAS CITY SPRING TO SUMMER 1835

I've decided to make the trip to Kansas City instead of going to Rendezvous and trading this year's fur for next year's trade goods and supplies. There are two reasons for this decision. First, I need to see Debra. I know by now her father has introduced her to someone, or many someone's, in her circle of friends, in their family's sphere of influence. I see now I never stood a chance, nor did I really want to. I understand that now and I am incredibly relieved. She used me to get at her father. That's alright. However, I owe it to myself to say hello and goodbye, if they'll see me. Chances are they will refuse me. And that too is okay with me.

The second reason is to sell to Mr. Richardson and get a better price for my furs and pelts. In that whole town he's the only man I trust. As soon as I load my packs with the necessities that Sees Far and Nate have asked for, I will head back to the mountains and my Cheyenne friends. I reckon two or maybe three more trips and I'll have enough to begin the horse ranch I've been thinking of and striving towards.

Four Cheyenne warriors and Nate help me until we leave the foothills reaching the plains. From there Nate and I are on our own. I hand our escorts gifts. They turn around and ride away without a word, but they do raise a hand and wave. I hope to see them in less than five months. Looking ahead at the trail to St. Louis I see Nate has not left but is still with me.

"Why aren't you returning with the others?" I ask him.

"Sees Far wants me to stay with you to learn the secrets of the furs."

"This is something you want to do?"

"Yes. I will be a help and not get in your way. I can..." he pleads.

"Okay Nate. You can stay and I'm glad to have you." With a smile on his face he rides for the lead packhorse, takes up the lead and begins leading the packhorses east.

I've got twenty-five packhorses carrying furs. Four packhorses carry camp supplies. We both have an extra riding horse. Nate is wary of making the trip with me. He does not want to return to the life of an American boy. He wants to stay with the Cheyenne, and I don't blame him one bit. I will claim him as kin and keep him with me.

We ride east along the North Platt River towards the Missouri River. I'm hoping to catch a ride on a river boat heading south. Traveling on the river to Kansas City will be a nice distraction. It will save the horses and us from walking but may take the same amount of time, unless we're really lucky. We'll see.

Our trip goes much better than can be reasonably expected. When we run out of camp meat, finding buffalo close to the river is fairly easy. No one said anything but I have a feeling the Cheyenne put out the word, we are protected. Sure, we see other Indians, but none come close. The only real trouble is with another grizz. Shortly after following the North Platte I get the feeling we're being followed, the short hairs on the back of my neck are standing straight. I decide to stop and let the horses rest an extra day. I've had enough of being followed, it's time to confront whoever it is. We've got a tight camp hidden deep in the trees along the river. About midday on our rest day I return with a deer on a packhorse. After arriving in camp, the grizz announces his presence. The horses sense him first. They begin fusing on that picket rope. They are hobbled and can't run, but that don't stop them from trying.

He's waddling into camp following his nose. He must have been following me. He can't make up his mind between the deer on my packhorse or the helpless horses tied by the creek. He ain't only hungry but ornery. It's been awhile since he has torn through a camp for the sheer exhilaration of a fight. With an unsettling bellow and a growl like thunder he stands on his back legs at the edge of our camp. His holler flings a wet cloud of drool from mouth and chin through the air. Standing to his full length, I recognize this is an enormous bear. I don't reckon I've seen a bigger grizz. He's old and experienced. It looks like he's chosen to sample the deer and raze our camp. His smaller front legs bat the air in front of him. He reminds me of a boxer warming up. Except this fighter has five-inch-long, sharp claws. I reckon he's simply warning us of what's to come.

With possibles over a shoulder, I'm unsaddling my horse. The packhorse carrying the deer squeals while pulling at his reins I've tied to a tree. He's doing everything he can to dump the bear bait secured on his back. With that scream, I drop the saddle to grab my rifle and a second pair of pistols. Nate is at my side with his bow and a quiver of arrows. As I'm bringing up my rifle, Nate begins sending arrows into the chest of that grizz. I shoot. The cloud of burnt black powder blocks him from my sight.

Each arrow penetrating his hide reaches his heart and elicits a howl and a grunt from the king of bears. He's game, standing to take the punishment Nate is lashing out. Nate has fired six arrows into that bear. The spread of arrows is no bigger than a supper plate. Until the rifle ball strikes his chest. That's the game changer. He drops to the ground. Now he's enraged, dead on his feet, but wrathful and unrestrained. All four feet are throwing grass and dirt through the air behind him. Saliva turns to red foam at his snout. His great head is swinging back and forth. He's chomping his jaws, the teeth making a horrible clashing noise. He's fixing to charge. He is cross and ready to set things right.

Nate moves to one side; I take the other. I'm reloaded and ready for a second shot. I add a second rifle ball to the front shoulder of the grizz. The ball of lead hits the grizz, plowing through and breaking the shoulder, he falls to his side. The broken bones will not support his weight. A cloud of dust rises as he hits the ground. I feel a tremor run across the campsite, through the bottom of my feet, in my moccasins. Nate looks at me with a wide smile on his face. I can't believe the short, yet intense fight is over. I find myself talking Cheyenne to my young partner.

"Be careful. Make sure he's dead," I tell him. We walk towards him together. Nate has an arrow on his bow string. I have a loaded pistol in my left hand. He looks dead. With my stronger right arm, I'm reaching out to touch the end of my rifle to an eye. When the end of the rifle's barrel is close to his eye, he wakes, opening both eyes. I draw in my rifle and jump back. Nate delivers another arrow to the great heart of the mortally wounded grizz. The giant bear releases a screech that makes my hair stand on end. He's angry and telling us. I fire my left-hand pistol. We're so close his chest hair begins smoldering, burning from the black powder explosion. The pistol shot elicits a deep growl. He tries to stand. Nate lands two more arrows. The great bear settles to the grass. I know he's dead but need to catch my breath before confirming it. Nate has another arrow ready, just in case. The body of the giant bear deflates.

He does not move. I can relax knowing he really is dead. I remember Micah warning me more trappers are killed by dead bears that live ones. I know what he means now. I reach out with my rifle barrel to confirm he's dead. There is no movement.

"He is your kill," I tell Nate. He looks at me as if I'm joking. I nod my head towards the great body. Slowly he walks towards the grizz. I watch as he begins skinning his first grizz.

I've got to see to the horses, I leave him with his bear. I need to pat each horse, reassuring them they are all okay. I check the knots on the picket line and the hobbles, before moving to the next horse. I'm finished before Nate finishes skinning the bear.

I bring out my sharp knives to help get the job done. Nate has made the initial cut along the belly from neck to tail. Moving to the legs he has circled around the pad of each foot and up the inside of each leg to the belly cut. Now it's time to pull the hide off. Like we do with a buffalo, Nate ties a rock in the freed hide at the neck. Securing the rock with a rope and dallying the rope to the saddle horn of a saddled horse, I lead the horse forward as Nate frees the reluctant hide with a knife. The horse pulls the hide off. We spread it hair side down to dry.

Returning to the bear we harvest the lard in a Dutch oven

sitting on coals next to the fire. We add more lard as it melts down. Nate is already slicing off long strips of bear meat for jerky. Some we will use for camp meat, and the rest we'll dry for jerky. Nate wants the skull and claws. I leave him working on the four feet and the head. I've done it, he's welcomed to them this time. I reckon we're having bear for supper. I keep the drying rack full making grizz jerky. That may not sound appetizing right now but come a hungry late night or a snow-storm I'll be glad to have it.

I keep the fire hot and the flames low through supper time. After washing my hands, I mix bread dough and make the back straps ready for skewering. As the sun sets bringing dark to the flat lands, the grizz is finished and we can eat. After supper it'll take both of us to move the debris and scraps onto a canvas tarp and haul it away from camp. I decide to camp an extra day. I don't want to waste any of the bear meat. There's been too many times when I'd have given a fortune for a plate full of bear steak or a fist full of bear jerky.

I will admit I find something to do upwind of the fire as Nate boils the skull. When he's finished it is a nice trophy and I'm happy for him. He is anxious to tell the village and receive a new name, a warrior's name. As the jerky comes off the fire and cools, we pack it in canvas bags. The claws are in a parfleche, Nate will work on them every night until strung together making a warrior's necklace.

With sunup an hour away, we break camp continuing our

journey east. We reach the Missouri River. We wait two days, before getting a ride south to Kansas City on a paddle boat. Ten days later we arrive in Kansas City. We are the first to unload at the docks. Both of us must be looking a bit trail worn, the kind citizens of Kansas City make way for us and our horses. We have an uneventful ride to Mr. Richardson's back gate. At my insistent knocking, the gate is opened. We are recognized and led in. The workers help lead our horses inside and quickly locks the gate. A runner is sent to find Mr. Richardson. As I am unsaddling my riding horse, he runs out to greet us.

"Welcome back my friend. Am I ever glad to see you and your furs. You brought a friend along this time. He doesn't look Crow. How was your ride? How well did your trading go?" he's asking me as I work. There are so many questions I give up trying to remember and answer each one. When he runs out of steam, I look at him.

"Are you okay? Why'd you stop?" I ask.

"Because I received no replies," he tells me. When I'm finished with my horse one of his men takes it with Nate's mount to the small corral where my animals are kept while in town.

"Now," I tell him. "This is Nate. He started as an interrupter between me and the Cheyenne, but now I consider him a friend." They shake hands while sizing each other.

"This is Mr. Richardson," I tell him making introductions.

"I'm very glad to meet any friend to Uriah," he tells the boy. "You're not Cheyenne. Are you a captive?"

"No, I live with them of my own free will. Turn me in and I will run away and rejoin them," threatens Nate.

"I will not turn you in. If you're happy with them, well I'm happy for you. I understand that Uriah is teaching you the trade."

"We teach each other what the other doesn't know," slowly answers Nate

"I see. What happened with the Crow?" he asks me. Nate continues working on the horses.

"I never reached them." As the three of us walk into the building, to Mr. Richardson's office, I relate running into the Cheyenne, up to leaving camp at late spring. He is quiet through the telling. I notice Nate is looking closely at the animals Mr. Richardson has displayed around his office. Especially the full-sized grizz and the full-sized cougar leaping down on a full-sized elk.

"Let's get the tally and get our business taken care of. You will be glad to hear that I have built four rooms above the barn for the use of my customers. I have had several, shall we say, not so pleasant experiences between the hotels in town and my trappers."

"You mean like mine last year?" I ask.

"Exactly."

"How much is the rent?" I ask with a grin.

"For the trappers that work with me, it is my gift to them for making me the busiest tannery in town," he laughs.

"Congratulations, we accept. Is that café still serving us mountain men and trappers?"

"Yes, they are, and that red-haired beauty that caught your eye last spring is still there. I have heard she earns more in tips than what the owner brings in each night. It seems that all of your trappers tip her well," laughs Mr. Richardson.

"She works hard for it. Any gal that puts up with the likes of me and your other customers deserve it. I'll tell her I'll keep coming to town as long as she keeps working." Mr. Richardson looks stricken. He cannot tell if I am joking. It is only half a jest. If more people treated us like she does, well I'd gladly give them my business. Unfortunately, she is the exception when it comes to merchants and business owners. Oh, they're happy to take our money but don't want us in the same café, general store, or hotel they use. Thinking about their prejudices gets me to seeing red. Mr. Richardson can see it beginning and building.

"My theory why all you trappers return to her café is that the lot of you are half in love with her." He is a wise man. There is probably much truth in that simple statement. It makes me smile, leading towards a laugh. The red haze slowly recedes.

We walk down the hall towards the counting rooms. To me the rooms are in chaotic disorder. But Mr. Richardson sees through the chaos to the underlying order. A foreman walks up to hand him the tally sheet. We return to the office.

Sitting behind his desk, Mr. Richardson slides a folded paper towards me. I carefully pick it up. It is a comfortable amount.

"Agreed?" he asks me.

"Yes. I'd like half in the bank and half in money to pay for trade goods."

"That's 12 and a half pounds worth of $20 gold coins," he tells me. In his head he's done the sums while we talk. Every time I see it, he amazes me. I reckon all that schooling ain't so bad after all.

"I see. Okay deposit half in the bank, and a bag of coins and paper checks that the general stores will accept for resupplying our trade goods."

"Agreed," he tells me. He opens the bottom drawers and counts out the gold coins. He writes a deposit slip and I sign it. "I'll get you bank checks to pay for your supplies and trade goods. They are much easier and safer carried than bags of gold coins. There you go That's more than enough to provide your needs while in town. We can deposit the remainder in your bank account. I have your bank book. Care to do that now?"

"How about in the morning? That will give us a chance to wash and change clothes. I've been on the trail seven weeks."

"Yes, you're quite right. Come along and I'll show you your rooms," he tells us.

Outside we stop to pick up saddlebags and bedrolls. We follow Mr. Richardson upstairs over the stalls. He opens two doors.

"All the rooms are the same. Pick which you want," he tells us. Nate takes the first one. He is followed inside by workmen bearing buckets of hot water. The water fills a tub in each room.

"Thanks," I tell them. Turning to Nate I continue, "once cleaned up we're heading for the café." Turning to Mr. Richardson, it's his turn, "I'll see you first thing and we'll go to the bank." He sticks out his hand to both of us and we shake.

"In the morning then," he tells us. I walk into the room.

———

Kansas City

I sit in the hot water until it cools. I find myself really relaxing for the first time since last year. Putting it off no longer I get out and dry off. That's when I notice the bundles on the bed. I look closer, unwrap, and dump them on the bed. I'm surprised to see the town clothes I bought last year. I shave before dressing. There is no way I can get the boots on my feet. It's just as well, I'm used to the moccasins. I add a pistol to my belt holding my big knife. With my possibles over a shoulder I leave my room to check on Nate. I knock on his door.

"What?" is his shouted inquiry.

"It's me. Checking if you're ready to eat," I tell him through the door. It opens as I stop talking.

"Sorry Uriah, I didn't know it was you," says Nate wearing new unfamiliar town clothes and moccasins. "These were on the bed when I got out of the water. They are for me, right?"

"Yes, they are. Hungry?" I ask him.

"Yes," he simply says, tucking a pistol in his belt and his possibles over a shoulder. We walk to the café. There are no bells over the door ringing as a customer walks in. She knows when someone enters. In all the summers I've been through here, I have not figured how she does it.

"Uriah, it's good to see you. Sit where you'd like. I'm bringing coffee," she tells us. True to her word as soon as I sit in the chair a heavy mug is filled and waiting on me. With a twinkle in her eye she places one in front of Nate. The way he's looking at her I can tell he's already half in love with her, just like the rest of us.

"We have buffalo steak on special tonight. That comes with baked potato, and a slice of dried apple pie. Two?" she asks. With a smile I nod my head. I'm afraid my voice ain't up to a reply. After she glides away Nate looks at me in wonder.

"Now do you understand?" I ask him.

"I do. Thanks," he says, watching for her return. Reluctantly we're finished. I cannot down another cup of coffee or another bite of supper. I leave three silver dollars on the table.

"See you in the morning?" she asks us as we're about out the door.

"You can bank on it," I tell her. Nate simply smiles.

"It's time to drop our list of goods at the general store," I tell Nate.

"Why do you say we and our when it is your job and your labor?" Nate asks me. I stop and look at him.

"I reckon we're partners," I tell him.

"How can I be a partner? I don't bring in anything," he says, shrugging his shoulders.

"That ain't true. You worked with me through the winter. All along the way here you worked as hard as I did, doing the same work I did. In my book that makes you a partner. I reckon I should have told you sooner. I aim on paying you for all that work."

"Pay me? What? I don't understand. The Cheyenne told me to work for you. How does that make us partners?" he asks, the confusion written across his young face.

"When you do more than what is expected, that makes you my partner. You didn't have to go with me on this trip. I wouldn't have blamed you if you didn't, but I'm right glad you did. That makes you a partner. I'm going to pay you in gold coins."

"I don't know what to do with them. Keep them or use them to buy me trade goods. I have no use for the coins."

"All right. Come with me just so you know what I'm

doing," I tell him. He may think this is over but it ain't. I'm not sure what to do, but I know I'll reckon something out.

We walk through the door of a general store and the hated bells announce us. A new man is working behind the counter.

"What can I help you with?" he asks us. I dig out the list I puzzled over during our ride east.

"I'll be needing everything on this list. I can pick it up this time tomorrow. If you can have it in back of the store, I'll load my horses," I tell him.

"I no longer allow you trappers to load your flea-bitten nags at the back of my store. I..."

"I done it like that for a few years now," I interrupt him.

"I'm the new owner and I don't do it like that. I can deliver them to you in a yard in town here. That's it."

"Can you take them to Mr. Richardson's yard?" I ask him.

"I can, but it'll cost you a dollar per packhorse. It's either that or load your horses in the street," he laughs at me.

"You don't give a man any good options now do you?" I ask him. I'm about ready to try another store.

"I don't need to and neither does any other store. You can go check but it'll be the same for all of us. And before you complain, the prices are higher too. Pay it or not, I don't care."

"Here's my list of goods. Show me how much things have gone up."

"Give me your scribblings. I hope I can cipher it." I hand

him my list. He gets a smile on his face. "At least you can write."

"I can do sums also," I warn him with a hand resting on my pistol's handle. He sees and loses a bit of color.

"Don't worry, I don't cheat my customers," he tries to assure me.

"I reckon you don't appreciate them much either," I tell him. The look on my face stops whatever retort he was fixing to give. "Deliver it to Mr. Richardson's yard. He'll be there to receive the load and he can do sums also," I warn the store owner.

"Ain't no call to letting things get ugly. You'll find me an honest merchant."

"I hope so, for your sake." My meaning is clear, he understands it.

"It'll be there tomorrow at this time."

"Good, we'll be expecting you. I'll pay you then for what's delivered." Nate follows me out the door. We start walking down the boardwalk to the gun store. I have a list of supplies to be delivered to Mr. Richardson's yard tomorrow. Not feeling like bucking the crowds, we turn around and walk back to the yard without dropping off the list. I'll do it come the morning. It's dark when we climb the stairs to our rooms. I've had enough for this day.

The morning starts off well. We break our fast at the café. She is working and the place is full except for one table.

"I been saving that table for you. Glad you both showed

up. Do you know what you want?" she asks us, filling our heavy white enamel cups full of hot coffee.

"What's your name?" asks Nate. The unexpected question stops her for only a minute.

"Bridgit. You?" she asks him.

"I'm Nate and this is my partner Uriah."

"Glad to meet you Nate and Uriah. I've served you for years and am only now learning your name. What are you going to have?" she asks with a twinkle in her blue eyes.

"Griddle cakes, eggs, ham, potatoes, and a slice of that pie," I tell her. With a smile she walks back to the kitchen to deliver our order.

Stuffed to the gills again, we walk slowly to the gun store. I hand him my list, he looks at it, and promises it will be delivered by the end of the day. With nothing else to do and nothing to see we head back to Mr. Richardson's yard. We sit around repairing gear until our supplies arrive.

"Uriah, do I have enough of them gold coins to buy me a rifle like yours? And maybe a couple more pistols?" Nate asks me as we work on cleaning harnesses.

"I reckon you have more than enough. You'll be needing possibles too."

"How about a saddle like yours?"

"Sure, anything else?"

"Not that I can think of right now. But the day is early," he laughs. I notice the store's wagon rolling in with my order. We get up to meet the driver.

Mr. Richardson walks over when he sees me arguing with the wagon's driver.

"What's the problem here, Uriah?" I explain my earlier conversation with the store owner. Now it appears the totals on everything are short from what I ordered. Adam takes my list, the wagon's list, and compares them with what is in the wagon.

"You can return all of this merchandise. And tell the owner that we, I will be doing business with a more accommodating store. That goes for all of the trappers I deal with. Tell him he has made a big mistake by trying to take advantage of my friends," yells Mr. Richardson. Without a word the driver leaves the yard.

"Come with me," Adam tells us. We leave the yard in his carriage. We stop at a large store at the edge of town. It does not look busy. "Let's see if we can get a better deal here," he tells us. The three of us walk in. Everything is neat on shelves or tables. The air is fresh, not smelling of musty air from coal oil and sweat. We walk to the front counter.

"How can I help you?" asks the younger man behind the counter.

"I am Adam Richardson. I own a tannery by the river. These are two trappers, two friends that deal exclusively with me and my tannery. I have a similar relationship with another dozen or so trappers. We are here to restock for their return trip to the Rocky Mountains. We have severed ties with several other general stores. We are here to establish a business relationship. Are you interested?"

"I should say I am. I've been waiting for just this opportunity. What do you need?" asks the owner-clerk. I hand him my list. He writes down the prices next to the columns of trade goods, then hands it back. We look it over. This is better than I had hoped for.

"If I bring my packhorses can we load out back?" I ask him.

"Certainly, if that's the way you want to work. Or I can deliver it to Mr. Richardson's yard," he tells us, anxious for the work.

"It looks like we can do business together. Let's lift the goods once. I'll return with my packhorses. If you can begin making a pile out back, we'll be right back," I tell him.

"I'll start on this right away," he says smiling. We shake hands, sealing the deal.

"Why don't I stay here and begin balancing the piles for the packs?" asks Nate.

"That's a good idea. I'll be back as soon as I can." I get our packhorses and two saddle horses ready while Mr. Richardson retreats to his office. He returns as I finish. He hands me a check from the bank.

"Here, use this to pay for your supplies," he says handing it to me. "Fill it out and it's the same as cash."

"Thanks for what you've done. I'll be back as soon as possible," I tell him.

"Don't worry, do the job right. I'll have someone here to open the gates for you and help unload your animals."

"Thanks," I tell him leading the pack animals out of his yard to the street. I follow the trail Adam used to get there and back. We circle the busy streets riding around the edge of town making good time reaching the store.

Nate has been busy. He's balanced out the loads for the three panniers per horse. The store owner has a clerk helping us. We add the panniers to the pack frames then secure the loads for the ride to Mr. Richardson's yard. We've loaded the horses, leaving the last pair to carry the load from the gun shop. We start back, reaching the yard as the sun sets. Unloading the filled panniers in piles of three with a pack frame, we are done quicker than I reckoned we'd be.

Cheyenne village Winter 1835

It is good to be back. The Cheyenne take to the trading as fast as I remember the first time. When word spreads from this village to other villages, they begin gathering their extra furs to trade for the goods we've returned with. The cast iron cookware, especially the Dutch ovens, are the first items I run out of. Next are the blankets. The weather convinces the women to outfit their families before the snows begin sticking. Many wives trade for sewing needles and thread. The men like the axes and surprisingly the tacks I brought along by accident. No one is interested in coffee. I bring all of it into my lodge.

Daily the pile of firewood grows higher and longer. Nate is a good worker. He stays busy doing the things that need doing. Many tasks he sees for himself and begins them without me having to ask. In no time I come to depend on Nate.

I ask him about how we are expected to make it through the long cold winter. He tells me the buffalo will stay close until the snows and the real cold weather hit. He says I need to plan a hunting trip. He can skin and butcher the animals, but as a hunter, well let's just say, he's not one, yet. I have a buffalo hunt to plan.

"We'll need to leave as soon as possible. After the snows stick, we won't be able to get after them," he tells me the first time I bring it up. He explains how the Plains Indians' hunt. After finding a herd of buffalo they get them on their feet and running. One by one the riders pick an animal. The kills can be spread over five miles. An experienced hunter can down enough animals to last his family through the winter. That is not for me. I decide to make a stand with Nate. For two days Nate gathers strong logs, long enough to act as travois runners. He reckons at least twenty buffalo will see us through the winter. To get an idea of the size of the hunt he tells me our lodge is made from twenty-five hides. I make preparations to down at least twenty-five buffalo. He enlists the help of widows and orphans to butcher and skin the buffalo. They'll work for a share of the meat.

The morning of the hunt we're up before the sun. Nate knows where the herd is holed up. We attach twenty-five travois to my horses. Nate has earned his own horses; he brings fifteen of his own. The last of the sun has cleared the horizon as we ride from the village to the hunting grounds. I can smell them first. Then I hear them and finally see the herd. As far as I can see the buffalo stretch. The land is brown and moving. I've never seen so many animals in one place at one time in my life. The sight is breathtaking.

We stop the horses a half-mile from the herd of animals. Walking upright and carrying two rifles, my possibles, and a canteen, I approach to within 30 yards of the herd. Without having done it myself I never would have believed it possible. I know it's true having done it many times. Nate takes up his own position.

I make my stand in an old wallow. On the lip of the high edge I pound two stakes into the hard ground. At the intersection of the two sticks I'll lay the fore end of my rifle. I've load it with a high charge of black powder, 100 grains. I run a patched lead ball down the barrel. The last step in the loading process is adding the percussion cap to the nipple next to the hammer of the rifle.

Laying the rifle's fore end in the V of the sticks, the stock finds the familiar pocket of my shoulder. I line the sights on a cow at the edge of the herd. She is one of the sentinels, the guards. These are always the first targets. Standing sideways to me I aim under her front shoulder. If the leg is in the way I'll need to wait as she steps forward, exposing the target. When the sweet spot is exposed, I set the first trigger. Taking a breath, I control the movements of the sights, limiting their movements to sideway, not up and down. Letting out half a breath, the sights are exactly where I want them. I tighten up on the second trigger, the hair trigger.

Completely unexpectedly the rifle fires. I do not feel the stock make its substantial kick back into my shoulder. Nor do I hear the explosion of the black powder charge. I do see the ball hit exactly where the sights said it would. As the rotten egg smelling cloud of burnt black powder is carried away on the wind, I see the first buffalo fall.

I set the first rifle down to take up my second. Repeating the aiming and shooting process I have a second buffalo down. I reload both rifles and repeat the process, ten times. I have 20 animals down before the herd begins moving. They are not scared and only walking away, very slowly. I move to the wallow in front of me, closer to the herd. I repeat the process stopping at twenty-six animals.

Now my ears are ringing, my shoulder is throbbing, my nose is closed with the foul smell of burnt black powder, and my head hurts. I take up both rifles and walk back to my horses. I have not noticed but many from the village have arrived to watch as we collect our winter's supply of buffalo. While I was shooting, Nate was shooting on his own. He has

15 animals down. There is no way the pair of us can care for that many animals. Nate has made arrangements for extra help. He has hired orphans and widows, along with several large families that have a need for extra winter meat. He's trading half the meat for cleaning and butchering the animal and brain tanning the hide. Other parts from the buffalo are traded for help in butchering. The bow maker has agreed to have his wife and three daughters tan five hides in exchange for all the sinew.

All the bones have been traded for a pair of dogs. The horns are traded to an artisan making cups, bowls, and spoons. The hooves are traded to the glue maker. In exchange for meat families will butcher five animals and brain-tan five hides. Everyone helps in loading the travois. In a group we walk back to the village. This is the first time something like this has been done.

I'm hoping it turns out well for everyone. As we leave, I notice the large wolves eyeing the scraps at the butchering sight. Nate tells me the wolves will be hunted later this winter when their fur is thickest. Their winter fur makes insulated moccasins and gloves. I will have to keep that in mind. At the village Nate takes charge of the travois, my horses, the buffalo carcasses, and the hides. He assures me it will turn out as he has planned.

The next morning, we begin building platforms in the trees to store the buffalo meat as it is brought to us. Two days later, using the travois legs for bracing, the chore is finished.

The next day families begin dropping off our half of the buffalo meat. At the end of the week we have the meat from twenty-one buffalo safely stored for winter's use. A week later the buffalo robes begin returning. I am well-pleased with all forty. I give Nate three and I use two as a covering at night. The rest are stacked away for our return to Kansas City come spring.

As many days as possible before the heavy snows stick, I'm out hunting. I bring in more buffalo and elk. One of the four braves that invited me into the village has become a friend. He is Grey Wolf, and his wife is Sunshine. One day I bring back two black bears. I ask Grey Wolf and his wife how to collect and render the fat. I remember from the grizz we shot. They begin teaching me everything I will need to know about caring for the game and the hides I hunt or trade for.

I'm returning to the village with two elk in a light snow-storm. When I left the village the weather was nice, now it's snowing, sticking, and progress on the trail is slow. Late in the afternoon I still have a couple of miles to travel before reaching the village. As I come around a corner of a small rockslide, there is a grizz standing in the middle of the trail. He is busy finishing dining on a deer. He looks up at me with blood dripping from his muzzle. Seeing me and the horses, he stands and begins growling. He begins bouncing on his front legs off the carcass of the dear. This is a new sight, something I've not seen until now. I find myself watching when I should be acting.

With front legs out and batting the air in front of him, the grizz takes a step. With a 40-yard separation I place a rifle ball in his chest. He drops to four feet and begins waddling towards me and my horses. I reckon he's eaten too much to be in a big hurry. He knows I will be helpless against his coming attack. I pull two .54 caliber pistols and deliver both balls to his chest when he stands. When the second ball hits, he falls to the ground. He's not dead yet because I can hear him still making noises. It sounds like he's mad and getting riled. I reload my rifle not taking the time to measure the powder but pouring it into my hand before I add it down the barrel. I ram a patched ball after the powder. I add a cap to the nipple. Taking aim, I pull the trigger. My sights are on his right shoulder. The sun is almost completely down, but there is still enough light to get a clear sight picture. The murky day is lit like midday. Sparks and flames shoot from the end of the rifle for four feet. I both feel and hear the shot. The rifle recoils into my shoulder, leaving it stinging. My ears are ringing. My eyes are burning from the foul cloud of burnt powder. I can't believe the shot. The bear is down and not moving. The shoulder facing me is shattered. The ball went through it and into the bear's body. He's down and bleeding profusely. I think that powerful load did the job. I will not repeat that shot. There was too much powder used. I need to check if he's really dead.

———

The Mauling

Micah always warned me more mountain men are killed by dead grizz than live ones. After all of them I have killed, a dead one comes close to killing me. I poke the bear's good shoulder. He does not move. He is lying on his side, his head is down, I can't reach an eye. The best test is touching an eye with the barrel of your rifle. If he is truly dead, he will not move. If not, well the fight will be on. I have to move his head. With a pistol in one hand, I try lifting the great head. It does not move. I hate to do it, but I must lay down the pistol and rifle to use both hands to position the head. So, I do.

I reach down, grab chin hair and lift while pushing with my other hand. It works. I let the head drop. That's when my problems start. The impact of the head on the ground must have brought him around. I step back and stretch my back. I bend down to pick up my rifle and possibles. I take another step back. The bear's front left arm moves. I see it move and take another step back. I reload my rifle. He bats the rifle away as it fires. The ball tears a path along his back. My trigger finger breaks as the rifle is twisted and tossed away from me. Too quick, the left front paw knocks me on my backside. When I stop sliding, I see the bear trying to stand. He can't, his spine is shattered. How is he still alive? He's growling. I aim and shoot three pistol loads below his shoulder into his chest.

I make it to my feet, shaking but standing. The bear tries

standing too. Except he can't remain on his hind feet. He flops towards me. I see his eyes. I see pain and a raging, burning desire for revenge. I know he's coming for me. I have one unfired pistol left. Too fast to see, a paw knocks me off my feet. I crash to the icy, sandy trail. The bear is laying over my legs ready to attack until his last breath. I stick the pistol in his eye and pull the trigger. He collapses on top of me. I feel a leg bone break. I scream. Everything turns black. I count myself dead.

———

The Trappers

"You reckon that man is alive?" asks the trapper Abner to his friend and partner Ellis.

"I don't know, but we'd better make sure. I'd hate to bury a living soul."

"I reckon you're right. Best make sure that grizz is dead first. I'll aim my rifle at him as you tap his eye," suggests Abner.

"It's a good thing we're old friends," adds Ellis.

"Why is that?"

"I just may believe you're trying to kill me," laughs his old friend.

"Stop talking crazy. Check that bear so we know if we're

burying the man or doctoring him." Abner pokes the bear in the eye, there is no reaction."

"I reckon this ol' boy kilt him. Can you get him? Or do we need to move that bear?"

"Hold on to this for me," he tells his partner. Bending down he works my body out from the grip of the bear. "Can you get hold of him?"

"I can," he says, laying the rifles down carefully. Grabbing me under the shoulders they both pull. That's when I wake. All I know is the pain shooting through my entire body. I scream. It takes the two trappers by surprise, they drop me, eliciting another scream from my battered body. The two trappers scramble to pick me up and move me away from the bear.

"I can't hardly believe he's still alive. He's shore tore up," says Ellis.

"He is but I think the majority of this blood belonged to the Grizz." I open my eyes, watching the clouds and treetops move by as the trio of trappers carry me to the creek. I know they try gentle like, but as I land on the grass I scream yet again.

"Dip this in the creek," says one to his partner, handing him my bandana. It's soaking wet as he begins washing my face.

"That ain't so bad now is it?" he asks me. I look at him and grimace.

"We best set up camp here for the night. Get a fire and the coffee pot going. This here boy can use some coffee."

Without a word the partners get working together. Ellis brings in their horses. He gets a picket rope stretched between two trees. As he unburdens the horses, they are secured on the picket line. To me it seems quick. The next thing I know the trapper doing the doctoring is holding a cup of water for me to sip. I drink it all down.

"Good, thanks." I tell him after that first drink.

"When did this happen? Do you remember?"

"This morning...hunting...returning to camp...thought he was dead...wrong."

"Sign says at least two days ago. You're lucky to be alive. What's your name? Where's your camp?"

"Uriah...Cheyenne."

"You're camped with the Cheyenne? Why?"

"Trading."

"Hey now, this ol' boy says he is trading with the Cheyenne. If you see them, don't shoot at them. They're probably looking for him."

"Okay. Is he going to make it?"

"I reckon. I'll need some bear grease to cover some of these deep wounds."

"I'll get some on the fire rendering." Finished with starting a fire, with the coffee pot heating, he returns to the grizz. Using his knife, he peels hide from the bear's side.

Reaching in he begins filling a Dutch oven with the fat. When full, he sets it on the fire to render it down. Before it's all melted, he scoops out a plateful and brings it to his partner.

"Sorry Uriah, but I'm going to cut this shirt from you. I need to get to those claw slices." All I can do is nod my head. Picking out threads and bits of dirt and grass from the cuts he covers them with the bear fat.

"That'll seal them so no insects or more dirt gets in." I nod my understanding. Ellis has collected my horse. He brings me my blankets, covers me, and I fall asleep.

Unknown to me the pair of mountain men unsaddle my horse, hobble him, and put him on a picket line with my pack-horses. The elk on the travois is cut into strips. Some of it is dried into jerky and some cooked for supper. I wake as the sun is setting. They save the elk hides for me. I'm going to need a new war shirt.

"Hungry?" I nod. Abner gets up, returning with a plate of grilled venison, bread, and a cup of coffee. I can eat okay but need help drinking. He helps me. I fall asleep. That night I have weird dreams, like I've never had. Dreams of old friends, older enemies, the men I've killed, and lastly of Miss Debra. I know she is no longer waiting for me. Deep inside I know it. I am unaware of everything going on around me that entire night.

Just after the sun breaks the eastern horizon, a six-man party of Cheyenne warriors led by Nate ride into the camp. They see me in a shelter, lying under blankets, my horses, and my weapons. Nate talks to the trappers using signs and some English. The trappers explain what happened. The Cheyenne thank them for their efforts in saving my life. The trappers saddle my horses, the Indians tie me onto a travois pulled by my packhorses. The trappers give the grizzly hide, paws, and skull to the Cheyenne along with a Dutch oven filled with bear fat. For their help, the Indians give the trappers the meat and the rest of the fat. As the sun rises, the two groups separate to go in different directions.

———————

Recovery

It is good to see my friends again as we enter the village.

"I reckon I can't let you go hunting by yourself," Nate tells me half kidding, half in earnest.

Never having been in this situation I do not understand why it is taking so long to recover my strength. Some of my friends in the village tell me it will take a while. Two of the younger warriors spend the summer and fall helping me recover. With Nate and Grey Wolf's help I make quicker progress in recovering my strength through summer and into fall.

By the beginning of winter, I am almost back to where I began and feeling whole. I'll miss a year of trading and the entire hunting season. It's a good thing Nate and I have collected a pile of buffalo robes and fur last spring. I slowly begin hunting as the weather changes into winter and the nights grow colder. I bring in deer and a black bear, which I can handle myself. I'll need help going after elk or if I run into another grizz. To avoid that, I hunt close to the village. We'll have enough to make it through the coming winter months. The old women in the village say it's going to be an easy winter. The snow will not grow as high nor will the air grow as cold as many years' past. I content myself with sticking close to the village. With Nate's help we trade away every last item in the packs. We'll be returning with two years' worth of fur.

Through the easy winter Nate turns into a first-rate hunter with bow and arrow or his rifle. Close to the village he uses his bow. He saves rifle hunting when he is well clear of the village and after buffalo. When asked by the elders not to shoot any more game with the rifles he agrees. This forces him to refine his hunting with a bow or a lance. In the long term, this is exactly what Nate needs to force him to improve his skills. He improves to the point of impressing the entire village, especially Sees Far. Nate begins spending a lot of extra time with the old warrior. I concentrate on getting better and increasing my strength. It is a long and slow winter.

———

Spring 1837

Spring is around the corner and I am more than ready to get active again. I dream of hunting, trapping, and even doing camp chores. The winter was not hard or too cold. Our buffalo is almost finished. We're ready for fresh meat. The nearby deer are waiting for us. We take our bows to hunt quiet, not wanting to attract people curious about the sounds of gun shots. I aim to begin slow, planning to camp out for two nights and return with full travois.

The hunt goes as planned. Nate and I return late the third day. Standing on the ridge above the village, looking down to where the Cheyenne village should be, we see nothing. No fires, no smoke, no cries of kids or barking dogs, no horse herd, no buffalo hide lodges. The village is gone. The only question is, by their own accord or forced? We leave the extra packhorses on the other side of the ridge securely tied to trees. We will ride in and see what the signs say.

All horse tracks are three days old. The exodus happened the day after we rode out. But why? All the lodges but ours is gone. The large horse herd is gone. All that remains behind are black fire rings. We circle the camp. Finding nothing, we ride to our lodge. In the thick trees behind our lodge we find the rest of our horses. They are tied to trees, close to grass and water, waiting on us.

"I'll bring in our horses. Why don't you see what's in the lodge and in the fur shed?" Nate tells me. Since the mauling, our roles have reversed. That's okay with me. It has gone a long way towards maturing Nate as a warrior, hunter, and friend.

I look inside the fur shed. Everything is inside, just as we left it. I limp my way to our lodge. Lifting up the door flap I have a war axe at the ready. It is cold inside; the fire has burned out days ago. Everything else looks untouched. Our rifles, the extra rifles, all our pistols and the possibles sit suspended from the lodge frame. Our buffalo robes are folded as we left them. The extra firewood is still in a pile. The cooking pans remain in their place. Our packs of food stuffs lay untouched. I light a fire, add the coffee pot, and head outside with our weapons. Whoever we meet we will see over the sights of our rifles. Nate rides in.

"Well" he asks me.

"Everything is as we left it. I started a fire and put the coffee pot on. Here's your weapons," I tell him, handing him his rifle and possibles.

"Any idea why they left?" he asks me.

"None. Any sign up there?"

"No. They must have ridden out to the south."

"Let's put these deer away and look for sign," I suggest. With a nod Nate gets to work. The deer are hanging, the packhorses are taken behind the lodge, we're ready to ride.

Nate is looking through his possibles. He returns inside the lodge, coming out with a handful of pistols and an extra powder horn.

"These may come in handy if we run into trouble," he says, handing me my extra pistols.

Armed and ready we follow the sign. At the village site the tracks and sign are easy to see. There is no mystery here. A war party of Sioux attacked the village. The Cheyenne defended the camp, killing all eight warriors making up the raiding party. They are older boys out as soon as they can get away from the confines of their winter camp. They did not reckon on running into a village of enemies. The Cheyenne are heading for their summer range, early.

I follow the tracks of a large group of horses into the dense trees. A half mile from the village site, hemmed in a natural corral, are over thirty horses. They are not ours, but we can certainly use them. I reckon some of the village couldn't take their extra horses. Nate and I will use them. We move camp next to the horses in the trees forming the natural corral. All our packs, pack frames, extra weapons, and most importantly all the furs traded for over two years are safe in our new camp.

"They won't return until next fall, right ahead of winter," says Nate looking over the horses.

"I reckon you're right."

"Why you reckon things are turning against us Uriah?" he asks, looking right at me.

"I reckon my luck is changing."

"You mean our luck, right partner?" he says with a straight face. "I ain't leaving you, so we're in this together. You treated me as a grown-up full partner. Thanks for that. I'm sticking with you."

"Thanks Nate, but after we sell this load of fur, I won't hold you too that."

"Well that's a fine...I don't know what. I reckoned we were partners, and you go and say something like that. If you don't want me hanging around just come out and say it."

"I didn't mean that."

"Then what?"

"I've made enemies of Blackfoot and some Cheyenne southwest of us. I don't want to involve you in my mess."

"That ain't new news Uriah. We all knew that as soon as you entered our camp that first time."

"You did? Why didn't someone say something about it?"

"It didn't involve us, just some hothead warriors. The chiefs decided to let it go, as long as you treated us fair. I feel the same way now. All that don't matter to me. We're partners as long as you stay square with me," says Nate with heart felt meaning.

"I agree. You know, for a young man how'd you get so wise?" I ask him.

"I had some good teachers. What do we need to do first?"

"We need to take another look around the village site. If they left these horses, there may be others in smaller groups."

"Or maybe extra supplies or furs. Looks like they left in a hurry."

Leaving the horses, we circle the village finding discarded

packs of furs and debris from their flight. We collect what is salvageable.

We begin repacking the furs and robes we took from the shed. We make packs, add them to panniers and spread out three per pack frame. We end up with twenty-five packhorses carrying seventy-five bales of fur. We have twenty horses carrying buffalo robes. Four horses carry our camp gear, and five horses carry the extra bales of fur we found. We make new clothes and moccasins out of our well-cured lodge hides. The lodge hides are slowly smoke cured daily by the fires inside the lodge. These hides are highly prized to make clothes.

Nate shows me how to make pack frames from elk antlers. We'll need them to carry the last of our gear and fur. I'm glad he's here to help me trail our fifty-six horses. A week spent working from sunup to sundown and we're ready to ride.

"Where do you reckon on taking the fur Uriah?" asks Nate, looking at the loaded horses strung out on the trail.

"I reckon we'll get more at St. Louis. We're heading to St. Louis Nate," I yell. He adds his war cries. The horses all look at us like we've gone loco. Well I reckon in a way I have. My luck has changed for the worse this past year. If yelling like a crazed ol' mountain man can change it then I'll yell until my voice goes raspy.

I decide to go to Kansas City instead of taking our furs and hides to Rendezvous. We will be trading two years' worth of fur for supplies and trade goods. I hope my luck will change during our journey. It'll be a fast trip there and a faster return to the Yellowstone Valley and our winter camp. We roughly follow the trail to the Yellowstone River turning south towards the steamboat landing.

Mountain Man V Cougar

We need fresh meat. It's time to hunt. An unexpected, late season, freak, snowstorm has dumped a foot of fresh snow on top of the couple inches of not yet melted snow. We can put it off no longer. The night before is cloudy. This morning there's not a cloud in the sky. The tradeoff for the clear sky is plunging temperatures. At least I didn't have to get up in the dark and venture out before the weak sun rose. I wake as the sun began its rise. I've positioned my pile of cedar boughs covered by soft tanned buffalo robes where the rising morning's sun shines through a strategic crack, and directly in my eyes. Every morning the rising sun gets me up.

I stoke the fire from the buffalo robes, being careful not to burn my bedding. Small sticks next to the night's coals gets the fire and heat going. Feeding in larger sticks gets the coffee pot boiling. I've made it a habit to get the coffee pot ready the night before. That way I can enjoy that first cup in the warm robes. As soon as things heat to the point where I can tolerate rising, I'll begin my day.

"Get up old man," yells Nate.

"Quiet down you young savage. I ain't ready to get up, quite yet. "Sides I've already been working," I tell my young partner. He is not affected by the cold. Every injury I've suffered in the mountains and the railroad camp cries out in the cold weather, especially the wounds from Mr. Grizz. Why do I feel like this I'm only...twenty-five or so? Nate is about nineteen. He'll learn quick enough.

Dressed, warmed, and fortified for the day I emerge from under the pile of buffalo robes to saddle my horse. I ride to the horse herd for three extra horses. I can sense a successful hunt and I will need travois to bring back all the meat. I'm hoping for deer or elk. Leading the three extra horses to the fire, I fasten the travois on two of the horses. The last will carry two packs of just in case essentials, enough to pass a comfortable night out in the woods.

I load the four pistols. Two go on my belt and a pair in the pommel holsters over the saddle horn. A second rifle is secure in the pack horse. I carry my favorite rifle, the one I repaired with Micah's help, and have my possibles slung over my left shoulder. The powder horn is full, and I have an extra tin of percussion caps in a pocket of my wolfskin coat. I'm ready. Setting comfortable in the saddle I lead the horses out of our camp.

"You know what to do while I'm gone, right?" I ask Nate.

"I reckon so, you've talked it to death." I swear he gets to talking like me more every day. He's coming into his own being away from the Cheyenne and civilized towns. He's a good partner.

Riding away from the last of the ice covering the river, I am vigilant. I'm thinking the animals will come out now that the sun is up. I ride down the valley, through the trees, slow, making the least amount of noise possible. After four miles I stop. There is a clearing under the trees on the opposite side of the river from me. I always see deer and sometimes elk browsing under the trees. Today? Nothing. I'm fixing to nudge my horse forward with the heels of my wolf hair-lined elk hide moccasins when I see movement out of the corner of my eye. I sit still. There it is. I see the flicker of a white tail, a deer. It's behind me, on this side of the river, good.

I sit still as the deer lowers his head to take a bite out of the exposed grass. I've been tricked before. The buck's head is immediately up and looking around. When he's satisfied he's alone, he gets to enjoying the grass. Slowly I slip from the saddle. Stepping through the new snow as lightly as possible I get in front of my horse. He is used to rifle fire and has seen this played out many times. I walk to the edge of the tree line stopping at the last large diameter tree. The buck is still there, eating, but wary. I time my movements after he drops his head.

Taking a solid stance behind the tree, I slip the rifle's barrel out the right side. My left hand is locked onto the tree and supports the rifle. I double check, making sure the cap is still in place, tight on the nipple. It is. The end of the stock finds the pocket where my right arm joins my shoulder. I settle the rifle until it feels comfortable, solid in the pocket. I place the front sight blade behind the front leg of the large Mule Deer buck. I move the hammer back, covered by my glove so the click is not loud in the silent, clear, frosty morning air. I set my cheek against the stock. In seconds, the hold feels solid and familiar. I need the buck to take one step forward. I keep the blade on the spot and wait.

The deer lifts his head. He stomps his right leg, slowly moving it forward enough to expose his vitals. I'll wait until he resumes his grazing before shooting. His head goes down... and stays in place. My finger begins taking up the slack. When the rifle fires I do not expect it. I'm watching the buck, I do not hear the report, nor feel the familiar slap back into my shoulder. I smell the rotten egg cloud of burnt black powder as it drifts past me on the slight breeze. I hear a wet slap. As I'm watching, the deer jumps into the air. Hitting the snowy ground, he tries taking a step. The leg gives out. He crashes to the ground. A back leg kicks out, once. The big-bodied deer is still. The echo of the shot is fading.

I move the rifle off my hand to reload. Keeping one eye on the six-point muley and one eye watching me reload, I pour the powder charge down the barrel. I take a ball from the board hanging from my neck, placing it on the dark hole of the bore. I set the ball using the hardwood ball, turn it around and force the ball down about six inches. Using the ramrod, I push the ball down to the powder, with just enough force to seat the ball over the powder, then pull the ramrod. I replace it in its spot under the barrel. Bringing the rifle up I dig out the capper from under my wolfskin coat. Setting the cap... from the corner of my eye I see a grey blur heading towards my deer.

Taking a steady brace on the tree and supporting the octagonal barrel I aim at the downed deer. What was that grey motion? Anything? Or...oh no, it's a full-grown cougar. He's running to my deer. I see the tail swaying as the cat is running. On the end is a dark black puff of fur. The head. There it is, I see black at the top of each ear.

"Don't take a running shot," I tell myself. The cat stops at the belly of my mule deer. I set the front blade behind the front shoulder. Pull back the hammer, I'm not concerned about the click in the still morning air. The cat hears it. I know...he did. Steady the sights, take a breath, releasing, pulling the trigger, it falls. For the second time this short morning a shot echoes across the frozen river. I see the ball part the grey fur exactly where I was looking. The .54 caliber round lead ball knocks the cat forward and off his feet. He's up.

"Did he really fall?" I ask myself. I reload quicker this time. I'm watching the cat stagger, trying to turn, taking three steps, and he's down. I can see the snow under him turning red. I add a cap to the nipple. I pull both pistols checking

their caps, replace them, and start across the new snow. There's a tree over the creek that is clear of snow. Prints from small animals have knocked the snow off. I notice it as I walk to both of my animals. I stop after reaching the deer. The cat has not moved. There is no steam escaping his mouth.

I approach the cat first. His eyes have lost their sparkle. Even so, he is a magnificent animal. I touch an open eye with the barrel of my rifle. No change. He's far enough away from my deer, I leave him where he lay.

Slowly approaching the deer I'm sure he's dead. He didn't move as the cat watched him, but I make sure. I touch his eye with the barrel, no reaction. I begin on the Mule Deer first. I lean my rifle against the tree, standing with my possibles, and the powder horn. I dig out my sharpening stones, take off my coat, and get to work. Starting at the neck I run the sharp knife down the belly without puncturing the pouch holding the innards. At the back hip, circle the vent. Back at the belly I pull out the sack of guts, reach up as far as I can and cut the tube in the throat. I pull the deer away from the bloody snow, belly down and begin skinning the sides and the back away from the head. When the hide is off, I spread it out. I pile the large cuts of meat on the hide to keep clean. The last thing is the head with the skull and the antlers. The brain will be used to tan the hide and I'll cut the antlers off the skull later. When that's finished, I walk for the horses.

I load and cover the deer meat with the hide, onto one of the travois. Now it's the cougar's turn. At the throat I run the re-sharpened knife down the belly to the hips. I slice up each leg leaving the feet attached to the hide. Work around the hips. And peel off the tail. I work back up to the head. I want the head included. With a smaller knife I peel around the ears, nose, and mouth. I peel it off the back, and once off the body spread it out to receive the meat. I load the hide and meat on the second travois. The sun is past midday when I'm ready to wash and ride back to our camp. Nate sees me leading the horses to our camp he runs over.

"Can I help?" he asks.

"Always," I tell him. While I was gone, he was making racks to dry most of the meat into jerky. I'm getting hungry. I cut the venison back strap into steaks, add wood to the fire, throw on the coffee pot, then the steaks. Stopping to eat, we're almost finished. I've not had cougar jerky; I'm looking forward to it. We spend the rest of the day and half the next drying the meat from my kills into jerky. Nate makes sure to save out at least two weeks' worth of fresh meat to cook and eat on the trail. When we're finished adding strips of meat over the fire, he shows me how to finish skinning the cougar's head and paws. It will make a fine cape or wrap. I work on it while the jerky dries.

I can't believe it, but I find myself looking forward to reaching St. Louis.

6

TO ST. LOUIS

WE MADE OUR WAY DOWN THE RIVER. I'M HOPING TO catch the paddle wheeler south for a quicker trip to St. Louis. We have no idea how many days we'll have to wait before the captain sails by heading south. If it's too long, we'll continue riding and stop when we see the ship. Fortunately, we only wait for three days. Long enough to shoot a buffalo providing us jerky and fresh meat for the voyage to St. Louis.

I fire my pistols in the air to alert the captain. He acknowledges my request with a couple pulls on his steam whistle. He aims his boat to the sandy beach. He'll load firewood and us at the same time.

We get our horses, carrying packs of furs and our supplies, on board and settled at the bow. In return for the trip to St. Louis, we agree to hunt and defend the boat. The captain is impressed with the buffalo meat I give to his cook.

He asks us to supply more before heading further down river. Taking ten packhorses, our two riding horses, and a crewman, Nate and I set out for a two-day hunt. I leave the crewman in our temporary camp to watch our gear and keep the boat from leaving. We find buffalo close, so close the captain sends part of the crew to help skin and butcher the dozen buffalo we've got laying in the grass. That should be more than enough to see us back to St. Louis. I'm glad to help. It also means we ride for free. Can't beat that.

With the crew's help, the meat is loaded on our horses for the short return to the boat. With the help of the boat's crew we return loaded with meat and hides. The only trace of the hunt left behind is the gut pile. Varmints will see to it. The flint hides dry for the day and a half, about half the required time to turn the flint hide into a dry hide. We carefully dry them for another two days while sailing, to not damage the valuable hides.

Halfway to St. Louis, trouble and disaster strikes. The ship is stopped at a wood depot, to take on more firewood. Nate and I take out our horses to do a quick scout and to settle the short hairs on the back of my neck that are standing straight up. I'm returning when I hear the sounds of the boat and gunfire. I ride to the river and sure enough it's the boat.

———

Pirates

"Why did they sail unexpectedly?" I wonder to myself. Then I see the reason why. We receive warnings about pirates on the river every time we board. I scoff at the idea. Well, right there before me, I can see them, Black Jolly Roger, and all. A smaller more manageable boat is chasing the steamboat down river. We follow on our horses. I can see some of the crewmen trading shots with the pirates. The pirates are much better shots and are clearing the decks of the larger steamboat. Smelling victory, the pirates roll out a small cannon on a swivel. They load it with bits of chain and all the pieces of metal they have scrounged together. I can't let them use that against the boat and my horses. Nate and I begin shooting the men bringing the gun to bear on the flailing steamboat. Three shots take out the first gun crew, before they realize it's me and Nate shooting at them from the bank. The pirates try shooting at us. Nothing comes close.

Their next surprise is totally unexpected. They have strung a cable across the river. I'm not sure if the boat can see it and there is no way I can warn them. With the shouting and the rifle fire it's too noisy. The boat floats into the cable, creating havoc on board the craft. The pirates successfully clear the top deck of the steamship. I hope the captain and our horses survive.

The boat hits the cable. The cable shears off the top deck and the smokestacks. The boat driver must have been hurt because the boat is now floating unguided straight towards a sandbar. The cable only slows the steamboat for a handful of minutes. Once the current catches it, the boat is heading faster and faster towards the sandbar. When it hits, I can actually see the decks shift, moving forward. The boat crumples. The bow hits the sandbar first. That's where our horses are. Most of our horses land in the water. The pirate crew swarms on the heavily damaged boat, shooting the wounded crewmen, then stealing everything they can carry away. They cry out when they find our furs. The head pirate organizes their theft himself. I memorize every feature of him and all the crewmen I see. There is more loot than what they can haul off before dark. They leave our furs and our supplies cached on the bow of the damaged boat. The pirates gather loot floating down river from the wreck, and what has stopped along the side of the banks. In their greed they wait on our furs, horses, and have forgotten about Nate and me. We will wait them out. As the sun begins falling, they leave the stranded boat. We have to work fast.

We leave the saddle horses behind with our rifles. Taking four pistols each, our fighting knives, and Crow war axe, we cross the river to the boat. The dead lay everywhere. I'm heading to the bow, to the captain, and the horses. I find him dead. He was helping my horses off the boat when he was killed. His rifle and possibles are gone. I move him to the deck edge. Two horses are badly wounded. I hate to do it but must. I slit their throats. I don't want to risk a loud shot. I free our horses one at a time. Nate leads them to the edge of the deck, helps them into the water, and watches as they cross the river.

They gather around our riding horse, just as I hoped. The last horse is freed. The furs and our supplies are next. We work until the sun threatens to rise, taking what we can to a camp close by in the trees. Bundles of supplies and furs have spilled open during the crash. We leave them to attract the pirates, a trap.

We bury the friendly captain in a bank away from the river. Revenge is burning through me like I've eaten something rotten. Everything is tinged in red. I cut a rope into lengths to tie the pack horses together we need the packhorses to stay with us. Our saddle horse won't run off. We check our weapons. One rifle, four pistols, knife, and Crow axe each and our possibles. That is all we have.

We set out down river after the pirates. I know we're close when the hairs on my neck stand up. I stop the horses, from here we'll approach on foot. We tie them snug to a tree. I smell their fire before seeing the river pirates. I slow our approach. Using all the tricks and skills learned in the years living in the mountains with the Indians, we cautiously approach the small camp. I see four men, packs of furs, ten horses, and enough supplies to outfit us for a year. We can't wait. I want to be away from here when the sun sets. We both need to eat and rest. Anger and hate power both of us.

We creep forward. They build up the fire against the spring night's cold and the river's humidity. No guards. They are lazy men. They are still sleeping. That's all the better for us to even the score.

I have gained control of the red berserker haze. Now it's mine to use as a weapon. Three men lay closer to the fire. I take them, the lone man is Nate's. I don't wait as Nate delivers a quick knife to the throat of his target. He's no longer a threat. The next pair die in similar fashion at my hand. The last one must have sensed some change in the air around him. He wakes, sits up, and begins drawing a knife. I throw my war axe. It lands in his belly, a perfect shot. He won't die quick. He'll live long enough to answer my questions. First, I need to silence his screaming. He's not as tough as he thinks. I kick him in the face. He falls back flat on the sandy shore. He's quietly cowering.

"Who's the captain?" I ask.

"If I tell you he'll kill me. I can't..."

"I will kill you if you don't. That's a promise."

"You'll let me go if I tell?"

"Sure."

"Maxwell is the captain of the Rouge. Everyone knows him."

"How many crew men does he have?"

"Two dozen, but six were killed stopping the boat." I do the math on my fingers, *"Twenty-four minus six is 18. Minus these four is 14."*

"Where does he sell the furs and stolen goods?"

"In Fort Pierre."

"How long until he's back?"

"A trip takes ten days. You going to let me go now?"

"Soon."

"Who's the buyer?"

"I don't know his name, never met him. His warehouse is between the cat house and the Salty Dog Saloon."

"Let me get you something to wrap that wound in," I tell him. Walking behind him I pull my knife and end his raiding days. As I was talking, I began pouring through the goods piled, without thought or pattern, in the sand. I find our extra weapons, both rifles and pistols with our extra possibles. I couldn't let that skunk escape.

On Nate's return with the horses we begin loading, well everything. Three more horses that lived through the boat crash have gathered with our riding horses. We fill every pack frame and load our horses with furs and supplies. We work until we've carried all the supplies to our camp in the trees. It's time to eat and sleep. Later this afternoon we'll separate everything according to what it is, packs of fur, food, camp supplies, and everything else we can carry away. We push the pirates out into the river.

This Captain Maxwell will probably return with more men. In his place, I would. There is no way we can fight that many. We will hunt them. I'll give them a taste of what they gave my friend. We have ten days to prepare. Finished, we cook buffalo steaks and make a pot of coffee. While it's cooking, I pour through what is piled in our camp deep in the woods near the river.

I sleep poorly that first night, waking up in a malicious

mood, callous, and I'm ready for a fight. Nate shares my feeling. We are both mad clear through. The pirates will pay for what they have done.

During the night more horses wander into our camp, joining with our horses on the picket line. We work the second day loading more horses with packs of supplies gathered from the wreck. Nate takes a dozen horses and heads down river picking up whatever is useable. It'll take too many horses and too much time move our camp. Instead I work on reinforcing it while Nate is gone. Pouring through the last load of supplies salvaged from the boat, I find more rifles, pistols, kegs of powder, a case of flints, and 50 pounds of lead. All of it gets moved into our camp in the woods.

I climb into the saddle to reconnoiter the prairie on both sides of the river. About a mile away I see trees. Might be a creek or a spring there. I ride to investigate. It's a spring. There's a small wash. It's worth noting.

We return. Everything useable we ride across returns to our camp. I aim to clean these pirates out of everything they've stolen from us and the ship. It takes another day, but everything is gone from their camp. All traces of the men and supplies are gone. We gather the horses letting them rest. We have a week to wait on the returning pirates. We ride the river looking for spots to ambush the boat. They are expecting to take the rest of our furs and goods. We leave a rifle, water, and possibles at every site. We're going to hit them as they return to collect their evil gains. We're going to hit them as they stop to load...nothing. I chuckle to myself at the thought. And we're going to hit them as they try sailing away. We're going to take down as many as we can. I'll get the ones that escape to town, to Fort Pierre, but not one of them is getting away.

We have our packhorses cached at our camp in the trees. Nate takes the time to hunt a buffalo for camp meat and to make more jerky. We're as ready as we can get. The morning of their expected return we have five cache sites along the river. Each ambush site has an extra rifle, possibles, jerky, and water. The site in the middle holds an extra horse for just in case.

Mid-morning, I hear the boat's crew before seeing them. I take up my spy glass. I need to be sure before I begin a war with this Captain Maxwell and the crew of the Rouge. I can plainly see the captain, the devil that shortened the life of a good man out of greed and laziness. He is my first kill, a quick and easy shot. His death begins the battle.

We reload and take out the next man trying to organize the crew. He did pick up more men. They are out of my range, but not from Nate. Nate knocks down three more before they move to the center of the river. I ride ahead to meet Nate. I watch another man go down. The crew is on the verge of panic. A fourth man tries organizing the crew. I meet Nate as he lowers his rifle after killing the fourth would-be leader. Working together we begin on the crew.

With ready rifles we wait at the next ambush spot. I can hear the pirate's small steamboat chugging up the river. I can hear yelling. Can't make sense of the words. I wait. There it is. Not a single crewman is in the clear. They might not be as slow as I reckoned.

"Whoever you are, why are you shooting at us? What do you want?" asks a voice from the pirate's boat.

I take out the speaker, then the driver, and the man next to the driver. Nate is dropping crew members, keeping them from steering the boat. The boat hits the bank before someone grabs the wheel and takes the boat back out into the river. I shoot him and I reload. The boat is barely making headway. I wait with five loaded rifles and ten pistols. Nate is at the next position, waiting.

Someone begins shooting at me, but the balls come nowhere close to my position. The swivel gun is pointed at the bank and fires. It's a wasted shot. I know Nate is nowhere near where the shot from the swivel-gun lands. I take out the gunman protecting the swivel gun's crew. Next is the swivel gun's crew. I reload and wait. That must be close to half the crew down. The small boat moves ahead at a faster clip. Nate hits three stupid crewmen on the deck carrying rifles ready to shoot at us. It's time for me to move.

As I move, I hear Nate begin shooting again. I know each ball will account for a pirate. I reach the next position waiting with five loaded rifles. I watch through the spy glass as they steam ahead. Then I get a random thought. *What if they sent men ashore when the boat hit the shore? Surely there are some hunters on board.*

I look slow and careful around me. My horse is undisturbed, munching grass. I divide my spying between the boat and my horse's ears. You can learn a lot by watching a horse's ears. They'll swivel to pick up sound. A prey animal, a horse's survival instincts are outstanding. His ears stop. They focus on the bank down river. I look through the spy glass. I see a movement through the grass. This guy is good. He may be a hunter, but he's not faced many Indians. He's moving too fast. He's plowing through the grass and sagebrush without moving it from his path. I spot him by the moving grass. I look for a second hunter. No one. The boat is in Nate's range. Time to go to work. I wait for the man hunting me. I find him.

My first rifle shot takes out the crew's hunter. The next three rifle balls take out the boat's driver then two-man crew behind the swivel gun. I have one loaded rifle left but no exposed targets. I reload. The next stop is the pirate's camp. Before moving on I collect the weapons from the hunter. It's a nearly new Hawken, a .54 caliber percussion cap rifle. It's the first I've seen. I'll pack it away until I can practice with it. He's got two pistols on a belt and two more stuffed into the belt. I take the belt, with his pistols, and his possibles. I ride to my next spot as Nate keeps their heads down. This is almost over.

Looking over the old pirate camp I'm as prepared as I can get. As I count my weapons, Nate begins shooting again. Now I wait. If I make all my shots accurate, I can account for the rest of the crew. I have a feeling things will be settled today. I try to get a count on the crewmen, but Nate keeps knocking the foolish ones down. I can see ten men left.

"*Make each shot count,*" I tell myself.

I decide to shoot the Hawken. It's loaded and ready. I aim at the wheel man. Good sight picture. Solid hold. Take a breath, release half, pull the first trigger, begin pulling the hair trigger. Pop, much different than these flintlock rifles and similar to my cap rifle. The quick shot takes me by surprise. The .54 caliber ball hits the doorframe by his head. Close but not a clean kill shot. Splinters from the hardwood door frame, exploding into the man's face. He's blinded and as good as dead. Another man takes the wheel. The wounded man stumbles out of the cabin guided by another crew member. I take out the guide, then the new driver. The wounded man is shoved overboard by the new wheel man in a hurry to reach the wheel. His plan is to put as much distance between the boat and us. I easily shoot three more pirates just standing in clear sight. There can only be about one or two men left. I reload. And listen to Nate finish off the crew.

I leave the Hawken and the other rifles with the horses. I add lead balls to my possibles and a second powder horn. I stick two pistols in with the possibles. I have two stuck in my belt. Carrying two pistols I decide it's time to end this. Slow and careful I walk down the bank to the river's edge. I can see no one. The boat is not moving. The wheel has stopped turning. The boat has run aground at the pirate's favorite sandbar. I watch the boat and the shoreline. I smell him before I see him. A sickening mix of an unwashed body, fish, cheap stogies, and alcohol leaching from his body. I don't look forward to this.

"I know you're out there. What is it you want? Money, furs, provisions?" he asks.

"Revenge."

"On who? For what?" he asks. I change positions. When I'm settled, I'll tell him. Let him wait on me.

"Your pirate gang stopped a steamship last week, killing everyone on board. You killed the captain. He was a friend of mine." I move to another spot.

"Who was this captain?"

"Why's he talking so much? Behind me? Someone new is joining the party," I think to myself.

I hear a stick break, then a stone rattle downhill. I've placed him. Aiming one of my pistols I wait.

"The captain was my friend," I tell the last pirate.

"I remember him. I'm sorry for your loss. How can I make it up to you?"

"Who are you?"

"My name is unimportant. I am the new captain of the Rouge. How about throwing in with me? I can use a man with your skills. I pay well," he laughs.

I crawl forward to meet the man in the grass. I hold a pistol in front of me. I see the top of his hairy head rising from the prairie grass. Then his face and shoulders, that's far enough. I pull the trigger. The ball enters his forehead and explodes out the back. I turn as I hear a step behind me. There is the new captain; he tricked me. With a wide smile plastered over his evil face he fires his pistol. It explodes in his hand. He holds a stump out in front of him. Now I begin laughing. In shock, he's now staring at the open barrel aimed at his right eye.

"Are you the last of them?" No answer. "Did you stuff two loads in there or was there dirt packed down the barrel?"

"Must have been mud when I dropped it getting out of the boat. I am the last. Two jumped ship at the first shot. Two more when we were at the other bank. They will not pose a problem to you. Now what?"

"I'll take your pistol and all your weapons, mount my horse, and head to St. Louis. I'm not coming back this way."

"What about me? You can't leave me like this."

"Why not? You were going to attack me. You tried killing us. It's your tough luck."

Picking up all the loose weapons I walk to my horse. I stick all the new to me pistols and knives in my saddlebags. A second pair of pistols, freshly cleaned and reloaded, ride in the pommel holster. I ride away. I'm meeting Nate in our camp in the cottonwoods. As I'm climbing from the saddle, I hear a pistol fire. Nate got him. Ten minutes later my young partner rides into our camp.

"I took a look at their boat. It's loaded with furs and trade goods. I reckon it's ours now. We got more than what we can carry. What are we going to do with the extra?" he asks me.

"We'll cache the trade goods. We'll sell the furs in St. Louis and resupply what we don't have here. I want to visit this middleman in Fort Pierre. He's outlived his usefulness. Then we'll dig up our cache and return to the mountains. That suit you?"

"Only if we put a stop to this middleman," he tells me. "What about their boat?"

"After taking what we want off it, we'll burn it."

"Sounds good to me," is all he says. Leaving our extra weapons in camp we begin unloading everything from the pirate boat. The flames light up the night. Thinking back, I ain't too sure it was a good idea to burn it at night. Fortunately, no one bothers us.

Six weeks later we get our first glimpse of St. Louis from the trail. Riding past the docks we ride for Mr. Richardson's tannery. The gate opens for us. As we're tying the horses to the hitchrail men begin pouring out to the yard.

"Do you have furs to sell?" asks a man in an exceptionally nice suit.

"Yes, I do." I recognize him; why doesn't he recognize us?

"What do you have?"

"Buffalo, some beaver, wolf, bear, with deer and elk leather."

"Excellent. Can we help you unload?"

"Surely."

"All right boys take only the packs of fur, line them up in the first room. We'll open and spread them out in there. We'll get a tally on each species. Care to watch Mr. ah, excuse me we haven't been introduced. I am Mr. Richardson. And you?" he asks coming closer in the late afternoon sun. He looks into my tired eyes.

"Uriah and Nate? I don't believe it. We heard you both were dead," says Mr. Richardson grabbing me in his arms.

"And you believed the reports?" I ask hugging him back.

As his men work separating our furs we talk.

We get top price. Thirty of our packhorses carry beaver pelts. Ten horses are carrying other furs and hides, and fifteen horses carry buffalo robes. In addition to our two years' worth of fur, we inherit a year's worth of fur and his horses from a trapper that didn't make the trip. He is a casualty of the pirates. Nate and I settle with Mr. Richardson. We've brought in three years' worth of fur.

In his office Nate and I recount the pirate's attack, the bear attack, and two years' worth of stories. He sits in shock, fascinated by our words. In his office I glance at a picture protected in a glass frame. I do not recognize the man looking back at me. For the first time I see the damage the bear wrought. I smile. A long scar starting in my hair runs over my left eye down to my chin. Two smaller scars start at my hair line and stop at my nose, both on the right side. My once faded red hair is gray. My red and glowing mustache is now gray and stops at each corner of my lips. The bear put an abrupt end to my long and flowing facial hair. Oh well.

"*How would that Miss Debra like to see me now?*" I

wonder to myself.

The foreman knocks on the office door, comes in, and lays a slip of paper on the desk by

his boss. Mr. Richardson opens it. He stares at the figures, adds some of his own, then turns it so Nate and I can see the total. Sitting in front of us is three and a half years' worth of fur. Nate looks at me. I am speechless.

"Is that right?" I ask.

"It is. You both better walk with me to the bank and I will settle this as you wish."

"Can we do it in the morning? I'd like to clean up and change these buckskins," I ask my friend.

"Very good. We will walk to the bank together in the morning." He stands. "You both are welcome to use the rooms over the stables during your stay. The tubs are being filled with hot water as we speak. Enjoy your supper at the café. Until tomorrow, my friends," he tells both of us, extending his hand and shaking with both of us.

After breaking our fast at the café, Mr. Richardson escorts us two blocks to the bank he deals with. We are invited into the back office. After the introductions, we get down to business. Mr. Richardson helps Nate open an account. At the end of the visit I stand holding a book saying I have much more money sitting in the National Bank of St. Louis, $500 in gold coins, and two checks in my pocket for supplies. I thank them both for their help.

Nate is staring at the bank book telling him how much he

has in his account, a bag of $200 in gold coins, and a check for...whatever he wants.

"Can you take us to the general store to order our supplies and trade goods for next season?" We've made more than expected and while I thank you for the use of your rooms for last night, I want to show Nate the city. Can you help us get a hotel room?" I ask of Mr. Richardson.

"I can certainly help you with that, Follow me." We get into his carriage. We end up in front of the St. Louis Hotel. A foot man helps Mr. Richardson out of his carriage. We are escorted inside stopping at a big desk, which is the domain of a well-dressed young man. I let Mr. Richardson do the talking.

"Robert my old friend. I'd like to introduce you to Uriah and Nate. They'll be needing a room with a bath for, let's say for the next three days while they are in our city," says Mr. Richardson to the man behind the fancy counter.

"That's $24," says the counter man after adding up all our charges.

"Is that the best you can do Robert? Uriah and Nate have been in the mountain for over two years. They both are business partners with me. What can you do for me, Robert?" asks Mr. Richardson.

"For you, and only you Mr. Richardson, and do not ever tell anyone about this price. Let us say $10 for both rooms."

"Thank you," I say, as I place a five-dollar coin on the counter.

"My thanks also," says Nate laying down a five-dollar coin.

"That will be room 110 and 111. Bottom floor in the back on the left. Anything else Mr. Richardson?"

"No, nothing else, Thank you Robert. I will remember this," says Mr. Richardson.

"Thank you, Robert," I add. "We'll be back with our saddlebags and possibles."

"Very well you can pick up your key here at the desk on your return." We walk out of the hotel heading for the general store. Another friend of Mr. Richardson.

"Good afternoon William. This is Uriah and Nate. A pair of my Mountain Men trappers.

Both will need town clothes. I suggest high quality work clothes, three sets, and boots, with a

hat."

"Follow me and we'll get to it," says the counter man. He's not as well dressed as the hotel man but is wearing a suit. To me it looks hot and uncomfortable.

On a table clothes begin piling up. I'm measured, poked, and prodded. Jeans, long handles, three cotton shirts, a vest, a sheepskin coat, socks, two neckerchiefs, and boots.

"What's the damages, my good friend?" asks Mr. Richardson.

"The total is $45 even."

"Is that the best you can do, my friend? Both of my friends have been trapping for two years. They will need more supplies before returning. What's your best price?" He's looking at me and thinking very deeply.

"You bought supplies from me two years ago, correct? Yes, now I remember. I owe both of you a heartfelt thanks. Since then my business has flourished. Will you be resupplying this year? No matter. Of course, I can do better and tell every one of your trapping friends. How about $23 even?" he asks.

"Thank you," I tell, him handing over my list of needs. We gather our packages to return to the hotel. Mr. Richardson helps us to our rooms. I watch Nate enter his before opening the door into mine. I've never seen anything like this. A feather bed, a chest of drawers, a bowl and pitcher, and rugs cover the wood floor. In another room is the bathtub full of hot water. He produces a bar of soap and a towel.

"Stop at the office after you're washed up. We'll go to supper," he tells us.

"I will and thank you for your help," I add.

"My pleasure, and Nate too," he says.

After he leaves, I enter the hot water. It's nice to get clean and soak out the aches and pains but it is not as nice as the hot springs in the Crow winter camp. I soak until the water turns cold. That's when I notice my pile of dirty buckskins are missing. I dry off, get dressed, and head down to the big desk.

"How can I help you?" There it is, the slightly arrogant undertone. Like scraping off the bottom of your boots, undertone. Now I know I don't care for this man.

"Where'd my buckskins go?"

"We are in the process of trying to clean them," he snaps.

"All right, don't use water, just brush them off..."

"I assure you that our staff knows its job. Anything else?"

"No, that's it."

"Good day." In my room I finish dressing. I sling my belt around my waist adding two pistols, my knife, and the war axe. I miss them when they are gone. I check the loads in both pistols, then the edges on the knife and war axe. They'll need touching up tonight. I add my possibles over a shoulder. I leave out the back to check if our horses have arrived yet. Both our saddle horses are here. I enter the stall and brush him for a bit. I notice two packs sitting with my saddle. Then I remember, they hold the extra pistols I took from the pirates. I'm looking through my saddlebags when Nate walks into the stable.

"Oh, those snooty dudes in the fancy suits sure took their time telling me where their stable is. I don't reckon they care for us much," he complains to me. Nate is not one to complain, this must really bother him.

We ride slowly to Mr. Richardson's office. Looking at the packed boardwalks, the streets are lined with wagons, and everyone hurrying about. All these people sure look to be in a hurry. We ride into Mr. Richardson's yard. Everyone is busy working. I knock on his door.

"Enter," echo's through the solid wood door. I open the

door. "Uriah and Nate, I'm glad you're here. I'm ready to eat. Are you?"

"We are. Where are we going?" asks Nate.

"I thought the hotel's restaurant would be a good choice," he gets up from behind the desk. He's about 30 years old, slim, with very lightly colored skin. He would not do well under the prairie sun. He drives his buggy while we walk our horses back to the hotel.

"We will visit the gunsmith and his gun shop after we eat," I tell Nate.

"Do you need new weapons?" ask Mr. Richardson.

"No, I don't, we have a lot of extras taken from the river pirates that I'd like to sell. And we both need to refill our possibles."

"I see." All talk of stores and buying supplies is dropped in favor of inhaling the smells emanating from the hotel's restaurant. We walk in. In front of us is another front desk, smaller than the ones at the bank and hotel. The man behind it is in a very fashionable city suit.

"Can I help you, gentlemen?" There it is again. The next time I hear it...I breath in to settle myself.

"I have a reservation under Mr. Richardson."

"I see it, but unfortunately it is for dinner not lunch. Dinner is not for another half hour.

"Let me speak to Henry, the manager. I know he's here because I talked to him earlier this afternoon," counters Mr. Richardson.

"There is no need. I see we have a table in the back."

"Is that really the best you can do?" Mr. Richardson begins walking towards the offices.

"No, wait, there is one other. Please, follow me, gentlemen." There it is again, he's talking as if he's cleaning the bottom of his boots, again. I walk to his side.

"If you slur a word against us one more time, I'm going to stuff you into one of these potted plants. Do you understand me?" He looks at the closest potted plant, shudders, and turns to me.

"Forgive me, Mr. ah...Please follow me." We do. Watching from outside of the building are two men. Both are on opposite sides of the building and the opposite side of the law from us. Henry the manager walks up to us as we are sitting.

"Mr. Richardson, good to see you. And how are the both of you?" he asks me and Nate.

"I saw some sort of problem out front. Is there something I need to know about?" he asks Mr. Richardson.

"No, we took care of it. In the future your men should not judge a book by its cover. For instance, Uriah and Nate here. You may think they're out of place but believe me, one day you'll need someone like them. And on that day, you'll hope and pray someone like them is around and on your side. Besides, you would be very surprised at their bank accounts," boasts Mr. Richardson.

"Thank you. I will take care of this myself. Enjoy your

meal." I watch him walk to the front desk. I cannot tell the words, but I can understand their meaning.

We are enjoying white cake with chocolate frosting when another man approaches our table. I've seen him and have been watching him. I pull a pistol under the table, kick Mr. Richardson and hand it to him. I'm holding the second.

"My name is Rufus. I was the mate on the Rouge. I understand you killed everyone and fired the boat. Is that true?"

"Yes, it is."

"Why?"

"Because you killed my friend, the captain of the paddle boat. You stole four of my horses, and destroyed three pack-horses' worth of supplies and fur," I tell him.

"I see. Too bad for you. Now get up. We're going to finish this outside." To reinforce his demands, he pushes his knife into my belly. Now I'm seeing red. That cake was the best thing I ever tasted. Half of it is on the table with my coffee. I get up.

"You stay here, Adam, this won't take long," I tell Nate and Mr. Richardson. I get up, hiding my pistol behind me. We start to walk outside.

As we pass a table with a very respectable middle-age couple, she begins screaming, "He's got a gun." The mate turns to me ready to embed his knife into my guts. Before he does, I move closer and introduce him to my pistol. He falls to the floor bleeding out. Two patrons jump on me forcing me to the ground. Now I'm mad. Throwing them off, I stand, drawing my knife and war axe. In a fighting crouch, now I'm ready. The two on the ground stay there and bleed. Mr. Richardson walks up to me, slowly talking to me. The red haze is fading. I take my pistol from him. I holster the fired one. Henry the manager arrives on the scene.

"Mr. Richardson, what has happened?" he asks almost hysterical.

"This man came to our table, threatening us and escorting Uriah outside with the intention of killing him. A woman screamed giving Uriah the time and opportunity to pull a weapon to defend himself." He stops, bends down, and picks up the knife. It is quite the weapon. Eighteen inches long, weighing at least four pounds, and very sharp.

I take it from Mr. Richardson. I turn the mate over, taking his belt, and look for papers. In a leather wallet I find them. I sheath the knife and put it in my shirt. I'm looking through the papers when the town sheriff runs in.

"I heard a tramp was killing patrons. Who's this," he asks out loud, looking down at the body. Looking at me he draws his pistol, aiming it at me. I can see his finger tightening on the trigger. Mr. Richardson is trying to talk to him. He is ignored. I look in his eye and shake my head. He stops pulling on the trigger long enough for me to pull my war axe. As he watches it come to his forehead, his eyes grow large. His finger falls off the trigger. He drops the pistol. I drop my arm.

"What in blazes is going on here?" shouts an authoritative

voice. I pick up the pistol.

"John, I was here I'll tell you what is happening," says Mr. Richardson to the town's marshal. He does, the deputy's eyes grow large, his body shrinks.

"I have received reports about that steamship on the sandbar. You're telling me you killed them all?" he asks Nate and me with skepticism.

"That's right. All but the four who jumped ship," I tell him.

"Reports say there were 27 men killed."

"I already said I did it."

"Why?" asks the marshal. I tell him about the captain, the attack, the horses, our furs and supplies, all of it.

"We best finish this at my office."

"If you have intentions of arresting Nate, then we are not going to comply. I will hire the two best attorneys I can find. And I will fight this, the town, and you, Marshal."

"Understood Mr. Richardson, but I can't have him running loose in my town."

"For defending himself and getting his personal property back? Tell me, John. What's the odds of the law getting his property and bringing the pirates to justice?"

"But still," hems the marshal.

"You do this, and I will run Nate as Marshal for St. Louis come next election. And after the town hears what you did, instead of thanking him, well, you'll be out of a job and nothing but a laughingstock."

"Now you just whoa up here Mr. Richardson. You can't threaten me," blusters the marshal. The sheriff cowers behind the marshal, quiet and hopefully unobserved.

"John, getting your feathers ruffled is only going to make it worse. What are you going to do?"

"All right, you win. Uriah and Nate, I want you out of town..."

"As soon as I resupply, I'm leaving your little bit of heaven." That silences the argument. I push past the lawman. Mr. Richardson is at my side. We walk towards the hotel. That's when I remember I need to stop at the gunsmith's shop. Outside the building we thank Mr. Richardson. He goes his way, back to his office, and we go ours.

Two blocks over and on the corner is the shop. The sign says open. We walk inside. I talk with the gunsmith. He will buy them but will have to see them before he can quote me a price.

"We'll be right back," I say, asking him to remain open until we return. The gunsmith is talking with Nate as I walk out to my horse.

"I'll be here," he says. I ride to the hotel's stable, then to Mr. Richardson's yard. I bring out ten pirate rifles, in a haversack are all the pistols. I return to the gun shop leading a packhorse bearing the extra weapons. Laying everything on the counter we begin.

Nate and the gunsmith have a pile of weapons on the counter Nate is buying. He looks over the ten rifles and a dozen pistols. All are .50 caliber. Nate and I fill our possibles and our powder horns. We add a case of percussion caps, casting lead, and a keg of black powder to the counter. We both leave the shop re-armed and happy with the price received from the pirates' weapons.

We slowly ride back to the hotel. The next morning, we bring the pack string to the general store. I buy more frames and replace worn out panniers. By early afternoon we have twenty loaded packhorses, four carrying camp supplies, and a dozen unburdened. I think we have done well. Nate asks to take supper at the café. I agree. I can see something is bothering him. We are greeted like old friends. Taking a table in the back we order the special.

"What's the matter?" I ask my young partner.

"I do not want to return to the mountain and trade for another winter. I want to do something different," he tells me.

"Do you have something in mind?"

"Not really, I want to ride some place warmer during the winter. I might head to Santa Fe and see how my luck holds over there."

"That's part of Mexico. I've heard tell of rowdy and drunken Americans getting into trouble with the Mexican authorities and losing just about everything. I'd hate to see that happen to you. What about our partnership? I can buy you out and give you some horses. What do you need?"

"I'd like an extra riding horse and four packhorses, that's it."

"How much do you need for your part of our success?"

"Not a dollar. Like I said I would have helped you for free. I have more money than I could ever spend in the fancy bank in St. Louis."

"If you ever need help reach out to Mr. Richardson. Here," I tell him handing him a leather bag. It clunks heavy on the table.

"What's this? I told you I can't accept..."

"Take my gift, please Nate. If you ever need help, get word to me. I'll be in St. Louis every summer. I'll help with what I can."

"Thanks, my friend," he says, hiding the leather bag in his shirt. He extends his hand to me. "If you ever need my help I'll come running too." We shake and he leaves the café. I'll give him some time before heading for the yard. After a second slice of pie and more coffee I walk to the yard.

I can see Nate took his horses and his gear from the room over the stable.

"Where's he heading?" Mr. Richardson asks me.

"I don't know. Fighting the pirates shook him up, but I did not expect this."

"What are you going to do?" asks Mr. Richardson.

"I'm on my way back to the mountains."

"Which route are you taking?"

"I've had my fill of steamboats and rivers. I'm going to ride. I have three months. I should arrive as the Crow finish setting up their winter camp."

"I've got refunds for you. From the hotel," he says handing me a small leather bag filled with coins. "Nate only used his hotel room to take that first bath. He slept in one of my rooms. I have refunds for him also."

"Save it for him if he ever shows up needing help. I told him you will help him and to leave word with you if he needs to find me. Hope that is okay."

"Of course, it is. When are you leaving?"

"First thing in the morning. Once again thanks for all you've done. Expect to see me next summer," I tell my old friend.

"I'll be waiting for you next summer," he says, sticking out his hand. We shake and I climb into the saddle. I ride back to spend a last night in the fancy hotel room.

Nate left last night. He rode out alone, on his best riding horse leading a single pack horse. I offered him the value of half of the pack string and supplies but he refused to take it. I paid him not near what I feel I owe him, but he was content with the leather bag of coins I gave him. Something changed in my partner after the fight with the river pirates. I can't lay a finger on exactly what it was, but he was different. I know a seeing the boat wreck, watching friends shot down, and being in a gun fight can change a man, but I did not see it in time to help him.

We part ways. I'm returning to the mountains to trade with the Cheyenne. Nate is heading towards Santa Fe, New Mexico. I hope he can find what he's looking for.

Nate's Story

I did not dare tell Uriah, and I can't reckon why I feel this way. Knowing him like I do he probably would have let me keep the saddlebags I found full of gold coins and paper money. It was pirate loot and I kept it. Half my attention was on the journey to St. Louis. The other half was thinking how easy it was for the pirates to gather booty. After the gun fight a seed was planted. It took root during the ride. I saw the beginnings of the plan take shape during our time in the city. I saw how the only thing that matters to city folk is how much money you're worth and the clothes you wear. Right then I decided to head my own way.

I snuck out of my hotel room the one night I used it. I made my way to a saloon. I sat and watched the men coming in and more importantly going out. To make a long story short I made over two hundred dollars that night by rolling drunks. It was a heady experience. It changed my life.

I heard conversations about Texas. About how it was the next big thing, but first we have to take it from Mexico. A fight was brewing. I can feel my blood singing. I want in. On the walk back to my hotel room I make the decision to head for Texas. I now know how to make my fortune. Where there's a war there is money. I am going to steal more than my share. The thought made my stomach tighten. I can hear the blood pouring into my head past my ears. I get the same feeling as after a gun fight or fighting Blackfoot. And I like it.

After making my decision all feels right with the world. I fall asleep as soon as I land in that big hotel bed. I wake refreshed and ready, when I remember I owe it to Uriah to tell him in person. I will do that today and be on the trail by midday.

———

Uriah

I'm up before the sun. Nate joins me. We ride to the café for a last meal until next year. During the meal Nate tells me he will be heading for Santa Fe. He tells me he has no plan but needs to be on his own. Well, I can't argue that. I let him know he's welcomed back any time. I assure him Mr. Richardson feels the same. In the yard I get busy. I don't want to watch him make his own preparations. Later I see him approaching me and stop what I'm doing.

"Uriah, I just want to thank you for all you done for me. Look me up if you ever get to Santa Fe," he tells me, sticking out his hand. I brush it aside and engulf him in my arms.

"Take care of yourself. If need be, you know where to find me. Ride safe and good luck."

"Thanks." We watch him ride away leading a single packhorse.

In the yard I finish loading fifteen packhorses, four horses carry camp supplies and an extra riding horse. As the sun peaks over the eastern horizon I set off on the Santa Fe Trail, returning west, to the Stonies. I will turn north towards Yellowstone. I see no one during the first week on the trail. I'm making good time. After passing the marker announcing the turn off for Bent's Fort, I begin seeing people. One evening I am hailed from the dark. I move into the shadows with my rifle, possibles, and gun belt.

"Hello, the camp," yells someone from the trail.

"What do you want?"

"A seat at your fire and the chance to throw on a pot of coffee."

"Who are you?"

"Traders from Santa Fe. We are well known along the Trail. I assure you we are friendly. I've got women and kids that could use the fire."

"All right, come ahead, but heaven help you if you're not who you say you are." I watch as they ride in, stopping their horses and wagon outside the light of my small campfire.

"Who might you be?" they ask me.

"I'm Uriah."

"The same that rode with Micah?"

"Yes, do you know Micah?"

"Those are two names we'll never forget. We met a few years ago. Is Micah with you?" they ask me, walking into the light.

"No, he......"

"I heard about you. You're him? Uriah that settled the pirates, right?" asks another man.

"That's right. Take a set. Your women and kids are safe."

"I have word from the Crow for you. Let's talk after we eat." And eat we do. They have the last of an antelope quarter on the fire. I add potatoes and coffee. As the women are cleaning up, their wagon boss motions me to follow as we walk around the camp.

"I hate to be the one to tell you, but your bunch of Crow were attacked by the Blackfoot.

Luckily, no Crows were kilt. But they are living with the greater Crow nation. Word has come down from the chiefs that all the white hunters not married to Crow women are not allowed into their camp this winter. Something about getting their Medicine back. You know more about that than I do. I'm simply passing along the news."

"Thanks, good thing Micah ain't here to hear that news," I say.

"Doesn't apply to him. He married up with that little Crow gal he wintered with."

"Hadn't heard that. I was thinking on wintering with the Crow, but I reckon not now."

"What are you going to do now?" asks the wagon boss.

"I don't know. I'll have to ponder on it."

"You're welcome to fall in with us. We can always use a rifle like yours."

"Thanks for the invite. I'll think on it. Where you headed?"

"St. Louis."

"I just left there and ain't in a hurry to go back."

"If you don't mind a suggestion, Texas is a good place for a man to make something out of his life. You could do worse than ride with the Rangers. Give that some thought."

"I will, thanks."

I leave early the next morning before they are up and about. I am heading for the winter camp of the Cheyenne. The trail is easy and the trip quick. I am shown to my lodge. I pay the widow that packed it, moved it, and set it up for me. It is ready on my return. She is pleased receiving the trade goods, I am pleased I have a lodge ready for me.

———

The Crow

The Blackfoot attacked the Crow village during the summer while I was away. I was making the long journey to St. Louis to sell my furs to Mr. Richardson. I missed the fight. I'm not sure how I feel about that. On one hand I'm glad I missed it. A fight against Blackfoot, whether it's one on one or like this time, a war party verses a village, is never an easy thing. They are fierce warriors and make terrible enemies. As I understand things, the animosity began with Lewis and Clark on their Voyage of Discovery. I heard that a member of the Journeyers fired at and killed a Blackfoot warrior. I misremember the why behind the confrontation. I only remember that from then on, the Blackfoot carry no affection for Americans. The British however have made peace with the Blackfoot Nation and conduct business with them. I wish I could remember the small things but alas at this point in my life they don't matter.

———

Cheyenne Winter Camp Fall 1836

There was also a summer raid by the Blackfoot on the Cheyenne village for horses, increasing the perpetual animosity between the two peoples. The Blackfoot were busy this summer. I reckon the Blackfoot don't get along with very many others. The Cheyenne warriors were not waiting on my return to repay the Blackfoot, the timing just works out that way.

On my return I learn the warriors are planning a retaliatory fall raid. I understand I need to go about this very carefully. I do not want to reach above my place in the village, but I feel like I can make a contribution and have a role to fill. I begin by asking my friend, Grey Wolf. I approach him before supper the afternoon of my return.

"Standing Bear, I understand the village is preparing to

make a raid on the Blackfoot that raided your village this summer. I humbly ask if I can play a role in the raid."

"Uriah, my friend. I will welcome you on the raid, but the decision is not mine to make. It belongs to the main war chief. I don't believe he has considered taking you along on this raid."

"Will you go with me when I ask him?"

"I will."

"Thanks, when should I do this?"

"Soon. Plans will be concluded by tomorrow. We expect to ride in two days."

"Can we see him now?"

"We can try." Walking to the war chief's lodge with Standing Bear, I am quiet. I'm turning over the arguments that should see me become a member of the raid. I try to think of counters to his arguments. I do not know enough to ask permission the correct way. I'm going to rely on my friend Grey Wolf to do it the proper way. We arrive and I have not settled the questions in my own head. There is a guard outside the lodge.

"We seek the war Chief."

"He is busy. Go and return later."

"Uriah seeks permission to accompany the raiders," says my friend. The guard, a warrior I do not know well, looks me over slowly from head to toe.

"I will see if Grey Wolf wishes to talk to the trader. You both wait here." The warrior guard scratches on the hide door of the buffalo lodge. An answer bellows from inside. To my ears it is only a shout but Grey Wolf bends to enter the lodge. He is gone for less than a full handful of minutes.

"He will see you, Uriah the trapper, only you. He will hear your words. Go inside," he tells me, holding the oval door flap open for me. His entry opening is smaller than my own. I have to crawl to enter. I reckon that's the idea. If the visitor is unexpected or an enemy, he can be dealt with while crawling on all fours. For the first time I clearly understand this intention. It gets me to thinking. Once fully inside I stand. Grey Wolf and two other warriors are sitting around a small fire. It is clear they welcome the break from their meeting. I only hope things progress well and they are in the frame of mind to accept me.

"What do you want to ask of us?"

"I want to ride with my Cheyenne friends when they attack the Blackfoot, repaying them for the summer's raid."

"Why? You were not here when they made this attack. You have no one in the village that could have been killed. You had no hides, no furs, and no horses in the camp that could have been stolen. Why do you wish to become an enemy to the Blackfoot?"

"I am already an enemy to the Blackfoot. One of their young war chiefs is responsible for the wound and scar I carry. I wish to help my friends. It is because I was not here that I want to help now. You accepted me and we've helped each other in the good times. Now, I wish to help my friends in a time of need. I have benefited from your friendship. I will be honored to ride with my Cheyenne friends and hosts."

"We too have benefited from your trades. We are equal in that regard. The fight is a fight between Cheyenne and Blackfoot. Why take a hand in this fight?"

"Because I consider you friends, because you allow me to winter with your village, because we trade together. These are the reasons. I think I can help."

"You will use your fire weapons?"

"Yes." For the first time the warriors sitting by his side show agitation. They whisper to each other. There are angry shakes to their heads. Hands fly through the air. I have a suspicion that was a wrong answer. After a double handful of minutes, they stop deliberating and face me.

"Sit," orders the older warrior on his right. I've been standing. I sit facing the trio. "We cannot allow you to bring your weapons. The noise is great. This raid depends on stealth." The others nod their heads in agreement.

"I will use Cheyenne weapons, silent weapons."

"Can you?" asks the older warrior on the left. I do not know him well. I've not talked to him, having not been introduced to him we've not talked.

"I can. Standing Bear will help me trade for a bow and a quiver of arrows. I practiced regularly when I lived among the Crow. They have taught me the ways of the knife and lance. I've fought others using Crow weapons. I can quickly learn to use Cheyenne weapons; there is very little difference."

"Can you ride your horse like a Cheyenne? Can you dress like a Cheyenne warrior? Will you?" he asks me, looking deeply into my eyes searching out the truth behind my answers.

"I can and I will."

"I am not in favor of allowing you to war with us. I do not want the Blackfoot to see an American fighting with us against other Indians," says an older warrior. I feel shattered inside.

They wait. I wait.

"If you can look like another Cheyenne warrior and can use Cheyenne weapons, I will cast my vote for allowing what you ask. But I will be a hard judge. I will inspect you before we ride. If I like what I see I will favor your request," says the older warrior. It's hard to keep a smile from breaking out. I force the muscles to remain still, unmoving.

"I too, will find favor if you can blend in as a Cheyenne warrior. I have the same concerns. If you can actually use our weapons, ride like one of us, and look like one of us, I too am in favor," says the younger warrior war chief.

"I think there is much wisdom in what has been said. If I can see you as a Cheyenne warrior, with Medicine signs in paint, using our weapons, riding our way, and fighting as one of our many, I will be in favor of this thing, also. We will ride in two mornings. When the sun rises tomorrow, we will call for you and see for ourselves if you are Cheyenne. Is this agreeable to you?" asks Grey Wolf. On hearing the question, the answer is obvious on my face. I hear my name repeated by the warriors outside "Angry Bear will serve as your Cheyenne name too," simply says the oldest war chief. I can't help myself. The smile breaks out. I cannot hold it back any longer. The trio stands. I stand. They exit the lodge in order of age. I follow after them. The village is assembled around the lodge.

"If our friend Uriah can change himself into the Cheyenne warrior Angry Bear, then we will allow him to accompany us on the raid in two suns. He may need some help. Can some of you help him?" asks the oldest war chief. Pandemonium breaks out. I am hustled to my lodge. Inside I change from my trapper clothes into my buckskins. I'm transforming into a Cheyenne warrior from moccasins to lance, dressed in Cheyenne buckskins, moccasins, and war shirt. Under the war shirt I wear one of my cotton shirts. I take the pistols off my belt adding a large fighting knife and a war axe. I tie a headband around my head. Sees Far brings me one of his older bows and a quiver of arrows. I'm ready to step outside.

Only warriors greet me. Someone places a lance in my hands. The fighting end is deadly sharp metal. My saddle horse looks on barely interested in the transformation, until a new horse is brought to me. I watch as the old saddle is taken inside and replaced by a Cheyenne saddle made from hip and shoulder bones of a buffalo and covered in one of my trade blankets. Reins are exchanged for a rope simply tied around my new horse's nose. I climb aboard, my feet find the primitive stirrups, and the lance is passed to me. This horse is going to teach me to ride Cheyenne style. With bow and quiver safe over a shoulder I follow a handful of warriors out of the camp.

They put me through the paces. It's a good thing I know the Cheyenne language and have already fought using Indian weapons. It is all coming together today. We ride until supper time. I must admit I'm tired. New and previously underused muscles are crying out. I visit the hot springs and call it an early night.

There is an early morning scratch on my door, a very early morning. Standing Bear and Grey Wolf enter bearing bundles. I dress in my new buckskins and they get to work. I am meeting the three war chiefs planning this raid at mid-morning today. Grey Wolf unveils his burden, pots of paint. The weather is cool enough that I'll be wearing long-sleeved buckskin war shirt and buckskin pants covering arms and legs. He uses the paint as camouflage to hide my light-colored face. Even though I am tanned I am not as dark as the Cheyenne. Using horizontal lines, he achieved the effect. Grey Wolf adds two eagle feathers into my hair. I'm awarded them for killing two Blackfoot. Two others are added to my headband. Four more are tied to my lance, along with other decorations of porcupine quills and bead work to the rawhide sleeves along the length of the lance. My buckskins and saddle sport very little decoration or bead work. That will come with more experience.

When they are satisfied with the results, we gather my weapons, climb aboard horses, and set out for the war chief's lodge. Behind us follow most of the residents of the village. A crier is sent to announce our coming. Young warriors in training take hold of our horses as we stop in front of the lodge. As the horses are led away, the three elders come out to meet us. The three walk around me looking from the soles of my moccasins to the tip of my lance. Ready to announce their decision they stop at their place around the firepit outside the lodge. Part of a buffalo hump is cooking over the fire. The smells of roasting meat is making me hungry.

The oldest elder bids me and my three friends to sit. Another warrior cuts strips from the buffalo hunk slowly cooking. That's when I notice the coffee pot boiling on the fire. Another warrior pours and hands me a cup. Unsure of the protocol, I wait. When they begin eating so do the rest of us. As I finish the coffee, my cup is refilled. All the conversation around me is in Cheyenne. I surprise myself in understanding without linking the words to their English equivalent. Greasy hands are wiped on rawhide leggings. I am handed a second slice. With the reassuring nods from the three elders I eat and sip the last from my cup. All eyes move towards the elder when we finish. He stands.

"I am pleased with your look Angry Bear," he says using my Cheyenne name. "We will welcome you to ride with us in our raid on the Blackfoot tomorrow," he announces. With words of agreement floating through the crowd he sits. As the voices quiet, warriors begin talking while sitting around the fire.

"Remembering the cause of our celebration and knowing we will ride early, let the celebrating begin," announces the primary war chief of this raid. Instantly the village is engulfed in noise and talking friends. More freshly roasted buffalo are passed to warriors and village members. I help myself to more coffee. We sit, eating and enjoying the company of friends and family until the sun sets. Slowly the wives and families of the warriors begin leaving the fire. The warriors will stay to prepare for tomorrows battle. I stand to leave, unexpectedly tired from yesterday's strain.

I bring in my weapons left in front of my lodge to keep them from the night's mist.

Entering my lodge, I see a fire lit in the rock-lined ring. The air is a bit warm but will be good for the quickly cooling night. I prepare my coffee pot for the morning.

I am surprised to wake in the early morning dark. I add wood to the fire to get the coffee boiling. When I return from washing up Standing Bear renews the paint work that Grey Wolf designed for me. Wiping our hands after eating we walk outside. He helps saddle my new horse the Cheyenne way. Climbing into the saddle he hands up my weapons. I add my canteen and a parfleche of jerky to the saddle.

"Thank you for helping me," I tell him.

He smiles and slaps my horse on the rear. The horse is instantly running. I quickly lean forward keeping my seat.

The slap surprised both of us. I ride to the assembly area with Grey Wolf.

From the winter camp we ride west by north out of the Yellowstone Valley towards the Blackfoot. As the sun rises, I access the extra gear on my saddle. I look inside my possibles. Inside is my fire-starting kit and a hollow wood jar of home-made salve. I reckon it's a first aid treatment. I see a second canteen, a larger parfleche with a coffee pot and grounds, and additional jerky. Tied to the back of the saddle is my Hudson Bay blanket coat. Standing Bear is riding next to me. We are traveling fast and quiet.

When the forward scouts can no longer see the trail in front of them, we stop for the night. It will be a cold camp. We are too close to our enemy to alert them to our presence by a fire. I find a bag of pemmican in my gear. Standing Bear must have slipped it in there. The hearty thick paste, jerky, and creek water makes a surprisingly filling evening meal. Besides, I'm too tired to care.

Standing Bear wakes me in the dark. For a moment I am unsure where I am. As my head clears and my eyes focus, I remember, and things look familiar. I wait to eat until we begin riding again. Last night Grey Wolf felt confident we will find our enemy before the morning turns old. I can feel a difference in the warriors riding close to me. Most are grinning in expectation. Me, I'm excited about meeting the Blackfoot while hoping I give a good accounting of myself. I do not remember feeling this concerned prior to a fight when with other trappers. I reckon I'm not as confident of myself fighting like a Cheyenne warrior, yet. To take my mind off the worry, I dig out a long strip of jerky.

The sudden stop wakes me up. I wasn't sleeping, just kind of resting in the saddle. Now I'm wide awake. I watch as warriors renew their war paint. I follow their example. Standing Bear and I work together. We claim our weapons and leave the horses with young horse handlers. Slow, quiet, and careful we make our way on foot due north. The scouts have located the camp, but I have no idea where it lay. I focus on walking cautious and noiseless. I can feel strength entering my limbs. My eyes and hearing are growing stronger. I can see and hear farther.

My bow and quiver of arrows bounce gently against my back. I can feel the knife and war axe against my legs as we run forward. I carry a shield in my left hand, lance in the right. Instead of growing heavy and tiring, they grow light and I feel strong. I smell smoke on the wind. We slow to a walk. Another one hundred yards and the scouts stop us. They glide forward to locate the camp. I can't stand still. It's like the blood flowing through my body is singing. I like the feeling. I've been in gunfights where I've had to kill Indians and Americans, but I have never felt like this. I think because gunfights happen faster, without anticipation. If I ever felt the same, I did not notice it.

The scouts are back. The Blackfoot are fifty yards in front of us. The morning's sun is halfway between the horizon and straight up. The breeze moves towards us carrying the scent of fire and of horses. The weak sun is not warm on me, but I do not feel cold. The scouts divides us into three groups. I am part of the center group. Hastily I drink from my canteen. The hand command, forward, is flashed to all of us. We carefully walk ahead. Tall grass hides us from view. It reaches our shoulders. The Blackfoot camp is in a stand of trees. A small creek flows through the grove.

My hands are shaking. I hear the sounds of flies in the air and bugs in the grass. I see about ten feet ahead, through the grass. I'm ready. We crouch down hiding our heads as we walk forward. I see a Blackfoot warrior directly in front of me. He does not see me or the others. My left foot rises for a step. The shaking in my hands stop. The foot hits the ground, I hear and feel the thud. I can see the warriors on both sides of me looking ahead. I don't think they have seen this enemy. I draw my knife as my right foot rises from the ground. I let go of my shield and lance. The warrior catches sight of me from the corner of his eye. My right foot falls to the ground, pushing me ahead. I see the Blackfoot about to scream a warning. I grab him with my left arm as I swing my right hand with the knife. Before my left foot begins its step, I force the Blackfoot on my knife. I thrust, again, and again. He goes limp in my arms. I turn him around and slice his throat. I drop him as my left foot hits the ground. I sink to my knees. The warriors to either side see what has happened. They keep walking. As the dead warrior hits the ground, I grab my shield and lance. I keep walking finding myself a step behind the two men at each side of me.

The buzzing through my arms and legs has stopped, leaving me feeling strong. My ears hear the Blackfoot talking at the fire only yards from my group. I see two warriors in front of me. The quiet is broken by a shout. I launch my lance at the man on the left. I do not watch it hit. I'm drawing my war axe and charging the man on the right. Three steps and I'm on him. He is standing in place. Surprise is written across his face. I plant the war axe at the junction of neck and shoulder. He collapses. I can't draw out my weapon. I'll come back for it. I collect my lance, only to launch it again. I block a sideways slash of a Blackfoot war axe. It buries itself into my buffalo hide shield. I drop it. My knife puts an end to that warrior. I pull my bow, string it, and draw four arrows.

Standing in the clearing of the Blackfoot camp I look for targets. I have an arrow on the sinew string and three in my left hand holding the bow. From the side two young Blackfoot rush towards me. The first arrow takes the one on the left. I quickly add a second arrow to the string, draw, and release without aiming. At less than ten feet away the arrow flies true. I add a third arrow to the string. The sounds of fighting have stopped. I look but cannot see a live Blackfoot.

I check the dead, making sure they are truly dead. I collect my weapons as I walk. That's when I remember to collect a weapon for each of my kills. I've got knives and war axes from each man, and two hand carved war clubs. When I turn the fourth man over, he has a coup stick in his belt. I've not seen one this finely carved. It is a deadly work of art. The owner carved a bear with a ball in its mouth on one end of the stick. The stick itself is three feet long. Along the length is a spiral made from tacks. The tacks are similar to the ones I carry for trade. A wolf's head is carved at the other end of the stick. A rawhide cord fits between the eyes of the wolf. The cord goes around my wrist as I swing it. The wood is hard, dense, and almost black. The entire length of the stick shines in the sun. I add it to my belt and make a pile of the loot I collect. Next, I check the dead close by.

I make a second pile of weapons taken from the dead warriors I did not kill. The youngest leader of the war party walks by.

"These are all your kills?" he asks me.

"No," I tell him, "only this pile of warriors here," I say pointing. "All of these were killed by others."

"Who? What others?" he asks me confused.

"I don't know who. I noticed they were dead. After finishing the pile for my kills I gathered them," I tell him pointing to the other stack.

"You've earned seven horses. Go to the horse herd and collect your seven. You've done well fighting as a Cheyenne warrior today.

"Thank you," I tell him. He waves me off, in a friendly way. He's got more men to check on. I leave my lance and shield on the pile of seven men and their weapons. I walk back to reclaim my horse. The horse handlers are on their way to the battle site. I take my horse, climb onto the saddle, and ride to the Blackfoot herd. I'm wondering how many Blackfoot were in the camp. And how big the horse herd is. I see one of our horse handlers, a young warrior in training guarding the Blackfoot horses. I ride to him.

"Hello, I have been given permission to collect seven horses. One for each of my kills."

"Good for you. I can't wait until I become a warrior and can collect horses to buy a wife with," he tells me.

"You will make a good warrior," I tell him looking over the herd. I see the seven I want. He points to a pile of neck ropes. I ride to the pile, tie my horse to a tree and take up seven ropes. I notice the horses shy away from me. I reckon it's because I smell different. I return for my horse, mount, and try it again. This time I'm able to collect the seven I want. Carefully I lead them around the camp to the edge of the grass where I did my fighting.

I see others have made packs from blankets in the camp. I'll need to do the same for my plunder. I surprise myself; the work goes much easier than I expect. I have packs on two of the horses, with my weapons loaded, and I'm ready to ride. I hope we ain't spending the night in this camp but will be riding soon. The sun its past the halfway mark. I expect to hear the order to ride at any moment. Until then I'll eat the jerky in my bag. I take the horses to the creek for water. Still no order to ride. I lead them to a grassy spot, secure them to a picket line and go looking for my friends.

All the work is done, everyone is ready to leave this place for a camp of our own. I cover the whole camp without seeing my friends or the leader of this war party. I make my way to where I left my horses. That's when I catch up with my friends and the war party leader.

They are looking over the second pile of weapons I gathered. Those from the kills of other warriors.

"Where are the warriors belonging to these weapons?" asks the one of the war party leaders.

"I moved them out of the camp along with the Blackfoot warriors I killed," I tell him.

"Who is responsible for them?" he asks me.

"I do not know. I didn't see anyone kill them. I found them when I double checked on my kills."

"Good. You got your seven horses?" he asks me.

"Yes, and their weapons. Will we be riding soon?" I ask him.

"I'm thinking about spending the night right here. There's water and grass for the horses. The camp has meat for a small celebration. What do you think?" the younger warrior asks me.

"I'd rather not stay here. I'd rather ride away with our loot and horses to make our own camp. Other Blackfoot may show up looking for this first bunch."

"Those are good points, but I don't feel like riding. I'm

still thinking about staying here for the night." He must have seen the expression in my eyes. "Don't worry, we are a big enough war party to punish another bunch of Blackfoot if they should come by. Yes. We are staying here. Pass the word. Get fires cooking the buffalo we've found. Once again, good job Angry Bear," he tells me.

Well orders are orders. I walk to my horses to check on them. They are fine. I move them from the creek, off the short grass, to the edge of the high grass. If things turn bad, I'll be ready to ride east, through the tall grass, back to the Cheyenne winter camp. I make a small fire, put coffee pot on, and begin looking for a share of the buffalo they are issuing to the warriors. I'm almost through the camp before I find it.

"What do you want with it?" asks a particularly belligerent warrior, one I've never got along with.

"The war party chief said it's for all of us to share."

"He's not here. I took this as a prize. It's ours and we are not sharing."

"Okay," I tell him and turn around to walk back to my camp. I do not expect him to attack me, but I should have. I hear steps behind me. Turning, I drop my shoulder. He takes my shoulder in the beginnings of a rounded belly, a sign of easy living. I reckon he's not exercising as hard as he needs to, to stay slim and trim. His fetid breath woofs out of him.

He does not straighten up but holding his stomach he falls to the grass. That gets the attention of his friends. They both stand. I ask them to make sure they want to continue the fight before they begin. Both of them say yes. So far this has not called for weapons, I hope it continues that way. They rush one at a time. I'm able to block the rush. I deliver abuse to their face and stomach. Both end their fight by rolling on the ground unwilling to continue. I learned to fist fight in the camp of the railroad gang. That's something these Cheyenne warriors haven't seen. I turn my back on the trio to walk back to my camp. My friend Standing Bear is watching.

"Did you see all of that?" I ask him.

"I did. I was looking for you to invite you to share my fire," he tells me.

"Does the offer still stand?" I ask.

"It does."

"Where is your fire?" I ask. Without a word he leads me in the direction of my fire and camp.

"Do I need to be watching my back trail?" I ask my real friend.

"No, but to make sure, I will ride closer to you and your seven horses. You must promise to tell me how you earned your name?" I promise him I will. There are six warriors waiting at the fire when we walk in. I have returned to my fire and camp. Standing Bear is smiling at me.

"How did you know this was my camp?" I ask him.

"We saw you walk away. I thought you were looking for me. At least until you found yourself a diversion," he laughs.

"There is room for your horses at the edge of the grass next to mine," I tell them. Like me they want a camp at the edge of the long grass away from the Blackfoot camp under the trees. These experienced warriors do not like spending the night here.

"Do you expect trouble tonight?" I ask them. I hope I'm the only one. I do not want to fight in the dark.

"It is a mistake to remain here for the night. We should be riding east, away from here."

"I agree."

"Enough of that, come in and sit. Cut off some meat. Enjoy your coffee," says my friend. After eating we all turn in. I reckon all of us share the feeling of dread. I roll in my blankets with my weapons. Come daylight I'm surprised when I wake. We've passed a safe night. I rebuild the fire. When it's going, I set the coffee pot on and lead my horses to water. As they drink, I head back for my coffee cup. I finish that first cup watching my new horses drink creek water and chomp grass. All of a sudden, I feel the hairs on the back of my neck standing straight up. I look around but can't see anything.

"Standing Bear," I call, leading my horses back to the high grass. He sits up and looks at me. I begin signing that I feel an enemy is close. That gets him and the rest of them up and moving. I gather my weapons when I hear the first war cries.

"Blackfoot," I shout climbing onto the back of my saddled war horse. I lead the others into the grass and tie them as secure as possible. I ready my weapon. This morning I will fight differently finding myself on the edge of a mêlée. I stick to my war horse, using my lance and shield. For most of the short fight I do not have time to think, only thrust or parry then withdraw to ride on. I lose track of how many Blackfoot warriors I strike from their horses, ending their lives, but it's more than the first clash. I harness the red berserker rage, using it, clearing the field, and moving on. I do not feel my blood singing, the fight happens to fast. The end comes in an instant. Looking for my next victim and then, field is clear. I stop my tired horse, climb down, and drop my shield from a weary left arm. I plant my lance in the ground to lean on while I catch my breath. That's when things hit me. Slowly in my mind the scenes replay. I see each strike. I feel my lance hit. I see each warrior fall to the ground. Helpless I watch the scenes replay themselves.

Finished, I fall to my knees trying to empty my stomach. My horse nudges me with his wet and warm nose. His touch breaks the brawl's spell. I stand revisiting the dead to take a weapon from each and move on. I gather the horses waiting at the bodies of their former owners. I feel the wind but do not hear the smallest sound, everything is quiet. I end back at my string of horses still hidden in the tall grass. Without conscious thought, like I'm watching someone else's actions, I add more horses to my string. I watch as Standing Bear walks to me. His slap to my shoulder breaks this unique experience.

"We are leaving, gather your horses and your weapons. We ride," he tells me before moving on spreading the word. I am so tired but dare not close my eyes for fear of seeing...everything.

7

BLACKFOOT CAMP

WE HAVE SUCCESSFULLY DRIVEN OFF THE BLACKFOOT. However, the Cheyenne war party pays a heavy price. Four warriors, three warriors in training, and four horse handlers have been killed. We throw their bodies across their horses to bury them away from the hated Blackfoot camp. The toll from the second fight takes the glory from the revenge war party. The three leaders lose face for staying in the Blackfoot camp instead of riding out and making a new camp. It is too late to argue over what is done. The three war chiefs will not lead another war party for a long time, if ever again. They will not be trusted; few warriors will follow them.

Standing Bear's little brother is one of the horse handlers killed. Standing Bear takes his death hard. I ride with my friend in his pain. Well away from the Blackfoot camp, we find a gully with a dirt bank. We lay out our dead and cave the bank over them. We ride our horses over the dirt to hide their resting place. If the Blackfoot ever find it, they will dig up our dead warriors to desecrate their bodies. They believe this will keep our dead from chasing after the Blackfoot in the forever hunting grounds. We make our solemn way, returning to the Cheyenne winter camp before snow flies. There is a buffalo hunt to organize.

When the guards see us returning, we are not dressed in our finest buckskins or wearing paint and displaying feathers, they know something distressing has happened. We have lost our Medicine. The criers walk through the village preparing the people for bad news. I ask Standing Bear what I should do. He ignores my request. I make my way to my lodge to ask Lark. At first, she is glad to see me ride in. That changes when she learns of the death of her little brother. I keep my horses with me in case I am asked to leave the Cheyenne winter camp. I do not unload my horses nor carry my gear into my lodge. In addition to the change I smell on the air, I am worrying about the coming winter months. The village is not prepared. Standing Bear comes to talk to me.

He asks for permission to enter my lodge. Of course, I give it and bid him enter. He takes a seat by the fire Lark has left burning. I offer him a plate of the buffalo Lark has left on a spit over the low fire. We share a meal and talk.

"Uriah, you have been a friend to the Cheyenne but there

comes a time when even close friends can be considered outsiders. I'm afraid that time has come. I'm sorry to admit that many who should know better consider you an outsider. Adding salt to the wound is knowing you were correct about leaving the Blackfoot camp. We should have left and made our own camp. However, we did not do that, and we paid a terrible price. It is not your fault but..."

"Go ahead and tell me, my friend. What has happened?"

"I have been tasked with asking you to leave our village. There will be no further trading this season. I am deeply sorry."

"What about next fall? Can I..." I stop. I can't continue. I will not beg. I see the answer in his eyes. "How long do I have?"

"The council wants you gone within three days."

"I will bring in the rest of my horses to pack my belongings and be gone by dark."

"Thank you, my friend," slowly and sad says Standing Bear. He sets down his plate and leaves. He asks a horse handler to bring all my horses to my lodge. I begin loading my gear into panniers after he leaves. I pass a long night without much sleep. I'm up early securing all the pack frames I own on my horses. I stop for coffee only; I do not feel like eating. I work until every pannier is secure on a pack frame and all my trading goods, weapons, and well in short, everything I own, is in on my string of horses. Last, I take down my lodge. Using the frame poles, I make travois to carry the twenty-five-skin teepee. I know things have changed. I feel like I'm intruding. I line out my packhorses and leave the Cheyenne winter camp in the late afternoon.

I need to find a place to establish my winter camp well before snow falls. I use this as an opportunity to locate that valley deep in the Yellowstone Valley I have dreamed about. I consult the notes and directions in my journal towards the three valleys that may suit my needs. I travel to each, compare them, and make my choice. I settle north by west of the Cheyenne winter camp, close to the Crow winter camp, south of the Blackfoot winter range, deep in the Yellowstone area in a protected boxed canyon. I passed through one time never forgetting its location. It is remote and will suit my needs. I hope to avoid people for many, many years. The joy at finding this valley turns to ash in my mouth every time I think of my Cheyenne friends.

I raise my buffalo hide lodge and quickly build a smaller shelter to hold my fur and extra trade goods. The next project is building a large sturdy corral for my forty horses. I build it over a large grassy field with a creek running through its center. Next, I set out buffalo hunting. By the first snow fifteen buffalo lay securely cached on platforms in the trees around my lodge. I finish these projects as the snow begins accumulating in earnest. For weeks I keep busy cutting down additional trees. Dead trees for firewood and bigger live trees for the cabin I plan to build come spring. I leave the cabin logs where they fall after trimming off all their branches. They will season during the cold months. I stack firewood between the trees I leave standing providing shade and platforms. I keep myself busy. I do not think about how I landed in this valley while I work. I don't want to think so I push myself daily to retire at night too tired to dwell on my problems.

As it always does, and I hope always will, spring slowly arrives melting the snow around me. I've planned my cabin during the days I cannot work in the cold and snow. I reckon on living here for many years, so I want to do this right the first time. When the design is straight in my head, I set to cutting down more trees.

I lay a rock foundation and begin setting logs. Using the horses to move the logs and help muscle them in place, the cabin quickly takes shape. There are tools I need to finish the roof, to build doors and windows, and to build a hide shed. I load ten packhorses with fur and begin a ride to Bent's Fort to trade for my necessaries. I leave my horses in their corral sure they will be there on my return. The extra fur and supplies I leave in my lodge. I write a note and post it to the door of my lodge warning travelers who may stumble on my home to leave everything alone. I promise I will track them down if they don't heed my council. I am deep into the Yellowstone where few Indians and no mountain men have traveled through what I lay claim to. I leave knowing my things will be here on my return.

––––––––

White Buffalo Hunters Fall 1837

Two weeks into my trip to Bent's Fort I hear rifle fire in the early afternoon. I stop to see who's fighting. If someone is fighting Blackfoot, Sioux, or Pawnee, I may lend a hand. Otherwise I'll leave them alone. In the frame of mind I find myself, I will not pass on an opportunity to fight and release some of the resentment, rage, and frustration I carry at my circumstances.

I know it's probably not Indians. Not very many Indians have rifles, yet. After thinking things through I reckon it is a group of white men fighting Blackfoot, Pawnee, or Sioux. If so, that will be their fight, I will stay out of. I leave my horses behind creeping towards the rifle fire to spy the matter.

"*As you thought it is a group of white hunters,*" I tell myself. "*Who are they fighting?*" I creep closer to answer my own questions.

"*No, they are hunting buffalo,*" I reply to myself in anger. I'd rather not watch a hunting party killing buffalo for the army or...anyone. But done right this meeting could be of benefit to both parties. I wait for a lull in the shooting before announcing myself to the white hunters. They have located a small herd of buffalo on a wide grass field between two ridges with a clear creek running along the south ridge. When the shooting stops, I slowly ride closer until the hunters see me. There are two shooters cleaning rifles and six skinners working on the downed animals. In their camp I see a fire and two more men. A wagon is hitched to a team of four large mules. The skinners have just begun working. The two shooters watch as the small herd of buffalo walk away, out of the killing field, onto the open plains and beyond. I ride to the men working on the dozen buffalo they have down on the grass.

The hunters and skinners look at each other not recognizing me as a trapper or mountain man. From their reaction I reckon they see me as an Indian, maybe even as a warrior.

"Looks like you've had good luck," I say to the leaders, the two hunters holding rifles. One of them, the older of the pair, nods his head in understanding.

"Do you understand me?" I ask the hunting group leader in English.

"I do," he says back. "It's just sounds funny coming from a man dressed as you are," he tells me.

"Why you hunting buffalo here?" I ask.

"We are making meat for the workers at the new fort. We did not know there are trappers in the area," he tells me.

"What fort? Where is it?" I ask. Maybe I don't have to make the long ride south and east to Bent's Fort. This must be a new fort I've not heard about.

"You want to know where the new fort is and where we're taking his buffalo," repeats the old hunter. I nod my head in agreement.

"Didn't know there was a fort other than Bent's out here," I tell them. They are still looking at me funny.

"What's on your horses?" asks the other shooter, avoiding my questions.

"Furs I gathered this winter. I have need of tools and supplies and was hoping to trade for them. That's why I was heading to Bent's," I tell the hunting group leaders. The skinners have stopped their bloody work to listen.

"Where's your camp?" he asks me, still avoiding my questions. I decide to avoid his.

"Oh, behind me a ways." They don't like that answer. "Can you give me directions to this fort?"

"What do you need? If we don't have it, I can save you the trip."

"How many did you kill?" I ask the hunter's leader, again avoiding his questions.

"We have two in the wagon and ten on the ground," he tells me frustrated at the cryptic back and forth.

"Are you taking the skins and all the meat? Or just the tongues and humps?" I ask.

"No, we're taking it all, meat and the hides. We ain't wasting any of it. We'll be taking it to the fort."

"How far away is this fort?" I ask. I'm getting a bit concerned. The skinners can tell something has changed making the hunter's a bit unfriendly. I see hands closing on weapons

"What's the matter with them?" I ask the leader of the white hunters. I've reached my fill of this. "We can get mad at each other and that will lead to shooting. Or we can trust each other. My name is Uriah. I started trading with the Crow and I've been trading with the Cheyenne. My winter camp is in the Yellowstone Valley. I'm hoping to trade for another big axe for dropping trees and a couple of saws, a draw knife, and tools to make roof shingles. Satisfied?" I ask annoyed enough they can see it plain.

"I reckon I am. The fort is called Fort Union and is a three days' ride east," says their leader.

"We need to be careful here Russell," says the other hunter.

"No, I've heard of the trader Uriah. I trust you. Is that good enough?" he asks looking me square in the eyes.

"Yes, it is," I tell them.

"Okay, my name is Russell. We ain't trying to deceive you, just being careful. We were told there were no trappers in this area. You can ride to the fort with us. I know we'll have the things you need. We have coffee and food supplies also. We'll need to finish these buffalo and fill our wagons before returning to the fort. If that is acceptable you can ride with us," says the hunter's leader.

"I agree. I will look forward to meeting and talking to others at this fort," I tell the older hunter. "Your work will not be finished before the sun sets. I reckon we'll camp here tonight?" I ask. With his nod I move my horses into the trees closer to the creek for their overnight stay. The skinners work until dark finishing their grisly tasks. They retreat to their camp in the dark. All the hides and meat have been loaded. They will be riding come morning's light. We may not be friends, but we're not enemies. We watch each other cautiously throughout the night.

I wake before first light, as is my custom on the trail, in case enemies are waiting outside my camp. This morning I smell coffee on the wind. I can't help myself. I pull my blue enamel cup from my possibles and carrying my rifle and possibles over a shoulder, walk to the buffalo hunter's camp. My long hair is covered by the cougar hide shawl thrown over my shoulders.

"Look what we have here," says the cook to the buffalo hunters just getting out from their blankets.

"Can you spare a cup of coffee?" I ask the cook.

"We can, help yourself." I do.

As the sun breaks the eastern horizon, I am ready to ride. The hunter's camp is cleaned, they are packed, and ready to ride. We return to the fort in four days, just as they said, bearing an abundance of fresh meat. They receive a hero's welcome. I am shown where to put my packs of fur and my horses. But before unloading I want to see if they have what I need and how much they are paying for fur. I leave my horses inside the fort to walk inside the store.

"You must be Uriah. Russell told me about meeting you. What do you need and what did you bring for trade?" asks the clerk behind the counter.

"I've got thirty packs of prime fur I collected myself. I need a large axe, sharpening files, a foe, ropes, chains, a block and tackle if you have one, a draw knife and a spokeshave. I'll use what's left over on coffee, powder, caps, lead bars, and such."

"I have all of that. Let's go take a look at your fur. That will give me an idea of what we're trading for," says the trader thinking he's shrewd.

"Just so you know, I ain't a Pilgrim in my first year on these mountains. I have been here for a double handful of years. I've traded with the Crow and the Cheyenne and wintered with them. They know me as Angry Bear. I've fought Blackfoot, Sioux, and Pawnee. And they do not care for me. I've fought mountain lion, wolf, and grizz. I'm a good friend to those who treat me square," I tell the pompous traders. My words deflate them some. I see a change in their eyes. They see no backup in mine. Without a word we walk to my horses. Two of them look through my packs.

"Just a minute there. I don't mind you looking but stop tearing up my packs. If I choose not to trade, I'm riding out of here with everything I rode in with." They both stop and turn to face me. I hear the door slam behind me but do not turn around.

`"Well I'll be, Uriah, as I live and breathe. It is good to lay eyes on you old friend," says a voice I recognize from the past. I do not turn around. "I can see you're making friends the hard way, as usual," says Micah.

"You know this lump of buckskin and fur?" the head clerk and trader ask Micah.

"I should shout, I do. This is the man I rescued all those years ago. Together we lived and trapped with the Crow. I've kept track of you, old friend. Last I heard you was living with the Cheyenne." I turn to face my old friend.

"I was. Until a raid against the Blackfoot this fall. Things went bad and I was asked to leave the village."

"You still have your hair, your horses, and your plews. They couldn't hold you to account for everything. Seems I heard about that raid. You say they named you Angry Bear?"

"That's right."

"Russell you'd best set aside any foolish notion of cheating my old friend here. He is not a man to trifle with. If he says his fur is prime, then it is. I'd believe him without looking through them."

"That ain't how I do business," says this Russell.

"Well I reckon it was good seeing you Micah. I have a lodge deep in the Yellowstone. Stop by some time, alone," I tell my friend. I walk to my horses to leave this fort.

"Where are you going? I thought you wanted to trade" says this Russell.

"Trade, yes, not be taken advantage of. Bent will treat me

right. I know them and they know me," I say climbing onto my saddle.

"You want me to stop him Boss?" ask his helper.

"You do and both of you will be dead in less than a blink of an eye," I tell them. I feel the red berserker's rage closing in.

"You'd best back down Russell. You're in the wrong here. If Uriah leaves so am I," says Micah.

"Okay, everyone, take a breath," says Russell. "I may have acted hasty Uriah. I'll give you full value for your fur," he tells me.

"And your prices?" I ask. There is little benefit if he's fixing to raise them prices.

"Better than Bents, guaranteed," he says holding out his hand to shake. I think, looking over the fort's walls, into the sky and the floating clouds. I notice Micah nod his head.

"All right. I'll reserve judgement until we have reached an agreement."

"You are a hard man, Uriah."

"You'd best remember that, all of you," I tell the group, climbing from my saddle. I follow them inside. Russell scribbles on paper. When finished he slides it to me to read. He has agreed on a fair price for my fur. I nod in agreement.

"Now what is it that you need?" he asks me. As I list my needs, his men get it from the boxes scattered around the store making a pile on the table next to the counter. I keep adding supplies of food, powder, and lead, until both papers balance. His men take in my panniers to count my furs.

When empty, I load them with what I have purchased. Other men, good men who know how to pack a horse, balance each horse's load. With the sun at its daily midpoint we shake hands sealing the deal. I walk outside checking the knots on the pack frames. His men have done a very good job. I climb onto my saddle. Micah and Russell walk out the door.

"Feel free to return. There will be no more haggling with me. One thing, if you have horses or can get horses, I will buy all you bring me," says Russell.

"How much will you pay for a horse?" I ask him.

"It depends on the horse but if you're as good a judge of horse flesh as you are a trapper, I will pay top dollar."

"I will bring some with me this summer," I tell him.

"Uriah, would you mind if I ride with you? I'd like to talk and see where you've set your lodge," asks Micah.

"I welcome you old friend." With a smile Micah runs to his horse. He returns leading three loaded packhorses. We ride out of the fort. I hope I am truly a friend to the fort and it's not just words from Russell.

My Home

After a week on the trail we ride into my valley. It has been a good week. Micah and I catch up on the doings of the other. We are old friends once again. Along the way we skirt a trapper's camp and another hunting camp, they are close, maybe too close. I will breath deep only after they ride away.

We decide to harvest a couple of buffalo for fresh camp meat and to make jerky. I'll need much more fresh buffalo to keep Micah fed while he visits and works with me. We load a couple packhorses free of packs with our buffalo. Three days later and the short hairs on the back of my neck are standing straight. This is never a good sign. We ride west using the land to hide our presence. We take advantage of barrancas, gullies, and dry water courses to cover our trail. I do not want to be found by an unfriendly group of white hunters or Indians. Riding horses on the Plains our silhouettes will stand out...well plain. You see very few trees live on the prairie. Those that do will be found along creeks and rivers. We'll stick to the hills and valleys using the trees as cover. This is not a race, we take our time, staying out of the notice of our enemies.

Until... One afternoon the barranca we are following ends and we are forced to ride across a flat and open space. Before exposing ourselves, I look through my spy glass. I notice a grove of trees which means there is a creek which we can follow and stay hidden. Unfortunately, we'll have to cross about 200 yards of open land to get there. Not seeing anyone between us and the next ridge, we prepare to set out. That's when the shooting starts. We hunker down in the gully as the shooting continues. Whoever is shooting is not aiming at us.

From the sounds it appears that at least a half dozen rifles are involved. I can't see them. They must be in a depression.

"Who do you think it is?" Micah asks me.

"White hunters. But too much shooting for hunting. They are fighting others. We need to carefully move forward to find out."

"If you think we must. I say let them be. We can leave the horses here and go on foot," grumbles Micah. I nod my head in agreement. Checking the cap on my rifle and making sure my possibles are on my shoulder I am ready. Micah is similarly armed. A sneaking animal is instantly noticed as a predator. We walk upright but careful, heading towards the shooting. A grey cloud of burnt black powder is about 100 yards to the north. Using tall sagebrush and grass as cover we begin walking. The rifle fire is consistent. I don't hear any war cries from either side. Something ain't right.

I notice a pattern to the rifle fire. After six rifles fire, the sounds of the next weapons are much different. I'm thinking while some reload others are shooting pistols. When reloaded, the rifles fire and the pattern repeats. Whoever is out there is trained and disciplined like a squad of good soldiers. Their fire does not let up but remains constant. We are halfway to them when I see the first warrior attacking the shooters. It's a Sioux warrior. I point him out to Micah. He points out two more to me. Using our quiet signs, he tells me to take out the single warrior. He's taking the pair. We separate heading towards our targets. I'm glad it's the Sioux attacking and not two parties of white hunters. It would be too difficult to determine who is attacking who and why. This way I know my enemy, the Sioux.

At 30 yards I shoot at the first Sioux. I bring up my rifle. *"Should I wait for Micah to shoot?"* I wonder to myself. When I settle my sights on the warrior, I fire. He falls. I do not see another brave. I'll wait.

I watch where the hunters are shooting. Whoever they are after is south of me. Taking three slow and quiet steps I head south looking for more attacking Sioux warriors using the sagebrush as concealment. Another three steps, then stop to observe. Slowly I move my head to look ahead and to both sides. Nothing, three more steps. On the third repeat I see grass moving 20 yards ahead of me. This grass is moving against the wind. I lift my rifle to set the sights on the warrior hiding from my sight. I see a darker shade of brown pass through the grass, a body moving. Following along its length I find the shoulders. I aim, looking at a point above the ribs and below the arm pit. When I settle the sights on my target, I shoot. The ball flies true. I reload. The warrior stands when the .54 caliber ball hits him. Hit with my rifle ball, he is falling dead to the ground. I look for more warriors.

I hear Micah shoot. The rifle fire from the camp slows when they realize someone is out here helping them. I have a feeling there are a couple more Sioux warriors out here. Staying in place I work my eyes, looking for movement of a body, grass, or of sagebrush. Micah shoots a second time. All the shooting stops. The short hairs on the back of my neck keep rising. I turn slightly to look behind me. As I'm turning, a body slams into me, knocking my rifle out of my hands. I'm tumbling to the ground. As I slide along the grass, I pull my knife and a war axe. I roll to my feet behind a tall sagebrush. I don't want to get shot by the camp's defenders. I see him coming towards me, crawling in the tall grass. I take a knee to wait for him. I see the tops of the grass move. Judging distance, I spring towards him. Landing on his back I begin my attack with both knife and war axe. He is unable to defend himself. As he stops moving, another Sioux warrior flies at me knocking me off the first and to the ground.

The fall's taken the breath from me. I wait kneeling hoping my breathing will catch up with me and the prairie stops spinning. Things are returning to normal when he launches himself at me again. This is an older warrior. I have my hands full now. We tumble in the grass. When we stop, he's sitting on top of me. I've kept my weapons but can't bring them up to use them. The Sioux warrior has a big grin on his face. He's beginning to laugh when a rifle ball passes through his head. I shove the dead warrior off me and lay flat without moving. I do not want to be shot.

"Hello, the camp," I yell out.

"Yeah?"

"We got four or five of them."

"Come on in."

"Don't shoot, there's two of us."

"We won't, wouldn't be neighborly to shoot the very ones which helped us out of that jam, now would it?"

"No, it wouldn't. There's two of us. We're coming in," I remind the camp.

"Come on in but keep your hands away from your weapons, until we get to know you."

"All right we're coming in." Micah brings me my horse. He's holding the horses from the Sioux warriors. I enter their camp with weapons held high. I will admit I am nervous.

"I thought you said there were two of you."

"I did, and there is. My friend is waiting to see how you greet me before coming in."

"Can't fault him for that. Where'd you learn the English?"

"From Ma and Pa," I answer, wondering why he asked me that. I signal Micah to ride in.

"Coffee's on if you want to help yourselves," says the oldest man in the camp.

"That'd be good, thanks." We dig into possibles for our cups. That gets the six hunters a bit nervous. "Easy, I'm just getting my cup."

"Put them up boys. I reckon they done us a good deed. Hold up your cup," says the leader.

"But they're Indians. How can we trust them?"

"We ain't Indians you idgit," says Micah. "You were fighting Sioux. They are our enemy too. We're trappers. Ain't you never seen a trapper before?"

"See there. Now relax. They are here because I invited them to come in. Understand?"

"Yeah, I got it, but I still don't like it," pouts the slow one in the bunch.

"Would it make a difference if I told you I'm American as you?" I ask the resentful man.

"How can I believe you?" he asks me.

"You won't take my word for it?"

"No, I don't trust any Indians," he says getting puffed up.

"I'll be going then. My name is Uriah this is Micah. Ask around, people know us and will vouch for me. And what's your name?" I ask the Indian hater.

"None of your business. I feel the same for a white man that's gone Indian. You just as well be gone," he spits out.

"All right," I tell him. Turning to the camp boss I continue, "There's another Sioux hunting party about five to ten miles ahead of you. I'd be careful if I was you," I tell him walking away. The hateful one grabs my arm.

"What do you..." he doesn't finish his thought. I have him on the ground with my knife at this throat.

"I should kill you now. It will save me the trouble in the future. But I ain't going to do it," I tell him. I let him up. Turning to the camp boss I say, "This one is going to get all of you in trouble. But what I said is true. Be careful as you leave from here. The Sioux are out there."

"He's lying Boss," he screams. Micah looks on with his hand close to the hammer of his rifle.

"And if he ain't?" asks the camp's leader.

"I still don't believe them." We put away our cups and walk out of their camp. I begin speaking to Micah.

"We are not welcome in their camp. Let's be on our..." a rifle ball missing my head but passing close to my right ear stops me from finishing. I grab my war axe, turn, and release it at the shooter, the Indian hater. The axe lands in his forehead. Micah waits sitting on his horse with his rifle aimed at the hunter's camp, ready to shoot. I walk back into their camp. I stop at the dead man.

"We helped you by killing more Sioux warriors than your bunch does. I will not help you again. You can thank this man," I tell him bending down to get my war axe. I wipe the blade on his shirt. I take his rifle, possibles, and belt with a pistol and knife. "We could have been friends. You let one man ruin it for all of you. I wish you well against the Sioux, you're going to need it." I turn to join Micah. Together we walk to the dead Sioux warriors. We take the weapons from each man we killed. We walk to our horses. As we ride away from the hunting camp they are still standing there. They haven't moved. They will not last long out here on the prairie against the Sioux.

"Some men should not be out here," says Micah. I heartily agree.

Knowing they are there, we ride a wide circle around the camp. Right about that time shooting from the white hunters starts up again. Hearing the shooting we use the time to ride away, far away, and quick. I reckon it a shame that five men have to pay with their lives for the ignorance and fear of one man. We ride away without looking back.

Micah spends two weeks with me helping me work on the cabin and the fur shed. When he's reached his limit he tells me he is riding on.

"Feel free to visit any time, old friend," I tell him.

"Thanks for the invite. I'll be back."

"Where you heading?"

"I think I'll winter with the Crow again. I'm going to make my way to them."

"Thanks for the help. Ride wary," I tell him. With a wave he is gone. I work arranging things inside the cabin. Fur and trade goods go into the shed. When finished, I look out over the corral at my horses.

"I reckon they would winter better if there were less of them," I tell the wind. I walk

over to begin the cull. I will start by taking ten to Fort Union. If I get a good price I may try selling more. If not, well I can still collect fur. I'll bring five horses to return with my supplies.

Having made my choice, I join them together with a lead rope. I set out for Fort Union, leaving the same dire warning promising trespassers retribution if they choose to raid my home and horses.

I make the ride in ten days. I want to arrive with the horses strong and filled out. I'm aiming for top dollar. When I ride through the gates, I notice the place is crawling with people, trappers, hunters, and Indians. I make my deal without coming down from my price. I am offered money or credit. I hand over a list of supplies and ask for gold coins to cover the remainder. I do not want to receive the coins with others in the store but cannot wait for all of them to leave. I accept the coins. I will be extra observant tonight, my last night in the fort and on my return ride.

"Uriah," yells the leader of the twenty-five trappers sitting down by the fire. They have turned in their plews here rather than at rendezvous. "Join us. You know if you didn't have bad luck, you'd not have any," he tells me, handing me a bottle of the house-made whiskey. I do not drink. I pass the bottle to the man on my left.

"That may be true, boys, but it always works out for me in the end," I tell them laughing at my calamities.

"How's that Uriah?" asks the leader of this pack of free trappers.

"Well, after everything is ironed out, I always end up with what I was after and a bit more," I tell the trappers in the company.

"How does that work?" asks the bully of the bunch. If anyone is going to end up with more, he wants to be close so he can get a part of the loot. Me, I seem to attract the bullies.

"If I remember correctly, on your way to the mountains that very first time, you was way laid by the Blackfoot and Cheyenne. And you told us yourself that pirates robbed the paddle wheeler carrying your horses and your fur. You told us you've lost your rifles, your pistols, and all your possibles. All your traps and plunder was gone, stolen by the pirates. Ain't that right?"

"Yes, and no. Micah saved me two days after I was left by the Blackfoot. He took me to the Crows. They helped me recover. Micah took me in as a partner. The next year we sold more fur than ol' Micah had ever trapped in a season."

"And yes, the pirates took everything. All I was left with was the clothes on my back and the weapons I carried on me," I admit. "But like everything else you only listened to half the story. You left out Nate and I killed all the pirates, fired their boat, and reached St. Louis with more horses, fur, and weapons than we left with that spring. So, you see that no matter what, I came out ahead," I tell the bully

"I don't count that coming out the better after suffering like that?" announces the bully.

"Well then that's where you and I will disagree," I tell him ending my part of the conversation, at least with him.

"Well sir, I was robbed one time," begins another trapper. "Two days later I come across those same two hoodlums. They'd made a camp. Somehow or another they got their hands on a bottle of moonshine. When I came across them, they was all but dead having drank a jar between the pair. Well the first thing I did was truss them two worthless outlaws' hand and foot. Then I cooked bacon and made coffee. I had plenty of time, the sun had just gone down. I took a look at what they had in their packs. I separated mine from theirs. I saddled my horse and repacked my loot on my packhorses. Of course, I filled the packs to the brim from their stores. I set aside their weapons and possibles. Then I topped off my possibles from their stores. Everything else I spread out on a sheet of canvas. Anything that would get me in trouble if found on my packhorse, I kept out. The remainder I repacked and loaded on their packhorses. Next, I looked at their weapons. They had plenty. I took all their knives and war axes, all their powder and the lead that fit my .54 caliber. The lead that was a different caliber I packed away to melt down. I packed away all the flintlock weapons, keeping out the percussion caped. I was going to trade the flint shooters for capped weapons. Any clean clothes and blankets I kept. The dirty stuff I left behind to burn before leaving the camp. I cut their moccasins off their feet, then sliced their pants and shirts. Now I was ready to go. I threw their cut-up clothes and blankets on the fire then rode off."

"I can see you got back at them, but you still suffered at their hands?" says that same bully trapper. "Ain't nothing you can say that will change my mind."

"Well, in addition to my horse and packhorses, I now had two extra loaded packhorses and two extra riding horses. I had four extra rifles and six pistols. I had provisions for two months and I was not feeling the winter's cold. I left their camp with more than I had."

"How long did that last you?" laughs another in the company of trappers.

"It lasted only until I ran into the grizz that killed the four extra horses and nearly killed me," says the youngster.

"That's exactly what I mean," says the bully.

"Since you ain't listening I ain't talking to you," the young trapper tells the bully who sees this as an affront.

"Why I ought to whip your..." he blusters until I interrupt him.

"These are our stories and if you don't believe them and refuse to sit quiet, it's time for you to move on," I tell him. At first, he can't understand I'm standing up to him. He doesn't understand what I said. All he knows is I took him down a peg in the eyes of the others. That will certainly not do, no sir. He's been with the company too long to put up with such insolence. Besides, he knows I'll be on my way tomorrow. By fall, everyone in the Stonies will know I told him off. He can't have that. He stands up.

"I reckon you have me to answer to. You and your tall tales," he laughs at me.

"Sit down I'm not in the mood to tangle with you," I tell him.

"Ain't that what I was telling you boys? Pure yellow," he laughs. I take a good at look at the bully trapper. He got a couple inches on me standing in boots like he is.

"*Why is he wearing boots?*" I ask myself, "*he should be wearing moccasins like the rest of us.*" He outweighs me by at least fifty pounds but all of it is plainly extra weight, pure lard. His nose has been repeatedly broke. I know why now. I stand to my feet.

"How do you want to do this? Fists and stop at first blood?" I ask.

"No, that's for sissy boys," he yells drawing a knife and axe. I don't recognize the make of either. I hand my gun belt to the man sitting next to me. I pull my Cheyenne knife and war axe. All the trappers sitting around the fire stand to their feet. This gets the attention of the brigade's captain.

"Not again. John if you fight Uriah, I'm going to throw you out of our company," he tells the enraged bully who is making a show of cracking his knuckles.

"Uriah...never mind," he tells me. I take off my cougar cape, my blanket coat, my Cheyenne war shirt, and my last good store-bought shirt.

"What tribe did you winter with?" the captain asks me, looking at my war shirt.

"Cheyenne for longer than I can remember," I tell him warming my muscles.

"How long you been up here?"

"Since 1833." He retreats from us shaking his head. "You're a fool John."

"I'll take care of you after this little man," boasts the bully.

We circle each other. I like to wait to plant my shoulder in my opponent's stomach and toss him over my head when he rushes me. I find this takes the starch from most men. I know I can do it to the tub in front of me, then rethink my strategy. I rush in delivering the fist holding my knife, to his jaw, then my second fist to the other side of his jaw. He is too slow to block either blow. The cracking is clear enough for all of us to hear. John does not say a word. Without disruption, I begin pounding under the reversed V of his rib cage, one blow after another until I tire. I watch as the light leaves his eyes. He crumbles into a still pile. There is no sound or movement from my victim. All the pain of Nate leaving me, of the forced separation from Micah and the Crow, up to the Cheyenne asking me to leave their village, fires my rage. I thought I worked through it all, well apparently not. John pays with his life as I erupt, my seething, pent-up fury and anger finding release.

I stand, mad he will not absorb more abuse. I scream out my frustration. Russell and the captain throw a bucket each of freezing creek water on me. My rage boils the water turning it to steam as it dries on my body. Once dry the cold draws the frenzy and fury from me. I drop my bladed weapons, docile. I'm pliable as the captain dresses me against the cold night air. Dressed, he helps me to my seat. The company of trappers look on in shock. They have never witnessed such a spectacle. Two of the wiser trappers tow the body away from the fire. Slowly the red haze and berserker rage leave me.

"Where'd you run into Grizz?" I ask the young trapper, taking up where our conversation left the rails. It takes a minute for everyone to process what they've seen, but the youngest member of the free trappers takes up his story from where he left off.

"It was after Rendezvous. I don't remember where exactly because I was lost. I cross a river riding north. Many days later, I miss-remember exactly how many, I was on the prairie. One night I hear the most awful growls I ever hope never to hear again. The horses are fussing. They couldn't run off because I tied them to a picket rope and hobbled their front legs. Well those horses attracted that grizz. I kept my riding horse close to my blankets, just like I was told. After shooting that Grizz, I meet up with this bunch..." he continues on. I do not hear anything but the wind in the trees.

"You won't believe me but, well that Grizz lit into them horses like he was killing mad. I jump up and commence to shooting him. I emptied three rifles and six pistols, all .54 caliber, all capped weapons. Halfway through the shooting, that Grizz turns to me and begins walking towards me on his two back feet. After that last pistol ball hit his chest he falls forward. Just like a tall tree as it's cut down. I remember the dust flying up and making a cloud as he splats. He kind of bounces up, but only an inch or two, then falls flat. I reload my best rifle like Hugh told me to, and check if that Grizz is dead or not."

"How'd you check, Kid?" asks one of the trappers.

"I poked the Grizz in an eye."

"Yeah, that's good. I reckon that's the best way," agrees another.

"What about them horses?" asks yet another.

"Well, two are dead right off. I try doctoring the other pair but can tell they ain't going to make it. I shoot all four to end their suffering. Then I pack up the camp."

"What about the Grizz? Didn't you skin him out?"

"To tell you the truth I was feeling so poorly about them four horses that I plumb forgot. Right about then a pair of buffalo hunters ride into my camp. They heard all the shooting. It woke them and they came to see if I was alright or attacked by Indians. They could see what happened. One of them went back for four horses and a couple skinners. They help me load my plunder on their four horses while two skinners take care of that Grizz. That's the rug I keep with my blankets. These are his claws," says the kid, rattling the necklace made of grizzly claws.

"The skinner cuts up that Grizz and pack him to their camp. This buffalo hunting camp was less than a mile from my camp. I couldn't sleep so we made coffee and throw strips of that Grizz on the fire to cook. At first, I wasn't too sure I wanted to eat that dang Grizz but after watching them buffalo hunters, I got hungry. That's where I learned to cook. Their cook also showed me how to bake bread too."

"Did you ride off come daylight?"

"No, I stayed with them for about a year. The hunter paid me for skinning buffalo. He also gave me a flintlock rifle and two pistols they had extra. I learned how to kill buffalo, how to skin them, and how to cook hump steaks. Yes sir, truth be told I should have paid him, he taught me so much. But he paid me gold coins for that year's work. I used the gold to reoutfit the next fall and headed back to the mountains."

"Have any other trouble like that Ol' Pete?" asks the captain of a different company of trappers.

"Well as you know, yes I did. I'd only been in the mountains about a week. I had no idea where I was. One night the Blackfoot come into my camp. They caught me. They took everything for themselves, except for the knife in my moccasins. They tied me to a tree for the rest of the night as they poured through my packs. They ruined everything. They didn't see a couple pistols in the bottom of a pannier. All the pack frames and panniers they threw in a pile. All my supplies they threw on top of the pile. When they ride off, they leave behind the pile of goods."

"Come morning they are riding as the sun is rising. I'm running behind them tied by my own rope to my horse ridden by one of the warriors. Three days I run after them Blackfoot. I eat a couple pieces of jerky and water while they're feasting on buffalo, my buffalo. In the middle of the fourth day they stop at a creek to get out their foofaraws. They gussy up for their arrival into the main camp. In the middle of their camp I'm tied to a post. A young girl gives me water and jerky. The older women beat me with sticks."

"I got to admit things were looking bleak. I kind of lost

hope. And I forgot about the knife I had hid away. The late afternoon on the fourth day I hear horses thundering towards the camp. I know they ain't Blackfoot. Young and old are grabbing weapons. No one is paying attention to me. That young girl comes back and cuts me free. She pulls me into the lodge behind where I'd been sitting. Inside are my weapons and possibles. I grab them up. I see empty parfleche, so I grab them and load up all the extras, the pistols, some jerky, and grab my haversack. I'm in desperate need of clean clothes. Inside the haversack is my buckskins. Grabbing all I can hold, we run. She's leading and I follow. We stop in the trees. I load my rifle and my two pistols. Then we wait."

"What were you waiting for?"

"That's what I wanted to know but I can't talk with her. Well the noise dies down. The Blackfoot have been driven away. The drivers are feasting at the fire. The girl wants to leave but not me. She grabs my hand and pulls. Well, I go. We walk to the fire. All the talking stops. She see's someone she knows, a warrior. Turns out they are Shoshone, and this is her brother. Well, they take me with them, after I change into my buckskins. They give me a horse and finds someone who knows American. A warrior tells me I can ride with them or stay here. I choose to ride with them. I convince them to ride to my old camp. I sort through the mess them Blackfoot made of my goods. I find the pair of pistols, my possibles, and my traps. I stay with them for a couple of months learning their language and hunting with them. Now it's winter. I'm given a small lodge. Through the winter I can come and go. I hunt and ride with them. Come spring I tell them I want to find white trappers. They tell me where Rendezvous will take place. Six warriors will escort me to Rendezvous. I'm ready, leaving the Shoshone camp with six horses, but I'm almost out of powder. Four of the horses carry the furs I collected through winter. Friends and family of the girl bring me four more horses carrying furs. That's how I resupply myself for this year."

"That's an interesting story, but is it true?"

"Yes sir, it is. There's some at Rendezvous that know me at different times. They stood up for me when I explain my story to the Booshway at Rendezvous."

"That's true Captain. I seen them and I heard the stories at the time. I couldn't believe it and wanted to double check it for myself. And I did. What he says, it happened. The only thing is, well, don't take it wrong, but I won't be riding with you. No sir. I wouldn't wish what happens to you on anyone," laughs his friend joking.

"I understand. It's okay." The rest of the hardened trappers are laughing, but quietly.

"There ain't too many that want to ride with me. Except for one old trapper that all the others hold in great esteem. He walks to the fire and stands in front of me. I'm thinking, how'd I make this man, this legend among trappers mad at me? I'm ready to receive his best punch. Well he looks down at me and with a slight smile on his face extends his hand down to me."

"I'll welcome you in my camp. You can ride with me if you want," he tells me. "Well now, I look him up and down really good. I'm wanting to make sure he's real, not one of them figments. He's real enough. I nod my head in agreement because I can't trust my voice. I pack my gear and fur on nine horses and riding my buffalo horse, move to his camp. I unload my furs and cover them, stake out my horses, except for my buffalo horse. He stays close to me, right where I'm sleeping. I add my supplies to his. I reckon I'd better contribute so I cook supper, buffalo, and bread. I get the coffee on first. He watches as I add the grounds to the old sock I use. He looks up at me with an obvious question on his face, but don't ask me."

"I don't like grounds in my coffee," I tell him. "I have him figured to be a man of few words. If it's good for him, well then, it'll be good for me."

"He's watching me thread strips of buffalo on them skewers and get them to sizzling next to the fire. When I begin mixing bread dough, he's especially paying attention. He don't pack flour. Says making bread takes too long in a trapper's camp."

"He's watching me twirl that thick bread dough around a skewer and add it close to the fire. He looks up and shakes his head at me. I can tell he's getting ready to say something, but it takes him awhile to get the right words sorted."

"That there is a neat trick. Mayhap I need to learn me it," he says.

"I'd be right glad to show you. It ain't hard, especially if you like hot bread at night or come a morning," I tell him. "I turn the buffalo and the bread. When it's done, I begin eating directly off the stick. He does the same. In between bites I can see a smile on his face. I reckon I'd better explain myself, to him."

"You know Hugh, I like to pull supper directly from the skewer because it saves me from washing dishes. That's something I hate to do. All I have to do is put away the skewers and I'm done."

"That's good," he adds. By the time the sun has set, the coffee pot is empty. I prepare it for the morning before hitting my blankets. That thoughtfulness earns me another nod from Hugh. He's awake before me, but that's okay. I smell coffee, buffalo, and bread cooking. From then on, we get along well."

There is a quiet after the kid recounts his story. I reckon this is a good time for me to break in.

"I'll be leaving come the sun. Sorry for disrupting the peace of your camp. Sorry for losing my temper. I've had a bad year," I tell the surprised group. They do not say a word as I walk away.

I find the bully's horses, packs of furs, and weapons, next to my blankets. I leave as soon as the company of trappers fall asleep.

The Mountains

Things have been quiet for a couple of years. Well, truth to tell, I have lost track of the years. But that don't mean I've grown lazy. I remember the hard-learned lessons from the Crow, the Cheyenne, and Micah. I continue to trap some beaver but mostly other critters. I've been away from the cabin for two days. I'm planning on returning come the morning. I reckon I let my thinking overpower my carefulness.

I notice the sagebrush in front of me part to reveal the first Blackfoot warrior. The Indian is pulling back the arrow on his bow's string. I shoot stopping him in his tracks. Dropping my plews I shrug my shoulders moving the rifle from my back into my hands. Glancing at the cap as it passes by my eye, I make sure the rifle is ready to fire. It is. Grasping the fore stock with my left hand I bring the rifle up, planting it in the pocket of my shoulder. As the rifle settles in, I thumb back the hammer. Each move is automatic, having been performed many times during these past seven years. Moving the blade of the front sight to the chest of the warrior in front of me, I pull the trigger.

The cap sparks, there's a small crack, the spark travels through the nipple landing on the seventy-five grains of black powder under the round ball. The powder catches fire pushing the lead ball down the barrel. I do not notice the

307

recoil; I'm concentrating on keeping the blade of the sight centered on the warrior's chest. The lines bored into the barrel during construction begin turning and accelerating the lead ball. The explosion pushes the tightly bound ball out of the barrel. The ball spits out accompanied with two feet of still burning black powder and a blue cloud. I hold the rifle still through the shot, from pulling the trigger until seeing the ball connect with the Blackfoot warrior's chest. As the warrior is pushed to the ground, I lower my rifle to begin the reloading process.

To speed up the process I pour powder directly down the still warm barrel from the powder horn. Yeah, I know I've been warned not to reload from the powder horn like that but I'm in a fight and I need all the breaks I can make for myself. I have no way to measure the charge. However, having done this before I have a hunch when enough is delivered. Placing the board holding a patched round ball over the rifle's open barrel I force the ball down the tight space. Using a starter, I get the ball about five inches deep. Dragging the ramrod from its spot under the barrel it forces the ball to seat on the unknown quantity of English FFg black powder. Jerking the rod from the barrel I drop it on the ground. Taking the capping tool in hand I add a percussion cap to the nipple. Finished I bring the loaded rifle to my shoulder.

It automatically finds the pocket of my shoulder as I watch a second warrior rise from the grassland. Pulling the hammer back I line the blade of the front sight, on the warrior's chest. Satisfied with the alignment I pull the trigger. With this shot the rifle slams back into my shoulder. This time I notice the recoil. Pushing it away from my mind I'm keeping the front sight on the Blackfoot. The ball travels up the barrel a bit faster with this load. As the ball clears the barrel it is followed by four feet of still burning black powder and a much bigger foul-smelling cloud. The Blackfoot is picked up off his feet and slammed backwards, to land in a mud puddle.

From the corner of my eye I see more movement. Turning my head, I see a third warrior charging towards me. Unable to reload in time, I drop the rifle, pulling a fighting knife with my right hand and a Blackfoot war axe with my left. I left behind all my pistols not thinking they would be needed. For a brief part of a second, I chide himself for the omission. I reckon I almost deserve what I'm getting. "No" I scream resolving never to repeat the mistake. As the rifle falls from my hands time slows down. My hands act without specific input from my mind. I'm watching the warrior charging towards me.

Feeling as if I'm swimming against the tide, I bring up both bladed weapons. Squaring both shoulders to meet my attacker head on I bend my knees. As I'm watching, my vision narrows until all I'm looking at is the Blackfoot running at me in a tunnel. With a primal yell I begin running towards my adversary. The action shatters the swimming feeling. The yell shatters the tunnel restricting the sight of warrior in front of me. Both of us are screaming.

We meet. The crash alarms the birds taking refuge in the nearest trees. They fly off. The squirrels are no longer heard. Meeting together, chest to chest, both warriors are forced to the ground. Gaining my knees before the Indian, I grasp the legs of my opponent. Bringing up the war axe over my shoulder I bury it in the Indian's shoulder. The Blackfoot, ignoring the war axe buried in his left shoulder raises the knife in his left hand. Reflecting rictus, the knife slams against my arm. The knife cuts through my buckskin shirt, the flannel shirt under, and the hard muscles of my arm. With another great scream, I lift the war axe for a second strike. This one is deadly, ending the short but intense fight. Chest to chest I watch as the fires of hate are extinguished in the face of the warrior. Supporting only a body, I let the Blackfoot fall to the grass.

The fight has leaves me exhausted. With a Herculean effort I rise to my feet. Spying my rifle in the grass I bend to retrieve it. Noticing the ramrod, I bend a second time and pick it up. Reloading quickly, I stand, looking around for my next fight. My shoulders slump, finally, at not finding another Blackfoot. Slipping the rifle over a shoulder and onto my back I pick up my furs and beaver skins. Six to an arm I trudge toward my camp.

"Coffee ready?" I ask myself, smelling the refreshing aroma as the reviving begins. I look up noticing the white clouds in the blue sky. Why is it I only notice clouds after a gunfight? I stand to pour my cup full and take a sip of the hot coffee. Now I know I'm alive. I made it through another fight. Finishing that first cup I begin loading the camp on my pack-horses. After four days off they are ready to return home also.

I leave the campsite after collecting 57 beaver plews, two spring black bears, five wolves, and three buffalo. Not bad for a four-day camp. Now it's time to ride home to the cabin. "I'll need to bring in buffalo to make winter meat and the wood pile is almost finished," I think to myself climbing into the saddle for the two-day ride home.

8

MICAH RETURNS

I NOTICE TWO RIDERS APPROACHING THE CABIN AS IF they have an invitation. Behind the much smaller second rider are over a dozen heavily burdened packhorses. I stop counting at twelve and concentrate on the riders. There is something I recognize about the large Mountain Man riding in front, leading his partner and their string of horses. I can't put a name to him. I am not alarmed. The short hairs on the back of my head lay flat. I cannot place why I feel a sense of familiarity. I watch them approach through the opened door from well inside the cabin. I am still a cautious man. Walking to the open door, I take two pistols from the table by the door thrusting them in my belt. I slide my possibles over a shoulder, take up my rifle, and only then walk out the door. I stop in the center of the rock floor I painstakingly laid on the ground outside the door. The rock floor cuts down the mud I track into the cabin. Today it gives my feet solid purchase in case I find myself in a gunfight with the two strangers.

The leader stops twenty yards from me. I see a deeply tanned face. A fox fur covers the upper half of his face. The wolf fur around the collar of the buffalo coat hides the bottom of his face. His partner is dressed in the same fashion, only a smaller version.

"Good day to you," he says to me. The scales fall, recognition shoots across my mind. I can almost feel it when I understand. I know who he is, but not the smaller man to his side.

"Micah, been awhile. How are you? Glad you found me?" I ask my old friend.

"Everyone in the Stonies is talking about you, Uriah," he tells me.

"Why?" I simply ask concerned at being the center of mountain gossip.

"We've heard about fighting with the Cheyenne and the bad deal they gave you. No one knows where you are but me. Only that you rode out deep into the Yellowstone's. When I remembered riding past here a few years ago I recalled you saying you'll return some day. For me it was easy to retrace our steps and find you. It will not be so easy for anyone else."

"What others?" I ask without moving.

"Don't worry no one is interested in you more than in spreading gossip. You're safe."

"Who'd you bring with you?"

"This is my Crow wife Rainbow." She throws back the

wolf hair collar and takes off the fox fur cover and shawl so I can see her face. I recognize a Crow woman, a young Crow woman.

"How did a dried up, ne'er-do-well, ol' mountain man like you end up with a young wife like Rainbow here?" I ask with a smile.

"I was lucky, I reckon," he laughs.

"How many horses did this miscreant pay your poor father, Rainbow?" I ask her in Crow.

"Eight," she laughs with a hand in front of her mouth. I walk off the rock floor to their horses.

"Since you're here you may as well make yourselves at home," I tell him. Micah throws his left leg over his saddle, slides down to the ground, and envelopes me in a giant hug. He lifts me off my feet while squeezing.

"Easy old friend, I feel a rib or two close to breaking."

"When did you grow soft?" he asks, me setting me down. "How's your meat bag?"

"Bare, I was fixing to go hunting here in the next few days."

"It's a mighty terrible thing when a guest has to supply the fixings. "Rainbow," he tells her, "where is that haunch of buffalo?"

"I will find it. You unload the horses and let them roll," she tells him sliding to the ground from her saddle.

"Add your flea-bitten nags with my horses. Just so you

know, mine are the healthy-looking ones. Unlike the bags of bones, you're calling horses.

"Well now, since you're so concerned about the condition of my horses, we'll take yours when we leave to go hunting come the morning," he tells me, leading the horses to my large corral.

"If you have buffalo hump why we going hunting?" I ask him confused.

"We'll finish that off tonight. You can't expect me to work without at least feeding me, now can you?"

"Work? What work are you talking about? Have you gone addled in your old age?"

"Me addled? You're the one making your guests hunt their own meat. I thought I taught you better manners than that," roars Micah, then exploding in a fit of laughter. Rainbow pays us no mind carrying half a buffalo hump inside the cabin. I hear the door slam closed.

"It's good to see you old friend," I tell him.

"Same here," he says accompanied with a hearty slap to my back. I lead the packhorses to the fur shed. We unload Micah's panniers before releasing his packhorses in the corral.

When we're finished, Rainbow has a fire under the buffalo hump on a spit, in the outside firepit. My coffee pot sits on the rock, almost to the boiling point. Micah and I catch up, the years seem to disappear. While we talk, eat, and drink coffee Rainbow erects their fifteen buffalo-hide lodge. She joins us at the fire as the sun sinks below the western horizon.

When my canyon is covered by the night's black, we separate. I head inside. Micah and Rainbow head towards their lodge. I fall asleep glad they are both here.

The three of us sit our saddles as the sun begins rising. Micah leads. He says he knows he can relocate the game spotted on their way to my valley. We set up camp off a feeder creek, off a creek that flows into the Yellowstone River. Micah deems it important to rest the horses for a couple of days. The weather is excellent, the game abundant, and we have nowhere else to be. I am returning to camp with a freshly killed Mule Deer slung over one of my packhorses. He is nervous carrying this burden smelling of fresh blood. Reassurance from me in the form of pats and a soft voice settles his nerves enough to carry the burden. I sling my rifle over a shoulder thinking my shooting is finished for the day. That is until we ride past a large boulder, part of a substantial rock formation. The horses know something I didn't but should. I would have noticed the fear and urgency displayed by the horse's ears, if I was paying attention. But I wasn't. My thoughts are stuck in the past.

When the packhorse starts pulling on the lead rope I pull back. When he stops and refuses to move ahead, I climb from my saddle to reassure him some more. This time, nothing I do will settle him. I should know something is not right. If my steadiest packhorse is feeling anxious, well something is not right. As I check the ropes tying the deer to the pack saddle, I see a shadow from the corner of my eye. As the shadow moves, I turn my body in the direction my eyes are looking. I hear a snarl, a warning I will never forget, the shadow launches itself at me and my packhorse. I drop the reins to my saddle horse to pull a pistol from my belt. A mature male cougar is flying towards me in very slow motion. Several things happen during the short flight. My saddle horse runs down the trail, away from the danger. My packhorse tries to run off. I'm watching the grey body hurtling towards me as I'm working a pistol from my belt, left-handed. My right hand is holding the packhorse's lead rope. I notice the black fur at the tip of his ears, nose, and tail. I see a white patch centered over his chest. That's when I see the claws are extended ready to kill.

I finally have a pistol out. As I raise it to aim and shoot, the packhorse decides to run. Holding the lead rope, I'm dragged forward. The angry cat lands in the middle of an empty trail. As the cat lands, he turns. Now I swear he makes that turn without a paw touching the ground. I stand, amazed at the dexterity and grace of the cat. He is now standing facing me fiercely indignant after not securing a meal and mad at missing his target, either the packhorse or me. He lets out another aggressive violent growl with a snarl. The clearly enraged cat is facing me, defiant. He launches himself at the only target left, me.

As he leaps, clearing the ground, I see the white patch. Using that as a target I fire my pistol. I drop it, immediately grabbing for my second weapon. My right hand grasps the war axe, my left fumbles for a pistol. At the shot there is a quick growl then a long, drawn out roar. The cat is within touching range. I raise the war axe and deliver it to the cat's head as he flies into me. The collision drives me to the dirt. I lay trapped, struggling to drag in a fresh breath of air. I'm at the point of panic when the sweet breath of the wind fills my lungs. I quickly exhale and draw in a second breath. Only then do I remember the cat. Both hands are empty of weapons. The second pistol is laying in the dirt, feet from me, useless. I see the war axe buried to the handle in the crown of the cat's head. The only weapon left is my knife. I pull it, just in case.

The feline eyes stare into mine, separated by less than two feet. I watch as the fire and rage burn out. With a sigh, the last breath leaves the magnificent cat, the body deflates. The sight reminds me of the time I seen what's called a flying balloon crash to the earth, lose its air, and deflate. I move a hand to an itch on my chest. I look down, it comes away red. I fumble pushing the cat off my chest as time resumes its normal course.

The front of my last cotton store-bought shirt is in taters and slowly turning red. Laying in the dirt I pull the shirt open to survey the damage. There are eight scratches down my chest. I think these are the rear claws. The front feet hit my arms. Those scratches are not too bad. It could have been much worse. Usually the rear claws rip open the stomach of their intended victim. This time I stopped the attack in time, with the pistol shot and the war axe. I count myself extremely lucky. Seeing the wounds melts the lethargy I was feeling only minutes ago. The attack renews my love of life. I have to lay back down. I don't know how much time passes, but I hear horses up the trail heading my way. The sounds force me to my feet. There is Micah leading my two horses.

"I reckon you lost these horses?" he asks me. I do not reply. His eyes look over the scene.

"You best sit. Let me look at them wounds," he says, digging in his saddlebags. He comes out with a bottle of cheap, gut rotting, whiskey. Using the back part of my shredded shirt he washes the cuts to my chest, then arms.

"You was lucky to shoot him before he landed on you. The war axe in the head is a nice touch," he laughs.

"I wasn't paying attention. The rifle was slung over a shoulder. I've learned the hard way. That won't happen again. I reckon the past will stay in the past." Micah looks at me like I'm blabbering. I reckon mayhap I am.

"Good, you ready to get on with the next part of your life?"

"Yes I am. Thanks for your help." I'm thinking he means getting on with my life in the hidden valley. He was not.

"That's what partners are for," He tells me. He helps me to my feet then leads the horses off the trail to a patch of grass. I pick up my pistols and walk to a rock at the side of the trail to sit down. Using more of the scraps from my shirt I clean both weapons, my rifle and pistol, then reload them. Micah picks up the cat and brings him to the front edge of the grass. He hands me my war axe. I wipe it clean and add the weapons to my belt. Together we skin the cougar. Taking the prime cuts, we tie them to the skittish packhorse. With gentle but forceful encouragement Micah gets the horse to cooperate. Climbing onto our saddles Micah leads me to our camp. My packhorse follows Micah. He has a couple of superficial cuts but is otherwise unhurt.

As we ride in Rainbow is quickly at my side. At her encouragement I climb from the saddle handing the reins and lead rope to Micah. As he takes care of the horses I submit to Rainbow's care. She rewashes the cuts, making a paste of herbs and what looks like weeds, applying the mixture generously to each cut. I can feel the heat leaving the wounds. Rainbow hands me a cup of coffee and joins Micah in hanging the deer in a tree and slicing the best parts from the cougar for our supper. Adding the cougar meat that remains in a canvas bag, it quickly joins the deer hanging in the tree.

`"I reckon a couple more days of rest will not hurt us," says Micah as we share another meal. Rainbow nods her head in agreement. I ask for another slice of meat.

`"I noticed pan-sized fish in the creek," adds Rainbow. We both look at her, nodding our heads, she smiles. After supper I watch Rainbow making a fishing spear. She is going fishing first thing in the morning.

As the sun begins thinking about rising and starting the day, Rainbow is fishing. After a cup of coffee, I follow

Rainbow to the creek, to watch. Careful to keep her shadow away from the water, she slowly approaches the creek. She knows right where the fish hide. She is wearing pants fashioned from old and well-cured buffalo hide lodge coverings. Taking off her moccasins and rolling up the legs of her pants she slowly and carefully enters the cold water. I've not tried fishing with a spear. For now, I'm content to simply watch Rainbow. Holding the tip of the spear just above the water she readies for a quick strike. It does not take long before a fish swims by. I see the smile beginning on her face. I pay closer attention to what she's doing. The thrust of her spear is faster than my eyes can follow. It's a blur. With a wide smile and a modest screech, she lifts and twists her spear, throwing a fish on the bank. I run over and trap it from flopping back to the water. I'm so caught up watching her fish that I don't hear Micah walk up behind me.

"What..." he begins, but before he can finish the thought, Rainbow hisses him to silence, without taking her eyes from the water. In a second flash, another large trout is flying out of the water to the grassy bank. Micah grabs it and delivers a blow to the back of its head with a knife handle. I point to the first one. His eyes light up. We both turn to look when a petite cry comes from Rainbow. Her eyes grow big, with great effort she flings a third fish to the grass. The last is clearly the biggest, larger by several inches in length. With a wide smile and laughing, Rainbow begins climbing out of the water.

Micah walks over to help her out. I knock the fish in the back of the head, like Micah did.

I take the fish to the edge of the creek and begin cleaning them. After a rinse I hand them to Rainbow. Taking a long stick with a fork at the end, from a back pocket, Rainbow threads her fish through a gill. Still laughing she heads back to camp. Along the way she stops to pick up additional long sticks.

"What are those sticks for?" I ask Micah.

"That's how she's going to cook them," he tells me, like I should already know this. At camp Rainbow takes her fish off the forked stick. Threading a stick just a bit into the head of the fish she places the trout over the fire. Quickly six skewers holding bread dough join the three holding the fish. As the coffee heats I watch, hungry and actually anticipating a meal for the first time in many moons.

After the feast we sit back sated, enjoying the morning. I rest most of the day letting the claw wounds close and heal. Micah and Rainbow ride off with their rifles looking for game. Two shots wake me. I must have fallen asleep next to the fire. I gather my rifle and pistols, checking their loads and the caps. When ready, I wait to see what trouble my friend has landed in. The wait is not long. They return with two deer slung on packhorses. I relax and lay back down watching them ride into camp. Without talking, Rainbow and Micah clean, skin, and hang both deer. Rainbow collects the sinew from the legs and back of the three deer. She adds it to a leather bag holding many more. Since we will be here for a few more days she adds the hooves of the deer to a boiling pot to make glue. I remember repairing my rifle many years ago with buffalo glue and sinew.

Micah and Rainbow set the extra venison on a platform for later use. Micah noticed a bear on a hillside as they rode by. Accompanied with Rainbow, they ride to hunt the bear. Rainbow says my wounds will heal quicker with bear grease. I find myself alone. Knowing my friends will return stalls any loneliness. I will face it alone after they leave for their summer range.

They return with a travois filled with a black bear. Micah helps Rainbow clean and skin it. The black bear is actually brown. A deep shade of brown that will make a nice bed cover for the cold mornings. She begins working on it later that day. Micah collects the bear fat in a Dutch oven to render it. I sit in the shade watching them work. The scratches are beginning to itch. I reckon that means I'm healing.

After harvesting a buffalo, which we split, my friends ride off. The three of us have finished the last of the cougar. Micah and Rainbow decide to go hunting for a couple of days. I am left by myself. Taking extra packhorses and a last look back at me at the cabin, they ride from my camp. They are after buffalo.

The wounds are healing better than expected. Rainbow has worked the hide of the cat into a shawl for me to cover my head come winter. She also gave me the soft tanned brown hide of the bear. I tell her thanks, cannot convey with words what their help and friendship mean to me. They are true friends.

I take my rifle with me later for a long walk around the cabin. I can use the exercise and am curious about what's changed around me. I don't want to be surprised because I'm living near a path used by the local Indians. All I find is more trees. The next two mornings I wander around the cabin. In the afternoons I begin cutting firewood making ready for winter.

A week later they return. It is with bittersweet feelings I watch them ride to my cabin. I'm truly glad to visit with Micah and Rainbow and I am happy my friend has found a good wife. Following after Micah are friends, trappers and mountain men, friends to the three of us. Old friends ride or walk in to say their hellos. I know most of trappers by sight if not by name. I help unload their horses. Micah is busy visiting with old friends as Rainbow begins setting up their lodge. I don't know how long all of them are going to be here, but by supper time there are eight old friends camped in four lodges, in my yard by the corral.

After the hubbub and commotion, first raised by friends greeting Micah and me, fizzles out, I am approached by a right fancy dude. He's standing at my side watching as I unsaddle my horse that first day, just watching. I'm wondering to myself where he came from.

"Is there something you want?" I ask the dude. He takes off his hat, which I learn later is called a derby.

"Yes, yes there is. If I may be so bold as to inquire, that is, well, I have heard of you, and Micah has told me much about you. Uriah correct?"

"Yeah, I reckon I am, why."

"I have heard that you lived with the Cheyenne. Is that true?"

"Yes, but what has that got to do with me?" I ask growing a bit agitated. "Come out and say it."

"All right I will. I will purchase, for a good price, all of your Cheyenne Indian paraphernalia."

"You want to buy my Cheyenne trappings and trimmings?" I ask him.

"Yes, and I will pay top dollar."

"Why? What are you interested in?" I'm a bit more interested now.

"All of it, everything." I'm staring at this English dude not really believing what I'm hearing.

"All right. Come with me." I have kept everyone but Rainbow out of my cabin. There has to be some things that are private to a man. I lead the way allowing the dude to follow me inside my cabin. He hesitates at the door.

"It's alright, come on in." He does. He stops inside the room to stare and look at everything. I begin by laying out a buffalo robe on the floor. I pour through my packs and saddlebags adding everything associated with my Cheyenne life on the robe. I add weapons starting with my bow and quiver full of arrows. I add extra knives, war axes, war clubs, the Blackfoot coup stick, horn cups, bowls, spoons. I keep my war shirts and buckskins but display everything else. He shows interest in some of the extra trade items I still have. They land on the robe. Hanging on my walls are my Grizz claw necklaces and one made from eagle claws. Old traps, a shiny bronze mirror, a couple beaver plews on oval frames, and my Medicine feathers.

"Is this what you have in mind?" I ask him.

He is too excited to reply. He nods, yes.

"How much will you offer?" I ask him, not having any idea what a fair price would be. But I do need supplies before snow starts. He blurts out a number. I have to ask him if he is serious. He is. This is more than I would make for a season's fur. I take it and begin packing it all in panniers for him. I reckon he'll need a packhorse or two.

"Would you be interested in the Mountain Mustang I stole from the Blackfoot?" I ask the dude following me to the corral. Like a hungry dog eyeing a bone, he's looking over my horse before he pronounces, "I'll take them."

We settle inside the cabin. For the first time in over two years I'm carrying coin money. I have forgotten its importance during my time with the Crow and Cheyenne in the mountains. It's only importance to me is buying trade goods. Now that I'm no longer trading it doesn't hold any value for me. That's when I remember I can buy my winter supplies. I reckon it does hold some value. I help the English dude load the packhorses with my past life. As he leads our friends, the trappers away, I vow not to return to the Indians.

———

Word About Nate

After everyone left, Micah and Rainbow stay one more night. Rainbow has grilled venison, bread, and coffee ready. I ask Micah how long he plans on staying.

"I haven't really thought it through yet. Why? Don't tell me you're ready for us to ride out."

"I'm not. I'm thinking about ..."

"I hate that I'm the one that has to tell you, but I've got word of Nate and it ain't good," Micah interrupts me. This must be something important. Micah does not usually interrupt me when I'm talking.

"What is it? Is he in trouble?" I ask.

"No, nothing like that. He's the one causing the trouble. You see he's in Texas..." Micah tells me all the news he has heard about Nate, and it ain't good.

Nate stays in Santa Fe long enough to collect a number of like-minded thugs and ruffians. He and his gang of hooligans begin robbing people on the trail between Santa Fe and El Paso, Texas. The gang is slowly making its way deeper into Texas. They attract the attention of the rangers but elude their traps. A couple members of the gang know the border area and stay a step ahead of the rangers. Nate leads his gang towards San Antonio robbing and killing as they travel. He has truly turned into a desperado.

"Well I reckon it's up to me to put a stop this trouble. I'm the one that taught him how to shoot and fight," I tell Micah, after hearing the story.

"I can do it for you, if it's too tough for you?" offers Micah.

"No, I will. He's my responsibility. Where is he?"

"Like I said Texas. Last I heard, which was this spring, he and his gang of outlaws were near San Antonio. I been there. I ain't in a hurry to go back. When we ride out, we're heading for Santa Fe. I ain't never been there. What do you say? Want to ride with us?"

"There ain't anything there that I need except to find and stop Nate. No, I reckon I'll head directly to San Antonio, get this done, and return home," I slowly announce.

"You sure? Well I reckon you know your own mind the best. Hate to go but, well good luck to you," he tells me, sticking out his hand to shake.

"I hope to see you both back here sometime in the next couple of years. Watch your hair down there, old friend."

"I'm sure you will," he tells me. Turning to Rainbow he continues, "We'll be back some time. Probably sooner than you think. You best not come looking for us. I'll be back." As soon as he's done talking, I wave good night to Rainbow and walk to my lonely, dark cabin. I sleep uninterrupted through the night. Early the next morning they ride from my canyon.

After finishing a morning meal of coffee, bread, and venison, I load panniers for the trip ahead of me. I lay out a line of pack frames. I add two loaded panniers to each frame. This journey will be longer so I'm taking it easier on my packhorses. Early before the sun breaks the eastern horizon, I secure the loads on my packhorses. I leave eight horses in the corral. It is large enough and the grass is tall enough to carry the horses until I return. I hope to be back before snow flies.

Taking the leads to my packhorses I set out, alone once again. This time I'm more able to meet whatever comes.

———

To Texas 1848

The Mexican war is over before I learn it even started. All anyone can talk about, or rather speculate about, is what changes will be felt in the towns and the surrounding areas of Texas. It's true that the Mexican's running the state, especially Santa Fe, before the war, took advantage of American merchants and their wagons and pack trains. Each load of goods entering the city was taxed $500. But now, no one is clear about how the new city leaders will be treating the stores and their wagons or pack trains. I spend one night in town. I leave the next morning, south by east for El Paso.

This town is also celebrating the end of the war. They are also wondering about their future. No one is clear on how it will all shake out. I strike south towards San Antonio. Following the trail from El Paso to San Antonio, I arrive at Horsehead Crossing in the late morning. The sounds of approaching horses drive away the dark thoughts of why I'm here. I jump onto the saddle and take up the lead rope on my packhorses. I hightail it into the brush. I secure the pack-horses to the biggest and sturdiest brush available. If I have to fight, I don't want to worry about my packhorses running off. There is nothing I can do about my tracks. I check all four of my pistols and both rifles. With my last Cheyenne fighting knife and war axe on my belt, I have done all I can do.

A small band of Comanche appear from the Mexican side of the border. They stop at the Crossing to water their horses. I take the opportunity to look them over. There are six of them. If I make each shot count, before they ride me down, I may come out of it. I decide against opening up this partic-ular dance. The leader of the pack is an older warrior, carrying a lance filled with scalps and eagle feathers. There are two young warriors displaying no honors. The other three are displaying plenty of war honors, but not near the amount of their leader. I sit back to wait this one out.

The leader addresses his men in Comanche. They line up in single file and cross the river to the US side. The leader is riding in the rear. He's turning his head from side to side inspecting the crossing. I have a feeling he's looking for tracks,

I hope not mine. He stops, rides back, and looks into the brush where I'm hiding. Without a change in expression, he charges my hiding spot. My rifle knocks him from his horse. One down. The cloud of burnt black powder gives away my position. The three experienced raiders turn towards me and charge. I take down the lead rider with my second rifle. My first pistol shot misses as the second experienced warrior swings down hugging the side of his horse. I shoot his horse instead. It lands skidding along the rock-strewn crossing, crushing the rider. I've lost sight of the third experienced warrior. The pair of inexperienced young warriors are left to deal with. My last pistol shot takes the first inexperienced warrior, the leader of the pair. The second young warrior makes a mistake by stopping to look after his partner. I reload my rifle, as fast as I can. I have plenty of practice fighting Blackfoot; however, a fast reload does not include measuring out the correct powder charge. I pour from the powder horn into my hand, dump down the barrel what's there, and send a patched ball afterwards. Add a cap to the nipple, looking up ready to take aim and, the last warrior is nowhere in sight. Is he looking for me? I reload two pistols as fast as possible. For some unknown reason I notice the sun is setting.

The last inexperienced warrior charges out from the surrounding cactus and chaparral. He's racing towards me brandishing a knife and a war club. I don't have time to aim. I bring my rifle around, when I thinks it's close to where he is, I trip the trigger. The fading daylight is replaced with full daylight. Flames from the extra black powder reach out to the advancing warrior. Hie eyes open wide as he's engulfed in the flames and smoke of the overpowered charge. The .54 caliber ball plows through him, stopping him in place. I'm holding the rifle at waist level. The rifle flies out of my hands landing behind me, stinging my hands. I pull a pistol, just in case. I hear another pistol shot from behind me.

"Is that another bunch of these Comanche? How'd I get surrounded?" I ask myself, picking up my rifle. I hear movement in the sagebrush behind me and make another hurried reload. I have my pistol aiming at the sounds of movement. I can't finish loading my rifle. I set it down to draw my war axe and turn to face a new enemy. I'm as ready as can be.

"Don't shoot. We're Texas Rangers. Careful now, I'm coming in," cries a voice in the brush.

"Come ahead and be careful. I'm still a might skittish," I tell the voice. I hear the sounds of many plowing through the brush before I see them. There are a horde of them.

"That was some good shooting," says the man leading the others.

"I've had plenty of practice."

"Against Comanche?" he asks.

"No, this is a first. Mostly against Blackfoot."

"You one of them mountain men, trappers?" asks another voice. The remark is tinged in, maybe not hatred or envy, but something mighty close.

"I was a trader and hunter more than a trapper. I lived in

the Big Stonies with the Crow and a time with the Cheyenne," I tell him after taking an instant dislike to the fellow. Another one hands me my rifle.

"A bit of an over-charge on that last shot?" he asks with a smile.

"I didn't have the luxury of measuring the charge. Things were kind of rushed."

"Yeah I saw that. You handle yourself pretty good. I know a lot of men that would have folded up and died."

"They took me once. I told myself no one will take me again."

"Who took you" Where was that at? When?" asks the first ranger, confusion written across his sun browned face.

"I'll tell you but let me check on them warriors and gather their weapons and horses first," I tell him. He nods. As I was talking, I reload both rifles. I walk to each body, even the one a ranger shot with his pistol. I will share that kill with whoever took the shot. I gather the weapons and the horse from each man. I notice the leader of this war party is wearing a thick leather belt with two holsters filled with a new kind of pistol. One I've not seen before. Over a shoulder is a possible bag. I take the belt carrying his pistols and a knife. I pick up a war club from the ground next to his body. I'll look these new weapons over later, alone. I lead the horses back to where my riding horse and packhorses stand eating the scant grass. The rangers have brought in their horses also.

"We were stopping for a water break. I don't like to camp

333

anywhere close to this crossing, too many Comanche for my tastes. How about you camp with us tonight. In the morning you can go on your way." I look into the eyes of the ranger, looking for truth of deceit. I see only truth.

"Sure, let me water these horses and I'll follow you. For adding your pistol shot, this last horse and weapons belong to you. We'll share the kill."

"What do you mean?" he asks me, looking confused. All the other rangers are listening for my answer.

"To the Crow the road to leading as a war chief begins at counting coup on a live warrior. And after killing another warrior, you collect his weapons and his horse. I reckon it's still a habit of mine. I know other Comanche will be looking for this bunch. Taking their weapons keep them out of the hands of them other warriors."

"Why ain't you with the Indians now?" asks the obnoxious ranger.

"That's personal, which I don't feel like explaining to you. Thanks for the help but if you're going to question me, then I'll make my own camp." I tell them.

"Calm down. Beebe knock it off. In fact, go check on the horses. If you can't keep it civil, I'll send you back to San Antonio," says the lead ranger. Beebe sulks away. I recognize I may have trouble with him.

"Don't pay any attention to Beebe."

"You rangers from San Antonio?" I ask, tying the weapons into a pack to add to a packhorse.

"Yes, we are."

"That's where I'm heading. One thing, what's a Texas Ranger?" I ask. The other rangers laugh and snicker. I recognize it as friendly and not antagonistic.

"Where you been that you ain't heard of Texas Rangers?" asks another ranger with a smile.

"Like I said, in the Stonies lately with the Cheyenne. I've got a cabin in a valley up the Yellowstone's. Been in the mountains for just over twelve years. Before that I came west from the east. I was captured by Blackfoot, before getting to the mountains on my first way west." I relate while stringing together the new horses with lead ropes. Gathering the leads together I climb into the saddle. "I'm ready, let's ride. I don't like it here."

"Let's go boys," yells the head ranger. I ride at his side; the others follow behind us. "How'd you get caught by the Blackfoot?" I tell him the story, the whole story as we ride. Four miles until it's dark, then we stop. I can smell a fire and more horses. This must be the camp.

"Take care of your horses before we eat, boys." Around the bend in front of us are many horses. I see the fire and places away from the fire claimed for the night by other men. I walk to the outside edge.

"This will do for a night," I tell my horses.

"Does he ever answer you?" Surprised that someone walked up on me I let the pistol slip back into the holster.

"Just wanted to invite you for supper. You keeping your horses close for a reason?" asks the lead ranger.

"More of a habit. Warriors always keep their best horse close to where he sleeps. In the village they're right outside the lodge. On a hunt or a war party they're hobbled right next to where we lay. I reckon it's a habit. 'Sides I've found a horse to be a better night hawk than many men we rode with."

"We?"

"What?"

"You said we when talking about a hunt or war party. Did you go on war parties with the Crow? The Cheyenne too?"

"Yes, I did but it was only against the Blackfoot. While I was with the Crow Micah asked them to teach me their ways. He taught me what I needed to know to live on my own before we reached the village."

"Did you like it with them?" he asks, as we walk to the fire.

"I did, until my friends turned against me." I tell him the story of the last Blackfoot fight, and Micah. I grab a plate; it's filled with a slab of meat and piled full of beans. I fill my cup from the coffee pot on the fire.

"I want to thank you boys for coming along when you did," I tell the group. They all nod their heads. I reckon supper is too important to interrupt with talking. When they finish, I sit and listen to their stories. When I get to missing Micah and Rainbow, I get up to leave.

"We'll be heading south in the morning. You're welcome

to ride with us if you want. That'll give you the opportunity to see what it is we Rangers do."

"Thanks, I'll do that," I tell him. I turn to walk to my blankets. I hear a voice behind me.

"Lieutenant, is that a good idea? We don't know who he is. We don't know what he's doing out here," says the cantankerous young ranger, Beebe.

"That'll be enough from you Beebe. I know his story. He told me. We seen how he handled himself in a very uneven fight. I may even invite him to join the Rangers. I don't want you to be a problem. You may find out you're tangling with more than you can handle," warns the Ranger Lieutenant. The ranger Beebe only scoffs.

The next morning I'm the first one up. I get my horses ready for the trail and clean my camp. I'm sitting on a stump when the lieutenant walks by.

"Hey Lieutenant, just who I wanted to see," I begin. "Yesterday I took these off the leader of that war party. They're just like the ones you boys are wearing. I've never seen them before. Can you show me how they work?"

"Their leader had them?" he asks, taking one of the pistols in his hand.

"Yeah. They were in these holsters on a belt around his waist. He didn't use them. He might not have known how." The ranger looks at me before answering.

"These were issued only to Texas Rangers during the Mexican War. He either killed a ranger or traded for them from the Comanchero. If you agree to ride with us, I'll tell you everything you'll need to know about them revolvers."

"If I don't?"

"Since taking them from you may prove to be more trouble than benefit, I'll let you have them and you can find out about them on your own."

"I see. I was figuring on riding with you but now..."

"What?"

"I don't want to be pressured into doing anything."

"Okay. Let's try this a different way. Ride with me, no questions asked about anything, and I'll tell you everything you want to know, about anything." I look at him, unable to stop a smile and a laugh.

"Lieutenant, I'd consider it a privilege to ride with you and your boys. Truth be told, if I don't find what I'm after in San Antonio...well I'd ride along until I do find what I'm looking for."

"Good. These are called Walker Colts. They are six shot revolvers. This is the cylinder; it holds six shots and rotates as the shot is fired." The lieutenant tells me their history, how to load them and how to clean them. I start the day by cleaning them. They are filthy, dirty from mud and dirt, not from firing. I show him the possibles and he shows me how to load them. "Later today on the trail I'll show you how they shoot."

"Until I learn that, I'll keep them put up. I'd best use what I know if we get into a gunfight."

"I smell coffee. Reckon it's ready?" asks the ranger.

"Let's go see." At the fire we sit down to eat. I am ready to ride before the rangers, but because of my pack horses and Comanche horses I ride at the end of the column. In camp at night I work on cleaning each horse of dirt, feathers, and dried paint until they fill out and look like good horses. So, good that when two horses come up lame on the five-week journey, each rider is forced to buy one of my horses. I sell them at top dollar because it's the fault of the riders that their horses are injured. The lieutenant takes my side using the situation as an example of how to care for your horse. I'll nurse the horses until they recover. Beebe is one of the men. His dislike of me grows daily. It explodes the day his horse turns up lame.

I notice the horse is limping as we camp for the night. I tell the lieutenant, and he tells Beebe to buy one of my horses. I take his horse in trade. Along the way I treat him, getting him trail-ready before we reach San Antonio. The fight starts when I explain the injury was easily preventable. A little inspection of the hooves in the morning and evening on a limping horse can make all the difference. As I turn my back to walk back to my horses and our place in line, Beebe jumps me.

I fling him off my back without effort. I take exception to Beebe attacking me behind my back. I look to the lieutenant; he nods affirmative but with a raised hand unseen by anyone else. I take it to read, don't hurt him, too bad.

Beebe picks himself up off the ground. Unseen by the

others but in full sight of me, he pulls his knife. I don't have time to pull mine. Beebe rushes me, hoping to end this fight quick. I stop him with a shoulder planted into his soft middle. As he struggles for breath, I grab his right arm and hand, the one holding the knife. I twist the arm behind him, almost to the point of dislocating it.

"Enough, let him go. Do not break his arm," warns the lieutenant. I realize he didn't see the knife. I drag the helpless man by the arm, holding his hand tight to the knife so he can't drop it. In front of the others I move my hand and the knife falls free.

"That ain't my knife. It's his. He tried to kill me. Stop him," cries Beebe. Several of

the men take a step to me. I'm still holding his arm.

"Stop or I'll tear his arm off. Lieutenant check the name on the knife and tell us all what it says," I order. The lieutenant doesn't like the fact that I'm issuing orders. To his credit he picks up the knife. As he reads the name his continence changes.

"It's Beebe's knife. You boys step back." I let go of his arm. He flops to the sand. I turn and head for my blankets. I begin packing my camp.

"What are you doing? We know it's his knife," says the lieutenant.

"That's what I told you, but until you saw it for yourselves you took his word over mine. You must have recognized Beebe for what he is, all of you should have. If you didn't none of you are aware enough to ride with me through Indian country. I will not ride with men who do not trust me or my word." When I'm done, I line up my packhorses. They are securely tied to a small struggling tree.

"Uriah, wait. You're right. A little bit of me didn't trust you. I do now. I saw Beebe for what he is, but we need rangers. I still want you to ride with us."

"And the trust?" I ask. As soon as the words are out of my mouth, I see a pack of Comanche cross the river coming right at us. No one else sees them over the commotion in the camp. I jump on my saddle horse and pulling both revolvers, charge them. I hope this move stops the Comanche long enough for the rangers to organize their defenses. I pass through the Comanche with the reins in my teeth, and both hands filled with revolvers that are spitting lead at the massed Indians. They can't escape. I plow through them. As I clear them, both hammers hit on spent cylinders. I put heels to my horse to get safely away. I need distance and time to reload. I holster both weapons. I look behind. No one is following. I pull my horse into a thicket. I climb down. Before the reaction hits, I need to get busy reloading. Concentrating on the process keeps the shakes at bay. I take a drink of water. Then remount. I am hearing steady firing, until now. I'm not sure what that means. Holding a single pistol, I nudge my horse forward.

Once out of the trees I start seeing the bodies. Scattered along the sandy riverbank are many Comanche. I did not get a count. I don't know if there are many more. I stop, letting my ears hear what's ahead. I hear horses splashing across the creek. I ready both pistols. It's Rangers, I lower my weapons and ride to them.

"Any left?" I ask the lieutenant. He just looks at me.

"What were you thinking?" he asks me. "Why didn't you say something to the rest of us?"

"It would have taken too long. I knew that if I could slow their attack the rest of you would get ready for them. That's what I did. Now, about the other. I'll not be riding with you Lieutenant, it's time I get the job done and return to my cabin in the Stonies."

"And Beebe?"

"Keep him away from me. 'Sides I'll bet you within a year you'll be after him. His name will find its place in your range books. I don't reckon he'll be honest for much longer."

"I hope you're wrong. Let's police them Comanches. Did you get all of them?" the lieutenant asks me.

"No, a couple of them got away. You'd better put out guards tonight. If it were me, I'd be back wanting vengeance," I warn the lead ranger.

I think the Comanche hold off their attack, until I take over night hawk duties. At the fire I help myself to a cup of coffee. Taking it with me I make a slow tour of the camp. I notice where everyone is sleeping and how the horses are doing. If the Comanche are going to hit us, as I expect, well I reckon it'll be similar to a Blackfoot raid. Before they try for the horses a couple of them will make a feint against the sleeping men. But the real attack will be on the horses. If they take our horses we're stuck and at their mercy. We still have a long way to travel before reaching San Antonio. I hide in the brush where I can watch the horses and the camp. I really like these six-shot revolvers. They make being outnumbered less of a problem. Shooting them for the first time I missed half my shots. I reckon that's allowable, this first time. With my rifle slung over a shoulder and a revolver in my hand, I wait.

The fighting begins after a quail call. It's answered from four different directions. I cannot get up and warn the camp. They'll be coming. I see shadows moving in the trees and scrub brush. I need to warn the others. A shot will be best. I don't want to waste a shot, so I wait. There, from the corner of my eye I see the outline of a Comanche warrior slowly walking to the horses. Taking aim with my first revolver I wait. When he's out of the brush I shoot. He falls to the ground. The bushes erupt with more screaming Comanche. Blankets are thrown off as rangers gather weapons and enter the fighting.

I carefully move after taking that first shot. The cloud of foul-smelling black powder giving away my position. I walk around the horses, away from the ranger's camp. Twice more I shoot careless Indians. The sound of firing reaches a crescendo, then falls to silence. My ringing ears fail to pick up the sounds of movement in the brush. I slowly continue around the horses. In ones and twos, rarely in threes, I hear more shots. I come across two bodies; both are Comanche.

They got too close to the camp. Continuing on I'm at the rope corral keeping the horses together. The knots are tight. I move on. I hear crashing brush behind me. Slowly moving only my head I turn to look. I see a body hurtling towards me. We crash to the ground together. Instead of seeing buckskins, I see a hat and jeans. I don't want to hurt the man wrestling with me.

"Stop," I shout. He does. I pick myself up, checking my revolvers, and help up one of the rangers I don't know well.

"I thought you were an Indian, sorry," he says.

"The Comanche are in that direction. Be careful, they are slipping into camp from the sagebrush," I try telling him.

"I know what I'm doing," he murmurs, walking away in the opposite direction than the one I pointed out. I watch him go. The shooting stops. I find a place and step back into the brush. The hairs on the back of my neck are standing; this ain't over yet. I check the three Comanche bodies I come across. I take their weapons, so they don't end up in the wrong hands. I hear horses racing away. They're close and heading my way. I stop to get ready. As they run by, I shoot as fast as I can. I'm pleased watching two bodies fall from their horses to the ground. The ones with them don't stop, they keep on going, escaping.

I check on the bodies. Both are young warriors. *"Why are so many of the Comanche warriors young?"* I ask myself. The others escape, unharmed.

"Stay in place until dawn. Be sure of your targets," yells

the lieutenant. The dark sky in the east is slowly fading. The sun will begin its rise in about a half hour. I make the rounds by the horses, inspecting each of the Comanche laying in the sand and rocks. I'm not certain where the rangers are waiting. I will stay by the horses, for now. The rising sun will confirm what I found. I watch the sun peak over the eastern horizon. I watch the sun rise from where I sit behind a sage brush.

"How many hit us?" the lieutenant asks me.

"I shot five myself. I reckon the ones from earlier today brought friends. I'd bet at least

four rode away. I don't know how many of those attacking the camp we stopped. I found one

ranger killed. There was two warriors next to him. He put up a fight."

"I hate to ask you, but can you stay here next to the horses while I check on my men?" he asks me.

"Of course, I will," I tell him. He walks away. During the next half hour I hear low conversations in the brush. I hear a shrill whistle spreading out away from the camp.

"Come on in boys. Meet me at the firepit. Coffee's on," promises the lieutenant. I

carefully head that way. I'm the last one in. Looking around I see we're two men light.

"I know where Harry is, has anyone seen Tom?" asks the lieutenant.

"Last I seen him was behind the camp, in the trees," says Bill his saddle partner.

"Uriah come with me; we'll look for him. The rest of you finish the coffee and grab some jerky. I want to be on the trail in half an hour," orders the lieutenant. Together we look through the patch of woods behind the camp. We find him, so did the Comanche. We bring him back to the camp.

"We'll leave after burying these two." The graves are shallow, the ceremony short. Within that half hour we are riding away from that camp. I'm still riding drag when the lieutenant rides by. He has a book in his hand.

"This is for you. It's for keeping notes. Like the description of outlaws. I drew maps in mine. I make notes at the camp spots, water holes, where we fight, or only see Comanche or Comancheros. Where the water holes are is the most important information. The best areas for hunting. You know things like that. Here's a pencil. Have you been to San Antonio?" he asks me out of the blue.

"No, not yet."

"We'll be there in about five days. After cleaning up you can meet the other officers and more of the men. I hope you decided to stick," he tells me, then heads for the front of the column.

Just like he said, five days later we enter town. The ranger camp is outside of town. Close enough to enjoy its services but far enough away not to hear the loud noises issuing from the saloons every night. I'm shown a corral for my extra horses and a stable for my riding horse. Next is the wash house. Washed and dressed in clean clothes, only then do we head for the tables in front of the kitchen for supper. The coffee is good, the steaks perfect, and the apple pie afterwards, the best.

"You must be the Uriah I've been hearing so much about," announces the Ranger Colonel sitting behind an ornate wooden desk. I find out later it is a souvenir from the Mexican War. How they got it all the way back to San Antonio, well I bet that's an interesting story. Any ways I'm standing in front of the Texas Ranger's Commander in San Antonio. I reckon this could be an interview, if I was interested in joining the rangers. Sitting by the desk is a ranger icon, Major Ben McCulloch. Hero in the Mexican War and a legend in the Rangers. In 1852 the major becomes a US Marshal for the Eastern district of Texas. During the Civil War McCulloch receives a colonel's commission from Confederate President Jefferson Davis. He is killed at the Battle of Pea Ridge, in 1862. However, I did not know all this at our first meeting, early that morning.

"I heard good things about you from the lieutenant and most of his men. What's this about your trouble with Beebe?"

"Ain't nothing, just keep him away from me. If you do, it won't be me ending his lack luster life."

"What do you mean by that?"

"I mean the man's a fool. He won't last long fighting the Comanche."

"I see. And you will?"

"I've fought plenty of Blackfoot and I've held my own so

347

far. I reckon I'll learn Comanche ways if I stay here long enough."

"I believe you will. Tell me about your time with the Crow," he orders. I start with

Micah and end with the reason I'm here in Texas, looking for Nate. I leave nothing out.

"I believe you'll do. Rangers provide their own horse, gear, weapons, and powder all for $1.25 a day. Pay days can be far apart. In camp you'll eat with us; on the trail you'll cook for yourself. We'll provide beans and coffee. Anything else comes from your pocket. Any

questions?"

"Yes sir."

"What," he asks, standing.

"I can't ride for you Rangers. I would but I came to Texas to find an outlaw. It's time for me to ride. I need to find him." The surprised ranger looks at me.

"Exactly who is this outlaw you're chasing down?"

"I know him as Nate. He's a young man that came from the mountains, same as me. He was living and working with me when he went bad. I took him under my wing and taught him to be a trader." I see the confusion their faces I start at the beginning and tell them the story about Nate. I do not leave anything out. Not the pirates, St. Louis, or any of it.

"That's interesting. I know one outlaw named Nate. Here's what we know..." says the Ranger Major.

9

SAN ANTONIO, TEXAS

TWO NIGHTS AFTER LEAVING THE RANGERS I RECEIVE more visitors. This bunch ain't near as friendly or as sociable as the rangers proved to be. The ears of my riding horse alerted me to their approach. I am too hot and too tired to fuss with whoever these ol' boys prove to be. I check the loads and caps on both Walkers, then refill my coffee cup with the last from the battered old pot. I reckon I have time to ready the pot for morning, before these fellers ride in. So, I do. I have the pot sitting next to the fire where I can reach it from my blankets come first light.

Well, as I sit back to take a sip from my last cup of the day, in rides trouble. There are three riders. They look as hot and tired as I feel. I do not like the feelings I perceive as they intrude. They ride into the light from my fire, raising dust in my camp. Now I really don't like them.

"You boys can stop right there. I ain't interested in entertaining tonight. I simply want to finish my coffee and close my eyes," I tell them. My left hand is gripping the smooth wood handle of the Colt on that side of my belt. They cannot see it.

"I don't particularly care what you want old man," threatens the rider siting his horse centered between his partners. I'm guessing he's the one that fancies himself in charge. "We're tired, hot, hungry, and thirsty. What do you got for us?"

"I've got nothing for you boys. You best back up them flea bags you're setting and leave me alone," I warn him.

"Them's fine words for a man outgunned and sitting down," opines the rider on the right side. The man on the left is quiet, just watching. I reckon him to be the most dangerous. He will receive my first pistol ball. I put my cup down. I'm making ready to stand.

"No, I don't think so. Just sit right there and put that coffee on while we tend to our horses," says the leader. I'm inching out the hidden Colt.

"No, I don't think so. You see that is for me come first light," I tell them. That brings a chuckle to both of the talkers. The quiet one moves his hand to his single pistol. "I would stop right there. Any further and I'd take that as unfriendly," I tell him, looking directly in his eyes, watching. Then I see it. I pull my left side revolver, aim in his direction, and fire the heavy single action revolver. The .44 caliber lead ball flies true, finding the center of his chest. I roll away from the fire. Along my way I knock over my coffee pot, dumping out the fixings so carefully set for morning. Now I'm angry. I pull the right-side Walker. As I'm rolling, I evade two lead balls thrown my way. Coming to an abrupt stop against my saddle on the ground, I aim and fire. I'm lying flat on my back, my thumbs are working the hammers on both revolvers, and I'm shooting as fast and accurately as I am able.

I watch the first outlaw, the quiet one fall from his saddle. His horse bumps the others trying to get away. Their shots are landing all over my camp. When the first one hits the ground, I send him another lead ball. Now to the other two.

One is wounded, I let him be, for now. The leader earns two lead balls to the belly. He drops his pistol to hold his belly. I switch fire to the wounded man as the boss falls to the ground. It ain't much of a gunfight. With the trio on the ground I stop shooting. Each of them has a pair of leaking holes, earned from my Walkers. The wounded man has three. I check how many shots I have left, two. I missed three shots. Not too bad, I reckon.

Getting to my feet I gather the reins to the three horses. They are calmer now that the shooting has stopped but still showing a lot of white in their eyes. I calm them with a combination of soft words and a couple pats. It works. I move them out of disaster that is now my camp. Securely tied to some kind of a sagebrush, it's time to collect weapons and see to these outlaws. I laugh at calling these three outlaws. They were not so tough. I'm sure in their minds they held themselves in higher esteem than deserved. I collect three pistols.

There are additional examples of dirty percussion caped single shot pistols in their holsters. I unhook their gun belts, turn out their pockets, and line them up on the sand. I'm holding about one hundred dollars. I add it to the coins in my bag. Next? Remove the vermin from my camp. Using one of their own horses and rope I tow the trio into the sagebrush fifty yards from my camp. Returning to the fire I unsaddle each horse and tie them to the picket line with my packhorses. At the fire I pour through their saddlebags. I keep their possibles, powder, lead, and caps. The rest is of no use to me. I pile it across from where I lay my blankets.

I'm ready to lay down for the night when I remember I need to reload my revolvers. I set to the chore. While reloading I notice the coffee pot. Finished with both Colts, I refill the even more battered pot, making ready for first light. At least the coffee grounds in the sock are still useable. I cannot get myself ready to ride without it. Finished, I look around for the last time looking for a chore I missed. There ain't one. I lay down and fall asleep before I realize it.

A stagecoach roars past my camp waking me from a light slumber. On waking I'm surprised to see the sun beginning its ride. Breaking camp is easy, I simply load the packhorses and saddle my riding horse and my packhorses and three new horses, gifts from the desperados. Coffee is good now; I will stop for food later. Anxiously I resume the trail and the deed I do not look forward to. I'm leading my pair of packhorses and three horse that belonged to the three outlaws that came into my camp last night with ill-intentions. I follow the curve in the road and right there in front of me is a stage stop. Good, now I can eat and rest the horses. I attract the attention of the family running the station. I reckon they don't often see a man leading two packhorses and three extra horses all wearing saddles. I ride to the barn. A weather-beaten man meets me at the door.

"Mister, I don't care who you are. I won't tell anyone you been through here. I have a wife and family. Just go on, while you can," he tells me.

"What do you mean, go on?" I ask. I understand I must look trail weary but do not understand his reaction.

"Like I said, I don't want your kind of trouble. My oldest boy has you in his sights and he's uncommonly good with that old rifle. Just keep riding," he pleads.

"I don't know who you think I am, but these are all my horses. I began this journey with this horse I'm riding and the two packhorses. It's true I had to kill to get the others, but these three here I got last night after three men attacked me in my camp. I'm a law-abiding man. I don't want trouble either. I can pay for a days' keep and feed. What do you say?"

"If you ain't who you say you are, I'll kill you," promises the work-worn rancher.

"Maybe I should be wary of you," I laugh. "If you don't want my money, I can trade a horse and saddle," I tell him.

"Just not my saddle horse or the two packhorses. I'll lay down in an empty stall if it'll make you feel better and take a meal outside."

"I reckon you are what you say. Climb on down. I would be interested in buying a couple of these horses," he tells me. I climb wearily from the saddle.

"Where can I put them?" I ask.

"Right here. Take the first empty stalls." I do. Later, I look over the rifles and pistols I souvenired. I'll keep a genuine Hawken .54 caliber rifle. I trade two rifles, the three t pistols, and the three extra horses to the man running the ranch-stage stop for two nights in the stalls and feed for me and my horses. He has two sons and a wife he's been wanting to arm and outfit with horses. However, every time he gets to the point of having extra horses, outlaws always arrive and steal them. I make him a good deal. I'm lighter by all the extra weapons, their possibles and three horses with saddles. Safely stashed away in my saddlebags is a leather bag slowly growing heavier, holding my coins and paper money.

I've lost the morning by the time we complete our business. The stage stop manager invites me inside to eat. I'm tired of my own cooking, I accept. The next day the horses rest. I take the time to inspect and repair my gear. Leaving early the next morning I continue my journey rested and resupplied. The stage stop manager gives me the names of the more discrete stage stops. These particular stops will not ask questions and will provide me and my horses a restful stay. I take advantage of those stations. They work out to be about three days ride apart. It works as he told me, no questions asked and a genuine welcome after seeing gold coins.

We arrive in San Antonio rested. It's time for me to run down Nate and his bunch. No one is willing to trust or talk to what they see as a busted up ol' mountain man riding a young horse and leading two packhorses. They reckon I ain't fit for company but I ain't down here to make friends. I quickly move on without explaining my circumstances to anyone. I'm heading towards Austin.

In Austin it's the same story. In a café I overhear two mule skinners talking about outlaws stopping mule trains between San Antonio and Santa Fe. I soak up their conversation, all of it. I sit drinking coffee until the pair finish, pay their bill, and step outside. I follow them outside.

"Excuse me, I couldn't help but hearing about your troubles on the trail."

"Mister, you shouldn't listen in on other folks' private conversations."

"I wasn't listening on purpose."

"What do you want then?" asks the older, grumpier man.

"What I mean is..." I try explaining. I grow frustrated trying to do it nice. I give that up. "This is what I want to know. Do you know the name of the gang that's preying on your pack trains? Or the name of their leader?"

"Can't say I do. Don't believe we ever heard a name. Why?"

"I'm looking for a young outlaw by the name of Nathan. I don't know what he calls his band of outlaws."

"Are you a bounty hunter? Aiming to collect the reward?"

"No, nothing like that. I knew Nate when he was younger. I taught him a lot of what he knows. I feel responsible for what he has become."

"What do you aim to do about it?" the mule skinner asks me.

"I aim to put a stop to him and his gang. I am not going to allow him to continue. I'm going to put them all out of work, just as soon as I find them."

"That's commendable stranger, but I think the rangers are more capable than you at that sort of thing," says the second mule skinner laughing.

"That may be, but I got it to do. I'd better ride," I tell the pair.

"Good luck stranger."

"You reckon he has a chance?" one says to the other.

"Not even a slim one, my friend," he responds as I walk away. Further up the trail towards Austin, Nate and his gang have made camp. They have cleaned up after supper on the trail. Nate assigns night hawk duties to each man. Satisfied each gang member knows his time and will be awake to man their posts, Nate crawls into his blankets.

———

Nate

It has taken awhile to train these men, but he is satisfied with the results. Before he came along, they were an unorganized bunch, without a plan, unable to work together toward a common end. Nate changed all of that. After making examples of the more cantankerous outlaws the others fall into line.

"A .54 caliber lead ball is proven motivation," Nate says to himself with a small laugh. After seeing Nate assume the reins to direct the gang according to his will the others follow along. Nate is just a little too free with his new revolver to argue with. Not long after Nate relaxes and falls asleep, he is woken by the night hawk.

"Nate, I have a bad feeling. I think someone is fixing to attack the camp," the youngest member of the outfit tells him.

"Have you seen anyone?"

"No."

"Then get back to the horses and only wake me if we're actually under attack."

"Won't that be too late?" asks the young outlaw confused.

"Don't sass me boy. Get gone." The Kid returns to the picket line.

"Regardless what Nate may think I know someone is out there," the Kid tells himself. As soon as he makes it back to their hobbled horses, he sees three Indians trying to untie the hobbles on the gang's horses. The Kid fires his rifle and sees one of them fall. The Kid hurries behind the animals to get at the other two Indians. He sees them both sneaking toward the horses.

Nate rises from a sagebrush shooting both of his single-shot pistols at the pair of Indians.

Ten feet away from their targets both fall to the ground. They are hit good. Nate can hear the others in the camp waking up. There are a couple of shots, some cries, and many screams as he frantically reloads his rifle and two pistols. He circles around the horses waiting out the night. As the sun rises, the other gang members find Nate at the horses' picket line.

"How many animals did we lose?" a gang member asks him. Nate stands to look him square in the eyes.

"Next time all of you had better get out of your blankets and back up the Kid. He tried to warn me before the attack, but I shook off the warning. I reckon I know better now. Sorry Kid. I should have taken you seriously. I am not impressed with the rest of you nor in the way you ran, not defending our camp. We did not lose any animals. I accounted for two of the Indians trying to steal our animals. I know the Kid got at least one. How did the rest of you fair?" He's looking at them with hate in his eyes. They all know he is in the right and not helping to stop the attack was a big mistake. Most of them are bullies and are not about to risk their hide unless the odds are overwhelmingly in their favor. Nate knows he needs to teach them all a lesson. A lesson none of them will forget. Before anyone begins lying to cover themselves, Nate sets in on them.

"I'm done with you all of you except for the Kid. Any man willing to let Indians take his animals and not join the fight to stop them is not a man I want to ride with. And a man that don't take his share of the blame when it is his fault but tries to blame others is nothing more than a bully. I refuse to risk my life working with a bully."

"I knew you were all cowards when I first set eyes on you. You're all nothing but..." One of his men launches his balled-up fist with the intention of stopping Nate's intentional insults. Nate is expecting it. He dodges the fist heading his way. Before the man can recover from throwing the missed blow, Nate sticks a pistol in his face, calmly pulls the trigger.

"You best stop right there, or I'll kill the next closest man," warns Nate. The next man is a lying bully paying close attention to Nate's Walker revolver.

"You disregarded my every word and most all my suggestions. You have three choices. One, pulling out. Two, start doing what I order done. And three, sass me. I do not want to lose my life with a bunch of green and incompetent fools as all of you. I reckon you owe me twenty dollars. And that is cheap for saving your miserable lives," he tells his gang.

"I have a question," shouts one of his men. Nate nods his head. "What happens if I choose to sass you?" he laughs. Before the gang understands what he's about to do, Nate pulls the trigger. The laughing gang member crumples to the ground.

"You put us all at risk just because you're scared or lazy," says an angry Nate. "Any other questions?" No one says anything but one of his boys is shaking his head. Nate walks towards him shoving the barrel of his .44 caliber Colt Walker revolver in his belly.

"You may want to rethink what you're contemplating," Nate tells him. Nothing, no more talking or laughing from them. He pulls back the hammer. That gets him talking.

"You're right. What you're saying is true. I didn't like nor trust either of them. I want to stay in your gang," he blusters. Nate's finger begins taking up the slack of the hammer.

"Wait Nate don't shoot me. I believe you. I will pay your fee. Just turn me loose," pleads the gang member.

"I will just as soon as I pocket the coins," Nate tell him. He pulls a leather bag from his vest. He spills coins into Nate's hand. Nate pulls away the pistol from his belly. He counts twenty dollars. Satisfied, Nate lets down the hammer. He's expecting some kind of trick. Sure enough, the humiliated gang member tries one.

While adding the pistol to his holster, the gang member tries delivering a roundhouse punch to Nates belly. Except, Nate steps back evading the blow. Now it's Nate's turn. Nate gives vent to all the frustration and anger he has been holding in since the pirate attack. The gang member is a faceless target. After a rapid series of devastating punches, Nate lets him crumple to the ground.

"Anyone else want to try me?" he asks the shocked gang. Nate teaches the bully that has never been beaten an important lesson. Don't be tangling with the boss either with pistols or fists. Without proving it, the lesson holds true for rifles and knives. His friends pick him up and carry the defeated tyrant to their camp. The Kid walks with Nate. Turning to the leader the Kid has a few questions.

"Nate was that really necessary?" asks the Kid. Nate stops to answer the Kid.

"Yes, it was. Absolutely. I have my eyes on bigger takings than stopping a stagecoach or robbing a bank. While the right bank will supply a pay day, I have something different in mind. Something that will not take as much effort. I want to take over a town."

"That seems a bit ambitious Boss, and uncertain," replies the Kid.

"That is part of the beauty to my plan. No one will be expecting it. I won't try it until we reach the perfect town. Something small enough we will not need a lot of men to help control. But something big enough to provide us with a steady income. I will know it when I see it. Don't tell the men, yet. We need to prepare for..." Nate cannot finish the thought.

"What do we need to prepare for Boss?"

"I ain't sure but I know something or a someone will be catching up with me. I'll need to defeat it or him when that time comes. I ain't waiting on it. We'll be riding out in the morning. I'll be looking for my town as we ride."

"You won't have to face it alone Boss. I'll help you," vows the Kid.

"Thanks, but if it happens it will be something I'll have to take care of myself. Tell the others we'll be pulling out come first light. I want you to take over assigning the night watch. I can trust you to take care of it, right?"

"You sure can Nate. I won't let you down," the Kid assures Nate.

"Good, thanks. You best see to the men and give them their watch times," suggests Nate.

"I will and thanks again, Boss." For the first time in his short life the young desperado has, if not a friend, at least someone who appreciates him and values his work. That is why he ran away from home. That is what attracted him to the renegade life. Too bad for the young bandit, but it is a counterfeit feeling.

———

Uriah

The Comanche are raiding during the Comanche Moon. This is an event I learn about later along my hunt for Nate. In my ignorance of Texas and of Comanche Indians I continue my way north and ultimately Austin. I'm beginning to miss

The Ballad of Uriah

my mountains. I'm ready to return to the Great Stonies. I've had my fill of the heat and prairies, but there remains the job facing me before returning home to the Great Stoney Mountains.

I stop at the edge of a river I do not know the name of to hunt and make jerky before continuing my journey. My first night near this unnamed river I down a pair of Mule Deer. I build a fire to dry most of the meat for jerky. Sunrise on my third morning beside this river I have my riding horse saddled and two packhorses loaded and ready to ride. I climb onto the saddle as the first edge of the sun breaks the horizon. I ride slow sometimes on an established trail and sometimes riding next to it. I ride wary not knowing the area and unwilling to fall into the hands of Indians or the outlaws I'm following.

I cross another smaller river at a gravel crossing. I can tell the local Indians regularly use this crossing. This place gives me a chill. The soonest I'm away from here the safer and better I'll feel. I leave the trail a couple miles past this crossing. I make camp in the midst of a pecan grove. I build a fire long enough to boil coffee, cook meat, and bake a couple sticks of bread, then put it out. I make extra for the next morning. I relax laying on my blankets, restless through the night. The dark passes. In the morning I do not feel refreshed. I spent most of the night waiting for intruders. Thankfully, they do not show up. I make a small fire to boil coffee. When finished, I put out the fire and load my horses. They enter my camp as I'm saddling my riding horse.

"That must have been your fire we smelled earlier," says a large trail-weary and dirty horseman. I have no idea who this bunch is, or if they will let me continue on without a fight. Everything in Texas either wants to fight, sting, bite, jab, or kill me.

"I did have a fire for a short time. Only long enough to boil coffee," I tell them.

"I smell fresh coffee. Do you still have some?" asks another.

"No, only some rolls and jerky I was saving for later today. Everything is gone or packed away. I was just fixing to ride out.

"What's the hurry friend?" asks another, climbing from his saddle.

"For some reason this crossing and this entire area leaves me with an unsettled feeling," I try explaining.

"That's for a good reason Pilgrim. This is a small east to west section of a larger Indian trail. The main trail runs north and south beginning well south of us at a place called Horsehead Crossing. On account of the skulls left by Indians," explains yet another gang member.

"That makes sense. What tribe are these Indians from?" I ask genuinely interested.

"Them be Comanche. Ain't you ever heard of Comanche?" he asks incredulously.

"Heard about them, don't know much about them, and don't want to meet up with any," I admit.

"It's a wonder you kept your hair this long. Crazy Pilgrim running loose alone during the Comanche Moon like you are."

"What's this Comanche Moon?" I ask.

"The Comanche Moon is the full moon of every month. That's the time the Comanche will raid and make war."

"That's right, it the three days before the full moon and the next three days after the new moon. A very dangerous time to be riding by yourself," adds another.

"The Crow and Cheyenne do the same thing, using the full moon to make their horse raids and making war on their enemies," I add.

"Now that you know, you're welcome to ride with us, if you want to."

"Thanks for the offer but I'm better off alone. I'm looking for a man I used to know. I heard he was around here somewhere."

"What's the name of this man? We know just about everyone around."

"He's not from around here. Like me he's from the mountains. He ain't a good man, it's better I do it myself."

"Is this man you're after an outlaw? Are you a bounty hunter?" still another asks.

"I'm no bounty hunter. I am after an outlaw. When I knew him, he was a kid captured by the Sioux then traded to the Cheyenne. We worked together until he decided to take the lawless path. I reckon it's up to me to make this good."

"What's his name?"

"I know him as Nate. I don't know if he's changed it or what he calls his gang," I tell them. "You boys rangers?"

"No were on our way back to the ranch. I sold a couple hundred head of cattle in Louisiana. We're on our way home," says the leader of the group.

"Good luck to you mister..." begins another rider.

"I'm Uriah." I watch them ride south. *"I forgot to ask how far north Austin lays and what's between here and there,"* I say to myself.

Unrulily Bartender

I follow the trail into a small town. The outlaw gang I'm after has passed through. I move on after talking to the town's law. I know I've gained on them. They can't be more than a half day's ride in front of me. I know I'm close. Knowing Nate, I understand how he thinks. That has truly helped me gain on them. I don't know if they realize I'm on their back trail.

I stop at the outskirts of the next town I come to. The town in front of me only has a single road and eight buildings. The general store, the sheriff's office, and the saloon are easy to pick out. I am surprised at not seeing the hitchrail out front of the saloon filled with tired Mustangs. I ride through the town looking for the livery or the town's barn. I do not see them. I backtrack to the saloon. I sit at the hitchrail catching my breath and looking around. There is no one on the street, no business doors open, and no sounds, anywhere. I'm beginning to wonder what I've ridden into.

As I climb out of the saddle, an out-of-tune piano begins belting out notes. The result of whoever is pounding the keys cannot be called music. I loosen the cinch of my saddle. There is a water trough under the hitchrail and a pump at the end of the trough. I work the handle. Slowly water pours out, a mere trickle. I keep working the pump. The flow increases. I stop when my horses dip their noses into the water. They need the water, but I limit what they take. I don't want them to flounder. Slow yet steady the trough fills. My horses return their muzzles into the water, and I can see the delight in their eyes. That is when I notice the way their ears are moving, twisting to find the source of the noises behind me.

That gets my attention, burning away the hot afternoon's stupor. My left hand takes over the water delivery duties as my right loosens the pistol in my holster on that side of my belt. I use the ruse of changing hands while pumping additional water into the trough to take a look behind me. I see a curtain on the window of the store fall back into place. The piano inside the saloon stops.

I hear a hand slap against soft flesh from inside the saloon and the piano starts up again. I've located at least two outlaws. I don't know for sure, but I believe it is Nate and his bunch. I've followed their trail for weeks. It leads here. I've been trailing four men. I need to find the last pair before starting after the others. Slowly, I inspect one side of the street then the other. I do not notice any difference from when I rode in. The trough is full. I stop pumping. It's up to me to get these pole cats to reveal themselves. Taking off my hat and untying my bandana, I dunk my head in the water. A good shaking and I lift up. Using the bandana, I wipe water from my eyes. Nothing has changed. If they are waiting for the right time, well it's here.

I wipe my face with the bandana, rinse it and rub it over my hair. Still nothing. With both hands full of hat and bandana I'd reckon now will be the time, but it ain't. Does that make these gents smarter than me or dumber than expected? I ain't sure. I rinse out the bandana before tying it back around my neck. I give a couple pats to my horses as I walk to retrieve my rifle. Still nothing. It's up to me. Saloon or store? One last look, up then down the street before heading to the...

The sound of breaking glass stops my wondering when they'll show themselves. The rifle shot tells me where one of them is. Burnt black powder escaping out the store's broken window confirms it. I run up the street before crossing over. There is not another shot. I reach the door and kick it open. The rifle is snug against my shoulder, a .54 caliber lead ball waits, sitting ready, the hammer is pulled back, and I move a finger inside the guard to the trigger.

I see the outlaw raise his pistol to shoulder height, like

he's in a duel. That fooling around gives me time to quickly aim and pull the trigger. The rifle ball hits him in the chest knocking him down to the wood floor. With a look of disbelief, he watches the red stain spreading over his shirt. He looks up from the floor, dropping his fancy dueling pistol. Keeping a loaded Walker on him I walk to the body. I check, there is no pulse. I pick up his pistol, tucking it in the back of my gun belt. I stop long enough to add his rifle and his possibles over a shoulder. Time to check the saloon. The piano player is pounding out what is supposed to be a tune. I cringe when a gal begins singing with more gusto than talent.

I drop the rifles and possibles at the water trough by my horses. I take the time to reload my rifle. Silently I climb the weather-worn wooden steps up to the boardwalk. At the saloon's door I stop, looking in both directions. I get that feeling. Knowing it's better not to bull my way through the door, I don't. I wait against the wall at the side of the door. I reckon I'm a better hunter than these outlaws. The second man gets impatient, opening the saloon door, looks out, and slams it closed. I know he saw me. Why didn't he shoot? That makes me anxious. Retracing my steps, as quiet as possible, to my horses, I'll wait a bit longer, letting them get nervous. A nervous man can be dangerous or make mistakes. I'm willing to gamble that these greenhorn desperados will make a mistake. A deadly mistake. After a handful of minutes, the door slowly opens, and he steps out.

"Hey Nate, did you hear those shots?" he yells back into

the saloon. The piano stops. In the afternoon's quiet I hear boots walking across the saloon's wood floor.

"What are you thinking Kid?" asks a voice inside. It's a voice I recognize. There's at least three of them in the saloon. Where are their horses?

"Did you hear that shot?" he asks.

"Of course, I did," says Nate.

"Think Adam's dead?" asks the Kid.

"Absolutely, Kid."

"What we going to do about it?" asks the youngest crook in a tight voice.

"I'm going to wait right here. Thanks to you he knows where we are. If I were you, I'd be ready and expecting him," shouts out Nate, the experienced outlaw leader.

"Okay Nate, sorry," says the Kid, breaking off conversation, knowing he's made a mistake. He's hoping it's not going to be his last. Making it easy for me, the young fugitive waits on the boardwalk with his back against the building. He's facing towards me, but two feet higher on the boardwalk. Now, it's time.

With my rifle in place, the butt firm against my shoulder, the hammer back, and it's pointed at the kid, I step away from my horses. The young, would-be gun hand sees me, stands up straight, and begins wrenching a flintlock pistol from his belt. The front sight and the hammer catch on a suspender, slowing his draw. He grows frustrated, further slowing the draw. On the dirt road, away from the door, I watch. It don't seem right to shoot this inept kid. I hold my fire.

"Lay down your weapons kid and you can walk away," I tell him. I have him in the sights of my rifle. He looks up as his pistol slides away free.

"*Don't do it,*" I say to myself.

"I can't, I've come too far," he says, raising the single shot to take aim at me down on the street.

"*It will be an easy shot with a pistol, if he makes it,*" I say to myself. I'm hoping he won't try it. If he does well...The ball hits a fresh pile of horse flop besides me, missing by five feet to the left.

"*He's twisting his hand when he pulls the trigger,*" I say to myself, critiquing his form, while pulling the trigger on my rifle. The shot interrupts him drawing a second pistol. He looks up, then down at me. My shot is fatal. Both pistols fall from his unfeeling fingers. As the kid loses strength he crumbles to the boardwalk. Before moving I reload my rifle.

"*Now the last two men,*" I tell myself, walking up the steps to the batwing saloon doors. The piano is still belting out a poor excuse for music and is joined by even worse singing. She matches his out of tune harmony perfectly. I hope they are both just nervous and this is not how the act always goes.

"*A couple of fighting cats sound better than that duo,*" I tell myself stepping to the saloon door. The music and singing stop. The town is absolutely quiet. I look at my horses. They are drinking water unaffected by my rifle shot next to them. About ten feet from the saloon's batwing doors I'm at the long windows. I can hear the outlaw's fancy Mexican silver spurs marking his location.

"*I wouldn't want some outlaw who fancies himself a gunman keeping track of my movements by them spurs,*" I tell myself. This is a habit I've noticed growing worse as I grow older, me talking to myself in stressful times. "*I reckon it keeps my mind off what may happen,*" I laugh at myself.

"Come on old timer, I'm waiting on you," screams the last outlaw.

"*I ain't more than four or five years older than him. Why for is he calling me old?*" I ask myself. "*Just for that he's going to wait a bit more. Waiting comes easier to us old timers.*" I listen as he walks back and forth. In my mind I see him walking from the door to the bar, taking a drink, and returning to the door. "*I reckon I can stay here longer than he can keep drinking like that.*" Sure enough, I hear miss steps, more cursing, and slurred threats.

Growing tired of the wait I peak through the side of the big plate glass window. While I'm looking, a gal I reckon the singer, makes a noise as she draws in a deep breath and her hand flies to her mouth.

"What's going on? What did you see?" he asks her.

"Nothing," she says knowing she's made a mistake. I hear a slap. I can't let that continue. While he's busy proving how tough he is by slapping a girl I quietly walk through the batwing doors.

"Try doing that to someone your own size hero," I tell him. He backs away from the gal clawing for his pistol. Except that the gal chasing after him begins getting in her licks as he's worried about me. She knocks him to the floor. As he's on his way down, he frees his pistol. A big grin takes over the frown. Laying on the wood floor he draws a second pistol. He aims, his hand are holding the flintlocks in my direction as I pull the trigger on my rifle. The ball flies true, to the center of his chest. I pull a Walker, aim, and fire. I'm making sure he's unable to shoot any of the captives in the saloon, now, and in the future. He's finished. I'm reloading my rifle with a ball from my possibles. I hear a horse racing out of town. I pick up the weapons from the floor and walk to the bar. I know Nate has escaped out the back and is racing away. I ain't worried. I'll follow him.

"How many of them are there?" I ask the bartender hedging my bet.

"I ain't telling you nothing." Some people I just can't figure.

"There was three of them here and the one in the street, stranger," says the gal wiping blood from her nose.

"Thanks," I tell her. I turn to the bartender. "You own this place?"

"Yeah, I do, why?"

"They rode into town, started a gunfight in the streets, and you're on their side?" I ask him.

"That's because I know them, and they are good for business. I don't know you and I don't like you," he says defiantly.

"Is that all of them?" He says nothing. The bartender, behind a rough wood plank bar suspended over empty beer barrels refuses to answer my questions.

"Answer me or suffer the consequences," I tell him, giving him one last chance.

"Consequences be dam..." he tries telling me. There are some folks you just can't help. I interrupt his unkind answer by grabbing a fistful of greasy hair on both sides of his oddly shaped head. I pull down as hard and as quick as I can with both hands filled with his greasy hair. His nose and lips meet the rough dry wood bar. Blood pours from his smashed features. When I let go of his hair, he spits out two teeth. I wipe my hands on a filthy, but wet bar towel. My hands still feel fouled and dirty.

"Why you dirty rotten bas..." he begins. In answer I send my left fist into his mashed nose. I save my right hand for the shooting I know is ahead of me. The poor man must have lost more blood than appearance indicates because he faints dead away, falling behind his splintery wood plank bar. As the bartender is sliding to the floor two men walk through the door.

"Now, you can't do that to one of our friends," the bigger of the pair says. To avoid the fight I know is coming, I pull both pistols. My rifle is slung over a shoulder. They stop in place. Behind them enters a third man.

"What's going on in here?" he asks. I see a shiny, town sheriff's badge, pinned to his vest. His right hand is resting on a single flintlock pistol.

"Glad to see you finally made it here Sheriff. Now that the shooting's over I reckon you're safe enough to come out of your office," I'm mad and getting madder with this peacock strutting in now that the shooting is over.

"That's just about enough out of you and..." he tries saying.

"I've been chasing these outlaws for six weeks. It strikes me funny they lead me to your town. Why is that? Do they feel safe here? Are you protecting outlaws in this town, Sheriff? I know the rangers will be interested in your answer."

"You murdered those boys..." he tries again.

"No Sheriff, they drew pistols first and it's their bad luck they tried shooting me. They paid a heavy price for the mistake." I tell him.

"I'm going to report this town to the rangers," I tell them as I search the pockets of the dead outlaws. I take what I find and their guns. I leave the saloon pushing past the trio in the doorway to search the one they called the Kid. I pocket his leather bag of coins, pick up his weapons, leaving them at my horses. I cross the street to the first outlaw. I check his pockets and collect his guns. I re-cross the street to my horses with my arms full. I add the different weapons I collected and the few coins in their pockets to my saddlebags. I buckle them closed.

The rifles go onto the top pack of first packhorse. At my saddle horse, the sheriff tries again.

"You're leaving me with this mess and riding away?" he asks me.

"That's right. Since you know them you can bury them. Oh, by the way, where are their horses?" I ask quickly, hoping to get the right answer.

"In the livery at the north edge of town, of course."

"Thanks Sheriff. You'd better keep a tighter grip on this town. Rangers will be riding by from time to time checking on you. I'll be seeing you," I tell him riding my horses to the livery. I expect him to try and stop me at any minute. At the livery I tie my horses to the hitchrail. The owner walks out.

"Can I help you?" he asks.

"Yes, you can. I want the horses from the three outlaws I just killed. They were stolen and I'm claiming them."

"I'd like to help but I ain't too sure..." I look into his eyes, apparently, he don't like what he sees. It helps.

"Well I reckon you're welcome to them."

"Thanks for your help. Not everyone in this town is inclined to help."

"I reckon that's true. What about the saddles?" he asks.

"All I want is the saddlebags and to inspect the saddles. You're welcome to them." I didn't expect to find anything on the saddles, and I don't. I quickly look through their saddlebags, finding nothing of value, to me. I climb onto my saddle and ride out of town. I find Nate's trail easily. It's as plain as day. I take out after him.

I can't believe I get out of town unopposed. Next stop...? I'll ride a couple hours away from that little town. I never did learn its name. Following Nate's trail, I ride until dark.

I make a dry camp, not unloading the packhorses before putting them on a picket line. I polish off the morning's bread with jerky and a can of peaches, no coffee. In the cool of the evening I drink the thick peach flavored syrup. It ain't the same as coffee, but at least it's wet. Finished with supper I ride ahead a couple miles before stopping for the night. I unpack the horses before stringing them to the picket line for the night

I'm not in a good mood. It's hot. I wake at the smallest noise. I'm surprised when the morning's rising sun wakes me. I feel more tired now than last night. I pack the horses and ride. I'll follow Nate's trail until I run him down or ride across water. Either is okay with me. When I finish this with Nate, I'll return to the mountains, a place I should never have left. If I ride to water, I'll stop long enough to boil coffee, let the horses drink, and refill my canteen.

Riding for a couple of hours with the sun beating down on me, I feel exhausted. I'm hungry. I need coffee. How can people live here? It is so different than around the Yellowstone Valley. It can get hot there, but this is different. The sun feels like it hates me and is fixing to crush me. When I'm ready to fall from the saddle I smell the creek.

I sit up, clutch my rifle tighter, and nudge the horse on with my knees. He doesn't need the extra encouragement. I keep the horses on the rocky bank. I don't want them to kick up sand or mud and I don't want them pissing in the creek before I drink and fill my canteen and the coffee pot. When they are sated, I make a quick camp under a pecan tree. A small fire of dry wood gets the coffee boiling with a minimum of smoke. I do not want to be attracting unwanted company. I thread a stake through the last lump of camp meat and mix enough bread dough, for tonight and the morning. While things cook, I unload the horses. I reckon if I need the break, so do they.

To stretch my legs, I walk the banks of the creek looking for Nate's tracks. I hate to admit it, but I lost them while I was feeling sorry for myself. Without finding them, I return to camp. Dang if he didn't trick me. Nate is helping himself to my coffee, bread, and camp meat.

"I didn't think you'd begrudge an old friend part of your meal," he tells me, with a smile on his face and a hand on the handle of a pistol in his belt. I notice his rifle laying on his blankets. When he stands, I see a knife in his left calf-high moccasin and a pistol in his right.

"I would never hold back on a friend, especially an old friend. But are we still friends?" I ask him, pouring coffee for myself.

"I reckon we are. I hope we are. After everything we've gone through together, we should be," he tells me, meaning every word.

"You need to help me understand what happened to you. Tell me what changed you," I plead to him.

"Can we set aside our differences and talk as partners for a while?"

"Fine by me," I tell him, slowly taking my gun belt off to set it with my possibles and rifle away from where we sit. He watches as I sit, then removes his weapons.

"I reckon you've changed since our fight with the river pirates. What changed you? You're not the same young man I took in and taught everything I know. Why the change?" I ask him.

"Can't rightly say Uriah because I don't really know myself. And that's the truth. But ever since killing them pirates I've been mad. Angry at the world. The only time my anger is tamped down is when I'm fighting. I know what I've done since then makes me an outlaw. I don't care. I can't go back to how I was before. I can't live with the Cheyenne, and I'm an outlaw to everyone else. You will not understand, because I don't, but I like the man I am now."

"You understand what that means, right?"

"I do. I reckon I've known it for a while now. I admired them river boat pirates, taking what they want and living how they want. They showed me how easy it is to take from them that's weaker than me. You understand. You're the only one sharp enough to find me."

"You're leaving me no choice, my friend."

"I reckon that's so." Looking up to the darkening sky Nate dumps the last from his cup, then tossing it to the side by the fire, out of the way.

"I always liked this part of the day the best," he tells me standing. He begins moving his head from side to side, loosing up neck muscles. He stops as I gain my feet. Looking me directly in the eyes he continues. "I don't expect you to give me any breaks. And you're too good a fighter for me to give you any. I'm going to do my best and I expect the same from you."

"I don't reckon you'll give an inch. I know I won't. You know what this means, right?" I ask.

"I do. I respect you as a fighter Uriah. I know it has to end this way. If you win bury me so the critters can't get me and I'll do the same," vows Nate.

"I will."

"How do you want to do this Uriah? Guns, knives, or fists?"

"I prefer not to do it but if we must, then I'll give you the choice." I watch as a small smile splits his face. He pulls the pistol from his moccasin. I watch as he picks up his Cheyenne war axe and a large fighting knife. He's made the choice.

"Any other way would be too quick. We've known each other too long to end this in a matter of seconds," he tells me, stepping towards me, away from his guns. I bend down to retrieve my Blackfoot war axe and Crow fighting knife from my gun belt. We face each other. I'm rolling my wide shoulders to loosen stiff muscles. I tense and relax every muscle I can control, getting the blood flowing through my body. I take in a number of deep breaths and let it all out. For some reason this always prepares me for battle. We face off.

At first, we circle each other looking for the smallest opening or mistake. The trouble is I taught him how to fight and we both learned the same things from the Cheyenne. Our moves are a mirror image of each other.

Nate stops the circling. With eyes full of pain and dreading the next few seconds, he charges me. I meet him with my left shoulder. It's an expected move. To mix things up I fall to my knees, grab him around the legs, stand, pick him up, and drop him on his back to the rocky ground. Trying to catch his breath, I jump on his stomach with both knees. Without expecting it, he grabs me, turns, and now he's on top of me. I was not expecting that move. I'm holding only a knife. I bring my knife up behind him, burying it in his kidneys. Nate's only indication of the wound is a sharp intake of breath. Leaving the knife where it is, I force a roll, and holding onto him, I gain my feet. For a second time I drop him to the ground. The landing sends my knife deeper into his body.

The mortal wound does not stop Nate. As he struggles to his feet, I lose focus. I feel a burning in my thigh. Looking down I find Nate's knife in the back of my left leg. I back up as he makes his feet wearing a wicked grin plastered tight across his face. His eyes burn with hate, envy, and defeat. I relax my leg to draw out his knife. I'm holding his knife and my war axe. His hands are empty. I do not know how he is still standing. We return to circling each other.

With a loud, explosive Cheyenne war cry and Cheyenne curses, Nate launches himself at me. I meet his charge with my war axe to his neck. Nate falls to the ground. I kneel beside him. He pulls the knife from his moccasin and hands it to me.

"I'm sorry my friend," he whispers.

"As am I, my friend," I tell him. His face softens, returning to the happy young man I know. I watch as life flees from his body. I leave him in the settling dust, rise and make my way to my horse and saddlebags. Slow and careful I care for my leg. With the bleeding stopped, I consider my wound care finished. I bind it tight.

I collect Nate's weapons, clear out his pockets, and fetch his horse. I lay him to rest wrapped in his blanket, in a shallow gully carved from a dirt bank by rain and flooding. I cave the bank over his body. Finished with my friend, I gather all our horses. Hobbling back to the fire, I pour a cup of coffee.

Sitting by my fire is when they show themselves. I recognize them this time. Six Comanche. I am too tired, too beat up, and don't care enough to grab my rifle laying at my side. I can only watch as they collect the knives and war axes from the scene of the fight. Shocking me, they sit at my fire. The oldest one begins using signs. He tells me they watched the fight. They followed me for two days hoping to steal my horses. He asks me why we fought.

Using signs, I try to explain Nate was my friend, he went bad, and it was my duty to stop him. They understand. They find my six bear claw necklaces in my saddlebags and Nate's pair. We both have Medicine. They examine my knives and war axe. Excitedly they talk among themselves, in their own language. Using signs, they ask for the story behind each set of Grizz claws. Each warrior has seen a Grizz but only one of them has fought and killed one. He is the leader of this band. I ask if I can put meat on the fire. My request spurs them into action. Two of them run to their horses returning with a buffalo hump. It is quickly cut into manageable chunks and strung over the fire. I thank them for sharing their meat.

I do not understand a lot of the next flurry of signs. Something about me being friends to Crow and Cheyenne and fighting Sioux and Pawnee. They piece together a lot of my history through the souvenired weapons on my packhorses. They say something about being the ones happy and willing to share meat with a warrior with my history. They have met many white men claiming to be friends to different tribes, but many do not have evidence of that friendship. I do. There is something about telling the story through signs that spreads the Medicine. It is too fast and too new for me to follow closely. I spend most of the night relating stories about Nate,

Grizz hunting, trading with and living with the Crow and Cheyenne. I fall asleep in the middle of an involved description of a fight with Blackfoot.

Once again, I am surprised and a bit shocked when I wake and there are eight Comanche sitting around my fire waiting on me to wake and continue the stories. One of the new arrivals is an old warrior. At first, he is cold and antagonistic towards me. After a description of Cheyenne life, which he also knows, he sets aside his prejudice. He is the one that invites me to their village. I explain I do not have any trading supplies. They understand. They do not want to trade; they want to hear my stories. Reluctantly I agree. All the warnings shared with me about the Comanche are not what I'm finding to be true with these men. Yeah, I know, under different circumstances I would have found myself a prisoner and things would be entirely different. All I know is what happened to me. I load my horses and follow the Comanche deeper onto a flat, hot, empty mesa stretching for miles in every direction.

With the heat beating down on me, I have no memory of a trail or how we arrived at the village. I begin paying attention when we begin climbing down into an extreme slash in the plain. It is a mile or more wide, by several miles long. Later I learn this is the Palo Duro Canyon, a Comanche stronghold, and I have traveled over the Llano Estacado. I lose track of the days I spend with them, but it was at least two weeks.

After an old woman sees to my wounded leg, I relate all my stories again, and again. My Grizz claws make the rounds, always returning to me. My Crow and Cheyenne weapons are examined. I trade my extras for Comanche examples of war axe and knives. When I see a sheep horn bow made by their master bow maker, I ask to shoot it. Not a one of them believes I can pull it back, let along hit what I aim at. By now I have picked up a bit of their words. I ask to use a regular war bow. One is quickly found along with a quiver of arrows. I surprise them all with my ability. The old bow maker lets me shoot his horn bow. Now that is an experience. Reluctantly I hand it back to him.

To see if I really am telling the truth I am invited to hunt a single buffalo. There are many in the canyon along with horses, deer, elk, cougar, and a few black bear. I ride my horse quickly, routing a group of buffalo. I release a single arrow stopping a dry cow. The herd stops running once I stop riding after them. The buffalo kill is observed by many of the warriors. The tale spreads through the village that night during the feast where the cow is the center of attention. I leave with my horses and gifts of weapons under the protection of the Buffalo Eaters. They point me in the right direction. I travel slow. Three weeks later I ride into Bent's Fort. I stay two days before heading towards St. Louis.

Summer has passed to its mid-point as I set my horses on the trail to St. Louis. I have coffee and enough provisions to reach town, if I hunt along the way. I want to outfit myself and return to my Yellowstone canyon before the snow falls. It will be close. I don't have a lot of extra time to lose.

Heading to St. Louis I replay the summer's events in my head; chasing, finding, fighting, and ultimately killing Nate, to my visit with the Comanche, which I truthfully hope never to encounter again. And my brief encounter with the Texas Rangers.

Reaching Mr. Richardson's yard, things become familiar again. I don't have fur to sell but I have money in the bank. I make my list and drop it at the general store. Mr. Richardson helps me buy packhorses. In four days, I'm ready to ride for the Yellowstone's. I have ten packhorses carrying three panniers each of trade goods for the Crow or Cheyenne. I have six packhorses loaded with winter supplies, and a second riding horse. For the first time since leaving the mountains this spring, I'm carrying enough powder and lead to hunt and defend myself, if I need to, through the winter. The horses and trade goods drained my account of two years' worth of profits. But like Mr. Richardson said, "That's okay because that is what money in the bank is for."

I leave St. Louis and Mr. Richardson's yard, refreshed, re-supplied, and ready to work through the rapidly approaching winter. I book space on the last paddle wheeler up the Missouri River for the year. I watch over my horses and goods like a mother protecting her young. I think I have successfully shed the tragedy played out over this spring and summer. The boat stops well south of the Yellowstone Valley. From there I ride leading my pack train. It is good to be home.

———

Uriah, the Last Mountain Man

I have most of what I need to live alone, undisturbed like I expect life. I do not trade with the Crow. The Cheyenne trade is about half of what it used to be. It is still enough to trade at Fort Union in the fall for coffee, sugar, and the like, my necessaries.

One fall, a couple years later I travel to trade fur for supplies at Fort Union and the fort is deserted. I have waited too long to make Bent's Fort and return before snow flies. I make a slow ride home unsure of the coming winter. Midway to home I ride across circumstances I hoped never to encounter in my mountains, immigrants. These travelers are on their way to Oregon. I stop at their camp made from circling their wagons.

"Hello, the wagons," I call about 100 yards from their camp as the sun retreats for its day.

"Who is it and what do you want?" is the answer I hear. Strikes me as a queersome reply.

"The name's Uriah. Are you folks lost? In trouble?" I ask, leading my horses closer to their camp.

"That's far enough stranger. What do you want?" They ask again.

"Just curious. Since you're all okay I'll be on my way," I tell him turning around. From the corner of my eye I see the speaker get an elbow from whom I take to be his wife.

"Hold up Mister. You're just in time for supper, if you care to set with us," he tells me.

"Thank you, I will," I tell them, tying my fifteen horses bearing furs, buffalo robes, and camp goods outside their wagons. At the central fire I am handed a plate heaped with a watery stew, potatoes, and hot bread with real butter.

"What's on your packhorses mister?" asks a curious young man.

"Josh, that ain't a neighborly thing to ask a stranger," scolds the elbow-stabbing older gal.

"That's okay ma'am. Ain't no secret. I was on my way to Fort Union to trade for my winter necessaries. But the fort has been abandoned. I'm returning to my cabin."

"You live out here?" asks the boy.

"I do."

"How do you live out here by yourself?" he asks, genuinely curious and wanting to know.

"I trap and hunt."

"You're a mountain man?" he asks in awe.

"No, he ain't no mountain man. I know they all left the mountains when beaver went out of fashion. He's telling you a windy," says an older brother, who should have known better.

"Boy, I'll excuse your ignorance because you ain't from around here. I came out here in 1834. I trapped the beaver, traded with the Indians, and hunted buffalo. If you're so set in your ways at so young an age, well I feel right sorry for you."

"You ain't..." he begins. He's leaning back on a wooden chair against a wagon. Quicker than any of these Pilgrims can follow, I draw my war axe and send it flying, landing with a loud thud in the wagon's side next to his slightly bleeding ear. The boy sits quiet, all the color from his face has drained away.

"You could have hit him in the head and killed my boy," says that same old woman.

"Ma'am my Cheyenne war axe landed exactly here I wanted it to land. If I was going to kill such an obnoxious spud, I just shoot him," I tell his Ma pulling a pistol.

"I'd appreciate it if you'd put away your weapons before someone gets hurt," says the man with the sore ribs.

"Mister, my weapons do exactly what I tell them and when I tell them to do what I want done. There ain't a way they can fire without me pulling the trigger. If I want to kill man or beast I do. I can see that not a single one of you if is fit company. Thanks for the watery stew. Time it right and tomorrow you can get a buffalo or two as you cross this ridge. They'll be right in front of you about midday," I tell him.

"We haven't seen a buffalo yet," says the boy's Pa.

"They ain't there, don't listen to him Pa," says the obnoxious older boy.

"Boy you're tempting me. Do you have a rifle and a horse?" I ask the man.

"I do, why."

"Come with me and I'll show you the buffalo. From there you folks are on your own."

"Call his bluff Pa."

"All right mister, show me these critters."

"Let me see your rifle first." He hands me his .40 caliber squirrel rifle. "In the east this may be a fine weapon but out here you'll need at least a .50, a .54 is better, to take buffalo. And if you happen to run into a Grizz."

"Mister, all the stories about fighting a Grizzly bear are Fairy Tales," says the boy, now that his color has returned. I reach into my possibles for my string of Grizz claws. That shuts them all up as they are passed around the fire.

"You want a buffalo?"

"Let's go," at least the Pa is game. I climb onto my saddle to wait for the sore rib man. He rides up. "Why you taking your packhorses with you?"

"I'm heading home after doing my last good deed for you folks."

"Uriah, I'll watch your horses for you if you have a buffalo robe for trade," says a young woman. I get the fire in my blood looking at her. I should know better but I recon I don't.

"And you are?" I ask her.

"Cathy."

"Cathy, I do have a soft-tanned robe I will trade for coffee when we return. Let's go." Within two miles I slow to a walk.

"See that ridge coming down onto the valley floor to the right there?"

"Yeah."

"Follow that ridge south and tell me what you see."

"Can't make it out."

"Let's get closer." I lead him within 50 yards of the bunch of buffalo and he still can't see them. "How bad do you want one?"

"I don't see them. But if you conjure one, I'll trade you coffee, sugar, and salt for it."

"Add flour and you've got a deal."

"Deal." I level my rifle in front of us on a cow watching us. The shot lights up the fading daylight. In the flash the Pilgrim's eyes are opened. The buffalo falls. The Pilgrim tries racing to the downed animal.

"Wait a minute Pilgrim, let the herd walk off a bit before we ride up there. I don't want them to scare off. It'll be easier for you to shoot them come the morning." He does not answer me. I give the herd about 30 minutes to walk away before riding up.

"I'll gut him. You can finish the job in the morning." The man

sits his horse watching me open the buffalo, pull out the gut sack, and cut out the tongue.

"Why you taking the tongue?"

"Next to the hump and the ribs this is some fine eating," I tell him. I wrap it in canvas to take it with me.

"It'll be okay here come the morning?" he asks me.

"Should be, I didn't see any coyotes or wolves tailing this bunch. She'll be here. Let's ride back, I'm ready for fresh tongue." He looks at me like I lost my mind. We ride to the wagon camp, getting out of the saddle outside the camp.

"See I told you there wasn't any buffalo. Why he's..." begins the loudmouth kid.

"Mark, say another word and I'll take a strap to you. There was a small herd of them just like he said. Uriah shot one and has brought back a treat for all of us to try." His son looks at his pa red faced and in shame knowing he's out of line.

"*But that's okay,*" thinks the older son, "*I'll get back at him,*" he thinks to himself.

I carry the canvas-covered tongue to the fire. "Cathy, in my saddlebags, on the right side, I have a half dozen wood stakes. Could you fetch them for me? I'll get this meat on the fire for all of you to try," I tell them. Instantly the camp is buzzing. I do not tell them what type of buffalo meat this is.

"You knew about the buffalo, didn't you?" asks the man's wife.

"Yes, ma'am I did. That's how I lived so long out here. Lived by learning everything I can about the country I'm riding through. I hope you'll believe that, because you will run into Blackfoot in about eight days if you keep on this heading. I would not recommend continuing on. Snow will start in two weeks. In three weeks, it'll begin sticking. I'd hate to see you stuck in a snowstorm. It can be mighty uncomfortable in the cold like that. I would recommend you winter at the empty Fort Union. You can defend it and pass the cold months in relative comfort. Of course, you'll have to bring in buffalo for meat and cut firewood, but you got time."

Cathy brings me the stakes. I slice the tongue, skewer it, and set it around the fire to cook. I watch it close, turn it, and when cooked how I like, pronounce it finished. I pull out the stakes and cut pieces for the immigrants to sample.

"That's prime eating right there folks. You really haven't killed any buffalo?" I ask, thinking it's hard to believe.

"Not only have we not killed any, we haven't seen any."

"I hope you follow my suggestions for staying at the old fort through the winter," I tell them, cutting the rest of the tongue into small pieces for them.

"Uriah, do you have that buffalo robe?" asks Cathy.

"I do. Come with me and I'll get it for you." She follows me to my packhorses. I drop the packs from one of the horses. I break open the bundle and after rooting around pull out the best one for her.

"Here you go. This is the best of the lot. Hope you like it," I tell her, watching as she looks it over.

"I didn't realize they were so heavy. How do you keep it from smothering you during the night?" she asks.

"Never worried about that. During the cold months I burrow down and don't come up until the sun is thinking about rising," I tell her.

"If I trade you for coffee, flour, and other things that you said you were going to the fort to get, will you lead us to this fort?" she asks me.

"For you I will."

"Did you hear that? We have a guide. I vote on staying at the fort. What do the rest of you say?" she asks them. They talk among themselves before answering me.

"We want to continue on our way. We won't be swayed. We'll be pulling out come first light," says the sore ribbed man.

"Sorry to hear that. Walk with me for a bit Cathy," I ask her. We walk out of hearing from the others.

"What?" she asks me.

"They will not make it to Oregon. They will get stuck because of the snow or the Blackfoot will get them. Either way they will perish. Don't go with them. You're welcome at my cabin."

"You're absolutely sure of this?"

"I was never surer of anything in my life. Please don't continue on. I ain't telling you this to keep a hold of you, but I don't want to see you perish with them. I reckon you're smarter than that."

"I have a hard time believing you, Uriah. I don't know. What would people say?"

"It's up to you, but if they push on, not a one of them is going to make it. I don't have any neighbors so no one will be saying anything about you staying with me."

"If I do, I will stay in my wagon, either until I learn more about you or decide to return back, to maybe St. Louis."

"You're welcome to stay in your wagon if you want to. Ain't nothing going to happen that you don't want to. That's a promise."

"All right I will. Let me add some things to my wagon and say goodbye."

"I'll be right here with my horses." Two men from other wagons walk up to me, I can tell they'd been drinking, and this is not going to end well, for any of us.

"You boys stop right there, turn around, and go back from where you came from. I don't want any trouble, but I will not be trifled with by the likes of you two," I warn them.

"Listen to the big man now. What do you say we trifle with him?

Joe?"

"I say let's do this." As they walk towards me Cathy sees what is about to happen and stops them.

"Both of you stop this right now," she commands. "Turn around and head back to your wagons."

"You boys have Cathy to thank for escaping injury," I tell them.

Both rush me at the same time. The Joe fella gets my shoulder in his gut. The other one runs into a work-hardened fist. Both of them react as if they'd run into a brick wall. Paying them no heed, I climb onto the saddle of my riding horse, take up the leads to my packhorses and lead Cathy and her wagon to my canyon.

Of course, it's dark when we arrive at the cabin. I start a fire in the outside pit and put on the coffee pot. Working together we unhitch her team after setting her wagon under a big cedar tree. The team of six big work horses enter the corral, roll, and begin eating the grass. I let them introduce themselves.

"I guess I should tell you that a pair of those work horses are a stallion and brood mare. I hoped to raise horses in Oregon," Cathy tells me. Her remark brightens the low burning spark of an idea I had of raising horses of some kind. If I can match up Mountain Mustangs with them work horses, what would be the results? I'll keep that to myself for now. After showing her around, which doesn't take too long, she retreats to her wagon for the night.

"Do you have a rifle in there with you? Do you know how to use it?" I ask her at my door.

"Yes, I have a rifle, but I do not know how to use it," she admits.

"We'll fix that directly. Here, take these two pistols. Good night." I give her two of my horse pistols hoping she will trust me. If I trust her with weapons...well I hope she grow to trust me

The next four weeks are a flurry of last-minute chores

getting ready for winter, the snow, and the cold. Cathy lends a willing hand. One of the first projects she asks for help with is building a chicken coop for her dozen hens and rooster. Second is a barn and smaller corral for her milk cow. We keep busy working on the many different projects in addition to teaching her how to shoot her rifle.

She has me start several short projects inside the cabin. When I finish them, I cannot believe the difference. It's looking like a home and less like a barn.

Six weeks pass before we talk about her moving inside the cabin. I reckon she's grown to understand me a bit. Love? I don't reckon that's the right word, yet. I believe it will come, but I reckon it'll be after winter. Maybe with the spring. For myself, well let's say I'm already lost.

When it does happen, it sneaks up on the both of us. After our first kiss she wonders why it took so long. I do not have an answer. I am happy and content with it happening.

10

I LOSE MYSELF IN MY NEW LIFE. IN THE SPRING OF 1854, I bring Cathy with me on a return to St. Louis and visit Mr. Richardson. I'm bringing in what used to be a single year's worth of fur. It took four years to accumulate what I sell. I return to the world of the white man. So much has changed. I promised Cathy a proper wedding in front of a preacher. Mr. Richardson acts as my best man and gives away the bride.

We both feel our place deep in the Yellowstone Valley is home. I buy the land with the money in the bank, with Mr. Richardson's help. We return to the mountains with supplies and a promise to return soon. I reckon every three or four years is soon enough.

At 60 years old I am found and forcibly removed from my valley by a bunch of government men and taken to St. Louis. Cathy died two years ago. Once again, I am sick at heart, I do not want to go. The mountains are changing. I sneak away from St. Louis after meeting with the banker and withdrawing enough money to buy more land surrounding my canyon in the mountains I love and call home. I remain alone, to live by myself, with my memories and reminders scattered around my log cabin, the barns, and in the corrals. The canyon is full of history yet empty of people, except of me.

Enough of an old man's ramblings. Winter is rapidly approaching yet again. I need to put up meat, wood, and grass for my stock. I enjoyed remembering. Even the hard parts that always crop up on my birthday. I miss Nate. Every year on my birthday I remember I shot and killed him, one of my best friends. I take the only solace I can in that at the end he was not the same man.

That is enough for now. The pile of firewood will not grow tall by itself.

I will recount my years in the Yellowstone Valley after giving up trapping. I will include the many years Cathy and I shared together. Some of our adventures may appear as repeats from the past, like a buffalo hunt, a grizz attack, or fighting with a mountain lion. Through this coming winter I will get my thoughts on paper. On those days too cold to work outside, I will welcome the diversion. If I get my words wrote down, I'll send them to Mr. Richardson. Oh wait, he now lives on his ranch in Texas, near the Devil's River. One thing I forgot to mention. Mr. Richardson is close to my age. I always deferred to him because he came from class. He told

399

me not to, but my admiration and respect is due him. I will send my dribbles to him and he will see if they are worthy of collecting, or not. One day someone needs to chronicle his story. It's different than mine but no less exciting. He knows all the old-time trappers, Morgan, and his son Ira. Caleb and all those ranching around him in Texas. And many of the old rangers. And of course, me.

Enough rambling I hear a stack of firewood calling. Until you read next words:

Uriah of the Yellowstone.

Printed in Poland
by Amazon Fulfillment
Poland Sp. z o.o., Wrocław

64743704R00228